Scipio Rising

Martin Tessmer

DEDICATION

To Scott, the latter-day conqueror of Tuscany.
Let the adventure continue!

CONTENTS

ACKNOWLEDGMENTS

Among 20th century historians, I am primarily indebted to Professor Richard Gabriel for his informative and readable *Scipio Africanus: Rome's Greatest General*, and *Ancient Arms and Armies of Antiquity*. His excellent books are the factual mainstays for the characters and events upon which I have expanded. Similarly, H. Liddell Hart's *Scipio Africanus: Greater Than Napoleon* provided many valuable insights into Scipio the general and Scipio the man.

Among classic historians, I owe a deep debt of gratitude to Titus Livius (Livy) for *Hannibal's War: Books 21-30* (translated by J.C. Yardley) and Polybius for *The Histories* (translated by Robin Waterfield). Cato the Elder's *De Agri Cultura* provided insight into the character of this plain yet brilliant and powerful man that so influenced the course of Western History.

Ross Lecke has written two fine historical novels about Scipio and Hannibal: they are *Scipio Africanus: The Man Who Defeated Hannibal*, and *Hannibal*. Ross showed me that a writer can spin a good yarn and still stick to the facts, where there are facts to stick to. Finally, I must give a tip of the hat to Wikipedia and the scores of websites and blogs about the people and countries of this period. Thanks to the scholars of our digital community.

Susan Sernau, many thanks for your proofing of the initial manuscript. Mercy Pilkington performed yeoman's copyediting work to make this book historically accurate and textually concise.

A NOTE ON HISTORICAL ACCURACY

This is a work of historical fiction, meaning it combines elements of historical fact (such as it is) and fiction. It is not a history textbook.

The book's major characters, places, events, battles, and timelines are real, meaning they are noted by at least one of our acknowledged historians such as Livy, Polybius, Plutarch, Gabriel, Mommsen, Appian, Liddell-Hart or Peddle. In those many cases where there is contradictory or contrary evidence, I have chosen the "fact" that best congrues with the rest of the story.

The books' Hellenic Party and Latin Party factions were created to capture the mood of the times, when there was real enmity between those favoring a more "decadent" Hellenic lifestyle and those of more agrarian sympathies who disparaged it. The parties are fictions, but their values and tactics are evident even today, as they were then.

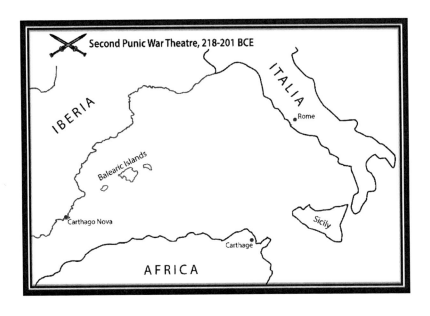

Second Punic War Theatre, 218-201 BCE

IBERIA

ITALIA

Rome

Balearic Islands

Carthago Nova

Sicily

Carthage

AFRICA

Italia, Second Punic War, 210 BCE

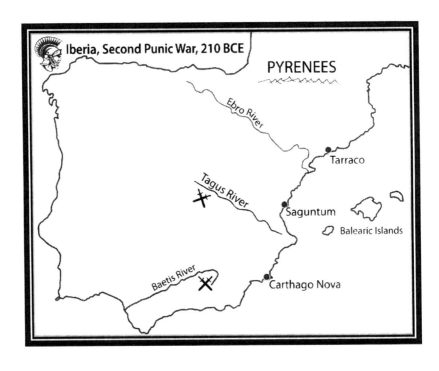

I. THREE VOWS

CARTHAGE, 237 BCE. The sword swooshes down at young Hannibal's head. The agile nine-year-old ducks the wooden blade and spins behind his stocky cousin Agbal, poking him with his toy dagger of ivory. The older boy spins around to grab Hannibal, but Hannibal dodges sideways and scampers behind the stone cistern in the mansion's walled courtyard.

"I knew you would do that, Agbal! You always make the same move!"

"Fight like a man, you little weasel!"

Agbal lunges for Hannibal, but the younger boy slides past him and grabs his purse on the way. Hannibal's foxlike face splits into a grin as he dangles Agbal's pouch in front of him.

"The weasel does not fight the bear, he tricks him." laughs Hannibal. "And steals his prey!"

Agbal's face darkens. He spreads out his arms and carefully stalks Hannibal into a corner, savoring the prospect of giving him a good sword paddling. Mago, Hannibal's five-year-old brother, watches the battle with wide eyes, hugging his silk pillow as if it were a doll, sucking on this thumb. A kind and happy child, he is the image of his older brother, from the light brown skin and high cheekbones to the emerald-green eyes and raven hair.

"You think this is funny, Hannibal?" says Agbal. "Just wait 'til I get hold of you!"

Hannibal's other brother, seven-year-old Hasdrubal, eases his slight frame into the courtyard and plops down next to Mago. With bulbous eyes and drooping lips, wiry Hasdrubal does not have the handsome features of his two brothers, but he is almost as cunning as Hannibal, and more ruthless. Though small for his age, he is fearless and aggressive, with a penchant for inflicting pain that keeps the local bullies at bay. Hasdrubal knows that his clever older brother is more than a match for big Agbal. He will find a way to outwit him, as he does to all his opponents.

"You can beat him, Hannibal," shouts Hasdrubal. "He's nothing but a fat-ass snail!"

As Agbal closes on him, Hannibal backs against the trunk of a tall date palm, raising his arms to fend off Agbal's attack. Just as Agbal raises his sword for the strike, Hannibal deftly scrambles between his legs and leaps onto his back.

"The weasel's got the bear! The weasel's got the bear!" Hannibal chortles as he wraps his arms and legs around Agbal's broad back.

Agbal curses and whirls about, trying to throw Hannibal off, as he clings on for dear life. Little Mago claps his hands, delighted with the show. Seeing Hannibal is in trouble, Hasdrubal rushes in and tackles Agbal from behind.

"Grab that bastard's arms, Hannibal!" Hasdrubal urges, as he clings desperately to Agbal's pumping legs. Agbal shoves at little Hasdrubal. "Get away, fish-face," he spits, a familiar insult which only serves to enrage Hasdrubal. He bites at Agbal's legs.

But Agbal has won many playground fights, and he has his own tricks. He vaults backwards and collapses on Hasdrubal and Hannibal, knocking them loose. As Hannibal disentangles himself, Agbal grabs him and throws him onto his stomach, capturing his right arm behind his back. Hasdrubal shoves vainly at Agbal's back until the older boy knocks him over with a quick swipe of his hand. Agbal starts to bend Hannibal's arm slowly backward.

"Give up, you filthy Roman!"

"Piss on you, fat stump!"

Agbal bends Hannibal's arm farther. Hannibal gasps, and tries to buck free. Mago's lip trembles as he tries to stifle his terrified sobs. When Hannibal screams, Mago throws down his pillow and dashes out the courtyard entrance.

"Father! Faaather!" Mago wails as his voice fades into the distance.

Agbal jerks Hannibal's arm tighter. Hannibal yells again, but his face registers no fear, only frustrated anger.

"Give up or I'll break it!" Says Agbal through clenched teeth.

Hannibal thrashes his head back and forth, looking for some part of Agbal to bite. "Get off me or I'll beat you up, I swear it!"

Now Agbal is scared. He knows the game has gone too far, but as a Carthaginian male he mustn't show the weakness of being merciful. So Agbal grits his teeth and begins to push Hannibal's arm farther. Hannibal's face contorts with anger and agony, his body convulsing. Yet his eyes still search for a weakness, a way to strike back.

"STAND!"

General Hamilcar Barca, Hannibal's father, stands in the archway, staring sternly at the frightened boys. Fearsome in his gleaming chain-mail armor, his ice-blue eyes glare like lamps from his dark, bearded face. Agbal leaps to attention and Hannibal rises beneath him, rubbing his arm and glaring at Agbal with teary eyes. Hamilcar and Mago scramble over to stand next to them.

"What is going on here?" Hamilcar demands.

Agbal is the oldest. He understands it is his duty to speak first. "We were playing Romans and Carthaginians. I pinned him, but he was too dumb to give up." Agbal pushes Hannibal, who kicks Agbal in the knee. Hamilcar raises his hand. The two boys snap back to their stance and remain silent. He walks about and studies the boys, fingering the jeweled hilt of his Phoenician sword, taking his time. The boys fidget and twitch, nervous with apprehension.

When he thinks they have suffered enough, Hamilcar nods. "Very well. The game is over. Agbal, go home. And give my salutations to your parents." Agbal dashes out as if pursued by demons. When he is gone, Hamilcar retrieves Hannibal's dagger and hands it to him. He looks at Hasdrubal and Mago.

"Hannibal did well," says their father. "It is important never to surrender, even when all seems lost. Remember, there is always a way out. Always a way to win."

Nodding solemnly, the boys stand quietly until their father

speaks again. "Mago, Hasdrubal: go to your mother." All three start to run off, but Hamilcar raises his hand. "Hannibal, you stay here." Hamilcar watches his other two sons scramble through the arched stone doorway, glad to escape him. He turns to Hannibal.

"I would have got him," Hannibal declares to his father. "I just had to get my head over to bite him in his fat arm. I would have done it!"

His father smiles at his son's words, knowing they so express his own heart. "It is no matter, we have more pressing business. Son, I must depart soon. I take the army to Iberia at the next full moon."

Hannibal's face drops. "But you just got back! Mother promised we could go riding with you. I have a new horse, father. It is a Numidian stallion. We could ride like the wind!"

Hamilcar gently strokes Hannibal's thick glossy curls. "I would enjoy that, truly. But the Romans have taken Sicily and Sardinia from us, and they will soon take Iberia if we don't stop them. Some of the tribes are rebelling against us, just when we need them to help us fight the Romans. Do you see why I have to leave?"

"But can't you stay for a while? It's not fair!" Hannibal stomps his foot and pouts, near tears.

Hamilcar's hand darts out and grabs Hannibal's shoulder, shaking him. "You are not to cry, you hear me? You are a Barca!" he says proudly. "You are part of the greatest military family in Carthage! In the world!"

Hannibal clamps his lips together, though his eyes are moist with tears. His father kneels in front of him, and smiles tenderly. "A soldier's life is not his own," he says softly. "You know I must go where the Council of Elders commands. Even though I command the army, I must follow orders."

"I want to go, too," exclaims Hannibal. "I want to be a general like you, and fight the Romans. Mother tells me the people call you 'The Thunderbolt,' because you strike so quickly. I can be General Hannibal Barca, son of the Thunderbolt!"

Hamilcar walks around the courtyard as Hannibal watches him. He considers his son's words, biting his lip. He looks back at his son, how he stands with the dignity of man, meeting his father's gaze with steady eyes. He takes a deep breath. "You truly wish to go with me?"

"Yes. I want to be a soldier!"

Hamilcar is not surprised by Hannibal's wish. Although his son is a gifted student of languages and military history, he spends all his spare time in concerted action: riding, sword fighting, and athletic competitions. Hamilcar is proud of all his sons, but he knows Hannibal has a will to win that sets him apart. The general has seen how other children naturally follow his lead, even ones who are years older. With another war coming against Rome, Hamilcar knows Carthage will need Hannibal's gifts as soon as possible. He searches Hannibal's eyes, and nods. "Then you may go. We will continue your military training in Iberia."

Hannibal bounces about with joy, but pauses. "Can Mago and Hasdrubal come?" Hamilcar grins at his son. "You always worry about them, don't you? Not yet, they can come when they are older. This trip is just for you, so you can learn how to be a Carthaginian general!"

Hannibal nods, looking solemnly at his father. "Can they be generals, too?"

"Yes, they will be generals someday." He laughs. "Even though Hasdrubal curses like a common soldier! But you will lead them both. That will be your duty. It will be hard work because you have much to learn. And you will be in Iberia for a long time. Do you still want to go?"

Hannibal stares up at his father. "Yes, more than anything!"

Hamilcar claps his hands together. "Then it is done. Before you depart, you must do one thing for me. Come."

The general leads Hannibal from the courtyard into the family's spacious atrium, following a stone walk lined with tall swaying papyrus and palm trees. Once inside the atrium, they go to a high stone platform set against one of the walls. On the platform is a gold statue of a bearded man with ram's horns, sitting on a throne. Hamilcar turns to Hannibal.

"Before you leave with me, you must take an oath to Baal, our supreme god."

Hannibal's stares up at his father, bewildered.

"You mean, make a promise? About what?"

"That you will never ally yourself with Rome, that they will be your enemy forever. You must take a blood oath. Will you do that?"

Hannibal nods mutely, his eyes large.

"Very well," says Hamilcar. He withdraws his dagger, pulls Hannibal's under arm next to his, and draws the dagger across his own arm. Blood trickles from the gash. Hamilcar pricks Hannibal's arm, opening a small bleed, and presses their wounds together. The boy trembles but stands resolute as their comingled blood drips down his arm onto the floor.

"Now, say, 'By the blood of my ancestors, I will never be a friend to Rome.' "

"By the blood of my ancestors, I will never be a friend to Rome."

"I will not rest until Rome is destroyed."

Hannibal gapes at his father. He gulps. "I, uh, I will not rest until Rome is destroyed."

Hamilcar gently disengages their arms and embraces his son. He sheathes his dagger, detaches it from his black leather belt, and gives it to Hannibal.

"My father gave this to me, when I completed the same ritual you have done. You are now a warrior of House Barca, on a man's journey through life. Some day you will lead Carthage to victory over Rome, I have seen it a dream."

"Me? What about you, father?"

Hamilcar gives his son a bittersweet smile. "The priests of Baal have prophesized, it is my fate to die in Iberia, never to get to Italia." Seeing his son's dismay, he kneels to face him. "Do not frown! It will be an honor to have a soldier's death, and join my ancestors in the Hall of Warriors. You and your brothers can carry on when I die. Is that not true?"

Staring raptly at his father, Hannibal raises his right arm. "Yes, Father. I promise."

"Be it so. I have one more gift for you." Hamilcar reaches into his side pouch and takes out a small clay figurine of himself. He presses it into Hannibal's hands.

"This is to remind you that I will always be with you. Even if

my body is gone, my spirit will be with you, helping you to
fulfill your promise to bring down Rome."

The boy studies the tiny likeness and eases it into a pocket in
his tunic. "I will bring them down for you. Me and Mago and
Hasdrubal, we will bring them all down."

AS TRUMPETS BLARE, twenty-six-year-old Hannibal leads
the Carthaginian army towards the hundred thousand Iberian
tribesmen who fill the wide plains in front of him. The armies
are only separated by the wide Tagus River. Although this is
only his first battle as a general, Hannibal is aware that
Carthage's chance to control Iberia hinges on its outcome. He
must win this one. If war breaks out between Carthage and
Rome, his men must believe that Hannibal can lead them to
victory against anyone.

The heavily armored Carthaginian cavalry is in the center of
Hannibal's front line, poised to ram the Iberians and deliver
maximum shock. A wall of twenty elephants is on each side of
the cavalry, arranged to occlude the Libyan infantry hiding
behind them. Although a fledgling general, Hannibal has already
learned the value of shock and surprise, tactics he will use for the
rest of his life.

Hannibal rides his war elephant, the massive and terrifying
Surus, an African elephant that stands fifteen feet at the shoulder,
providing Hannibal a high perch from which to view the battle
and give orders. The general wears the deep purple tunic that
signals he is the commander of the entire army, but it is sheathed
with the same stiff linen cuirass that his men use as chest armor.
Hannibal has eschewed the more protective chain mail preferred
by his wealthy officers. It is too Roman for his tastes, and would
give him more protection than he can provide to his men.

The young general rides across the front line bareheaded,

nodding at his soldiers and exchanging salutations. The veterans from Hamilcar's army cannot help but notice his uncanny resemblance to his father: the luminous, deep-set eyes, the high chiseled cheekbones, and the tall, lithe muscularity. His most notable feature, however, is his attitude; the air of absolute confidence and authority he exudes in every situation. He is so quick and decisive that he appears not so much a man as an elemental force for victory, determined to win at all costs. Although most of his troops are mercenaries, they follow him without question. They have fought with Hannibal in several battles. They know him to be a bold warrior but one who does not take unnecessary chances. The mercenaries have never been so outnumbered, but still they trust him, knowing he will somehow trick their enemy into defeat.

After trundling about to exhort the troops, Hannibal returns to the infantry center to join General Hasdrubal. His diminutive brother trots about on his nimble Numidian pony, anxious for a fight. Hasdrubal studies the enemy force, noting its size with obvious concern. As is his custom, Hasdrubal has a wry grin on his dark, lean face. He yawns heavily – and theatrically, before he yells up to his brother.

"Gods take you! Why did we have to march all night and sneak across this freezin' river when all we're going to do is just sit here?"

Hannibal grins, knowing this is Hasdrubal's way to ease the tension that gnaws at him before battle.

"You know why. We could not fight those lunatic savages out in the open. They greatly outnumber us, and we are slowed by all this damned plunder we are dragging along." Hannibal looks at the enemy hordes, and laughs. "Besides, being cocksure Iberians, they will think the only reason we sneaked past them at night is because we are afraid of them! They will be overconfident, and that will ease our way to triumph."

Hasdrubal makes a face, and points to a large group of enemy tribesmen who are screaming insults at the Carthaginians. "I can believe that. Anyone who can fight naked like those bristly-haired madmen must be overconfident. Especially with such tiny cocks."

Hannibal surveys the horizon-filling swath of his enemies. "Ah yes, the Olcade, not known for their tranquility or mercy," he says cheerfully. "And those in the center with the pointed helmets, those are all Carpetani. Must be eighty thousand of them, at least double our force." He watches Hasdrubal's eyes grow wide, and grins. "And there are the stone-eyed Vaccaei over on the left side, those bearded ones with the large spears. They will fight to the death, I am told. "

Hasdrubal rolls his eyes, and smirks at his brother. "So you think this will be a fair fight, because you have a river running near us? Brother, I think you have been eating those mountain mushrooms the priests take to bring visions!" He turns his horse about and faces behind the lines. "Maybe we should just drop all this booty and run," he says playfully. "We can make a run for Andora town while they're picking up the treasure. There is a prime whorehouse there with good wine, believe me!"

"Not necessary, we have the Tagus." Reaching to the side of his wide belt, Hannibal fingers the dagger he received as a child. "As our father said, 'Make the terrain your ally, and you will never be outnumbered.' Do you remember the story of the great Timoleon, the Greek general who defeated Carthage a century ago? Our army outnumbered his six to one, but he defeated us by waiting until we started crossing the river before he attacked. The river will be our ally, and it will give us the advantage."

Hasdrubal spits to the side, and scratches his backside while eyeing his brother. "I don't remember that story, but you were always the big scholar of military history, father's prize little piss-pot pupil. I can only say that fuckin' river had better fight well if we are to get to Rome! And get over those damned Alps, somehow!"

"For once, I have not given Rome my consideration," Hannibal says wryly. "See those Vettones over there? They swore they would crucify me if they caught me, as I did to their treacherous chieftains who deserted us. So forgive me if I concern myself with our more immediate encounter. When we win, then we can... ah, they approach! Get ready!"

The Iberians array themselves along the plain's edge above the river, poised to hurtle themselves at the Carthaginian invaders. Hannibal leans from his platform saddle and pulls his sarissa from its sheath, a fifteen-foot spear that allows him to fight from atop his elephant. He loops his circular wooden shield around his back and rides out to the center of his cavalry line, holding his sarissa aloft. The war trumpets sound throughout the Carthaginian ranks, and the air fills with the metallic slither of drawn steel.

Hannibal turns his elephant to face the hordes along the opposite shore. Bowing his head, he prays to Anath, the Carthaginian goddess of love and war, for a sign when he should spring his ambush – too soon and they lose all surprise, too late and they will all be slaughtered. He studies the bordering forests to see if he detects motion in them. Seeing none, he smiles and nods his head. Everything is ready.

A ram's horn blows from the opposite shore and thousands of enemy warriors storm down the plain toward the Tagus, eager for the kill. Backed to the edge of their tribal boundaries by the

Carthaginians, the Iberians know this is their last stand for freedom. They will neither give nor expect quarter. Their infantry lines tramp steadily towards the river, chanting their tribal battle songs. Many wave their gruesome falcatas in front of them, eager to show how their squat sabers can chop through shields and bodies. The Carpetani cavalry gallops past the flanks of their marching compatriots, riding two on a horse, rushing to engage the Carthaginian riders on the opposite bank.

Hannibal nods to Hasdrubal, who dashes over to the lead trumpeter and gives him a one-word command. The trumpeter blasts a series of three short notes, which are repeated across the half-mile troop line. The Carthaginian army pauses, stops, and then slowly backs up, as if retreating from the sea of oncoming Iberians.

When they see their enemy retreating, the Iberian infantry is further inflamed with battle lust. Their commanders shout in vain for them to maintain their lines as the main troops hurtle down the steep riverbank and start to wade across the wide river. The men shuffle through its forceful current, holding their swords and javelins aloft as the water swirls to their chests. The cavalry splashes through the river and emerges to clash with the waiting Carthaginian cavalry on the opposite bank. As the lead riders level their javelins at the armored Carthaginians, their second riders leap off to attack them on foot. Nearing midstream, the infantry watches their compatriots duel the Carthaginian riders, and they shout their encouragement.

Hannibal and Hasdrubal plummet toward the cavalry fight, joining their cavalry in the heart of the battle. Few Iberian cavalry can get near to Hannibal, because their horses bolt at Surus' terrifying size and strange smell. The frightened beasts dump their passengers into the turbid waters and make for the shore.

Hannibal checks the position of the enemy foot soldiers fording the Tagus and screams an order to his nearby trumpeter, who blasts another series of notes. The Carthaginian soldiers and elephants cease their brief retreat and return to the sides of the riverbank. Once there, they lie in wait for any Iberians who will make it to the shore.

Now tens of thousands of tribesmen are jammed midstream. Up to their necks in the current, their fellows shove them forward in their eagerness to destroy the Carthaginians. Hannibal rides along the riverbank, fending off javelins weakly tossed from his immersed enemy. He lances an attacking cavalryman and turns about to wave his sarissa at his riders upon the plain, signaling them to his side. The Carthaginian trumpets blare once more – one long, plaintive note.

As one, thousands of Numidian cavalry burst from the concealment of the forests bordering the river, galloping headlong into the Iberians in the Tagus. Bareback, with only a small shield for defense, the best horsemen in the world whirl from one immersed group of tribal infantry to another, stabbing some with their javelins, hacking others with their short swords, and knocking down many with their sturdy little horses. Hundreds of those knocked over are swept away to drown. Others sink silently beneath the weight of their wounds and armor. Many Iberians struggle to the shore, only to be trampled by the elephants or slugged down by the stone missiles of the Balearic slingers hiding behind them. Tens of thousands of the Iberian army are lost in the river slaughter, the dead swept from sight as the Tagus purges the horror from its waters.

Undaunted, more Carpetani, Vaccaei, and Olcade swarm into the river. By sheer dint of numbers, most make it to shore. They attack Hannibal's cavalry and the slingers, chopping through them with their falcatas, raining javelins onto their heads, pushing the Carthaginians back up the plain. Studying the battle from the opposite shore, the Iberian commanders foresee a victory. They direct their backup troops into the river. Helter skelter, the rest of the army wades into the fray.

The Carthaginian trumpets sound again. Their enemy looks up to see scores of concealed Libyan phalanxes striding toward them from the back lines, each phalanx a hundred-man square that bristles with sarissas. In the center of these men is a five-hundred man wedge of Hannibal's elite Sacred Band. These are wealthy Carthaginians who choose to fight on foot to demonstrate their prowess and win glory. All are superb at hand-to-hand combat; all are sworn to protect Hannibal with their lives.

The phalanxes delve through the Iberian infantry, marching and thrusting as a single being -- an impenetrable wall of death. The Iberian cavalry cannot ride to help their beleaguered comrades because the Carthaginian and Numidian cavalry have surrounded them and are closing their fatal circle about them. The doughty horsemen can only sell their lives as dearly as possible, charging headlong into their enemy with a final battle scream.

The implacable phalanxes move through their onshore enemy and plow on into the water, flanked by galloping Numidians. The Iberians in the river reverse direction and rush for their side of the riverbank, with the Carthaginians in close pursuit. Those tribesmen who make it to the shore dash for the sheltering fields and forests, shedding arms and armor to run as fast as they can. But not fast enough, as the pursuing Numidians scythe through them, slaying at will, herding others back into the threshing phalanxes.

Watching the battle from the opposite bank, Hannibal waves his remaining cavalry forward to follow him across the river and join the pursuit. Hasdrubal rides at his side, grinning with satisfaction as he wraps linen around a spurting forearm cut. They plunge their mounts into the Tagus and splash over into the widespread carnage on the opposite shore.

"We have 'em, Hannibal! We'll wipe 'em out!" Hasdrubal exclaims.

The battle rages for another half hour as tens of thousands of tenacious Iberians fight on. Hannibal turns back to the river, and waves at one of his Sacred Band officers.

"Sound the recall."

The officer rides to the waiting trumpeters. Two brief blasts repeat across the battlefield, and the Carthaginian army slowly returns across the Tagus, pausing only to dispatch wounded enemies. Hannibal watches the troops plundering the enemy as his officers ride in from each part of his army: Carthaginians, Numidians, Balearics, and Iberian allies. The young general raises his sarissa over his head, exuberant with his triumph.

"Victory is ours! Let the remainder escape. Kill any more and you will be eliminating our future allies. "

Several allied officers exchange dubious looks, but say nothing. Hasdrubal, however, cannot contain himself. "What horseshit is this? Our plan was to encircle them and wipe them out! To leave no one alive!"

Hannibal scrambles down a knotted rope and picks up a bloodied falcata lying nearby. Remounting, he hefts the dread cleaver, studying it as if it contained some important message. The men are puzzled but they wait silently amid the scattered screams of dispatched enemies and blood-maddened elephants. They know Hannibal is coming up with a new plan, and is measuring his words before he doles them out.

"Plans change, Hasdrubal," Hannibal says. "Those tribes will trouble us no more. Let them return to their towns and villages, to spin their tales of how our force outnumbered them and won the day. But eventually, they will come to us to make peace – and money. And we will conscript them to our ranks. They are deadly fighters with these," he says as he swings the falcata about. "They only need proper training."

Hasdrubal looks dubious but he only shrugs and nods, saying nothing.

Several of the chiefs now voice their disagreement, urging him to continue the killing pursuit. Hannibal knows he is on the cusp of a crucial moment in his budding leadership of these older men. He scrambles down and looks into each one's eyes before he speaks. "The issue is done. Gather what treasure we can find and bring it to camp. Tomorrow, we return to New Carthage and store our plunder."

All the captains ride off except for one-eyed Mehrbal, the chieftain of the Balearic Islanders. Unkempt, clad in stinking linens and skins, the savage repulses the meticulous Hannibal. But Mehrbal's slingers are deadly snipers, so Hannibal suppresses his repulsion -- barely.

"Hannibal, my men are not interested in shiny trinkets. You know what we want."

Hannibal steps back to distance himself from the smell, sighs with resignation, and nods. "Go to the Carpetani camp. Take what women you value." Mehrbal's snaggled grin splits his face, and he scurries toward his horse.

"Mehrbal!"

The chieftain turns to see the stern young commander staring him in the eye. "Kill only those who attack you. On pain of death."

The chieftain glares at Hannibal and spits near the general's feet. Hannibal fingers his sword hilt, and contemplates whether he should run his sword through the impertinent scum's remaining eye and be done with him. Mehrbal grasps the hilt of his sword, watching carefully for the young man's reaction. Observing the confrontation from atop his horse, Hasdrubal grins at Mehrbal's bravado. He has no doubt how this confrontation will end.

Hannibal walks forward and starts to withdraw his sword, his face free of fear or hesitance. Mehrbal blinks, pulls back, and springs onto his horse.

"Pha! It will be done."

The Balearic gallops away. Hannibal watches him depart, takes a deep breath, and slowly exhales. Hasdrubal trots over to his brother, chuckling with delight.

"For a minute there, I thought you were going to kill old dirty dick! Good that you backed him down, those Balearic dung-eaters would think you are a woman. But I'm with Mehrbal, I confess. I would chop them all down."

Hannibal draws the captive falcata from his belt and hefts it. "As I said, they are skilled and brave fighters. The gods know, the Iberians can be capricious allies, but we will need them if we are to defeat Rome."

"You think so? Just wait until Carthage finds out about our victory, the time will be ripe to get more money and troops from Africa. More Libyans – and they can fight like hell!"

Hannibal shakes his head. "It will not happen. The Peace Party controls Carthage, and they are nothing but a bunch of corrupt shopkeepers. They will not pay for any more troops, and why should they? They can keep collecting gold and silver here from Iberia's mines, as long as we control them. No, they are not interested going to war in Italia and fighting with Rome – it would be bad for profits!"

Hasdrubal winces with disgust. "True enough. Those dough-handed merchants spot their pants if Rome even farts in their direction! They'll wait until the Romans invade Carthage, and then they'll try to bribe them to go away. And Rome, Rome does not bribe."

A servant brings over Hannibal's horse and he smoothly vaults into the saddle, motioning for Hasdrubal to follow him. The two brothers jaunt back to base camp, away from the press of the thousands about them, far from the noise and stink of victory. They ride past their Lusitanian and Terduli allies, who are busily engaged in looting the corpses of their fellow Iberians. When the two generals reach a place where no one is within earshot, Hannibal leans over to speak quietly to his brother.

"The Peace Party will dither until it is too late. So we must make Rome declare war on us, it is that simple. Then we will get the men and money we need. The Peace Party will have no choice!"

"So we pick a fight with Rome, eh? An admirable idea." Hasdrubal looks carefully at Hannibal. "I knew you were cunning, but I did not know you were so devious. You might have made a better politician than a general!"

"And why not do it?" retorts Hannibal. "Eventually the Romans will manufacture a reason to declare war on us, just as they did in the last war. Best we fight them now, while we are strong and they are occupied with the Gauls and Macedonians."

Hasdrubal looks doubtfully at him. "And how do we provoke them? Planning to sail to Rome and seduce one of the consul's wives? Perhaps a comely daughter or two – or three?"

"Don't let your crotch do your thinking," Hannibal retorts. "Besides, it would not make a difference to those patricians unless I stole one of those young boys they so favor."

"Well then, perhaps I should be your special envoy to Rome," exclaims Hasdrubal, rubbing his hands together in mock avarice.

Hannibal makes a disapproving face at his brother. He withdraws a small papyrus map from his belt and points to a coastal town north of them, near Roman-held territories. "That is Saguntum -- wealthy beyond measure, and a staunch ally of Rome. If we conquer it, Rome will have to come to their aid."

Picking at a scabbed cut on his hand, Hasdrubal glances sideways at his brother. "Huh! It is a citadel with high walls and thousands of defenders. Not as easy as ambushing the Carpetani, I will wager."

"It will not be easy, but I know the hearts of our mercenaries. If we promise them the treasure within Saguntum, they will overthrow it, were they only wielding daggers and riding oxen."

"Hah! That would woo those sticky-fingered Carpetani over to us, for certain. Even so, we cannot attack Saguntum and start a war with Rome without reason. The Council of Elders would recall us to Carthage. And crucify us."

Hannibal rolls up the map and pats it into his belt, thinking. "Our spies in Saguntum have told me that the local tribes are always quarreling with Saguntum over land, and that these disputes break out into small wars between them and the city. If we sign a treaty with one of the tribes, such as the Edetani, they become our ally. And it will be our 'military duty' to protect them from any who attack them."

"And then we can attack, without being crucified?" asks Hasdrubal.

"And then we take Saguntum in defense of the Edetani, as we are obligated. Rome will declare war on Carthage, and the Council of Elders will have to commission us to attack Rome, Peace Party or not. Rome will fall, as we promised our father."

"And if Rome falls, Italia falls," says Hasdrubal. "But it will not be easy. They have their share of spineless city politicians, but many come from sterner stock, from the farms and fields. It is not their patricians I fear, it is their rustics."

*　　*　　*　　*　　*

SABINA VALLEY, NORTH OF ROME. 218 BCE The short, stocky youth doggedly pushes his ox-drawn plow through the stony soil of his small farm's border. *This will make a good olive grove*, he thinks, *it will give me much oil to sell at Rome's marketplace, I'll have money to buy more land.*

He shouts for his two laborers to come help him, cursing them even as they run to assist. "Get over here, you pumpkins! Clear out the rocks from these furrows!"

His neighbors call him "Cato," a word signifying natural sagacity and wisdom. Though he is only seventeen, this potato-nosed youth is a central figure in the local town forums, impressing the wealthy landowners with his plainspoken advice on property disputes and farming. They respect his forceful simplicity, that he takes direct action in all his affairs – whatever the consequences.

Proud of his "Cato" cognomen, the boy has adopted it over his family name of Marcus Porcius, which is unknown to anyone but himself. Certainly, his Porcii ancestors distinguished themselves in battle. Cato's father was a heroic infantry officer and his grandfather a valorous cavalryman. Nevertheless, Rome chose to ignore the Porcii once peace came, relegating them to the humble fields from which they came, without office or recompense beyond these twelve uncultivated acres. And the Porcii name sank into undeserved obscurity. Every time he works this small field, Cato promises himself he will rectify the injustice to his family, that the Porcius name will be spoken in the Senate and his ancestors known to the people they served. And he will be known to all as Marcus Porcius Cato, a man of substance, no longer ignored by the landed gentry ... or by their haughty women.

As Cato pauses to wipe his brow, he sees Lucius Valerius Flaccus picking his gangly way down the hill from his palatial villa, heading towards him. *Not a bad sort for an aristocrat*, Cato thinks, *at least he has no interest in that Greek nonsense pursued by most patricians.*

Flaccus' tall, thin frame is draped in the simple linen tunic that wealthy landowners prefer -- expensive but not ostentatious. A sociable and easygoing man, his languid manner is deceiving. Only five years older than Cato, Flaccus is a battle-trained veteran of the first Punic War with Carthage. He has watched Cato resurrect this little farm since Cato's father died two years ago. Since then the young man has worked stoically from dawn to dusk, clad in the same sleeveless woolen tunic through all the seasons. Flaccus knows Cato is a man of few words but many accomplishments. As a man who relies on ruses and rumor, he has a grudging respect for Cato's unbending honesty.

As Flaccus approaches, Cato briefly raises his hand in

salutation, and resumes his plowing.

Undeterred, Flaccus waves back energetically. "Salus, neighbor Cato. A minute of your time."

Cato yanks his ox to a stop, his shoulders slump with visible disappointment. His laborers continue ahead, clearing stones and limbs from his path, knowing better than to cease work under Master Cato's watch.

"Salve, Flaccus. What brings you to my humble field?"

Flaccus surveys Cato's land and turns back to him. He grins. "Humble? I only wish my grapes were as abundant as yours ... or my wheat as tall. My foreman says you are already one of the best farmers in the valley. I don't know how you do it."

Cato shrugs. "I use lots of poultry manure, as my father taught me. And I follow the old Latin rule: work your men as hard as your oxen, keep them both a little hungry and fearful. I hear it works for women, too."

Flaccus laughs awkwardly. "Yes, well, I'm not sure I would impart all of that homily to my wife! But you have done wonders with your acres."

Cato bends down and scoops up some of his soil, lovingly crumbling it through his fingers. He holds a mound under Flaccus' nose.

"Smell! It is good earth, black and moist. When this land spit was given to my father – in lieu of pay or magistracy – it was naught but feeble dust. He soon died from his war wounds, but he never complained about the little given to him. I have made it fertile in his honor."

Flaccus nods sympathetically. "He sounds like he was a true

Roman. Close to the land."

"It is from the farming class that the bravest men and the sturdiest soldiers come," [i] says Cato. "We are the backbone of Rome."

"Yes, yes, I myself feel close to the land." Flaccus exclaims proudly. "Having my hands in the soil keeps me in touch with Roman virtues: honesty, simplicity, and devotion to duty."

Cato frowns at Flaccus, resentful that a patrician with uncalloused palms would speak knowingly about farming. "For my father, that was indeed true," Cato says. "He could have been a tribune or a censor, but he had the humble ways of our Latin ancestors." Cato picks up his plow and shoves its blade deep into the earth, grunting with the effort. "You speak of Roman virtues? Rome today does not respect simplicity or frugality. No, they would rather mimic the ornate ways of the effeminate Greeks, like those members of the Hellenic Party. Pthaw!" Cato spits into the dirt near Flaccus' feet.

Flaccus jumps back and chuckles. "So you have said, friend Cato, so you have said! Your speeches at the village forums have made some of our neighbors quite uneasy. But I admire your respect for Roman traditions. I think you should speak about it at a larger venue. So I offer you this: come with me to Rome."

Cato carefully lays down his plow. He squints at Flaccus. "Go to the city? I have much work to do here. There are trees to plant, crops to harvest. No." Cato hoists up his plow, snaps his switch on the ox's backside, and resumes pushing his plow through the stubborn soil. Flaccus stares at him, then trots to catch up.

"I know you do not trust aristocrats, but there are many of us who agree with you that our traditional values are subverted by Hellenic ways, that we have drifted from our agrarian roots of austerity and simplicity. So we have formed a party to preserve the old ways. We are just starting but we already have a dozen senators and Fabius himself."

Cato halts his plowing. "General Fabius?"

"Hero of the first Carthaginian war!" exclaims Flaccus. "He is not much of an orator, but his presence lends credence to our movement."

Cato lays down the ox's reins, and studies Flaccus. "And why would you have me join such as you? Do you fancy me as your aide? I do not take well to serving others!"

"Yes, yes, I have noticed!" laughs Flaccus, flapping his hands. "But that's not the reason, on my honor. You are eloquently simple and direct – when you ever speak – and the Roman people will hang on your every word. You could lead our land-owning citizens, the plebs, to the Latin Party. Consider, Cato, you could be the first in your family to be a senator. The Porcius family name would be known throughout Italia!"

Cato's eyes light up, but his face remains impassive. "I will consider it."

Sensing an opening in Cato's wall of resolve, Flaccus grows more animated. "I only ask you to follow the trail that noble Cincinnatus trod a century ago, Cato. Put down your plow and save Rome!"

Cato turns and picks up his reins, steps behind the ox, and looks straight ahead. He snaps the reins and the ox plows forward. "That is a stirring little speech, but I have much to do here. Excuse me now."

Flaccus nods resignedly, starts to walk back to his villa, but he turns about. "Cato! Why not come to Rome after the harvest, when we bring our food to market? Surely, that would be a practical time to do it."

Cato yanks his harness. The ox stops. He turns to Flaccus with a look of smoldering anger. "Enough. We shall talk tomorrow."

Flaccus takes one look into Cato's eyes and walks off. Cato hefts the plow to resume his work. As Flaccus heads up the hill, he can hear Cato cajoling his laborers to keep up with him. No easy task, Flaccus thinks.

That night, Cato lies upon his sleeping mat, staring at the thatched roof of his small house. He knows Flaccus has given him an opportunity to fulfill his promise to gain fame, but seizing that opportunity might also immerse him in the ways of Flaccus' patrician allies. He might become the very person he despises – a self-indulgent aristocrat. Or worse, the Party would use him as a tool to curry favor with the citizens they covertly despise and manipulate. And what will they think of an ignorant farmer with shit on his sandals? The patricians are educated men, wise in the ways of art and philosophy. Will they respect him? Does he need their respect, or does he just need an opportunity to win it? Cato tosses, drowses, and finally sleeps.

Dawn slides over the green-shouldered Sabina Mountains as Cato rises from his mat. He pulls on his worn leather sandals, belts his frayed tunic, and walks out into the rising sun. He strides through his fields and up the side of a steep hill, never breaking pace, to tramp down into a lush grain field where a simple cottage stands, an island in a waving sea of wheat. The landowner has kept this rude hut untouched because to Romans it is a temple to Roman virtue. This was the home of Manius Curius Dentatus.

Cato stands in front of the sun-tinged cottage, staring into its doorway. The youth walks around the front yard and stirs the dirt with his toe, uncharacteristically nervous. He finally summons himself and walks slowly into the dim interior. Inside, he sees Dentatus' iron hoe and sickle lying on the floor, unmoved in sixty years. And there, built into the back wall, is the famous stone hearth.

 The boy knows well the legend of that fireplace, how the Samnites visited Dentatus in this hut after the war hero returned to it from his third year-long stint as one of the two consuls, leaders of all of Rome. The Samnites could not believe that a general who had earned four victory parades would live in such rude circumstances. They entered the shelter to ask the slave inside for directions to Dentatus' manse. But there was Dentatus, sitting next to the hearth fire, roasting turnips.

 The Samnites showed him the carts of treasure that would be his if he would but lobby for their interests in Rome. Glancing outside at their wagonloads of bribe, he said he preferred to rule the possessors of gold over possessing it himself, and returned to his turnips.

 As a child, Cato became breathless the first time his father told him that story: he found his hero. Cato found out later that Dentatus died happy as a poor farmer, uncorrupted by the fame and power he had achieved – and abandoned.

 Cato stands immobile, facing the hearth as minutes drift to an hour. Sunshine now blankets the valley floor, flowing up its grove-lined slopes. The youth walks out to stand in the warm sun, listening to the raucous starlings welcoming the day. He looks once more into the hut's front door, wipes the corners of his eyes, and marches up the hill toward Flaccus' villa.

 Cato locates Flaccus in the back of his garden, directing the field slaves in his vineyard. The youth strides over to him and blurts, "I will go with you to Rome, but it will be after the harvest."

Flaccus smiles, and slaps Cato on the back. Cato winces at the familiarity, but Flaccus doesn't seem to notice. "The gods be thanked! I will introduce you to our party members, I'm sure you will want to join us! There is Senator Marcus Gracchus, Tiberius, and Cassius…."

Cato raises his arm, cutting him off. "I would meet General Fabius. Promise me that."

"Of course," hastens Flaccus. "It would greatly please him to meet you! I have told him about your family's military service. I'm sure he would have a commission for you. So, perhaps we should go sooner than the harvest. That devil Hannibal has captured Saguntum over there in Iberia, did you hear? He's marching over the Pyrenees to the Alps, maybe heading towards Rome!"

Cato shrugs. "He is a Carthaginian. He means for our destruction. It will not happen."

Flaccus laughs. "Of course, he cannot cross the Alps in winter, but Rome is taking no chances. They will send Fabius' army to northern Italia before the winter comes, and Fabius will soon be departing. Why wait? My slaves can harvest your wheat and grapes."

Cato's looks at Flaccus, his jaw set in a manner all Rome will come to know. "I follow the path of Cincinnatus and Dentatus. I will finish my crops by the next new moon. Only then will I put down my plow and go to Rome."

Flaccus sighs. "As you will, after the harvest. But we leave immediately after it is done. Ah, you will love Rome. You will have many to help you free Rome from the control of those

Hellenic Party elitists: the Tullia, the Julia… and the Scipios!"

* * * * *

ROME, 218 BCE. Pomponia, wife to the consul Publius Scipio, stalks the marbled halls of the spacious family domus. Her son is late for his tutoring session, and he is nowhere to be found. She paces through the domus' frescoed hallways, looking into the study and peering about the inside gardens. A queenly woman with flowing red hair and blue-green eyes, Pomponia is rarely given to bouts of impatience, but now she grows more irritated by the moment. With her husband gone to war, she has had to manage the family farms and villas by herself, and she must prepare for a morning business meeting. Pomponia hurries through a rear corridor, calling her son's name.

"Scipio! Publius Cornelius Scipio! Your friends are here. Time for your lesson!"

As she passes a side corridor, a tiny head sticks out of it and watches her go. It is Barco, a Nubian child who is a slave of the Scipio household – and a spy for young Scipio. Barco darts down a hallway to the slave quarters, where he skids to a stop in front of an upstairs sleeping room, its opening covered with a worn linen cloth. Barco whispers loudly at the room's entry.

"Your mother is on the far side of the house! All is well!"

A lean muscular arm extends from the cloth covering, holding a nut-filled date. The hand flicks the date down to Barco, who snatches it in midair and dashes off, pursued by the sounds of muted laughter from the veiled sleeping room.

Inside the cubiculum, sixteen-year-old Scipio lays nude next to Jamila, an equally naked young slave girl. He smiles and puts a finger to his lips, signaling Jamila for quiet, and bends to her ear.

"It pays to have spies about. Now we don't have to worry about Mother!"

The slim African slave girl giggles conspiratorially and pulls Scipio down to her. She kisses him ardently, running her hands down his bare back, clutching his buttocks and stroking his cleft until she feels him rise and harden against her. Jamila smiles and lies back, awaiting his attentions.

Scipio is a practiced lover, having regular sex since he was thirteen. Like all Roman men, he believes frequent sex is necessary for health and fitness, something to be indulged in as regularly as exercise. But he is unique in that he studies lovemaking as an art, experimenting with the Greek and Egyptian techniques he's learned from the scrolls he purchased at the marketplace. And he has learned much.

Scipio lays back and pulls one of her legs on top of his. He thrusts into her with quick, short, strokes. Jamila moans into her pillow, clawing its cover. Her groans come shorter and quicker. She trembles, quiets, trembles again, and explodes in orgasm. As she spasms against him, Scipio feels himself throb, tingling with a delicious mounting pain-pressure. He comes violently and they roll together, convulsing until they are spent.

Scipio soon rises and wrestles into his tunic, giving her a final caress before he vaults from the cubiculum and hustles toward the central atrium. Jamila leans out to watch him go, smiling at how he strides as if his every step had an important purpose.

The slave girl hears footsteps coming. She withdraws into the loft, waiting to discreetly exit. She thinks about Scipio as she pulls on her shift and sandals, how he has always treated her as more than a slave, respecting her wishes, sharing his hopes and dreams. *May the gods protect him*, she prays. *His love for commoners and slaves will bring him in trouble someday.*

Scipio races through the mansion's passages to burst into the wide, airy atrium; almost falling into the fishpond. The atrium's vaulted walls are lined with paintings, some of Roman gods and heroes, others of the many Scipios who served as generals and consuls to Rome since its days as a kingdom.

His mother sits at one of the couches surrounding the pool. Arms crossed, she stares irritably at Scipio as he hurries toward her across the wide marble tiles. Next to her sits his two dearest friends, Laelius and Amelia, grinning at him because they know he's in trouble. Boltar, the family's two hundred pound Mastiff, lolls at their feet.

Laelius springs up to meet Scipio. "Late again, Scippy. Your mother has proposed adopting me in your place!" The curly-haired teen is tall, lean, witty, and graceful; the embodiment of manners and consideration. His elegant mien belies his common roots, as well as a strength and toughness that has laid low more than one male who mocked his effeminacy – and seduced others who were attracted by it. A boy of modest means, Laelius first met Scipio several years ago at one of the many city parks, places where the boys gather for wrestling and wooden sword fights. Scipio delighted in Laelius' sense of humor and sarcasm, oft directed at those who would mock his strange ways. They quickly became close companions and have been inseparable ever since.

On his first visit to the Scipio manor, Laelius was awestruck at the patrician wealth that surrounded him. Driven to escape his lowly upbringing, he soon adopted the aristocrats' dress and mannerisms, hoping to make his fortune by associating with them. Today, Laelius is dressed in one of the ornate Greek tunics scorned by many Romans because the style lacks the somber gravitas of the plainer native clothes, an overly serious attitude that Laelius finds both amusing and entertaining.

The two boys grasp hands, and Laelius gives Scipio a playful shove. "Late again, donkey!" Scipio returns the push, and a shoving match ensues. As he contends with Laelius, Scipio glances over at Amelia, who is watching them with amusement with her dark green eyes. Scipio can't help admiring her long brunette hair styled into a woman's coif, at the swelling breasts and hips that seem to have sprouted overnight from her coltish body. Was this the tousle-haired child of last season who followed him around all the time, asking him questions as if he were an oracle? My gods, he thinks amusedly, now she argues with me at every turn. Where did the girl go, when did the woman arrive?

Pomponia steps between the two roughhousing boys and stares into Scipio's face. "Where were you? I roamed all over this house looking for you!" Scipio flicks a glance at Laelius. "If truth be told, I was into something I couldn't get out of. I came as soon as I could after that."

Laelius grins mischievously as he bends over to pet Boltar. "I'm sure you came quickly, Scippy. You're known for that."

As Scipio snarls at Laelius, Boltar happily climbs onto Laelius' lap, bowling him onto his back. Laelius pushes futilely against the friendly behemoth. "Off me, dog! Sit!" Laelius' shoves only encourage the dog to further play. The beast leans his pot-sized head into Laelius' face, enveloping his face with tongue. For the meticulous Laelius, this is tantamount to being washed with a toilet sponge. His face is a rictus of disgust. Amelia and Scipio laugh at his wailings. Even dignified Pomponia cannot help but smile.

"Owgh! Sit, sit!" yells Laelius. "Scippy, I thought you taught that dog to sit!"

Scipio knows his friend is angry when he uses his first name, and decides he's had enough. Scipio stands behind Boltar and pulls him back by his studded leather collar as Laelius crawls out from under the dog.

"Dogs can tell when you are truly serious, Laelius," says Scipio in his best tutorial tone. "You need an air of command. Watch." Scipio stands stiffly, and affects a commanding air. "Boltar! Down! Sit!"

Boltar looks at Scipio, curious but unmoved. Scipio bends forward and starts shoving on Boltar's hindquarters. "Sit down, beast. Sit!" The dog mills about in confusion as Scipio hunches over and follows him, pushing against his hindquarters. Laelius bends over with laughter.

"Careful, there, Scippy, you look like you're trying to catch him for a sniff!"

Scipio's mother steps forward and gently intervenes, stroking the dog as she pulls Scipio upright. "That's no way to treat poor Boltar, you're scaring him. He may bite you, and I would not blame him if he did!"

"But he must learn, Mother," replies Scipio. "Father said a Roman should have a firm hand in all of his affairs."

Laelius rolls his eyes. "Your father often had a firm hand on your backside," he says, "and you still snapped back!"

Pomponia raises her hand, and the two boys fall silent. "You can be firm and still be kind. Teach Boltar to sit because he wants to, not because he's afraid of you. Here..." She breaks off a piece of bread from a wicker basket on a settee. She holds it above Boltar's head, forcing him to look up as she strokes firmly down his back. Boltar sits, and she gives him the scrap. Pomponia turns to her son.

"See? He sat willingly. If you make him afraid of you, he will not follow. He may even turn on you someday, because he has no love for you."

Young Scipio mulls this over. "Father punishes his men when they do wrong," he says sullenly.

"Your father is also merciful to them, and rewards them when they do right. That is why they are so loyal to him. Even the Italia tribes bear him respect for his fairness to all. Now try it again with rewards, not punishment."

With a doubtful look at his mother, Scipio repeats her trick with another piece of bread, and the dog sits. Scipio tries again, without food, and the dog repeats the act. He beams at his mother. "Look, it's working! Good Boltar!" The boy strokes the dog's head.

Amelia applauds, giving Scipio a wry smile. "I do say, Cornelius Scipio, you have already learned a lesson today, and we haven't even started the tutorial. You're ahead of the pack again."

Scipio tries to feign indifference to Amelia's words, but a pleased grin escapes him, which he quickly stifles. He knows that Roman men must always exhibit gravitas if they would be respected. Nevertheless, he is delighted with her praise, and his eyes sparkle under his furrowed brow.

Inconspicuously, Pomponia has been watching Amelia and Scipio today, as she has done for months. She is pleased at the ardor that blooms between them, and plots how she can help it grow. Pomponia intends that Amelia will be the next matriarch of the powerful Scipio family

Pomponia knows that Amelia's independence and quiet strength are the perfect tempering forces to her brilliant but headstrong son, that Amelia's practicality would be the balance to his growing propensity to follow the vivid dreams which come upon him at night, believing them to be messages from the gods. Amelia's father is the admired and powerful general Lucius Aemilius Paullus, and that makes the match even more appealing to the politically-minded woman. Their marriage would join two of the most influential families in Rome, both supporters of the Hellenic Party, the nemeses of the Latin Party.

Pomponia turns her attention back to young Scipio, who is repeating the trick with Boltar, trying to get him to lie down. "Very good. He will give his life for you if you but care for him, show him respect. Remember that when you are a general and command your own men."

"General?" Scipio makes a face. "Last night I dreamed I was a great scholar like Aristotle or Plato. I was walking about the Temple of Vesta, my students following while I lectured. It was wonderful!"

Laelius shakes his head, amused. "You and your dreams, always talking about your dreams! You'd make a better priest than a general, Scippy!"

"And you would make a better woman than man," Scipio retorts with mock anger, "the way you always dress up in those fancy Greek togas! If I am to be a temple priest, you could be the temple eunuch, guarding the virgins!"

"Pha! Now you sound like one of those Latin Party gasbags. They want everyone to dress like a farmer and smell like fertilizer! You think this finery hides a woman? I can bend your back any day, double-chin!"

Laelius jumps onto Scipio, and they fall to the floor in a

wrestling match. The fight is even. Slim Laelius is wiry and quick, while muscular Scipio is strong and determined. They laugh as they wrestle, but neither gives an inch. Neither holds back. Laelius eventually climbs on Scipio's back and pins his arms in a chokehold. "Got you! Give up!"

Scipio pitches over to land atop Laelius and knock the wind out of him. Laelius recovers in a flash and wrestles his way free until Scipio tackles him and pins him to the floor. Laelius squirms underneath him like a maddened snake. "Get off me, pumpkin!" demands Laelius. Scipio grins triumphantly. "Ha! I learned that move from you, toga boy!" Learn from your enemies, isn't that what they say?

Pomponia turns to Amelia with a look of mock anger. "Those boys would kill for each other, if they do not kill each other..." She claps her hands peremptorily. "That is enough." Scipio and Laelius stand next to each other, breathing hard. Pomponia points a finger at the couch. They walk quietly to it, elbowing each other, and return to their seats. After they sit down, Pomponia stares at Scipio until he squirms. "I just don't like him making fun of me. And I really could be a great scholar, I can see it!"

Pomponia shakes her head. "Your father, grandfather, and great-grandfather were all generals, you know that. As a Scipio, you are destined to lead men to battle and lead them in the Senate." She sees Scipio's face fall and instantly regrets her words. "But perhaps your dream will come true anyway. "Many things are possible over a lifetime," say the poets. You might be both."

Scipio looks away from her, his shoulders slumped. "If I must fight, I cannot be a scholar or teacher. I'll spend all my time learning battle tactics and stratagems, and logistics and weaponry. Just like Father does…"

Pomponia sits next to her sullen son, leaning her head in to talk softly to him. "War has its own thinkers and philosophies, that much I know. It takes a true scholar to learn the ancient warriors' ways, and mold them to your purpose. And to learn from your enemies. There is much wisdom to war, if you would but attend to it."

Irrepressible Laelius, silent through all this, jumps up and grabs a scroll, waving it like a sword as he prances about them. "General Cornelius Scipio, the fighting philosopher! Certain death to enemy thinkers!" Scipio laughs in spite of himself, walks over to place his hands on Laelius' shoulders, as if he is an officer giving a commission to a soldier. "And you will be my right-hand man. First Centurion Laelius, the fighting poet!"

Amelia frowns derisively at the two boys. She stalks over to a rack of practice weapons, grabs a blunted wooden spear and presses it into the hands of a startled Scipio. "Dolt! Do you not see? You can be like that Alexander the Great that Asclepius told us about. Alexander studied his Persian enemies. He learned their ways in order to conquer them. And he was the greatest general who ever lived! Do you not recall anything you have learned?"

Scipio expertly performs several feints and parries with the spear, and preens before Amelia. "I know enough of the military arts. I would rather learn about other lands and peoples, Amelia. Distant ones!"

Amelia glowers at him. "I hear Iberia is filled with wild tribes and unexplored forests, strange plants and animals, mines laden with silver and gold. If you go there, you would have so much to see, you silly boy."

"If I go there, I will be in the middle of an army! I'd have to go where it goes and do what it does. Oh, shit!" Scipio stalks over and shoves the spear to its rack.

Pomponia feels for her son, knowing his desire so differs from his destiny, that he prefers the life of the mind to the life of the sword, though he is adept at both. "Amelia is just trying to help you, my son, she knows your destiny as a Scipio. It is my heart's desire that you pursue your wishes, but Rome needs you for other purposes. This Hannibal may soon be at our gates. All Romans will have to answer the call of duty."

The sound of scuffling footsteps interrupts their conversation. The teens know that sound well, and they go to sit on one of the low-lying couches, facing the entryway.

A tall, angular, old Greek shuffles through the doorway, cradling a half-dozen papyrus scrolls against his plain white toga – one of the few foreigners in Rome that may wear that privileged garment. His face is seamed and his back is bent with age, but his arms are still sinewy; warrior arms that belie his current profession. It is Asclepius, the famed Greek sage. A retired brigadier of the Athenian army, Asclepius was once taught by the students of Aristotle, the greatest of the philosophers. True to his oath to Aristotle's Peripatetic School from which he graduated, Asclepius walks about and imparts his wisdom freely to others.

The ancient tutor's writings are known throughout Rome, but his favorite pursuit is teaching. To that end, he serves as a tutor to the Scipio family's two sons, and to their friends Laelius and Amelia. Even at seventy years, his gray eyes are clear and intense, his deep voice purposeful and sure. He nears the couch, waves his arm to bring the three teens up to face him. "Scipio, Laelius, Amelia! Time for your lessons. Best you be prepared this time."

Asclepius hands them each a scroll, turns to Pomponia, and inclines his head. "I trust you are well, madam."

"I am, Asclepius. I was talking with the children about the importance of scholarship to life ... and to war."

"All too true, madam. In our last tutorial we were talking about Alexander the Great and his genius at absorbing his enemies' tactics and weaponry. What a pity he became such a madman. He might have conquered the world!"

Pomponia nods her head toward Amelia. "I know. Amelia has just informed us about Alexander. She was very clear about that."

Pomponia walks out of the hallway entrance, her slave attendant following her. She motions for Asclepius to follow. He hands his lesson scrolls to Laelius and hurries out to meet her. The matron bends close to Asclepius' ear and speaks quietly but intensely. "I fear my son there has little appreciation for battles and conquests, tutor. He is very skilled at arms, but he seems more a budding priest than soldier, always talking about his visions and dreams. His father worries he will not follow the family line. As do I."

"Would that be such a waste, Domina? He has a mystic's eye," says Asclepius admiringly. "And he sees the future in his dreams. I myself have seen some of his predictions come true. He has more imagination than I have seen in a man – especially one who is a Roman!"

Pomponia winces at his words, aware of the Greeks' attitude toward the Roman intellect. "Amelia and Laelius talk about him and his dreams," agrees Pomponia, "how the visions come to him when Febris, goddess of fever, visits him in the night. They think he is touched by the gods."

Asclepius laughs. "Yes, and they are also a bit afraid of him! You know, those fevers of his started when we had that cursed infestation of mosquitoes several years ago. I think they passed something onto him, something that accounts for his 'visits by the goddess,' as you say."

Pomponia shrugs. "Perhaps so, but our doctors have found nothing to treat. But that is no matter. I wanted you to hear my concerns about my son, so that you may help resolve them. Encourage him to follow in his ancestor's footsteps, to serve Rome with both his arm and his mind. It is his destiny."

"I will do my best, madam," says Asclepius, with a slight bow. "But his peers in the military may not embrace his creativity and intuition. The boy is not one to follow a well-trod path."

"All the more reason he should be a general, he is so well read."

"What is the saying, Domina, *Cave ab homine unius libri*, beware the man of one book? Rome needs leaders with new ideas."

Pomponia turns from Asclepius, motioning for her slave to follow her. "I must go, Tutor. Our property taxes must be figured, and that is something I can resolve. Teach them well."

She walks back into the atrium to a table near the end of the couch, picks up several wax tablets of the estate accounts, and heads out the door as her slaves follow. Asclepius ponders her words about Scipio as he goes to sit on the couch, gesturing for the three students to sit at his feet.

"Now then! We shall continue last week's lesson on Greek philosophers. What did you learn from Aristotle's work on politics?"

Scipio's raises his hand eagerly. Asclepius' tutoring sessions are the high point of his day. Asclepius acknowledges him with a nod.

"Proceed."

"A good citizen works to preserve his country, but a good man works to do the right thing, to be a good person. And these two may come into conflict."

"Oh? And how may that be?"

"His interests in being a good person may interfere with his interest doing good as a citizen ... uh, doing good for others, for his country. Therein lies the conflict."

"And when these two interests conflict?"

"It is nobler to act in the interests of the state over the individual. That is correct, is it not?"

Asclepius ignores the question. "Even if the individual must commit dishonorable acts?"

Scipio pauses, looks over at his two friends. Laelius seems to have found a fascinating pattern on his robe which occupies his attention, but Amelia shakes her head in disagreement, further confusing Scipio.

"Yes, I ... I would think so."

"Well, you should hesitate on answering. Aristotle is not so clear on that point, is he? What if a man must sacrifice his personal honor, his beliefs, for the good of his country? What if he must kill or steal to save it? Could such a man – or woman – be a hero?"

Amelia looks puzzled and becomes irritated with Asclepius.

"How can such a man be a hero?" she demands. "A hero has character. What character remains to someone who sacrifices his beliefs? His morals? What is left of him?"

Laelius looks up, suddenly animated. "It is not so black and white. It's all a matter of compromise, I say, of reasonable accommodation. You give a little to gain a little, or give a lot and gain a lot. But you must always keep something of yourself, of what is most valuable. And maybe you give up one of your values to achieve another, as a farmer will steal to save his children from hunger. That is the way of those who would accomplish things."

Scipio and Amelia simply stare at Laelius, they have never heard him speak so seriously for so long. Asclepius breaks their silence.

"Ah, Laelius, you always have a pragmatic view of things. Now Aristotle, he would say that there is not necessarily a conflict between man acting as a good citizen and acting as a good individual, if the state is promoting the common good. But where it does not promote the good of the people, perhaps the man must act contrary to the state's interests, both as a good citizen and as a good man. Is that not so?"

Amelia fidgets with her wool tunic's edge. "Please be careful, tutor; you will be accused of promoting revolution. I would hate to see your head at the gates of Rome."

Asclepius nods, laughing grimly. "Ah yes, treason. A handy excuse to kill dissent by killing the dissenters! Do you know, the Greek state sentenced Socrates to death for corrupting the young; a man who was only interested in educating them? If Rome executes me for that I would at least be in good company!"

Scipio laughs. "Well said, tutor. I bet Socrates was a masterful teacher. I would be like him – and you."

Asclepius puts his arm on Scipio's shoulder. "Young Scipio, you are a general's son, as was Alexander the Great. You remember what we learned about Alexander?"

Before Scipio can answer, Amelia jumps in. "We talked of that before you came, tutor. Alexander was the greatest general of all time." She looks at Scipio. "The Macedonian was a great scholar, too. He studied his enemies, used their ways against them."

Asclepius nods approvingly. "Yes, yes. Remember, your enemy will teach you how to defeat him, if you but attend to his words and deeds."

A stentorian voice booms from the hallway. "Unless you are a Roman, then they must all attend to you!"

Asclepius turns to see General Publius Scipio step into the room. The consul has the wide, staring eyes and cleft chin that he passed on to his two sons, along with his dark curly hair and broad shoulders. Standing ramrod straight with head held high, Publius exudes an air of absolute authority, though he wears but a simple white tunic bordered with a wide purple stripe and a dagger attached to his leather belt. Lucius, Scipio's older brother, stands behind his father, lolling against the archway. The chubby young man has an easygoing and subdued manner, a trait that Publius has long tried to drill out of him, with little success.

Young Scipio rushes over to his father, who wraps him in a bear hug. "Father! You are back from Iberia!" He nods to his brother. "Salus, Lucius."

Lucius grins and waves, then drifts over to talk to Laelius and

Amelia.

"My heart sings to see you!" says Publius, holding Scipio at arm's length. "How fare you?"

"I do fare well, Father. Asclepius teaches us about Aristotle and Alexander the Great!"

Publius' brow narrows, though he maintains his smile. "Ah yes, mighty Alexander, master of the world. He is a worthy topic. But why would you study Aristotle, a fancy Greek philosopher? What good are his ideas to a future general?"

Asclepius coughs and studies the nightingales singing in the atrium's bronze birdcage.

"We are learning politics today," says Scipio. "Asclepius says that the might of a country lies in its wealth and military, but its greatness lies in its art and philosophy!"

Publius throws a cautionary look at Asclepius. "Well, there is something to be said for art and philosophy, when peace allows for such indulgences. But peace for us may be far away. Art may have to wait."

As his father talks, young Scipio studies the large atrium and its adjoining rooms, admiring the beautiful mosaics, statues, and sculptures that fill their living space. Scipio walks over to the far wall to a wooden bin that holds scores of papyrus scrolls; the writings of learned Romans, Greeks, and Persians. He pulls a scroll from the bin and cradles it lovingly in his hands.

"We have so much art and literature here, but the people outside have none. I wish we could share it with them, and I could be their teacher about it."

"Teacher?" says Publius irritably. "We have Greeks and slaves to be our teachers. What about being a general or senator, a leader of men? Would that be so detestable?"

Asclepius interjects, "Heed him. Your father is a revered senator. The Senate bends their ear to him when he speaks."

"I do admire you, Father," Scipio hastens to add. "I hear you will be one of our next consuls, leading all of Rome. But Plato says that a philosopher should be the ruler of the people, but that he is too good or wise to seek an office because he knows it will corrupt him. Is that true?"

Amelia and Laelius grin at each other, amused at Scipio's unwitting jibe at Publius.

Publius cannot help but laugh. "Plato is right about the wisdom of avoiding office. I should have read more of him! Perhaps Plato's philosopher-king would sacrifice some of his high standards for the good of his people. He who carries a heavy load must bend to bear it."

"I would love to be like you, but I do love scholarship. I would favor being a teacher and philosopher, if the Fates allowed it."

Publius studies his beloved son. He withdraws his dagger, and bends over to scrutinize its keen blade, as if it contains a message for him. He glances up at Asclepius. "The lesson is over," Publius says flatly. "Cornelius, come with me."

As Amelia files out with the others, she casts an anxious smile at Scipio, unsure of what his stern father has in store for him. Scipio looks at her and shrugs, mystified.

Publius walks his son out of the wide atrium to a small room adjoining it. Inside is a narrow temple of wood and marble, holding five human figurines on a wood shelf that is placed at eye level. It is the family altar, holding clay statuettes of the five spirits that guard the household. A small plate of meat and grain rests on the shelf in front of them – the Scipios' daily offering to their protectors.

On the wall next to the lararium hangs a wax death mask of Scipio's grandfather, Lucius Cornelius Scipio, former consul and general to Rome. A half-dozen other masks circle it like a halo, all of them ancestors who were military leaders.

Publius faces his son. "You are a Scipio, son, born to protect and lead. That must be your devotion ... your life."

"But I had a vision, Father. I saw myself as..."

Publius points to the first mask. "You see your grandfather watching us? He was a great general, as was his father before him. Even now, your uncle Gnaeus is in far-off Iberia, fighting the Carthaginians. That is what Scipios do, we protect Rome."

"Lucius could be the next general," Scipio says encouragingly. "He wants to be a great soldier – he told me so!"

Publius looks away from Scipio. "Yes, but Lucius is ... he is destined for other accomplishments. You are our only hope for succession."

Publius turns his son to face the altar, and stands in front of it. "Cornelius Scipio, it is time for you to take on the ways of men and do your duty. So now, before our gods and our ancestors, swear you will follow your destiny. Swear you will devote your life to preserving Rome from all who would destroy it."

Scipio looks down, swallows nervously. His right hand twitches, as it always does when he is anxious and indecisive. He can see a life of study and teaching for himself, a man serving all of Rome, peacefully. He does not fear punishment for denying his father's wishes, but loving him beyond all love of himself, he sorely fears to disappoint him. Young Scipio shifts his feet and stares at the altar and the mask. He finally turns to his father and squares his shoulders.

"I do so swear."

"Say it. 'I swear I will devote my life to preserving Rome from all who would destroy it.' "

"I swear I will devote my life to preserving Rome... from all who would destroy it."

"Whatever the cost."

Scipio's eyes widen and his hand twitches again. "What, uh, whatever the cost."

Publius kisses his son on the cheek and puts his hands on Scipio's shoulders. "I know you sacrifice your chosen path for this. I am proud of you."

Scipio bows his head, avoiding his father's eyes.

Looking around to ensure no one is near him, Publius speaks in lowered tones. "I have my own 'visions,' did you know that? No one knows but your mother. In a dream, I saw you entering Rome in a glorious triumph. Thousands chanted your name as you rode in a white chariot, garbed in a purple toga and wearing the victory crown of laurel leaves. You were a savior of Rome!"

Hearing his father's words, Scipio's eyes widen with excitement. "But then I saw your face," Publius continues. "You were oddly sad in the midst of your glory. I do not know why. Nor have the Fates shown me why you attained such greatness, just that it will come to you as a young man. As your father, I must help you attain it. Wait here."

Publius walks out, his puzzled son watching him go. Scipio leaves the lararium and returns to the bin of scrolls. He trails his fingers across the tops of them, as if caressing a lover goodbye. He abruptly pulls one out and reads over it, feeling the tears well in his eyes.

His father returns shortly, carrying an armful of gleaming bronze armor. There is a full-face helmet, greaves to protect the shins, a breastplate inscribed with battle scenes, and a small round shield. He lays them onto Scipio's cradled arms, and unscrolls an elegantly drawn lambskin map of Italia.

"Your service begins next week. Hannibal is now in Italia. That demon somehow crossed the Alps in winter, and he marches for Rome. The Senate has sent me to intercept him until more legions can be recruited." Publius points to the northern regions of Italia, near the Iberia border. "Hannibal will be somewhere in the Po River Valley, and that is where we will meet him."

Young Scipio stares incredulously at his father. "You are going to war again? So soon?"

"The harvest is almost finished. Our soldiers can leave their farms, so I can ship our legions up to the north." Publius points at his son's armor. "Go ahead, try it on." Scipio solemnly dons his new breastplate as his father continues. "You will be part of the cavalry, to ride along as an observer. You are an excellent horseman, after all."

Scipio tightens the straps on the sides of the breastplates, and waves his arms to test his freedom of movement. "So I am to fight the dreaded Carthaginians. Fight Hannibal the Great."

Publius grins, puts his arm around Cornelius and tugs him closer. "You still have much to learn about fighting, boy, learning that is not in scrolls or the practice field. As I said, you will only watch this time. We depart in four days."

Cornelius bows his head somberly, but then he brightens. "Can Laelius join us? Please?"

"You know the equestrian rules, boy. Anyone who joins the equites must buy his own horse and armor," Publius frowns regretfully. "And Laelius is not from a wealthy family."

Scipio pulls off his breastplate and flings it to the floor. "Gods be damned, that is nothing but shit! He is a better rider than any of the other boys, even better than me! He fights like a cornered weasel, is he to be denied simply because he is poor? Is the Roman way the way of privilege over talent? Wealth over skill?"

Publius blinks in surprise, and stammers an answer. "W- we have our traditions, and they must be respected."

Scipio looks into his father's eyes. "You asked me for a promise, Father, and I gave it. Now I ask you for one. Promise me, truly, if Laelius can provide acceptable horse and weaponry, he can join us in the north."

The consul stares at his son. Scipio returns his gaze steadfastly. Publius shrugs his shoulders, half in resignation and half in admiration. "Very well. If he can provide horse and armor, it will be so." Publius raises a warning finger. "But you must not give them to him. Nor give him money to buy them. On your honor."

Scipio barely represses a smile – he has an idea. "I do so promise. On my honor."

"Very well." Publius strides out as young Scipio gathers his armor and holds it at arm's length, studying it as if it were a costume for a party he does not want to attend. He carefully lays down the armor, picks up the scroll he was studying for today's lesson, and walks over to ease it into the bin. He returns to the couch, with Boltar following him, to slump forward with his arms resting on his knees. Looking at Boltar, he gives him the "sit" gesture and watches him obey. Scipio slowly strokes the dog's head as he stares into space. After several minutes, he smiles morosely at the dog.

"Well, Boltar. If I cannot be the next Aristotle of philosophy, perhaps I will be the next Alexander of war. Or something such as that. Pha!" Scipio slumps forward, and is quiet for several minutes. Suddenly he vaults up, face alight with mischief. "Come, Boltar, let us visit Laelius. We have a little trick to play." Scipio trots from the room, Boltar loping next to him.

That night, Scipio twists in his bed, sweating with the recurrent fever that so often comes upon him. After several restless hours, he plunges into a deep exhausted sleep. And then the dreams come to him, as they always do.

In the dream, he is sailing away from the Roman docks toward the rising sun, gliding out on a small Grecian sailboat. He sits in the back amid a pile of his paintings and scrolls, taking his treasures to a new home. Asclepius steers the boat. He smiles at Scipio, enjoying their venture to his homeland. Next to Asclepius is a small statue of Athena, Greek goddess of wisdom. Scipio knows it to be Asclepius' prized possession.

Wearing only an unadorned tunic and sandals, Scipio is relaxed and peaceful, enjoying the scene of his small boat sliding along toward the luminous eastern horizon. He looks back over his shoulder at Rome fading from sight. His father stands alone on the docks wearing full battle armor. He holds his right arm out, palm up, expressionlessly bidding goodbye to his son. Scipio returns the gesture, searching his father's eyes for a glimmer of approval or affection, but none is there.

A dark swarm of insects gathers behind Publius. It approaches him in a swirling cloud, but he does not see them. Scipio screams a warning, but Publius is too far away to hear him. Scipio yells for Asclepius to turn the boat around, but his tutor only grins and holds the tiller on a course to Greece. As Publius fades from sight, Scipio watches the cloud envelop his father, and sees him whirl his arms in futile defense. And then the cloud thickens, and Scipio sees him no more.

Scipio blinks awake in his midnight room. Bleary-eyed, he recalls the dream, pondering its significance. He knows his dreams are messages from the gods, and he vows to take his dream to the temple priests that day for interpretation. He lays back in an effort to sleep, but he tosses restlessly. The image lingers of his father in the swarm, alone and helpless as he sails away.

The next afternoon finds Scipio in his room, somberly preparing for his trip to Iberia. He folds several tunics and loincloths into the leather satchels on his bed. He stuffs in some scrolls about Plato, Alexander the Great, and the first Punic War against Carthage. *Scholar of war my ass*, he thinks to himself. *How much can you learn when you are dead?*

His mood brightens when Laelius clanks into the room, sporting new armor, sword, and shield. "That was quick!" chirps Scipio. "I see it worked."

"As you expected," says Laelius with a bow. "I told that wealthy snot Camillus that you were going to Iberia for the war against the Carthaginians – which is true – and that your father might recruit him to join you as an older protector – which may be true, who knows your father's mind?" Laelius grins. "While he was trembling at the prospect of death, cold meals, and dirty underwear, I told him I would go in his stead if he provided me with horse and armor, so that I may rise above my impoverished station in life. The poor sheep, he almost fell over rushing to get them! I hate to say it, but that was a clever idea, Scippy!"

"It was nothing," says Scipio, "I borrowed the idea from Aesop's fable about the Kite and the Swan. That one Asclepius taught us: that the desire for imagined blessings can mean the loss of your real ones." Scipio grins. "Camillus is imagining he saved his wealthy little skin, and all it cost him was a horse and a sword – and he is a much happier man for his loss!"

"Well, I am glad to join you, even if he would not." Laelius says, and clenches his friend's shoulder. "Were it not for you, Scippy, I could be toiling in someone's turnip fields, or enslaved in a brothel. I will never forget that. Never."

Scipio stares at his feet and awkwardly waves his arm. "Ah, it's all to my good. I need you along because your girlish ways make me look more the man, it's much easier to get women this way!"

"Goat face!" Laelius jostles Scipio, instigating a brief wrestling match. Pomponia comes into the room, and they look guiltily at one another. She eyes them.

"I heard you laughing. What was so amusing, boys?" She eyes Laelius suspiciously. "Is that your armor?" A flushed Laelius looks to Scipio, his eyes pleading with him to answer his mother.

"Uh, we were just laughing about Aesop's Fables," Scipio says brightly. "And yes, that is Laelius' armor, he got it himself!"

She cocks an eye, knowing she has half the story. "Yes, I know Aesop's fables well. One of my favorites was the one called 'The Mule.' Do you remember the moral to that story?"

Laelius smiles guiltily. "Uh, that there are two sides to every truth?"

Pomponia nods approvingly. "Just so. And that people may only give you one side of it, Laelius." She turns to her son. "Are you ready for northern Italia?"

Scipio forces a wooden smile. "Yes. Father and I go to the Senate this afternoon to affirm the final details. Isn't that exciting?"

"Is it?" Pomponia studies him. "Your face says otherwise, dear."

"As you have said, I need to do this. I want to make Father proud, to be as a great leader as he is. And as wise as you."

Laelius shifts his feet, looks about the room. "I think it is time for me to go. Scippy, I will see you on the morrow." He clanks out the entryway, brushing imagined dust off his shiny new breastplate.

Pomponia watches him go, then turns back to her son. "Cornelius, I am not the scholar you are, but I know that 'great' and 'honorable' are horses of different colors. It is very difficult to be a person of both power and principle. One leads to the dissolution of the other."

Scipio stands on tiptoe, arms spread as if teetering on a beam and mugs at his mother. "Then I shall just have to learn to balance them! To be both soldier and scholar, as Amelia said. Without taking a fall!"

Pomponia glances outside the doorway, waves at someone there, and walks out. Scipio hears a muted but animated conversation between his mother and someone else. Pomponia's tone becomes amused, then pleading, and finally urging. There is a brief silence and Pomponia reappears in the doorway, smiling impishly.

"Someone is here to say goodbye, son. I will see you soon."

As Pomponia walks out Amelia enters, wearing an ankle-length flowing cotton tunic. Her slender feet are wrapped in the flat straps of a dressy pair of caligae muliebres. Though her long brunette hair is curled into a matronly crown, she stumbles childishly into the room, awkward in her new sandal boots. Amelia teeters over to Scipio, eyes downcast, fingering a red rose she carries with her.

"I heard you are leaving soon."

Scipio summons a modicum of excitement. "Yes! Finally! Time for me to follow my ancestors' path and become the next General Scipio!" Amelia looks directly into his eyes, and the false bravado falls from his face. He gives her a sad smile. "Well, it will be an adventure, anyway."

She returns a tiny smile, blinking back tears. She suddenly steps forward and shoves the rose into his hands. "Here. For luck."

Scipio reaches out and takes it from her, stares silently at it. Amelia places her hand over his. "Don't be embarrassed. A lot of our soldiers wear them into battle. They stick them in their helmets or shields. To remember their children, someone they love…" She blushes and turns away.

Scipio takes the rose from her, lays it carefully next to his satchels. Not knowing what to say, he silently looks at her, his eyes soft. Amelia shifts about self-consciously, and Scipio breaks into a wide grin. "Well, perhaps all my studies are not done. Asclepius will be here if – when – I return. You must help me catch up when I come back."

"Oh yes, I would! I, you … I …" Amelia suddenly leans in and kisses him – once, lingeringly. Her hands touch his shoulders, then clench them. She abruptly pulls away, red-faced, and scurries to the doorway, pausing there to look back at him, a challenge in her eyes. "You will come back to me, will you not?"

Scipio reaches over to touch the flower's bud, raises his head. "Always. I shall always come back to you."

Amelia nods and whirls away. Scipio walks into the hallway to look after her, carrying the rose with him. He fits it into the belt in his tunic, studies it, and smiles. And then he resumes his packing.

II. FIRST BLOOD

As dawn's light illuminates the center of Rome, Publius and Cornelius Scipio tramp through the city's narrow side streets, heading for the Senate. Their sandaled feet trod along dusty byways lined with the tall, rickety tenements that house most of Rome's plebs. The Scipios navigate through the hundreds of shop stalls that line the base of the tenements: butchers, slave sellers, toolmakers, tailors, and prostitutes. The morning streets are already a cacophonous din of sales pitches, hagglings, songs, and curses. With a half-million residents, Rome is a bustling city from dawn to dusk, and its buzzing activity only increases as one nears the Forum at the city's heart, which is the Scipios' destination.

"Look out, son, we're being attacked!" shouts Publius. Laughing, the Scipios push through a swarm of frantic schoolboys rushing around them, stampeding to their community classrooms. Many are toting a breakfast pancake they bought at a bakery stall.

One of the boys stumbles into Scipio, scraping his honeyed breakfast against young Scipio's elegant Greek toga. "I am despoiled!" cries Scipio; "I cannot present myself in public this way. You must soldier on by yourself, Father."

The senior Scipio crooks his finger, gesturing for his son to follow him. "You will not escape politics that easily. That toga has so many colors in it, no one will notice another one."

A knot of patrolling soldiers passes by the Scipios. They raise their right arms to salute Publius. Many nod and smile at the general. Publius Scipio is a popular officer among most of the legionnaires because he is known to protect his men in battle instead of sacrificing them for glory – a rare trait in a patrician general.

Turning to their left, the Scipios enter the wide main street that takes them to the magnificent Roman Forum, an enormous plaza built between the seven hills upon which Rome was founded. The Forum is a graceful complex of sculptured temples, ornate government buildings, and open-air meeting rooms. Its field-sized open space is alive with acrobats, speakers, soothsayers, priestesses, and merchants. The air is redolent with the many spices, perfumes, and foods being sold there. Ever since his father first took him to the Forum it has been young Scipio's favorite spot, filled with cultures from all over the world. The Forum taught Scipio that there was a world waiting for him outside its gates if he will but seek it.

The Scipios walk down the grassy hillside to the base of the Forum, ascend its marble steps, and pass through its columns to approach the front of the massive stone Curia Hostilia (Senate chambers). Publius is coming to the Curia to finalize his expedition details with the ruling body of Rome, to make sure they agree on a delivery schedule for his supplies and reinforcements. When he has the floor, Publius will again ask the Senate for a legion of veteran soldiers to supplement the three legions of recruits given him to battle Hannibal's veterans.

Dwelling in the protected arrogance of the Senate chambers, the senators feel that Roman soldiers, however raw, can defeat the Carthaginians, however experienced. So the Senate has allocated the veteran legions to Publius' co-consul, General Tiberius Sempronius, because he is protecting their profitable groves and vineyards in Sicily, a land recently taken back from Carthage. Publius knows he will argue in vain, but he must try. If not for victory, for the sake of the vulnerable young men in his charge.

Publius pushes open the Curia's high wooden doors and turns to his son with invitation in his eyes. Cornelius surveys the city below, avoiding his father's look. Publius shrugs, enters, and closes the doors. Young Scipio exhales with relief and skips back down the Forum steps, greeting familiar senators on their way up to the Curia chambers.

Young Scipio has attended the boring Senate meetings for years, so he chooses to remain outside the Curia while his father pleads his case. The boy much prefers conversing with the plebs than listening to the patricians' pompous posturings. He knows his father would prefer to have him there, but he still resents the oath he had to take, setting him on a path that takes him from his heart's desire.

As he descends, Scipio spies the scarecrow form of Senator Flaccus, stalking his ungainly way up the Forum steps. He knows Flaccus only too well; he has heard his father Publius debate him and General Fabius about the future of the growing Republic. Scipio knows that both are members of the Latin Party that his father despises.

The Latins are the agrarian-values group who believe that Rome should be an army of farmer-citizens: men of plain, earthbound values who are ready to drop their plows and pick up their swords whenever Rome is threatened –and then return to their farming. As a Hellenic, Scipio's father has argued that the time is past for Rome to remain a simple insular society, that Rome must inevitably become an empire, with a full-time military to protect its territories from the imperialistic Carthaginians and Macedonians. And its citizens must become educated and acculturated, to become artists, craftsmen, and engineers.

In his speeches, Publius frequently restates the motto of the Hellenics: the power of a country lies in its economy and military, but its greatness lies in the education its citizenry and its benevolence toward the less fortunate. The Latins counter that such "greatness" would require increased taxes on the wealthy patricians, which for most senators is sufficient reason to oppose the Hellenics. There is deep enmity between the traditionalist Latin Party and the modernizing Hellenics, a rift that brooks no compromise in the eyes of either. It is a war no less virulent than the one against Carthage.

Walking with Flaccus is a young man Scipio has never seen, a stocky fellow who walks as if he was stomping on bugs, so forceful is his step. The youth wears a homespun knee length tunic, his dingy garb contrasting sharply with the patrician's shining white toga. The boy's eyes, however, they burn with uncommon determination or anger, Scipio cannot tell which. Scipio has always liked the quirky and effusive Flaccus, whatever his politics, and he rushes down to meet him.

"Salus, Flaccus. How fare you?"

"Salve, young Scipio. I do fare well, very well. Where is your father?"

"He is in the Senate chambers, waiting to discuss the North Italia campaign. We sail on the morrow."

"Ah, of course, of course. And you are going with him?"

"Yes, Senator. It is time for me to begin my apprenticeship into the military. Father says not a moment too soon."

"Yes, yes, of course, your father has always been an ambitious person! With lots of new ideas, I must say. Oh well... Cato, I must go to the chambers now. Are you coming?"

Cato stands, eyeing Scipio's elaborate toga, white with an intricately embroidered border of purple, the elite color worn mainly by officials and priests. "I will be there," he says. "Go ahead."

Flaccus rushes up the steps. Scipio stares at Cato, who is still surveying him. Scipio steps toward him. "You are interested in my clothing?"

Cato points at Scipio's toga. "What is that are you wearing?"

Scipio fingers his toga, looks at Cato. "This? This is a Grecian toga. My tutor gave it to me. I wear it today to honor my father!"

Cato circles Scipio. "Very fancy – as are the delicate Greeks you mimic. I would think a plain Roman toga would suffice. They are as simple and strong as our people."

Scipio casts a cool eye at Cato. "The Greeks have given us much. We copy everything from their architecture to their battle formations. This toga is a work of art – you do know what art is – and I wear it proudly. As I said, it's a special occasion. My father addresses the Senate today."

Silence falls between them, and lingers. Scipio summons his manners and extends his hand. "I forgot to introduce myself, forgive me. I am Publius Cornelius Scipio. My father is Publius Scipio, consul and general to Rome."

Cato eyes Scipio's hand, crushes it with a brief grasp, and drops it. "Your father is going to try to defeat Hannibal. That bastard with the elephants who made it over the Alps, yes?"

"He will do more than try. And who are you?"

Cato's chin goes up. "Cato, Marcus Portius Cato. The Scipios would not know my humble family, but that will change when I am consul of Rome."

Scipio cannot repress a smile. "Consul? Friend Cato, you are ambitious! True, I know naught of your family. But that matters little. A worthy man makes his own inheritance, does he not? "

Cato glares. "Easier said when one is privileged. My ancestors were simple farmers, but they drove the Etruscan invaders from our land back when Rome was a simple, uncorrupted town of men with calloused hands and broad backs. Now we are as soft and self-indulgent as the Greeks, thanks to the educated 'nobles' who run this country. I would restore Rome to our former greatness."

Scipio absorbs Cato's short speech, nodding where he agrees with him. Then Scipio spreads his hands.

"Under Alexander the Great, the Macedonians conquered the world by diplomacy, as much as by force of arms. And they absorbed each culture they encountered to create a rich new world. That is greatness, would you not say?"

"Diplomacy? Absorbed? They should have wiped their enemies from the face of the earth, as we will do with Carthage. The dead do not rebel."

Young Scipio grimaces at Cato's words. A conciliator by nature, he would like to find some common ground between himself and Cato, but he finds himself curiously repelled by his angry, destructive tone – he finds himself wanting to disagree with him even where he agrees. His reply has an edge to it.

"Carthage is a civilized nation. We can make peace with them and an ally of this Hannibal. We need powerful allies to help us drive the Gauls from our borders, or they may sack Rome again. Don't you see? The Carthaginians fight for equal trade rights, but the Gauls fight for our lands and our lives. They are the real threat."

"Not so," says Cato, with a firm shake of his head. "Hannibal took Iberia away from us, and now he is in Italia. He must be destroyed. Carthage must be destroyed!"

"You speak of noble values, but you would make Rome into a barbarian horde, wiping out all who oppose them. I admire your ambition, but not your ambitions." Scipio turns to leave. "We may differ on how to do it, but we both want to protect our homeland. There is that. I hope we shall speak again."

"We shall, Cornelius Scipio. I shall have my eye on you."

Scipio stares levelly at Cato for a few long seconds before he spins and strides off, clearly irritated by this stubbornly resentful youth.

Cato watches him go, then walks up the Forum to enter the Senate chambers. He takes a seat in the rear semicircle with the other plebs. He listens to the elder Scipio enumerate the troops and supplies he will take, his requests for additional veterans, and his strategy for combating Hannibal. At the end of Publius' speech with the Senate, the three hundred senators take a vote. His request for veterans is denied. After voting on several municipal issues, the Senate adjourns.

With the meeting closed, most of the senators stay to chat in groups. Cato moves quickly to join his neighbor Flaccus, who is speaking to a gaunt, scarred, elder senator. Cato tenses, knowing that it must be General Quintus Fabius, hero of the Gallic and Punic wars. Cato draws near to the pair. Flaccus is so deeply immersed in conversation he does not notice Cato's approach. A determined Cato quickly rectifies that problem. "Flaccus! I am here!" he shouts.

Flaccus jumps. He turns around to grin at his ward, amused at his uncharacteristic eagerness. "So you are… Hmm, I suppose introductions are in order."

Cato waits, holding his breath as Flaccus turns to Fabius. "General Fabius, I would like you to meet a prospective Latin Party member, the one I told you about. This is Marcus Portius Cato, known simply as Cato. Cato, this is Fabius Maximus, former consul and dictator of Rome."

Fabius bends down to eye Cato face-to-face and grasps his lower forearm. He speaks in the measured pace for which he is known, repeating his words.

"Ah yes, Cato. I hear you are a fine speaker, very fine. That you have your head in the right place … no Grecian frippery for you, eh?"

"Thank you, General. It is my life's desire that we instill our founding fathers' values back into Rome, before it becomes too … too… Grecian! I wish only to help – to serve with you."

"That is good … very good. Perhaps you will join me as an aide. Much to be done, on the battlefield and in the chambers!"

"Gladly will I serve, if I can have time to tend my fields."

Fabius bobs his head. "Hah! He is an old-time Roman is he not, Flaccus?"

Flaccus slaps Cato on the back. "He is, truly. Land first, politics later. Cincinnatus would be proud of him, proud I say!" Cato winces, looking sideways at Flaccus.

Flaccus and Fabius head toward the Curia's front door as Cato follows. "Well then, young Cato, it will be done. In accordance with custom, we shall check the portents and auguries before you join our Latin Party." Fabius winks at Flaccus. "But I am sure Fortuna will smile on you, yes she will smile…"

For the first time that day, Cato grins. "Thank you, Dominus. It will be a pleasure to serve you and the Party. Perhaps we shall serve together in the field, against the Carthaginians. That is, if Publius Scipio does not wipe them out before we get the chance."

Fabius bobs his head up and down. "Yes, certainly there is a … a good chance of that. A good chance. Naught but a bunch of Carthaginians, eh? With some nosy beasts and hired savages? Led by a crazy man named Hannibal?" He snorts a laugh. "This may be a short war, very short!"

*　*　*　*　*

PO RIVER VALLEY, NORTH ITALIA, 218 BCE. The vast Carthaginian force sprawls across this frost-tinged river valley at the base of the Alps. More town than army, there are cordons of elephants and their keepers, herds of oxen and cattle, and hundreds of tents occupied by armorers, doctors, priests, and blacksmiths. Acres of soldiers are there; thirty thousand infantry and cavalry, a formidable array of seasoned Iberians, Gauls, Numidians, Libyans, and Carthaginians. Yet this army is less than half the force that started over the impassable wintry Alps. The incredible exploit killed more of Hannibal's men than any foe he had faced, yet he regards the expedition as successful. Were he to wait for spring he would have lost the element of surprise, and with it his chance at taking Northern Italia – and Rome.

For all its size, the camp is quiet, with few fights or drunken revelries. Instead, the men are curled into blankets, playing dice games, listlessly practicing swordplay, or tending small cooking fires. The autumn cold of this northern clime has subdued even these doughty men, who know their next waking day is never guaranteed and spend their present ones in revelry.

Inside his command tent, Hannibal meets with his Carthaginian army officers and with the chieftains of his Numidian and Iberian mercenaries. They are all a bedraggled lot, dirty and exhausted from their ordeal over the frozen mountains. But Hannibal's spies have sent word that Publius Scipio's Roman army is camped on the other side of the Ticinus River. The Carthaginian commanders know a battle is imminent against the legendary Roman legions, and plans must be made. The officers stand in a semicircle about Hannibal, chewing on the bread and roasted ox set before them. Maharbal, Hannibal's cavalry commander, is complaining to Hannibal even as he gnaws on a rib. General Mago, Hannibal's younger brother, stands next to him, a slimmer duplicate of his one-eyed sibling.

"The Romans have pitched camp within a day's march. They will soon be upon us. I fear we are not ready."

Hannibal considers carefully the words of this leathery little Carthaginian. If Maharbal says the men are not ready, it must be true. He knows stoic Maharbal is not a man to accommodate weakness in any form. Without a word of complaint, he led an undermanned attack on the citadel of Saguntum, storming through its formidable defenses to crash down its gates. Hannibal respects him above all his men, a bold and fearless fighter who only takes calculated risks.

"We should quickly prepare, regardless." Hannibal says. "This is our first battle against the Romans, and they against us. We must make a strong impression, to breed fear in their ranks."

"But Maharbal is right, brother," says Mago. "The men are starved and tired. They have been fighting those pestiferous mountain tribes since we started over the Alps. I fear they do not have the stomach for another battle right now."

Hannibal rubs the back of his neck, frustrated. He stalks out of the tent, leaving his officers to wait for him. Out in the busy camp, he surveys the muted sea of men around him, most of them curled into sleep. Minutes pass as the young general stands immobile, oblivious to the din, thinking. He strides back inside the tent and faces the commanders and chieftains, his eyes alight. "Tomorrow, in the late morning, bring all our men to that shallow valley where we keep the Numidians' horses. I would address them."

Early the next day, the army's officers rouse the listless troops, directing them to go sit on the shallow hillside that rings the valley. A great clanking and cursing arises as thousands of infantry and cavalry stir themselves and trudge through the chill sunlight to the designated spot. Tired as they are, most of the warriors are grateful for the diversion from their nervous waiting. The men know that the army of Publius Scipio is now less than a half-day's march from them and that their lives may soon be in the hands of the gods of war and fortune. Tonight many will visit the camp's small temples of Baal, god of all gods, to offer a prayer that they live through the impending battle – or die a heroic death. But for now, the weary men seat themselves on the crackling grasses of the hoar frosted hillside. Some fall asleep as soon as they sit, wrapped in the coarse wool blankets they've dragged with them.

Hannibal enters the shallow bowl at the valley bottom, and the men's heads snap up. He holds his sarissa upright in front of him like a sentry, watching the rest of his army file in. Thousands of men encircle him, anxiously watching their leader. Every soldier stands in awe of young Hannibal, even the capricious and bloodthirsty Gauls who have recently joined him. They know the stories about him: that he will crucify his own officers for cowardice or indecisiveness, that he sleeps on the ground among the men and eats the same food they do, and that he lost an infected eye because he refused to stop for treatment, wanting his men to escape the Alps before another snowstorm came. They know he is a born general, a man fated to lead and conquer.

The last soldiers file onto the slopes, and the trumpets blare for silence. All eyes look down at Hannibal. He says nothing but points his sarissa at a spot in the crowd. There is a commotion, and the bottom rows suddenly part as his Sacred Band guards lead two dozen chained captives into the open circle, to bunch up behind Hannibal. The captives are Gauls from the fierce mountain tribes that fought against the Carthaginians when they intruded upon the tribes' dominion of the Alps. They glare at their captors, unbowed in spirit, ready for death.

The soldiers mutter curiously about the prisoners in their midst. A master showman, Hannibal lets the wonder build, silently turning in a circle to face every man on the hillsides. Then he commences his speech. "Men! You have fought bravely and fiercely. You have overcome every object before you. The path to Rome looms before us, a passage to treasure beyond your wildest dreams! But first you must overcome one final obstacle: the Romans, the famed Roman army. They gather near us to oppose our will, even as we speak here. And we will face them very soon."

A low wave of grumbling washes across the hillside, as the men vent their concern and weariness. Hannibal raises his sarissa, and the trumpets blow them to silence. He slowly turns, gazing into their faces as if he is talking to each one of them.

"Yes, for months you have labored like Heracles himself, across terrain so forbidding no one thought we could cross it! By all our gods, you deserve your rest, and you shall have it – but one more battle remains to you, one more contest before you take your leisure. Fear not, you are more than up to the task of paddling these Romans' downy bottoms and sending them back to their wet nurses in the city."

Laughter scatters across the crowd. Hannibal raises his hand again. "These men, these terrible Romans whom you hear about – do you know they are but new conscripts, who have not tasted the toils of war or the bitter fruits of battle? Are these the men whom you fear to fight? You have triumphed over the hostile tribes of Iberia, crossed the Alps in winter, and subdued the mountain tribes that fought us over every rock and precipice. Are you now to fear these pampered Roman boys, so recently pulled from the suckling teat? You will cut through them like a scythe through wheat, and harvest the spoils of their defeat. All plunder goes to you, and only you!"

The troops mutter their approval, but Hannibal knows these weary men are not yet primed. "And... and when we emerge victorious, every man will receive his own twenty acres of land, wherever he chooses: Africa, Iberia... or Italia itself, because we will rule all of them! Now is not the time for rest. Now is the time to grasp your dreams!"

A loud cheer erupts from the horde. Hannibal lets the roars echo until they begin to lose volume, and he quickly raises his hands for silence.

"Still, in spite of what I say, perhaps you fear you will die in battle, that all these riches would avail you naught. To answer that concern, I have prepared a show for you."

Hannibal gestures to several nearby officers, and they push through the crowd to return leading a stout young horse, fully caparisoned with food and clothing. One officer holds the horse near the crowd, the other fetches two sets of Gallic armor and swords. He places the outfits near Hannibal's feet. Hannibal can hear the men discussing this puzzling scene. He waits several minutes, and then he addresses the prisoners brought before him.

"Prisoners! Are there two of you prepared to fight a duel to the death? The winner will receive his freedom, to ride away immediately. The loser will die.[ii] Will any volunteer for this contest?"

The Gauls leap up together, eagerly shouting their willingness. Hannibal has them draw for the two black dice in an urn of twenty-four. The two who draw the black die shout in delight, while the losers sit dejectedly to watch the winners fight.

It is an incongruous matchup. A young and muscular warrior is pitted against a rotund older veteran. They don the armor and grasp their shields and swords, moving apart to stand at the edge of the forty-foot circle, stomping with anticipation. Hannibal stands in the center, holding his sarissa aloft.

"Commence!"

The two combatants rush to the center. They swing at one another with their three-foot Gallic swords, blades ringing against the stout round shields. The younger man's blows are strong; several times he brings his older opponent to his knees, only to see him scramble away as he raises his arm for a killing blow. The weary soldiers have now come alive, cheering their favorite and making bets. The hill becomes a bedlam of cheers and curses.

Finally, after ten minutes of chasing his scurrying opponent, the younger man knocks the veteran down and smashes his shield apart, knocking him prone. Filled with bloodlust, the youth throws away his own shield and swings his sword aloft with both hands, aiming to cleave his opponent's head. The wily veteran sprawls before him, feigning helplessness until the youth has his sword in full arc above his head. Then the older man quickly sits up. With one lightning sword thrust he pierces the young man's groin and twists the sword's blade in a wide disemboweling arc. The youth jerks his head back in agony, eyes bulging from their sockets as he screams and collapses to the ground, curling into a ball, cradling the intestines that snake from the yawning gash in his abdomen. Without a backward glance, the bleeding old warrior throws down the sword and limps over to the horse held by Hannibal. With a curt nod to the general, the victor takes the reins from him and mounts the horse. He rides away, waving his right hand at the riotous crowd – a free man once more.

Hannibal's men have become delirious. They cheer the loser as well as the winner, who is now galloping out of sight over the hill. The remaining prisoners encircle their lifeless compatriot and chant a prayer for him, rejoicing that he has escaped their miserable life. They lift the dead youth to their shoulders and carry him to camp, shuffling back over the hill. When they have disappeared, Hannibal moves back to the center of the circle and faces his aroused troops.

"Hear me, warriors. Did you see that those prisoners would eagerly risk their lives to battle for freedom, even though losing meant their death? Did you see that all of them, however weak or sickly, would rather die fighting for freedom than remain a prisoner? Did you see how they cheered their fallen comrade, as happy for him as for the victor, because he had escaped their future as slaves? Did you see?"

The crowd is dead silent. Hannibal stalks around the circle, head down as if in deep thought. When he completes the circle he raises his head to look at them. His eyes blaze with excitement. He stares intently at the men about him, and raises his fist as if taking an oath to the gods.

"I tell you now, men, your lot like is that of those prisoners. Fortune has limited your options here on this far-flung shore. You have the same choices that I offered them. Victory or enslavement."

Hannibal walks to the blood-stained ground where the prisoner died, stabs his spear into the discolored earth, and faces the men with his hands raised over his head.

"Just now you congratulated the dead man as well as the winner, and no doubt pitied those who remained alive to be bound in chains. As they did feel for themselves, is that not so? Men, I expect you to go into battle tomorrow with that same feeling for your comrades – and for yourself! Go to this battle determined to win, to gain freedom, glory, and untold wealth! But if that proves impossible, if victory be not yours, be happy to die rather than lose and face the prisoners' lot – a life of Roman slavery and abuse!"

Hannibal paces the periphery of the circle, allowing the men to talk among themselves before he resumes. "If we were to lose this battle, do you think you could escape and find your way home, back over those snowbound Alps? Back through the bloodthirsty mountain tribes we fought every step of the way? You have no hope for escape, no hope to run and hide. Victory or death, these are your choices! And they are why you will triumph."

Hannibal looks into the alarmed faces around him. "Whenever people had to give up the hope of losing and staying alive, they have always defeated their opponent. These Romans, they can hope to return to their homes should they lose by escape or ransom; they have hope in defeat. And that is why they shall fall to your sword and spear. You will fight with the ferocity of a bear backed to a wall. Rejoice! You have only victory or death, so victory will be yours!"

As one voice, thousands chant, "Han-ni-bal, Han-ni-bal, Han-ni-bal!" Hannibal raises his sarissa over his head, triumphant in their enthusiasm. The chant builds to a deafening crescendo as he walks into his men, the packed crowd slowly parting as he approaches. Hands reach out to touch his armor, to grasp his shoulder, to clasp his hand.

The young Carthaginian strides up the hill to his command tent. His officers and tribal chiefs follow, the chants still ringing in their ears. Inside the tent, Hannibal faces his commanders. "Tomorrow, before we decamp and move toward the Romans, I will lead an advance force to reconnoiter the Roman camp. Maharbal, you will join me with two thousand of the Numidian riders. Mago, you take three thousand of the Iberian and Carthaginian heavy cavalry. If there is a skirmish, we will be prepared."

Mago is puzzled. "What about taking infantry with us?"

Hannibal grins, turns to a cavalry chief from Iberia and claps him on the shoulder. "These are our infantry! Our Iberian friends will jump off their horses to fight on foot, as they always do." Hannibal rolls his eyes at the other leaders. "My gods, they are as bad as the Romans!" Amid the laughter, Hannibal continues. "Yes, they will be our foot soldiers, and none other. We must be very mobile for what we are to do. Look here!"

He unfurls a large hand-drawn sheepskin map and has two guards hold it open while the commanders study it. Hannibal runs his finger across the painted contours of the local plains and forests. "Our scouts drew this out yesterday. Here, about three miles from the new Roman camp, there is a wide plain between these low-lying hills. If the Romans move toward us tomorrow, we need to meet them on this plain where our cavalry have the advantage. We will use the terrain as our ally, and spring our trap!"

*　*　*　*　*

"THE PORTENTS! AH, the portents! The gods are angry! Evil is abroad, General Scipio!"

Inside Publius Scipio's tent, the ancient camp priest is apoplectic with fear, hopping about in his swirling long robes while Publius' officers observe him with wry expressions. General Scipio sits on a pile of furs, head in hand, studying the frenetic holy man as he continues his declarations.

"I have seen it! A hive of bees suddenly appeared on that tree outside your tent! Just yesterday, a wolf entered camp and attacked the soldiers! [iii] One of the camp dogs was heard to utter the word 'Triumph,' in the marketplace. Strange spirits are about, General, the gods must be placated!"

Without changing expression, Scipio mutters, "Commence the rites to appease the gods, priest. Make the proper sacrifices and say the proper prayers. You know what to do, why do you bother me with this?"

"I come to warn you, General. You must not venture out until the gods give us signs that they favor our enterprise."

Standing next to his father, young Scipio listens anxiously, worried that the gods are truly warning them. He recalls his dream of his father being surrounded by a dark swarm. "Father, perhaps we should delay our mission until the rites are completed, and there is a favorable sign for our venture."

"We cannot wait for such … activities. The Carthaginians are coming. I must pick a battle site and engage them so we can destroy them before we retire for the winter. Marcus!"

A short, block-hewn centurion steps forward, bows slightly, and stands ramrod-straight in front of his general. Young Scipio stares at him, fascinated. The older man seems to be made of nothing but sinew and bone, the boy can see every muscle and vein on his cabled arms. He carries an assortment of daggers around his worn belt, each a one-piece blade and handle that looks like an elongated leaf. Publius notes his son's interest and smiles. He rises and gestures at the centurion.

"Son, before I go any further, I should introduce you to my most trusted officer. This is Marcus Silenus, First Centurion of the First Cohort, the leader of my elite guard."

Without moving his body, Marcus Silenus turns his head to fix his feral yellow-green eyes on Scipio. "Salus, Publius Cornelius Scipio."

Young Scipio instinctively steps back from the centurion's stare, but he manages a conversational response. "S-salus, Marcus Silenus. Uh, what are those odd knives on your belt?"

Marcus glances down at the knives and snaps his head back to attention. "They are African in design. The Kordofani tribes throw them at prey – and enemies. I have them made for me by our armorer."

Publius smiles grimly and walks over to pull a knife off of the belt of his officer, tumbling it in his hand. "Yes, and he is very good with them. He has saved me more than once with his throws, is that not so, Marcus?" Marcus gives the briefest of nods, and Publius laughs. "For you, that is a speech, eh? And now to business. What have you to report?"

"Our scouts have seen clouds of smoke in the distance, General Scipio. Hannibal cannot be far away. I could send men out to find his exact position."

"No, centurion, I shall scout this barbarian myself. Assemble a striking force for a reconnaissance mission: two thousand cavalry and three thousand light infantry. Go now, all of you, and report to me before night's end."

The officers and priest rush out, leaving father and son alone in the tent. Young Scipio waits until he is sure no one is near and turns to his father. "I have been studying the Senate's records about the first war against Carthage, about Hannibal's father, Hamilcar."

Publius fondles the knife he borrowed from Marcus Silenus. "So?"

Scipio spreads his hands open, and talks excitedly. "Since infancy, Father, Hannibal has been raised to be a general, to defeat Rome. He must have learned all about history's finest generals: Pyrrhus, Alexander, Xenophon … and the Persian leaders such as Xerxes and Darius. Just like I did!"

Publius plays at throwing the knife, and then gives it to his son. Scipio eagerly stuffs it into his belt. "That is likely true," says Publius, "but why should we care?"

"Those Persians were masters of deceit and trickery," says his son. "They lured their enemies into ambushes and traps. It is said that Hannibal's father, Hamilcar, used such tactics to subdue the Numidian tribes in Africa. And I heard that Hannibal defeated the Carpetani and the Gauls in such a fashion at the Tagus River! He appeared from nowhere to surround them, it was an ambush. I do fear he has something similar in mind for us. We must be careful."

"I am sure such tactics work well on the disorganized savages they are used to fighting, but we are Romans. We maintain a disciplined attack formation, no matter what the circumstance. And we win. Do not worry yourself."

"I just wondered about being slowed by the infantry, that is all. Forgive my impertinence."

"You will be a great leader someday, but you rely too much on what you read about others, about the dead and defeated. Learn Roman strategy and tactics, and that will suffice. We remain unconquered."

Scipio bows his head, nods. His father slaps his back, giving him a gentle push. "Now go prepare yourself for tomorrow. You will be part of a turma of cavalry. You and Laelius."

Scipio looks anxiously at his father. "I ride out for battle?"

Publius smiles at his son's discomfiture. "Yes. As one of the rear guard, led by Quintus Tacitus, an admirable young officer. His turma has thirty men in it, all charged with protecting you while you learn our military operations. *You are there to observe, not to fight.* Understood?"

His son nods. Publius grins and slaps him on the shoulder. "Very good. Now report to Quintus, he will give you your position within the formation. And go to sleep early. We leave after breakfast."

Two hours after dawn, Publius Scipio leads his forces across the capacious Po Valley plain, its broad river lazily sweeping across it. It is a crisp, cold day. The bright alpine sun dazzles the mounds of snow speckled about the foothills of the surrounding Alps and Apennines. The velites march on foot. As light infantry, they take their place in front with the cavalry lined up behind them. Publius leads the cavalry, with Cornelius and Laelius part of Quintus' turma of well-armored young knights from the best Roman families. The highborn equites are eager for a fight. They anticipate an easy victory over these Carthaginians and their savage allies. Easy victory and easy glory.

* * * * *

Hannibal looks over the Po Valley expanse; his reconnaissance force of five thousand light cavalry waits behind him. He assesses the forest density in the surrounding hills and studies the clouds for wind and weather signs. He kneels and scoops up a handful of the dry plains, sifting it through his fingers, watching how it falls in a wispy cloud. Satisfied with what he sees, he remounts his horse and trots over to confer with Hasdrubal.

"The earth is dry and dusty, and the wind is up. Our company will make a large dust cloud when we ride. The Romans could see it far away."

Hasdrubal sniffs. "Let 'em see it. Those recruits will shit their pants when they see us coming."

Hannibal frowns at his brother. "No Roman will turn from the battle, Publius Scipio will see to that. We need the element of surprise to make this easier on us. We must make that dust work in our favor."

Hannibal gestures for his Sacred Band guardians to follow him, and he rides off to the nearby foothills. He soon gallops back, excited and anxious. "Quickly, before the Romans arrive. You see that small rise in the plain, over there? Take a thousand of the Numidians and hide in the forest hills next to that rise. Remain there until our trumpets blare thrice."

"It will be done. And then what?"

"My men will stay here, making the Romans come to this spot. Then their rear lines will be opposite your men. When they arrive we will charge immediately, before their infantry can make their standard attack. While they are distracted with us, you come out behind them."

Hasdrubal laughs, spits, and turns to his brother. "Workable, very workable. Those Romans are so easy to trick! Always the same damned formations. And their cavalry will probably jump off their horses to fight us on foot, as if they can't stand riding on them. Shitheads!"

"Their regular infantry are invincible against any foot soldiers," Hannibal replies. "But they only have light infantry today, and they have not seen the like of our Numidian cavalry. Now go!"

Hasdrubal wheels about and gallops away to prepare the Numidian chieftains. Soon the Africans riders are stampeding toward their hiding place in the hills. Hannibal stares straight ahead, anxiously watching for dust clouds, praying Hasdrubal's wake will settle before Publius' scouts appear.

An hour passes. The dust settles. Hannibal directs the men to eat a meal and drink water while in formation, that they may maintain their strength. As the sun rises higher, several small dust clouds appear in front of the Carthaginians, and the Roman scouts arrive. Once they see the Carthaginians, the scouts pivot and race away as the Carthaginians give chase.

Another hour passes. A faint clanking grows louder, joined by the machine-like pounding of thousands of feet in unwavering unison. Then the Roman army appears, heading straight at the Carthaginians. Maniples of a hundred twenty light infantry advance in front of the armored cavalry, each man carrying a brace of javelins. Neither their steady pace nor their determined expressions change as they approach Hannibal's force. It is as if the Carthaginians were not there, lined up to kill them.

Hannibal's heart races in spite of himself. These are the men he has sworn to conquer, the admirable warriors he must learn to hate. He glances to each side to affirm his troops are arrayed properly: heavy cavalry in front, and the Numidians behind them. He watches the Romans halt, so close he can see General Scipio staring at him across the plain.

The Roman cavalry close ranks, moving into attack position. The velites march out toward the Carthaginians. Before these light infantry can settle into their battle formation, Hannibal vaults up in his saddle, waving his sarissa above him.

"Forwaaard!"

The Carthaginian horns blare, and three thousand Iberian cavalry immediately surge toward the Roman lines. The remaining Numidians fly past the tank-like Iberians, guiding their horses with their knees as they pull out their javelins. The Numidians loop around the Roman's main force and attack the cavalry's flanks, aiming to distract and disorganize them. The first battle is joined in this second war between Rome and Carthage.

WHILE HANNIBAL WAS PREPARING his ambush, Publius Scipio led his army across the plains, chatting with his officers and his son. The relaxed mood quickly dissolved when the general's scouts appeared on the horizon, riding frantically toward him. Publius motioned for the lines to halt. The lead scout pulled his frothed mount next to Publius.

"General, the Carthaginians are near! By the Ticinus River, just ahead!"

Publius immediately shouts orders to his officers. The cavalry and velites are put on battle alert, weapons are drawn and horses readied. The army moves forward at a more deliberate pace, but soon the Carthaginians appear in the distance, unmoving in the midst of the wide plain.

Young Scipio is wide-eyed with excitement. "Is it them, the Carthaginians? Can you see Hannibal?"

General Scipio squints at the enemy force as he canters ahead for a better look, his son following. "See that tall fellow with the spear in the plain linen armor? Look at how he commands the others – that must be him." A puzzled look crosses Publius' face. "They have no foot soldiers, just cavalry and those half-naked savages riding bareback. Our men will cut them to pieces."

Publius hastily returns to the front lines with his son. "You must go now Cornelius, move to the rear with your squadron. Observe how our infantry engages this force. Quintus, where are you?" The young officer rides up to the general. "Quintus, take your turma back with you to the rear, and stay out of the conflict." Quintus nods his assent and waves for his men to follow him. Scipio and Laelius follow his return through the cavalry lines.

Publius trots over to his infantry commander. "Salvius, move your infantry to the front of the cavalry. Attack at my signal." Publius returns to the head of the cavalry, watching Salvius lead his maniples of velites out to face Hannibal's horsemen. Odd, thinks Publius, none of the Carthaginians are moving.

Publius sees Hannibal raise his spear; he hears the Carthaginian trumpets blast. The Iberians suddenly gallop at full speed toward the velites. Surprised by the abrupt attack, only a few of the recruits can hurl their javelins before the heavy cavalry are into them, trampling them down and lancing them with their long sarissas. The velites rush back to escape the enemy assault.

Publius rises in his saddle and shouts to his cavalry commanders. "Now! Charge now, charge!"

The Roman cavalry plunge forward and crash into the armored Iberians. Most of the Romans immediately dismount and fight on foot, thrusting their six foot javelins at the Iberians who ride in to spear them, chopping at the barbarian's legs as they ride past. Many Iberians quickly leap from their mounts, lusting to fight the Romans hand-to-hand, but the dismounted Romans down many of them with skillful thrusts of their two-foot blades. The mounted Iberians riders revenge their fellows, lancing the earthbound Romans from all directions. The Numidians harass the Romans with quick attacks on their flanks, riding in to make a javelin throw or sword cut and quickly riding away.

The battle rages evenly for some time, then the Romans begin to drive the Carthaginian forces back. The legions grow excited with the possibility of victory. Publius boldly rides out in front of his men and waves them forward. He spears an onrushing Iberian rider, shoving his pilum through his neck, and his men cheer wildly.

Far to his right, Publius sees Hannibal cutting down a velite who was foolhardy enough to attack him, the general's face almost bored as he pierces the young man's unarmored breast with his sword. Then he sees Hannibal raise himself in his stirrups, coolly examining the Roman lines. Hannibal waves twice to a nearby trumpeter. The soldier blares his horn three times, then again. The notes echo down the line, and the Carthaginians suddenly halt their retreat. Publius looks about, trying to identify the significance of the signal.

A movement to his right catches Publius' eye. To his horror, he sees hundreds of Numidians storm out of the trees behind his lines, riding like the wind across the plains and into the Roman's backs. The rear infantries are driven into their own cavalry, destroying the formations of both. The legions mill about in confusion while the Numidians encircle the army's rear and sides. The Iberians reverse their retreat and battle forward, slowly surrounding the Roman army. Many of Romans break through the encirclement but they are ignored as the enemy drives at a tight circle of defenders that has Publius in the center, targeting the general for the final kill.

WHEN THE NUMIDIANS ambushed the Roman's rear force, Quintus hastily directed his squadron away from the fray, regrouping on a nearby hillock. From there, Scipio anxiously watches his father in the middle of his dwindling army, battling the converging Iberians and Numidians. Publius bleeds from a dozen cuts but he fights on, refusing to yield to Fortuna's dire wishes for him. A javelin thunks into his upper chest and he collapses onto his horse's neck, only to pull it out and hurl it back at his foes. Marcus Silenus stands on the ground beside his general, killing any who dare attack with a few well-placed parries and thrusts, downing others nearby with his deadly knife throws. The surrounded Romans fight valiantly, but their numbers shrink.

Scipio watches in horror. He can see his father's doom is approaching. He gallops over to Quintus, who sits on his horse watching the battle. "My father is trapped! We have to help him!" Quintus turns to Scipio, his face set with resignation. "We are sworn to stay here, Cornelius, to protect you at all costs.

Your father is completely surrounded by the enemy. To ride into them would be your death. And ours. Apologies, but I cannot do that."

"What? You cannot just sit here! That is your General down there! Forget about me, you have to save him!"

Quintus looks away, resolute. Scipio stares at him in disbelief. Seeing no further reaction from him, Scipio whirls to face the rest of the turma. "General Publius Scipio – my father – is trapped down there. We have to rescue him! Who will join me?" The riders remain silent, awaiting Quintus' order. Scipio looks pleadingly from face to face, but each soldier avoids his eyes. Quintus rides closer to console him when Scipio abruptly wheels around and dashes full speed toward the battle, galloping at the enemy swarming around his father like the insects in Scipio's dream. Quintus starts in alarm.

"Scipio, come back! I command you! Now!"

Quintus watches him disappear and feels the shame of his inaction. As he bows his head another horseman flashes past him. It is Laelius, rushing to catch his friend. Quintus turns to his men. "Gods be damned, go follow them! For Rome and glory!"

The turma leaps into action as Scipio enters his first battle, riding into the backs of the Carthaginian cavalry. As he nears the fray, he is stunned by the overwhelming cacophony of war: the shouts of the victors, the screams of the dying, the smell of the dead's voided bowels, and the blurs of the many riders whirling about him. Forgetting all he knows about tactics and horsemanship, Scipio simply plunges ahead, slashing at the backs of any enemy that crosses his path. Laelius follows close behind, jabbing his javelin at anyone within arm's length, his eyes wide as saucers.

Quintus leads the charging turma along Scipio's path, and they wedge through the small hole he opened in the Carthaginian lines. The rear attack throws the enemy into confusion. Quintus waves his sword frantically at Scipio until he catches his eye. "We are here!" Quintus shouts. "Onward to the General!"

Cheered at the site of his squadron, Scipio redoubles his efforts to reach his father, hacking his way to the center as the turma follows him. Laelius joins him and they fight next to each other, wildly stabbing at the arms and legs of any approaching rider, causing several of the enemy to depart for easier prey.

Scipio turns to wave over his turma, and sees Quintus nodding his acknowledgement. Then Quintus' eyes start from his head as a spear point emerges from his right eye, dark blood streaming down his breastplate as he crashes face-first into the gory ground. Scipio gapes in horror as he watches his friend kick, spasm, and lay still. *He was only following me,* Scipio thinks, *he wouldn't be dead if I hadn't come here.* Wiping his eyes, Scipio mutters a quick prayer to Mars, god of battle, to guide Quintus' soul safely to the underworld.

Side by side, Scipio and Laelius battle their way to Publius. "Father! I am here!" he shouts. Publius' eyes widen at the sight of his son in the midst of this massacre, and he searches desperately for an escape. He shouts to his nearby men to follow him, and they slowly thresh their way toward Scipio and Laelius.

A Numidian rider appears behind Publius, riding toward him with an upraised sword, intent on bringing Hannibal the head of a consul. Young Scipio's eyes start in alarm, and he surges in past his father. Scipio rams the Numidian's horse from the side and swings his sword at the barbarian's unprotected head. The Numidian easily deflects the blow with his small round shield and thrusts his javelin at Scipio's stomach. As he was taught,

Scipio turns his shield sideways and the javelin skids off. Scipio chops into the Numidian's arm before he can retrieve it, and the barbarian shrieks with pain as blood gouts from the deep slash. The Numidian turns away to escape, but Scipio flings his javelin squarely into the Numidian's back as he starts to ride off, and he falls from his horse. The man rises and stumbles about, the javelin trailing from his back, looking at the battle as if surprised to be there. Then he falls again and his eyes become glassy. *I've killed a man,* Scipio thinks. *My gods, I am a killer.*

Marcus Silenus collides against Scipio's mount, grabs Scipio's shoulder, and shakes him from his reverie. "Come, boy, the hole is closing!"

Afire with the chance to live, the Romans mow through the broken ring of Carthaginians and rejoin their army. Publius organizes his cavalry into closed ranks in front of his remaining velites, and directs the trumpeters to sound an orderly retreat. The Romans slowly withdraw from the battlefield, picking up their wounded as they depart.

Hannibal sees his force has lost their opportunity for an easy victory, and curses with disappointment. He knows that his troops are still exhausted from their ordeal in the Alps, and a counterattack could be a disaster. Reluctantly, he orders a recall. The Numidians and Iberians abandon the fight and hurry to the dead legionnaires, stripping them of their chain mail hauberks and rifling their corpses for money and treasure.

Hannibal turns to Agbal, his cousin, the commander of his Sacred Band. "Gather what treasure those buzzards have not taken. And take all the swords and armor!" Agbal places his fist over his heart and bows his head, the sign he will comply.

Hasdrubal rides up, grinning through the grime and blood on his face. "We kicked their asses all over the plain! Those were the fearsome Romans? Pthaw! We would have had the General's balls were it not for that ambush behind us."

Fingering his figurine of Hamilcar, Hannibal shakes his head. "Have you forgotten? Our father taught us to respect our enemies, because defeat lies in underestimating them. Those Romans had many untrained recruits in this encounter, yet they fought their way out of a trap and never lost their courage. Next time we will face their veterans. That will be a truer test of our mettle."

SLUMPED IN HIS SADDLE, Publius Scipio leads his remaining force across the Po Valley toward the Trebia River, looking to camp in a more defensible position. Marcus Silenus rides on Publius' left, stern and silent. The tribune scans the countryside for enemy cavalry, expecting the Numidians to attack again. He knows the Carthaginians always pursue their enemy after a victory, bent on eliminating the remainders of the defeated. It is one of the few things he admires about them, and he wishes the Romans would do likewise.

Marcus does not know that Hannibal has indeed sent his Numidians to finish off the Romans, but they have stopped to loot the abandoned Roman camp, sparing the lives of Publius' surviving force. Instead, Marcus stolidly awaits a final conflict with the Numidians. He knows the decimated Romans can only hope to take many enemies as possible before they fall, but he is unperturbed by that thought. It is, after all, an opportunity to die killing his enemies, the death he has prayed for all these years.

Scipio rides to the right of his father, attending to his needs. He helps his father drink from the water skin and helps him tighten the bandages on his bleeding wound. "Where are we going, Father?"

"We go to make a new camp across the river, in the hills. We will use the Trebia River as a barrier. If the Carthaginians attempt to cross it, we can kill them when they wade in. A good place to defend ourselves against those damned cavalry."

"Did you see them, see those Numidians?" says Scipio. "They guided their horses with their legs, as if they were one with them. They rode about like whirlwinds. They were so fast and agile! Our cavalry should learn to fight like that."

General Scipio grimaces in pain as he turns to his son, clutching the wound in his chest. "The Roman cavalry are the best in the world! Hannibal merely surprised us with those cavalry hiding in the trees. Next time we will be ready for his little tricks."

Scipio turns his head and looks into the distance, saying nothing. Publius puts his hand on his son's shoulder. "Do not be stung by my words, Cornelius. I do hear what you say, but you have much to learn." When Scipio nods mutely, his father pats him on the back, wincing with the effort. "Be of good cheer, the troops have told me about you riding into the fray to save me. I am recommending you for the corona civica, our highest honor."

Scipio looks at his father, incredulously. "You want to give me a crown?"

"Yes, Cornelius. I would do the same for any soldier who acted so bravely."

Scipio's shakes his head. "Honors corrupt, Father. I want no such temptation."

"I act not as your father but as your commander," Publius says. "You deserve recognition for risking your life to save your commander."

Scipio shakes his head again, his face set. "The action was one that rewarded itself." [iv]

The elder Scipio grins in spite of his pain. "A patrician who does not seek recognition? Gods, you will be a rare bird in the Senate! Very well, it will be as you wish. You have earned that. And my respect."

Scipio looks away, embarrassed that his father will see his moistened eyes.

The company soon crosses a meandering stream and rides into the low hills on the other side, from which they can see the gleaming Trebia before them. As they ease out of the hills, Scipio mulls over the previous battle: how Hannibal exploited the landscape's features, and how the Iberian cavalry hacked through sword and shield with their cleaver-like falcatas. His father was right, there was much for him to learn, especially from his enemies.

He thinks of Amelia, how she talked to him about following the steps of Alexander the Great and becoming a scholar of war, to master the opponents' tactics and culture and absorb their ways of thinking. How could a girl know of such things, that little brat he would wrestle to the ground? Then again, she last came to him dressed in perfumed robes, a girl no more. And her kiss, her kiss was not that of a girl, so deep and softly probing. By Mars and Heracles, he would like to wrestle with her now!

Near nightfall, Publius and his men arrive at the Trebia. The resilient legionnaires immediately set about building a fortified camp, laying up a wall of trees and digging a trench around it. Publius lies in his command tent, attended by his Greek physician. As the physician ministers to his father, Scipio watches the doctor's face, searching for signs of encouragement. The aged medicus nods his head approvingly. He is pleased that the blood flow has relented and the wound is clean. Scipio breathes a sigh of relief.

He leaves the tent and wanders over to the scrubby trees and bushes at the riverbank, away from the specter of military life. Trudging through the crackling leaves, he recalls the face of the man he just killed, his look of pain and shock. There he lay, sprawled amidst the blood and corpses, a man terrified at the approach of death. Scipio wonders if he can bear seeing that expression again on the next man he kills, on the faces of dying soldiers he has led into battle, perhaps victims of a mistake he made. Has he vowed to live a life that will be a living death? Scipio squats by the river and puts his head in his shaking hands, overcome by his thoughts.

An urge comes upon him, so quick and strong it seems like a spirit possession, bending him to its will: leave this world of horrors, unbuckle your sword, shed your armor, ride into the protective mountains as a commoner, and head to the eastern coast. Sail to Greece and have the peaceful life of your dreams, far from the madness of this mercenary war. As if in a vision, he can see his life there: his country villa, his crops, and his eager students. He can see his life's work before him, his heart's desire.

Scipio lays his helmet on the grass, then his chest armor. He reaches for the buckle on his sword belt. Pulling the buckle back, something pricks the side of his hand. He looks down to see Amelia's rose, its naked stem still wedged into the side of his bloodstained belt. He glances back at the distant camp and sees his father struggling out to oversee the development of camp fortifications and his guard hovering to assist him. He watches his father looking about for him, hears him calling his name. Laelius comes to stand beside Publius, looking about as if he is searching for someone, too.

Scipio gazes into the river. He fingers the rose stem. He picks up his armor and turns back to camp, walking faster with each step until he runs up to stand beside his father, ready to support him, no matter what.

III. ALARM

ROME. "Did you hear? Did you hear? Hannibal defeated Publius Scipio's legions. The Carthaginians won! They head for Rome!"

Cato glares at the scruffy young man tugging on his toga, and thrusts the man's hand away. "Pha! Hannibal but killed some green recruits and intemperate Gauls, led by one of those soft-handed Scipios. You need not fear, Tiberius Sempronius has returned from Sicily with all his veterans. He will solve Hannibal forthwith."

Cato stalks on, but the wide-eyed townsman follows him, waving his arms about.

"This man they call the Carthaginian has brought strange, horrible beasts with him, tall as a tower! The beasts have a giant hand growing out of the center of their head, to grab and crush soldiers! He has ghosts for cavalry; they swarm like locusts and cannot be killed! Come with me, citizen. We must ask Mars to help us. We must make sacrifices to the gods before it is too late. Hannibal is coming!"

Cato stops so abruptly the man bumps into him. Cato thrusts him away. "Gods? The gods favor the quick and strong. Cease your womanish cries for divine intervention – join the army if you want to do something! Be off with you!"

Cato hurries to catch up with Fabius, who is rushing up the main street toward the Forum, late for a Senate meeting. Cato draws nigh to the general, who gives him with a quizzical look. "What was all that fuss, boy? A persistent beggar?"

"It was but one of our citizens, frightened by the news of Hannibal's victory over General Scipio. The idiot thinks the world is coming to an end."

Fabius nods impatiently. "Yes, yes, I have heard the talk. Even some of the senators are alarmed, they quack about making peace with Carthage. Peace!"

Cato stares at him, aghast. "Peace? We should burn Carthage to the ground!"

"Ai, ai, soon enough, perhaps. But for now we will find gold where others see dirt. Let us use Rome's anxiety to our advantage."

Cato and Fabius ascend the Forum steps. The older man glances about to ensure he is not overheard. "The Scipios must not be allowed to defeat Hannibal. Their political power would increase tenfold. But we are in luck. Publius is wounded. He cannot lead our men against Hannibal." Fabius' eyes light with enthusiasm. "Now, if Tiberius Sempronius can defeat Hannibal while Publius Scipio is incapacitated, the honor goes to him – and thence to us! Sempronius favors our Latin Party. And he is an ambitious man, so he can be manipulated. Yes, Tiberius Sempronius must be the hero."

Cato opens one of the massive Forum doors so Fabius can sidle inside. They pad through the spacious hallway and enter the semicircular Senate chambers. Fabius sits in the first row of the long stone benches that flank each side of the center open space, a position befitting his seniority and honors. As a citizen-observer, Cato takes a seat in the third row, off to the right.

Tiberius Sempronius stands in front of the senators. He is recently returned from a successful campaign against Carthage in Sicily, and proudly wears a dazzling white toga bordered with purple and gold stripes. Sempronius is a striking man, tall and sinewy, with dark curly hair and a prominent aquiline nose in his craggy face. His voice is deep and decisive, radiating confidence. His only flaw is his air of restless impatience, as if he is always trying to catch up to himself.

As Fabius sits down, the Senate leader commences the meeting. "Consul Tiberius Sempronius, we are honored to have you with us. I suppose you understand the reason we have asked you to return from Sicily?"

The consul nods his head. "Yes, of course, that northern affair with Hannibal. Things went badly for Publius Scipio, I am told. I can rectify that immediately."

The Senate leader nods. "Publius' legions were very raw. Your veterans should fare better against the barbarian rabble. But you must depart quickly, winter is coming."

"That will be fine," says Tiberius, with an airy wave of his hand. "I can set out for northern Italia within a fortnight."

The senators look at one another, unsure who should tell Tiberius the bad news. With an exasperated shrug, Fabius creaks to his feet. "Yes, yes, best if you had that much time for provisions and preparation. However, we must resolve this

Carthaginian pest before the northern winter ends all chance for battle, ends it 'til next year. You must leave in five days."

"Five days! It is not possible! My army has just returned from Sicily. My men have families to visit. They must take their rest. I am a man of action, but that is too soon."

Fabius turns to eye his other senators, who nod their heads as if knowing what he will say next. "Might I remind you, Tiberius Sempronius, the consular elections occur in two months, and your consulship expires thence? Should you not succeed by then, we will have to send the new consuls to finish your work, at the first spring thaw. The honor of victory will be theirs. And our gratitude…"

Tiberius hears the other politicians murmuring their agreement. His look of outrage is replaced with one of sullen resignation. "I will leave five days hence, on forced march, sustained until I reach Scipio's camp."

Without another word, Sempronius stalks from the chamber – his quick, stiff strides evidencing his mood. Fabius nods at Cato, and they hurry out to catch up to the fuming young general. As they near Tiberius, Cato whispers something to Fabius, who signals his agreement. Fabius puts his hand on Tiberius' arm, prompting him to stop and turn around.

"One last word, honored consul," says Fabius. "Certainly, Publius Scipio has won many battles for us, but he is at heart a cautious man. Perhaps he is a bit too cautious, if I may say. Do not be dissuaded by any of his temporizing about attacking the Carthaginians. Hannibal must be destroyed before our army goes to winter camp."

Tiberius listens patiently to Fabius. He is one of two consuls over all of Rome, a powerful man. Fabius, however, has many

Senate connections and can bestow large favors when he is so moved. His power demands respect.

"General Fabius, I am not a man to wait for Fortuna to come to me. I must return to Sicily within the year, to rid the island of the Carthaginian pirates that plague it. After I meet with Publius, I will attack the Carthaginians immediately."

Fabius grins. "Gratitude, Fabius, we would have no other for the task. I would ask that my young colleague, Cato here, accompany you. He has just arrived from his farm near Sabina and is the newest member of our Latin Party. You will find him an able soldier and assistant."

Tiberius examines the youth with a studied eye, noting his sturdy physique, the firm set of his jaw, and the unblinking stare of his eyes. A little short, he thinks, but a determined-looking young man. "You do look capable, Cato. As a landowner of Rome, you have the right to serve in the infantry. Very well, raise your right arm and take the sacramentum, the oath to give your life to me, to follow me unquestioningly."

Cato nods in acknowledgement. He raises his arm and repeats the oath that Tiberius gives him. After Cato is sworn in, Tiberius fixes Cato with a stern look. "You serve me now. Get yourself one of the red tunics my men wear. The red means any blood you spill for Rome will not stain you or your family. Report tomorrow."

Tiberius and Fabius briefly grasp each other's forearms, and the general stalks off. Fabius turns to a flushed and excited Cato. "Excellent," Fabius says, rubbing his hands together. "You have taken your first step toward the Senate." Fabius grins slyly. "Just remember who put you on that path. You are not some simple farmer fighting for Rome, you are a messenger for the Latin Party."

Cato looks puzzled. "Meaning what?"

"Tiberius will camp next to General Scipio's force. Learn what you can about the Scipios. Keep an eye on that boy Cornelius, who is supposed to be such a hero. Report anything that might discredit them."

The youth looks stonily at Fabius. "I lie for no man."

"Lies? We do not want lies. We want information. Some threads of information that we can weave into a fabric of truth. Just give us information. We will know what to do with it."

Cato walks onward with Fabius, still frowning. *Fabius is not fighting just the Carthaginians,* Cato thinks, *he is fighting the Scipios.* What would Fabius do were Rome held in the balance between them?

*   *   *   *   *

TREBIA RIVER PLAINS, DECEMBER, 218 BCE. From the top of the camp watchtower, Publius stares out over the staked earthen wall of his army's camp. He is there watching the Carthaginian army as they stand in battle formation a quarter-mile away. Hannibal is in front of them, sitting atop a rust-colored Numidian stallion. The Carthaginian stands unmoving, facing the Roman fortifications, seemingly staring into Publius' eyes, reading his distress.

Publius knows what the Carthaginian is up to. Hannibal has displayed his forces to challenge the Romans to battle. If Publius' weakened force engages them, Hannibal will wipe them out. If the Romans do not attack, Hannibal's men will think the fearsome Romans are afraid of them, and will gain confidence in their superiority. Hannibal cannot lose either way. *My son was right,* he thinks. *We must not underestimate this barbarian.*

There is much to learn about him.

Publius' eyes rove across the wide sweep of grim armored men when his scrutiny halts and he sneers at what he sees. On the far right side he sees three thousand Gallic infantry, the same Gauls who were part of his own army three nights ago. The Gauls murdered his camp guards and slinked away under cover of darkness, allying themselves with Hannibal's superior force. With their loss to Hannibal's side, Publius dare not confront the Carthaginian in open battle. He can only hope that Tiberius Sempronius will arrive on the morrow, as the messengers from Rome have promised.

Publius clambers down from the tower, leaning sideways to favor his wounded chest. He enters his command tent and sits on a wooden chaise specially constructed to ease his wounds. It is time to meet with his officers about camp affairs. Cornelius stands in the corner, studying a scrolled map of the Po Valley terrain. Publius sees him and thinks, *Studying, the boy is always studying.* He wonders if he erred in casting him into a military life, then he shakes his head as if to clear it. *He has a leader's air of command. That must not be wasted on scholarship.*

The officers' meeting goes on most of the day, across a variety of topics: what food needs to be bought from the surrounding towns, where new latrines should be dug, a progress report on the development of pontoon bridges to cross the Po River, and the results of the grain foraging expeditions – all vital affairs. As dusk approaches, the tower trumpeter announces that someone has entered camp. There is a rising commotion of voices in the camp, signifying the arrival is more than a messenger.

Publius ends the meeting and walks to the front gates, with Scipio and the officers following. As they approach the front they see Tiberius Sempronius riding through the open portal, leading his vast army into camp. Publius smiles a welcome, then looks across the plain to Hannibal's force, and sees they are withdrawing from battle formation to head back to their camp. Publius thinks, *he must have known that Tiberius was coming. He had no intention of battle; that formation was just a show for his men.* He grins to himself. *A crafty bastard.*

Tiberius leaps from his horse and embraces his fellow consul. Publius winces with the pain but says nothing, maintaining the stoic attitude that befits a Roman soldier. Arm in arm, they walk back to the command tent to confer in private, with Scipio following behind.

"Tiberius, you are indeed welcome," Publius says. "Your journey must have been very uneventful, you have arrived so quickly."

"We have marched for forty days so we could join you." Says Tiberius. I know Aquilon will soon bring his icy blasts to bear on these plains. I did not want to miss an opportunity for a final scrape before he sends us to winter quarters."

Publius nods, but does not say anything. He is well aware of Tiberius' ambition and drive; he has watched him quickly rise from city magistrate, to tribune and finally to consul. He knows Tiberius seeks the glory of defeating Hannibal before he relinquishes his generalship, to thus become the savior of Rome. But Publius likes this brave but impetuous young man, in spite of his overweening ambition. He is, after all, a true soldier.

"In truth," says Publius, "Hannibal was challenging me for battle just this morning. The Carthaginian army was but two javelin throws from here. But we had best approach this Hannibal very cautiously, he will lay traps for us."

Tiberius smiles patronizingly. This is what Fabius told him he would hear from Publius. "I have brought almost thirty thousand battle-trained veterans with me. What have we to fear from that African scum? Our fathers campaigned at the very walls of Carthage, what do you think they would say if we hesitated to engage this Carthaginian here, on our native soil?"

"I do hear you, brave Tiberius. And we will soon conquer him together, after I am well enough to fight. But I cannot even raise my sword arm. Within two weeks we will fight him, no matter how well I am. That I promise."

Tiberius waves his hand dismissively. "No need to wait, my friend. We can proceed on the morrow, after my men have a good night's sleep and a full meal. We will march across the Trebia and attack them out in the open, so we don't have to worry about any of these 'traps' that so concern you. Then we will be rid of these vermin, and return to the sunny south."

Cornelius has been watching the exchange silently in the rear of the tent, but he steps forward when Tiberius describes his plan. "No, you cannot do that! We would be ambushed!"

Tiberius eyes the boy with thinly veiled contempt. "Ambush? Where? We will be out there in the middle of the day, on the open plains. Do you expect the earth to suddenly open up and swallow us, sending us all down to the underworld? Feh!"

"You do not know him, general," says Scipio nervously. "He has a way of appearing from nowhere."

Tiberius sniffs. "Those savages can leap from the sky for all I care. If we maintain our ranks no one can defeat us."

"If you are going to attack him on the other side of the river," says Scipio, "let us first scout the hillsides about the plain, find the places where he can hide his cavalry – as he has done before.

I volunteer to do it."

Tiberius turns to his fellow consul. "Publius, is your boy to dictate strategy to us?" Knowing his son has spoken out of turn, Publius points for his son to retire to the rear of the tent.

After Scipio stands back, Publius nods to Tiberius. "Apologies. He has the brashness of youth, consul, though he oft has the wisdom of an elder. His words do bear some weight."

Young Scipio gives a despairing look at his father, who gives him the briefest of nods toward the tent exit. Scipio bows his head to Tiberius. "Excuse me, honored consul. I have spoken out of turn. I will leave now." As he walks out Scipio thinks, *This fool will lead us to our deaths. But if this is my last night on earth, I have well prepared for it.* He exits the tent, grinning. Once outside, Scipio encounters a slave boy waiting anxiously for him. Gesturing for the boy to follow, Scipio walks out of earshot and bends his head down, motioning for the boy to whisper. The boy leans close to Scipio's ear.

"At dusk, master. By the rear gate."

Scipio gives the boy a coin. The youth dashes off as Scipio heads over to visit Laelius. Scipio soon returns to the command tent. He hears his father conversing with an allied cavalry officer inside, a sign that Tiberius has departed. Scipio pokes his head inside the tent. "I will be back, Father."

"Where are you going?"

"I… I will be about the camp, looking at some fortifications."

Publius gives him a knowing look. "Very well. If your study of the 'fortifications' takes you outside of camp, do not leave without an escort."

Scipio's face reddens. "I will not, I promise."

As young Scipio leaves he smiles to himself. *It will be more a look at fornications than fortifications*, he thinks. But a promise is a promise; he will fetch an escort.

Scipio walks over his cavalry group and recruits several trusted friends to ride with him, telling them to wait by the rear gate. He leads his horse over near the gate and walks restlessly about it, looking for someone. Then he spies the person he has sought; an older, elegantly dressed man with a furtive eye, nervously kneading his hands as he waits for Scipio. His name is Commodus, a town merchant who is also one of the camp followers that attend every large army: seers, peddlers, prostitutes, entertainers — the people who profit from soldiers with money. Scipio walks quickly up to him.

"It is arranged, Commodus?"

The old man bows with dignity. "Exactly as you requested, Dominus. A most difficult arrangement to make, but not unheard of, I must say."

Scipio withdraws a bag of coins and drops it onto Commodus' outspread hand. "More when my encounter is concluded, if it proves worthy. She is alone, correct?"

Commodus nods. "Naught but her servants and guards." Commodus shifts uneasily, looking over his shoulder. "We should go, the hour grows late."

Scipio and his escort ride out with Commodus, heading toward the walled town of Placentia. With the merchant in front, they easily pass through Placentia's front gates and canter down a side street until they reach a large, well-appointed mansion. Scipio and Commodus dismount. Scipio signals for his guard to remain by the horses. The merchant leads Scipio through a side door and into a spacious entry hall adorned with statues and frescoes.

"This is not her house, of course, for secrecy is paramount. But fear not, the owners are gone, and they are friends of mine. You will not be disturbed."

Commodus leads Scipio into a large feasting room off the main atrium. In the middle of the chamber stands a red-haired young woman in a thin white gown, her face covered with a lace veil. She thrusts her arm toward the door, commanding Commodus to leave. As he exits, Scipio bows and steps forward.

"I am Publius Cornelius Scipio. And you are …?"

She bows her head, eyes averted from his. "Please, do not ask," she says, in her deep, soft, voice. "I know who you are, proconsul. The Scipios are known even in these northern reaches. But you must not know who I am. It could be my ruin."

Scipio cannot help but stare at her. The veil cannot hide the sensitive beauty of her features: her milk-white skin and carmine lips, the proud tilt of her softly pointed chin, her sea-green eyes. Commodus had provided Scipio with some intriguing generalities. The lady is from a respected family in neighboring Clastidium. To restore her parents' waning fortunes, she was matched in wedlock with the patriarch of a powerful Placentia family, an old man with a fiery temperament but an icy touch. She is destined to live in wealth and security while her womb withers in a loveless bond. It is worth her life if she is caught in adultery, but it is worth her life to feel a vibrant man inside her. One who will disappear, afterwards.

The woman's gown is made of diaphanous white linen. More a veil than a dress, its sheer layers shadow the rounded outlines of her heart-shaped ass and silhouette her slim legs when she moves. The deep shadow of her buttocks' cleft commands Scipio's eyes. As she walks away he can feel himself swell.

The woman goes to a long oaken feasting table in the center of the room, and turns to face Scipio as he follows her. She looks urgently into his eyes and her cheeks flame in embarrassment at her wantonness. She turns away from him and shakes her head, as if clearing unwelcome thoughts from it.

"I am sorry, truly sorry," she says tremulously. "But I…I cannot do this. I…"

Sobbing, she leans over the table, hands grasping its border, her head bowed in shame. Scipio says nothing as he steps in to her, his chest touching her back. He leans his head next to hers, lightly nuzzling her hair, his hands caressing her shoulders. He can hear her breath quicken, sees her neck arch with the advent of long denied pleasure. He trails his lips down the side of her neck, kissing the vein that throbs there, and glides his mouth along her shoulder. She gasps, clenches the table, and moans quietly.

"Oh my gods," she says, waving her hand as if shooing a fly. "Please go!"

Scipio reaches around to cradle her thinly-veiled breasts in his hands. A gasp erupts from her. Beneath his gently kneading hands, Scipio can feel her nipples harden, poking against the linen. He reaches inside the sleeve holes of her robe to fill his hands with her quivering breasts, cupping their undersides, rolling the nipples between his fingers.

The young woman grasps the table with a white-knuckled grip; face down, moaning with passion and embarrassment, wantonly thrusting herself against his center.

"Oh please, please," she moans, her face scarlet at her brazen plea.

While his left hand fondles her breast, Scipio lifts up the back of her sheer dress with his right, exposing the tight globes of her ass. His finger traces her cleft from top to bottom, first lightly and then deeper. She thrusts against his invading hand, groaning quietly until Scipio eases two fingers deep into her wetness, and she cries out in spite of herself. Scipio reaches up to stroke her clitoris and she spasms with the pleasure of it.

Sensing her approaching climax, Scipio withdraws his hand to part his robes, and eases himself through the tight folds of her nether lips, deep into her center. His hands clutch her hips as he rocks into her. She screams, arching her head back, grunting with pleasure each time he delves into her. Suddenly, she pushes him away, lays back upon on the table, and parts her legs. Scipio scoops her robe up to her waist and plumbs into her. She scissors her legs about him, pumping frantically. He slowly strokes inside her, enjoying her earthy cries, until he feels her mounting tremors. He quickens his thrusts, rushing to catch up, driving until he feels his nether head swell and split apart. He founts his seed into her as she shrieks with orgasm.

Scipio collapses on top of her and they lay together, listening to their breaths slowing and quieting. He raises himself and she quickly pulls down her dress and stands in front of the table. Her head momentarily bows in shame, but she looks up and gazes affectionately into Scipio's eyes. Standing on tiptoe, she gives him a lingering kiss, and hurries toward the door. Her tear-stained face looks at him for a final time. And she smiles.

The woman suddenly strides back to Scipio. Reaching into her dampened locks, she fumbles out a gold and emerald hairclip, opens Scipio's hand and places it into his palm, pushing his fingers closed upon it. "A memento, Cornelius Scipio. I shall not soon forget our time together."

She swirls out of the chamber. He can hear her soft footsteps pattering down the corridor, soon out of earshot. Scipio rouses himself and walks out the door in which he entered. The aged shopkeeper stands outside in the garden, waiting. His face is impassive but the gleam in his eyes tells Scipio that the woman's cries had penetrated even the staunch stone walls of this fortress. *By Jupiter*, Scipio thinks, *if some passing guards had heard that screaming I could have been killed – and I was worried about dying on the battlefield!* He tosses the shopkeeper a small purse of silver sestertii. The merchant snatches it out of midair, bows, and disappears into the night.

As the dawn moon slinks into the horizon, Scipio returns to camp. He enters the rear gate and heads to the praetorium, the general's central command tent. Once inside he flops on a pile of sleeping furs in the corner. Just as he starts to drift off, a voice comes from the darkened corner where his father beds down.

"Odd, is it not? Everyone in camp has the stench of an unwashed body, yet you smell like jasmine blossoms. Odd indeed..."

Cornelius lies quietly, pretending to be asleep. But his father continues. "I was a young man once, too. But remember, an officer who is a slave to his appetites will get neither trust nor respect from his men. Whether it is an appetite for battle or one for women, he must be in control. Sleep well."

Scipio says nothing but he is awake far into the night, thinking.

* * * * *

Hannibal and his two brothers halt their horses on a shallow rise overlooking the wide Trebia River plain, watching Tiberius' soldiers build their camp. The brothers can see the mounted guards staring at them but they are unperturbed, knowing no Roman horse could catch their swift desert mounts.

Hasdrubal trots off from his brothers, riding parallel to the Roman camps, looking for potential weak spots in their fortifications. Hannibal stands immobile, lost in his study of Tiberius' emplacements. Mago canters about restlessly, anxious for action. He nears Hannibal and spits into the dirt, clearing his mouth of the gum he was chewing. Hannibal rolls his eyes. He knows his brother is going to say something impulsive and irritating.

"Baal be damned," Mago grouses. "Now we have to contend with both those generals! My scouts said the new one must have at least thirty thousand men. That's more than forty thousand together! They outnumber us by ten thousand, do you know that?"

Hannibal looks across the plain, studies the forested hillsides and the many-tongued Trebia River. "I am well aware of their numbers, Mago. And I am quite competent at mathematics. It is not my main concern."

"Not a concern! We could have flattened Scipio's camp before Sempronius' legions arrived! We could have sent the elephants trampling through those whip-dogs and ambushed the other ones as they came prancing to their rescue like whores on a holiday!"

Coming up to join them, Hasdrubal echoes Mago's point. "Yea, he makes sense. It's too late for that now, but we can still attack while they're working on the new fort."

Hannibal waves his hand dismissively. "No, it does not serve our purpose." He faces Hasdrubal and Mago, becoming their commander instead of their brother. "We must break the will of Rome, that is more important than winning any battle. If we had ambushed Tiberius or crushed Scipio's wounded force, Rome would make excuses to continue their delusion of superiority. They would say we tricked them or took advantage. No, we must defeat them both, head-on, in open battle."

"That may not be wise," growls Hasdrubal. "I do not share my brother Mago's disdain for the Roman infantry. Publius Scipio's novices put up a good fight – I lost three tribal chiefs! And now they have at least as many infantry as we do, so a pitched battle could go either way."

Mago grows increasingly irritated at his brothers' reticence. "So what do you want to do, Hasdrubal? Should we bare our asses when they attack, so they can fuck us before they kill us? You have lost your testicles, I swear!" Mago wheels about on his horse, growing more excited. "I'll take my Numidians and ride on that new general's camp at dawn, we'll have it burning 'fore the sun is up!"

Hannibal raises his hand for silence. "No, we do not have the horses to defeat that large a foe. I have another plan."

"Which is what?" asks Hasdrubal. "Going to try to get them to wade into the river again, like you did the Iberians? It worked once."

Hannibal sighs, and rubs his brow. "I have told you before, your enemy will teach you how to defeat him, if you but pay attention. This Tiberius Sempronius, he is hotheaded and ambitious. He is not as cautious as Publius Scipio."

"So what if he is not?" Mago asks derisively.

Hannibal frowns at his brother. "So, cautious Scipio is too

wounded to lead the army. The impulsive Tiberius will be in command. We do not have to attack them, we can entice them to attack us, on our terms."

Hasdrubal tilts his head, puzzled by Hannibal's words. "How can you be sure of all this? How do you know all about this Sempronius?"

"My spies in Rome have told me much." Hannibal shakes his head in amused wonderment. "These Romans, they are too arrogant to ever use spies. They think it is cowardly. And yet they torture prisoners and bribe locals for information, as if that was as good as sending someone to find it for you!"

Mago stirs restlessly. "If we are to prattle forever about nothing, I would have wine." He reaches into his saddlebag and pulls out a flat brass vessel, from which he drinks deeply. "Took this from a dead tribune's pack. Excellent stuff! So what did you learn from your precious spies at Rome, Hannibal?"

"The Latin Party pressures Tiberius to upstage the Scipio family by defeating us." Hannibal says. "Tiberius needs to fight us while he still holds office as consul. He must be very impatient for battle. We can use that. Look here…"

Hannibal gestures for his brothers to dismount. Casting a wary eye at the Roman guards in the distance, they jump off their horses and crouch down to watch Hannibal draw a map in the snow-filmed dirt. He scratches out the Roman and Carthaginian camps, the broad plain fractured by the river branches, and the hills that border the plain.

"As you say, Mago, they have thousands more men than we do. To balance the scales, we must recruit four allies for this battle: the weather, the trees, and the river. And hunger, hunger is our most formidable ally. Here is what we do on the morrow of the next snowfall…"

As he describes his plan, Hannibal points to the map, and then points out to the surrounding terrain. Mago and Hasdrubal at first eagerly nod their assent, but then they begin to argue with their brother, drawing several new attack lines in his snowy sketch. The three finally reach an agreement, smiling with anticipation. Hasdrubal passes the wine about as Hannibal wipes the map off the soft snow.

They start to mount their horses when Hannibal stops. "I almost forgot, Mago. Pick a hundred of your finest cavalry and infantry. And have each one of them pick the ten best fighters they know. These will be our rivermen. Another little surprise for the Romans tomorrow…"

AS DAWN BREAKS on a snowy morning at the Publius Scipio camp, young Scipio drowses in the tent he shares with seven other cavalrymen. The command tent is no longer his regular abode. After overhearing a few comments about nepotism from his cavalry mates, he thought it best to leave his father's comfy tent and occupy the same quarters that they do. After a few days of Scipio sleeping on the ground, soldiers that had previously ignored him nod their greetings when they see him.

A sentry sticks his head into the small tent and beckons for Scipio to follow him. Rubbing his eyes, Scipio stumbles out toward his father's nearby command tent. As he enters he finds his father fully dressed and freshly bandaged. He sits at a table, eating flatbread dipped in wine with a small plate of cheese and olives.

"Father, what are you doing up so early? I have not yet even breakfasted."

Publius painfully raises himself and shuffles over to a small dining table, beckoning for his son to follow. "Here Cornelius, eat something quickly. We must go to Tiberius' camp as soon as possible. Something is afoot with the Carthaginians."

Scipio sits down at the table, and grabs a piece of bread. "Should I be riding with you, Father? I am but a cavalry soldier."

Publius frowns at his son. "Of course, but you are also an officer in training. You must learn about our enemy's strategy and tactics, and learn them quickly."

Shrugging noncommittally, Scipio pops a piece of roast fish into his mouth. "They are going to attack us soon?"

"Perhaps," says Publius as he spreads honey on his bread. "There has been much movement in their camp. But our scouts can only observe it. They cannot identify its purpose."

Scipio shakes his head in frustration. "Instead of relying on scouts, Father, we can bribe some of those treacherous Gauls to report to us, the ones who went over to Hannibal's side. We could compare their information to what little the scouts can see. I would wager that Hannibal is preparing another trap."

Publius drinks some watered wine and bangs down his brass goblet. "Romans do not need the lies of some sneaking barbarians! Hannibal will not catch us unprepared again. I alerted Tiberius about his trick of hiding men in the hills."

Scipio laughs. "Do not count on him thanking you for the advice! I swear to Jupiter, that man is as headstrong as a mule."

"Just so," says Publius. "So I have sent our men to reconnoiter those forested hills for any lurking Numidians or Iberians. We will be prepared for Hannibal, regardless of what Tiberius does." Publius points to a small covered dish. "Try the dormouse, they are the best mice I've had since I left Rome."

"But Father, you told me that Hannibal is a well-educated man. He has likely studied Alexander the Great and Cyrus the Persian. He will know not to use the same stratagem twice in a row. I think he will use those hills as a distraction."

"Perhaps, perhaps. But I have discussed this with my officers. The hills afford his only means of concealment. He has no other place for an ambush. If he tries to ambush us from the hills, we can …."

One of Publius' private guards barges into the tent. "A sentry requests an audience, consul. He bears urgent news." The general signals his assent and the guard waves the sentry in.

"General, the Carthaginians are attacking Tiberius' camp!" blurts the sentry. "Our scouts saw a host of riders circling his fortifications, throwing flaming spears into the timbers. They look like Numidians."

Publius grimaces at the news, and painfully raises himself from the table. "Gods above, I was afraid of this! Get Marcus Silenus in here! Rouse our men, we must get our men over to Tiberius' camp!"

The sentry rushes out. With Scipio's help, Publius eases into his armor and weapons, steadying himself on the table. Marcus Silenus enters the tent, his worn sleeping tunic sodden with the falling sleet. He glances at the armored Publius and smirks. "It is Hannibal, is it not? He attacks in the snow?"

Publius nods. "His cavalries are besieging Tiberius' camp. Get the tribunes in here."

Marcus turns to leave when another sentry enters the tent, smiling triumphantly. "General Sempronius has counterattacked.

111

The Numidians are retreating."

Publius' face tightens. "Damn him, he couldn't wait for us! Marcus, we must get every man over to him before he goes too far afield!"

Marcus nods, and stalks from the tent. Publius turns to Cornelius. "Who is the new leader of your turma?"

"Atilius," he answers.

"Tell Atilius that your squadron is to survey the hills south of the plain. See if Hannibal's cavalry are hiding there. Do it now, our army must depart soon!"

Scipio scrambles out of the tent and runs to the squadron leader's tent, then darts over to his own to clamber into his armor. His heart thuds in his chest, he knows he is heading for a monumental battle. And he knows that Hannibal likely has some plan to trick the Romans, if he can only figure out what it is.

At Tiberius Sempronius' camp, some four thousand Roman and Italian cavalry have given chase to the fur-cloaked Numidians. The African riders whirl in to engage them and then retreat full speed, only to wheel about and quickly attack another part of the cavalry before they can mount an assault. The elusive Numidians repeat this pattern as they retreat toward the river, drawing their vengeful enemies after them.

Sempronius' Roman and Italian infantry soon march out from camp, thirty thousand strong. The massive army is grouped into legions of thirty six hundred, each legion comprised of thirty maniples of a hundred twenty men. The soldiers double-time across the wide treeless plain, following their cavalry west toward the Trebia. To a man, they are bent on destroying Hannibal's camp.

Cornelius' squadron of thirty men gallops out from Publius' fortifications, hastening on to their scouting mission. They ride across the wide river plain, directly at the hills south of the advancing infantry. In the distance, Scipio sees Sempronius' soldiers tread into the chest-high frigid waters of the Trebia, carrying their weapons above their heads, their faces stoically impassive. On the other side of the river, the lightly armed Numidians skirmish with the armored Roman cavalry. The Africans slowly give ground as the Roman infantry crosses to reinforce their fellows.

Hannibal's army appears on top of a shallow rise a mile distant; a half-mile line of infantry and elephants. The army eases down the incline toward the Romans. Now the Numidians race to the flanks of Hannibal's attack line, joining the armored Iberian cavalry stationed on each side of the foot soldiers. With an entire army looming in front of them, the Roman cavalry halt their pursuit and trot back toward the legions. The Romans emerge from the chilly river and thresh through the thick vegetation that surrounds it, eager to annihilate their oncoming enemy.

Scipio's squad crosses the Trebia up near the hills, barely within sight of Sempronius' army. They trample through the waist-high brush and brambles, looking for enemy riders. Scipio dismounts to guide his horse through the tangle, and it occurs to him that a man might easily hide in this dense vegetation, were he to lie low enough. As is his tendency, Scipio begins to argue with himself. Could Carthaginians be hiding in here? Perhaps, but the brush is too thick to mount a concerted assault from it, and the plain is so barren that you could easily see them coming out from the brush. That would give the legions time to prepare for them. No, that trap would not work, but Hannibal has one in mind. Would he actually repeat his trick of hiding in the hills? He seems too shrewd to do that. He must know that even the headstrong Romans will not be fooled twice with the same ruse.

He has to have something else in mind. But what?

Scipio's turma scrambles up to a hillside clearing, and he pauses to scan the brush lands on the plain north of them, near the back of the Sempronius' army. He stares at it for signs of the enemy, but the vegetation is a featureless strip, no movement beyond birds hopping in the branches. He starts to return to his squadron when a distant flash catches his eye. Was that a glint of metal near the riverbank? Scipio cranes his neck, peering into the wide belt of green, but sees nothing. Still, the green oasis is very quiet. He can feel that something is amiss. He gallops hard to catch Atilius before he leads them into the upper hills.

"We should check the riverbanks for enemy troops," Scipio urges. "They could be hiding in the brush."

"What? The infantry just plowed through that scrub, and no one came out."

"But our men chased the Numidians through it. They could have led us where they wanted us to go. It just looks like a good spot for an ambush."

"Possibly, but we have orders to probe these trees, an entire army could be hiding up here! Proceed on course."

Atilius slaps the side of his horse and trots off, leading his squad up into the deep green hills.

BACK ON THE PLAIN of battle, new recruit Cato tramps out of the river brush with his legion, heading for the approaching Carthaginians. Because he is an inexperienced soldier, Cato travels with the hastati, the heavy infantry, a force of younger and poorer men who compose the front line. Cato is half frozen and starving, having to rush out to join his legion before he could grab even a scrap of bread for breakfast. Nonetheless, he is determined to do his forefathers proud by killing some Carthaginians. He glances to each side of him, certain he has kept the required three-foot fighting distance between each of his linemates, and six feet in front of the line behind him. He hefts one of his three javelins, making several mock throws. Cato smiles grimly, his eyes alight. *I will show them what a Porcius is made of,* he thinks.

Claudius marches next to Cato, a tall thin youth who befriended him when he first joined the maniple. This stableboy is an expert horseman, but his family was too poor to buy him a mount for the equites. So he starts his military career with the infantry, his gifts wasted, hoping to become a tribune and make his fortune in the world.

Claudius turns to Cato, his eyes wide with apprehension, his body shivering in the cold. "Cato, can you see them? I think I can hear their armor clanking!"

Cato peers ahead intently, staring through the light snowfall, more irritated than fearful. "No, there's too much snow. But the vermin are out there." He turns his eyes heavenward. "Oh Mars, god of war, bring them to us."

Cato's prayer is quickly granted. From out of the snow a hail of stones rains down on the Romans, flung by Hannibal's Balearic slingers. Anticipating the snowfall, Hannibal commanded the slingers to sling only light colored stones. The missiles fly through the dense falling flakes unseen until the last second, with deadly effect.

The rocks ring loudly off the legionnaires' sturdy brass helmets, counterpointed with the grunts of those felled by a crushing hit. Faint shadows appear, and then take on definition – the enemy infantry approaches. Northern Gauls lead the charge, men who are the Romans' mortal enemies. Hannibal recruited the tribes for the sole purpose of delivering maximum shock the Romans' front lines, hoping to break their ranks.

Tall, broad, and heavily muscled, the Gauls are naked to the waist in spite of the frigid conditions. They heft an ax or broadsword, most eschewing even a shield, showing their disdain for the hated Romans. Their chests and faces are streaked with multicolored war paints, giving them a demonic appearance.

The Gallic mob struts forward with eager grins, intent on the personal glory of splitting a legionnaire's head. Cato feels his heart flutter and curses his fear. *Would Cincinnatus tremble at this stinking rabble?* He asks himself. Cato's reverie is interrupted by a drizzling sound next to him and looks to his right. Glassy-eyed Claudius has soiled himself. The youth stumbles forward shaking with terror. Cato reaches over and grips Cladius' forearm. "Steady, friend. Maintain your position and all will be well. This fight will be over soon, and you can go home."

Cato does not know that the enemy is supremely prepared for this battle. While the Romans ran from camp without food or water and waded across the Trebia's freezing streams, the Carthaginian army rested, took breakfast before a warming campfire, and covered their bodies with olive oil to withstand the day's chill. Now they stand on high ground against an enemy that is cold, hungry, and weary. Hannibal has used his allies of weather, terrain, and hunger to even out his numerical disadvantage. But all of them have not been brought fully into play. He has several more surprises for the Romans.

As the Gauls draw nearer to Cato's line, the Roman velites dart out and hurl stones and javelins into the Gauls. Scores of the barbarians hit the earth but the rest stomp forward, unperturbed.

The skirmishing velites hurry back behind the lines before the Gauls can catch them, being too lightly armed to deal with the shield-splitting giants.

When the Gauls are within a javelin's throw of the Roman lines, they rush forward with roars of battle lust. They close the space between the Romans so quickly that Cato has no time to think about what is happening; the barbarians are upon him. He hastily throws his first pilum into the back lines of the Gauls and is rewarded with a yell of pain. Before he can hurl his second javelin, a Gaul is in his face. The Gaul lifts his mighty broadsword with both hands, and swings it at Cato, intent on cleaving his skull. Cato coolly raises his rectangular shield at an angle to deflect the blade downward. Even so he is almost knocked down with the blow's stunning force. *Strong bastard,* he thinks.

As the Gaul arcs back his broadsword for another strike, Cato lunges forward with his javelin, neatly puncturing his opponent in the middle of his hairy chest. The barbarian roars in anger and pain, and swings his sword wildly at Cato's neck before he falls upon his knees, clutching his breast and spitting blood. When the man falls flat, Cato stands back and surveys his first kill. "Not so fucking strong now, are you?" he says to the corpse.

Cato glances over to his right and his eyes start from his head. Claudius is crawling along the ground, trying to prop himself up on a half-severed shoulder. Cato shoves his way through the melee' to succor his friend. Before he arrives, a screaming Gaul straddles Claudius' back and arcs his axe down to fling off Claudius' head. Cato watches his friend's head tumble away, and he feels cold anger swell inside him. He leaps forward and hurtles his remaining pilum into the Gaul's side as he turns to fetch Claudius' head. The javelin strikes home, deep into the man's ribs. Streaming blood, the Gaul yanks out the pilum and stumbles back toward his own lines, cursing all the way. Cato rushes toward the Carthaginian lines to kill him. Before he can take three steps, he is yanked back by the iron arm of his centurion.

"Maintain formation, boy. Your linemates need you!"

The infantry battle is a fight between the organized and disciplined Romans who push a steady attack, and the powerful berserking Gauls who are trying to chop their way through the legionnaires' tight formations. The inexperienced hastati on the front lines are driven back by the sheer ferocity of their attackers. At a command from their centurions, the hastati retreat behind the second line of legionnaires, the elite principes. These skilled veterans step forward to engage their familiar opponents, and a new battle starts.

The principes patiently cut at any exposed part of the Gauls, knowing their wounds will wear them down for the kill stroke. Within minutes, the battle line is strung with wounded barbarians. Even so, the hunger and cold take their toll on the dauntless principes, and the Gauls fight their way to a standoff. Both sides pause to catch their breath, keeping a twenty-foot space between themselves as they patch wounds and hurl curses. The front lines are quiet for a while, save for the moans of the wounded and dying. Then Cato and the other hastati step forward to relieve the principes, and the fight is on again.

Hannibal rides about with his elite guard, dueling with any Romans who draw near him, wielding his sarissa and sword like the trained weapons-master that he was raised to be. In the midst of the fighting, he shouts commands to his officers and sends battlefield messengers to his outlying cavalry. He directs some army divisions to reinforce weak spots, others to retreat, and others to press their advantage, changing his plans to match the battles within the battle.

Hannibal sees that the Gallic infantry in the center are slowly giving way to the Romans, and he nods with satisfaction. Hannibal had intended the Gauls to only be assault troops, to occupy and tire the heart of Sempronius' army. They have accomplished that objective, but he knows they will soon tire and leave the fight. He looks to the far sides of the battle and sees that Maharbal's Numidian and Iberian cavalry are pushing the outnumbered Roman horsemen away from the Roman infantry, leaving their foot soldiers vulnerable. His eyes light with excitement.

The Carthaginian shouts a command to his nearby trumpeter, who blares two lingering notes that are relayed by others across the field. The Numidians leave Maharbal and his Iberians to battle on their own with the Roman cavalry. They race over to attack the Roman infantry's flanks, closing them in. Hannibal sees that the Romans are being surrounded from three sides, that only the rear lines are open. He shouts an order to a mounted field messenger. The man speeds east of the battle, across the wide barren plain, back towards the Trebia River behind Sempronius' army.

IN THE HILLS above the battle, young Scipio rides through the dense oaks and pines with his squadron, searching for signs of enemy cavalry. Peering out between the trees, he can see the river plain below. He watches the two armies clash, watches the outnumbered Roman cavalry fend off the Numidians and Iberians, and sees the Numidians wall in the sides of the Roman infantry. *Hannibal had many more Numidians than those below,* he thinks, *but where are they? They aren't up here. And the brush below is too low to hide horses.*

Then Scipio remembers how his riding teacher would bring his horses to Scipio's lessons, to show the budding equestrians how many tricks horses can learn when properly trained. Scipio remembers how the teacher could command his horses to lay flat, as if asleep, and they would remain immobile for hours. Now Scipio realizes the brush could hold thousands of horses, if they were lying down.

Scipio looks back at the plain of battle. He sees a lone Carthaginian rider speeding across the plain toward the river, waving a red cloth, as if giving a signal. Scipio's eyes bulge with alarm. He shouts at his squad leader. "Atilius! The trap! Down there by the river!" Scipio turns to head down the hillside, frantically waving for the squad to follow him. But it is too late. He can only watch the disaster unfold.

The riverside bushes quake as if an earthquake has hit them. Thousands of heads rise from the low-lying scrub, the heads of Numidian soldiers and horses. The night before the battle, Mago led his Numidians into the riverside bushes. As is the Numidian way, their mounts were trained to lie quietly until commanded to rise. The Africans lay low at each end of the green belt as their tribesmen lured the Romans between their hidden lines. The Numidians then waited for the signal to attack from behind. And the signal has come.

Mago is first out of the brush, pounding towards the Romans' rear lines. Two thousand horses follow him, each with two riders. They ride full speed across the undefended plain to crash into the back of the Roman infantry, each second rider jumping off to fight as infantry. The Roman army's unprotected back is beset by a surprise cavalry and infantry attack.

Now the Roman army is surrounded, but they maintain their ranks and fight with discipline, held by their unwavering centurions and tribunes. The Romans eventually repulse the

Carthaginian forces to the front and rear, driving them back through sheer dent of will. Iberians, Libyans, and Gauls all fall beneath the Roman blade, and victory is imminent.

Hannibal employs his last trick and sends scores of elephants stampeding into the Romans' flanks. The cavalry horses are terrified at the smell of the unfamiliar beasts. They drag their riders away from the battle, which frees the elephants to crash into infantry legions, trampling soldiers and disintegrating their formations. Several legions are separated from the center of the army. They break ranks and flee for the river, pursued by cavalry and elephants. The pursuing Numidians cut down the Romans and their Italian allies while elephants trample over many others. Most of those who make the river leap in for safety but many of them are soon drowned, too spent to overcome the strong frigid current.

In the center of battle, Tiberius Sempronius sees that his outlying legions are beyond rescue. He orders his center legions to tighten their lines, and for all remaining cavalry to protect the infantry's flanks. As one, the center legions push forward. They will fight their way out or die.

Cato's legion is in the heart of the battle. It is faring poorly against the Gallic horde that presses upon them. The exhausted principes are being slowly pushed backward, and the hastati have been decimated. The centurions order the principes and hastati to withdraw to the rear, and they quickly march back to stand behind the legion's last line of defense, the triarii. This third line is composed of the most veteran members of the Roman force, older warriors who have seen too much death to fear it. The triarii kneel down and plant their long spears into the earth, there to impale any enemies who are foolish enough to charge them. The velites and hastati behind them hurl their last pila into the oncoming Gauls, stifling their attack.

The triarii hold the Gauls at bay as the centurions ready Cato's line to return to the fight. The refreshed hastati step forward between the triarii and clash with the tiring Gauls. The Romans stab their short swords into the enemy's unprotected arms and sides, spearing those that fall or stumble. Where they cannot find an opening, they shove their bossed shields into their opponents to create one. Helter-skelter the Gauls retreat, leaving any lingering tribesmen as easy prey. The velites dash out to hurl the last of their stones into the retreating enemy's backs, hastening their rout.

Cato and his fellow hastati can see the tide of the battle turning. Their fear is replaced by determination to avenge their fallen comrades, and they quickly step to the front. They battle the Gallic remainders for half an hour, then step back to allow the principes to go forward and slash down any who are left to oppose them. Several mobs of Gauls run at the Romans but most have lost interest, and the Romans move inexorably forward. They join Sempronius' remaining infantry, fighting for escape.

Hannibal sees that the Roman army's center has reorganized, and that the Gauls are being decimated. His commanders urge him to mount a concerted attack on the center with their cavalry and Iberian foot phalanxes, but Hannibal knows that breaking that center would cost him too many men. As a lion will attack the weakest in a herd, he directs his army at the isolated legions on the flanks, cutting them off from their fellows, encircling them for the kill. The captive Romans fight with desperate strength, knowing their impending fate. But the circle tightens about them until there is no one inside.

LED BY TIBERIUS SEMPRONIUS, the surviving Romans battle north across the field, leaving more than thirty thousand dead comrades behind them. Cato trudges wearily along, so exhausted he feels neither relief or triumph at surviving, just a dull determination to put one foot in front of another until someone tells him to stop. He watches the surviving cavalry riding back in to join them and thinks about that Scipio boy he had argued with at the Forum. *Wonder where that patrician asshole was at? Probably hiding in his father's camp, reading Greek scrolls and lounging about in his fancy togas. If they were here we wouldn't have lost this fight!* He looks at the ravaged faces and bodies of the survivors about him. *We will soon purge Rome of those Hellenic puffs.*

At sunset, the Romans enter the fortress town of Placentia. The town's legion commander helps Tiberius down from his horse and leads him and his officers to a small stone house to use as his headquarters. Tiberius sits on a sleeping bench, hands folded in front of him and head bowed. Minutes pass silently, and then he raises his head and looks at his surviving officers.

"Rome must not know of another defeat. We must tell them that the weather prevented our victory."

"What of Publius Scipio?" says a tribune. "He will be there."

"I lay this defeat at his feet. If he had listened to me, we could have joined forces, and this tragedy would not have happened. I was told he would prevaricate. Rome will know of his temporizing."

Several of the officers look at one another, but say nothing. After an awkward silence, Tiberius tells them what they will say about the battle when they return home.

WHEN THE CARTHAGINIANS ambushed Tiberius' troops, Atilius knew his little turma could do nothing to save them, so he led his group back to Publius' camp. Publius had mustered his army to join Tiberius' force, but when he receives word about Tiberius' defeat, he knows Hannibal will soon attack his own outnumbered army. Publius immediately burns his base camp, divesting it of anything of military value. He leads his legions on a forced march to Placentia along the other side of the Trebia River, thinking it is the likely destination for the survivors of Tiberius' army.

After a day of marching through inches of new snow, Publius' army comes to rest at Placentia. Publius goes immediately to the town's military headquarters, where he finds the embarrassed but defiant Tiberius Sempronius. Publius is still seething about Tiberius' unannounced attack on the Carthaginians, but he maintains his composure.

"Hail, Tiberius."

"Hail, Publius Scipio. How is your wound?"

"I am recovering. It will soon be no more." Publius shifts his feet, thinking of the right words to say. "The battle did not go well, as I hear it."

Tiberius avoids Publius' eyes. "I sent word to Rome. The bad weather kept us from a victory." Tiberius waves his fist angrily. "If it had not snowed so much, my center lines would have turned the tide of battle. The Fates have cursed me!"

"Did the snow kill thirty thousand of our men?" asks Publius mildly. "It must have been very fierce weather. I dare to say Hannibal's stratagems played a larger part, consul."

"Hannibal?" Tiberius snorts. "He is but a cowardly trickster. He could not stand up to us in a fair battle."

Publius is silent a long moment before he speaks, composing himself. "As my son told me, I will tell you now, for the second time. Hannibal is a clever tactician. We must learn from him or that 'coward' will repeat his 'tricks' and slaughter us all!"

Tiberius face darkens with anger. "If you were not so worried about Hannibal's little tricks defeating you, we could have attacked him together. There would be no Hannibal to argue about, consul."

Scipio glares into Tiberius' flushed face. "And instead of waiting to plan an attack you rushed out to fight him, as if his army were a tribe of drunken savages! Do not let your arrogance blind you to his genius, Tiberius Sempronius. This is a foe like none other we have faced. We must change our approach if we are to defeat him."

"We change nothing! You and your Hellenic friends always want to change the old ways – the ways that made Rome great! Oh yes, the Latin Party is well aware of your sympathies, Consul Publius, and I shall make sure they are reminded of them!"

Publius laughs. "When you remind them of my sympathies, Sempronius, make sure you explain how your vast army was massacred by a snowstorm. " He stalks to the front door, pauses, then turns to Tiberius. "Hear this. I now command what is left of the legion I gave you, may the gods forgive me for that. I go to Cremona and sail for Rome."

As Publius opens the door to leave, Tiberius shouts at him. "Go on, take them then. Go back home and lick your wounds."

Publius smiles derisively. "A wounded wolf is twice dangerous. He has learned to be wary of the hunter, if he is smart enough to learn. I will see you at the Forum, Tiberius. This matter is not yet finished." He strides out without another word.

Publius returns to Marcus Silenus and Cornelius, takes the reins of his horse and walks him to a stable built into the town's walls. Marcus and Scipio dismount and follow with their horses. The consul says nothing until he secures his horse in the stable and feeds it, brushing it with a comb. Scipio fidgets about, anxious to know what they will do. Marcus merely waits, immobile. He knows his commander is deep into his plans even as he attends to his horse. Publius finally lays down the brush and faces them.

"Marcus, we will camp in the town streets tonight. Tomorrow we go to Cremona. We leave our main force there to guard the frontier. Your legion will return to Rome with me. Tiberius' men will follow."

Scipio cannot hide his surprise. "Leaving? We are to leave Hannibal out here? Won't he attack again?"

"Our forces will all be in fortified towns. He dare not try. Soon he must go to winter quarters. There will be no battles for months."

Scipio ties his horse to a stall post, and begins to brush him. "Are you going to return in the spring to lead our legions against him?" The boy pantomimes riding a horse. "We could take his Numidians out of the battle by luring them to chase our cavalry. Hannibal wouldn't expect a Roman to use tricks. We'd get him then!"

Publius smiles, he has always liked his son's audacity. "That is a clever idea, but I will not be fighting Hannibal. That will be the privilege of our two newly elected consuls, Gaius Flaminius and Servilius Geminus. They will face Hannibal in the spring, before he nears Rome." Publius allows himself a sarcastic smirk. "I do believe Tiberius will ask to go back to Sicily – he has had some success there."

Scipio scratches his head and looks confusedly at his father. "But what will you do? Will you join the new consuls? Go to Sicily?"

"I will petition the Senate to join your Uncle Gnaeus in Iberia, to wrest control from Carthage." Publius glances over at Tiberius' headquarters. "Gnaeus and I, we work well together."

Marcus nods. "To kill a lion, it is wiser to starve it than attack it. Iberia is where Hannibal's money is. And reinforcements."

Publius feeds his horse some handfuls of grain. "Iberia's tribes provide Hannibal with most of his heavy infantry, and its silver mines provide him limitless wealth. Now that he's come to Italia, Carthage can use that money to hire thousands of those Gallic mercenaries up north of us, and his army would double. We must retake Iberia, or Rome will fall."

A large shadow falls over Scipio as he listens to his father's words. He sees his father stop talking and stare behind Scipio, his mouth agape. Marcus Silenus draws his sword and steps toward Scipio, his face grim. Scipio looks over his shoulder and sees the largest man he has ever beheld standing next to him, arms crossed and glowering. A Celtiberian by his dress, he is one of the fearsome northern Iberians who are half Celtic and half Iberian. A foot and a half taller than Scipio, the giant is dressed in gold-trimmed white leggings and tunic, but he carries an oversized falcata on his gold-trimmed belt. *He could split a man in half with that* is all Scipio can think.

"You are Publius Cornelius Scipio?" asks a deep bass voice in broken Latin, its question a demand. "There is one who would talk with you…"

As calmly as if he were going to the fountain, Marcus Silenus approaches the Celtiberian, but Scipio halts him with a gesture. Scipio has a guess at who wants to talk to him. The Celtiberian nods over at a gold-gilt van some distance behind him, carried by four elegantly dressed slaves.

"Everything is fine, I think," Scipio says. "I will return shortly."

"I would be happy to accompany you, in the event some help is required," says Marcus Silenus, sheathing his sword while he glares at the giant. "My gods, what a trophy he would be."

Scipio follows the Celtiberian over to the heavily curtained van, just large enough for one person to recline inside. As he draws within arm's reach, the curtains part and a pair of sea-green eyes stare at him from atop a silk-veiled face. Scipio smiles tenderly. "Ah gods, I thought I would never see you again."

The woman motions for Scipio to come closer as she withdraws further into the van. When Scipio's head is inside, she pulls the curtains about his shoulders, drops her veil, and kisses him lingeringly and deeply. She pulls back and strokes his cheek, looking intently at his face, as if memorizing it. "I heard there were Romans returning from battle," she says tenderly. "I had to see if you were here, that you were well."

"I am twice blessed," says Scipio, "for returning unharmed and for seeing you again."

She softly fingers his hair. "Thank the gods it is so." She heaves a deep sigh, and her mouth tightens with reluctant determination. "Now you must go, beloved, I peril my life to talk to you." Scipio starts to withdraw when she grasps his tunic impulsively and pulls him forward, putting her lips to his ear.

"Your seed has taken inside me," she whispers breathlessly. "The priestess of Eki foretold it, though I said naught to her about us. You will have a son, my heart, a son! Now, though it wounds me to say it, please go!"

Scipio pulls himself out of the van and marches away, his eyes distant with thought. He sees his Roman compatriots waiting for him, heaves a deep sigh, and speeds his walk until he rejoins Publius and Marcus.

"What was that about?" queries Publius.

"Oh, just one of the women from town. She knew one of my friends who live here."

Publius' brow furrows. "A woman in Placentia knew a friend of yours in Rome?"

Scipio avoids his father's eyes. "He is a well-traveled friend."

"Ah yes, he must be. And she must really like him," Publius deadpans, "for her to kiss you for him." Scipio wipes his mouth and an orange-red streak of crushed gemstone powder comes off on his hand. He looks at his father embarrassedly, but Publius has turned back to the stable, putting his horse in the stable boy's hands.

Scipio and Marcus walk over to join him. Marcus sniffs the air and frowns at Scipio. "You smell like jasmine, girl," is all he says. Scipio raises his eyes heavenward and chuckles, shaking his head.

The three men leave their horses in the stable and walk toward the town commander's house where Publius will meet with the surviving officers. They pass hundreds of Tiberius' crestfallen legionnaires, many of them squatting under blankets to fend off the cold. One of the men they pass is Cato. He sits with his back against the fortress wall, chewing on a piece of dried cheese. The two Scipios walk past him but he says nothing, eyeing them resentfully. Cato notices young Scipio's armor is unblemished. *As I suspected*, he thinks, *he didn't even fight. Just another pretty patrician who is afraid to dirty his fancy Greek tunic.*

Cato hears the trio discussing their trip to Rome, and his eyes narrow. *The Scipios will make trouble for Tiberius*, he says to himself. *They'll blame him for the army's defeat, so the Hellenics can take control of the Senate. Time to mobilize the Latin Party.* He flings his cheese at their disappearing figures. "You will taste defeat too," he shouts angrily, "when next I see you in Rome."

IV. HOMECOMING

The trireme eases into Ostia, Rome's port. The ship's three banks of oars slowly stroke the water as it meanders through the empty channel, until it pulls up at the massive marble pier reserved for the military. Two marines pop out of the ship and quickly rope it to the dock columns. Several others leverage the wooden gangplank onto the wide stone walkway, and the ship is ready for disembarking.

Publius Scipio totters down the gangplank, clad only in tunic and bandages, bent double to favor his wounded chest. Publius' guards swarms around him like a flock of anxious geese but he refuses their assistance; only Scipio is allowed to help. Wearing a sword and dagger over his simple tunic, the younger Scipio holds his father's elbow as he totters down the worn oaken planks.

Pomponia and Amelia are at the pier walkway, waiting. When Pomponia sees her husband swathed in blood-mottled bandages, she cries out and rushes up the gangplank, shouldering her way through the guards. Pomponia wraps her arms around Publius' neck and cradles his head next to hers.

"Oh my gods, you are back! I had heard you were dying, I didn't know if I'd ever see you again! Please tell me you are getting better. Tell me truth or lies, but tell me you are well!"

Publius gently pushes her back and smiles into her eyes. "Pluto himself could not keep me from returning to you, my heart, much less the spear of some barbarian. I am well. I sacrificed often to Hygeia, our goddess of health, and she is taking care of me, although she does seems to be taking her time! "

Pomponia sobs with relief and leans in to kiss him again. Scipio stands alongside, eyes moist at seeing his parents together again.

Pomponia eases back from her husband and looks at Scipio. She turns to hug him but hesitates. Looking at his stern posture, at the mix of sadness and happiness in his eyes, she knows that her boy is gone, replaced by a man. With a sad smile she steps over to hug him, embracing him as a beloved adult instead of clutching him protectively as her child. Cornelius holds her against him, saying nothing until he steps back.

"Mother. I am so happy to see you again. Happy we are all together."

"Are you well, son? Amelia and I have been praying at the temple of Febris, hoping to placate her so that she would not visit you out there."

"I am well, Mother. The fevers have not come at all."

"Our son is better than well, he is a hero!" exclaims Publius. "He saved my life." He waves his good arm in a circle to take in his guards. "Ask my men! Ask anyone!"

Pomponia looks proudly at Scipio and then a shadow of worry crosses her face. "Where is Laelius? Is he all right?"

"He is back with our squadron, marching down here with the rest of the legion. For all his fancy dress, I think he loves being part of the common citizen's infantry." Scipio grins at her. "But I'm going to get him back on a horse. He can join me in the cavalry!"

Cornelius looks over his mother's shoulder and sees Amelia standing back on the walkway. Pomponia catches the direction of his glance, turns him toward her, and gives him a gentle shove. "We can talk later. Go."

Scipio starts walking toward Amelia. She stares avidly at him and then looks down, not knowing what his heart will be. His walk quickens and he breaks into a run, only to disappear into her arms and whirl her up and about him. A sob of relief and joy escapes her. She pushes his head back and buries her mouth upon his.

Scipio lowers her and strokes her hair, looking softly into her face. He reaches his hand into the purse tied to his swordbelt and pulls out a battered rose stem, only a few broken thorns clinging to it, and holds it up in front of Amelia. "This never left my side, carissimus. Even in the heat of battle."

"That is the rose I gave you?" she says, looking at the forlorn flower.

"Yes, and it saved my life!" He grins. "Well, it at least saved me from making a very bad decision about my life. It was my treasure."

Amelia takes it from him and stares at it, her eyes large with emotion. She looks into Scipio's eyes. "You kept it all this time?"

"I said I would bring it back to you. And bring myself back. As

I always will."

As the two youths hold hands, Pomponia escorts her wounded husband along the dock walkway, heading home. As she watches the soldier and maiden, she offers a prayer that peace will come soon.

*   *   *   *   *

LAKE TRASIMENE, NORTHERN ITALIA, 217 BCE. Hannibal stands on the Trasimene lakeshore with his battered helmet dangling from his hand, exhausted from his latest battle with the Romans. Hasdrubal and Mago stand at their brother's side, letting their horses graze on the lush valley's tender April grasses. The three brothers survey the narrow valley that borders the large lake, conversing about the steep forested hills on the opposite side, at the beautiful turquoise waters of the giant lake. Then Mago and Hasdrubal resume their game, counting the Roman dead that sprawl around them in the wind-rippled fields.

Hasdrubal turns to Mago. "How many, do you think?"

Mago stretches his lanky frame, and rubs the bandaged cut on his shoulder. He turns his head right and left, bobbing his finger as if he is counting a flock of sheep. "Not as many as Trebia, when we stomped Tiberius' balls into the snow. But I'd wager we got ten thousand of them. Not many of them escaped."

Hasdrubal hoots. "Ten thousand? My infantry killed that many of those fuckers! Those prissy Numidians of yours must have killed another two thousand just by trampling them as they rode by! There's fifteen thousand there, if there's a man. How many do you think, Hannibal?"

Hannibal pulls his weary eyes from the field to stare at his brother. "There are more than enough. We did not lose many of ours – that I value most of all."

Hasdrubal barks out a laugh, rolling his eyes. "They walked right into your little setup – again! We were on them before they could even pull their subligaculum over their little phalli." Hannibal nods gratefully at his roughshod brother, knowing that is his version of praise.

Hannibal's battle strategy was simple but brilliantly effective. It was a version of the tripartite tactics he deployed at Trebia and Ticinus: use the terrain and weather as allies, play upon the opposing general's weakness, and ambush the enemy when they least expect it. In this case, the terrain was a narrow valley bordered by steep hills on one side and an enormous lake on the other, with a high ridge at its terminus. It would be a perfect place for an ambush, if Hannibal could lure the Romans and their Italian allies into the valley. That was the challenge.

Fortunately for the Carthaginians, the Roman general helped them spring the trap. While Hannibal was marching near Lake Trasimene, heading south toward Rome, his scouts notified him that Gaius Flaminius Nepos, Rome's new general and consul, was leading his army toward him. Through his informers in Rome, Hannibal knew that Flaminius burned with the same temper and ambition that possessed his defeated predecessor, Tiberius Sempronius. Flaminius would be confident of Roman superiority on the field of battle, and eager to engage Hannibal and gain the political glory of defeating him. Hannibal had only to put his army in a vulnerable position to be the bait for a trap. Given half a chance, Flaminius would blunder into it.

To set the stage for his ruse, Hannibal ravaged the countryside about Trasimene. With their crops and livestock seized by the Carthaginians, the local populace came begging to Flaminius for succor. Flaminius was inflamed at Hannibal's brazen attack, and he quickly set forth to engage the Carthaginians. Once Hannibal found out that the Romans were on the march, he took his army to the far end of the Trasimene valley – there to build his camp on a high ridge, awaiting the onslaught of the Romans and their Italian allies.

Fog from the lake blanketed the lakeside valley those early spring mornings, a fact that did not elude the Carthaginian – this was perfect weather for an ambush. That night, Hasdrubal strung thirty thousand infantry and slingers along the forested hills that bordered the valley floor. Mago followed suit with thousands of his cavalry. When Flaminius' army arrived at the valley entrance early the next day, the legions could see a huge Carthaginian camp on the ridge above the fog, packed with soldiers moving among the cooking fires and the tents.

What the Romans did not know was that Hannibal had scattered his remaining five thousand men along the front of his camp, most of which were injured soldiers and support personnel. This "army" built countless cook fires along the ridge, giving the appearance that the full Carthaginian army was waiting there. While several thousand of these soldiers attended to the fires, the remaining men marched about the ridgeline, making them visible to any Roman scouts who were reconnoitering the area.

When the sun came up, Flaminius could see the Carthaginian camp prominently displayed on the ridge above the soupy fog. Flaminius was certainly an impetuous man, but not a fool. He led his main force to the valley's mouth, but only after sending out a vanguard to skirmish the enemy and ascertain their strength. Knowing they could not assess his numbers in the fog, Hannibal sent a reduced force to fight them, with orders to retreat at his command.

When the Roman vanguard reported that they were driving the

Carthaginians from the field, Flaminius rushed the rest of his army into the narrow valley. The mist concealed the silent enemy hordes that stood but a stone's throw from the Romans as they marched toward the Carthaginian camp at valley's end.

When the last of the legions were in the valley, the Carthaginian trumpets sounded throughout the hills. Hannibal's men swept down upon the Romans. The Libyan and Gallic infantry totally surprised the marching Romans, penetrating them before they could organize into maniples. The Iberian and Numidian cavalry weaved through the broken lines with lances at the ready, almost invisible in the fog. They speared men from all angles and threw the legions into confusion.

Flaminius' veteran legionnaires had never tasted defeat and they fought ferociously, but their disorganized groups were surrounded and they were soon decimated. The Carthaginians drove the hundreds of surviving Romans into Hannibal's ally, deep and frigid Lake Trasimene, and it became the bane of any heavily armored Romans that fled into its waters.

One legion survived the deadly ambush, maintaining battle formation and beating back all who opposed them. These unconquerable warriors fought their way back to their own camp, rescuing survivors even as they fought. Five thousand Romans made it back to their fortified camp, but fifteen thousand would never return.

Having lost only a few thousand warriors – most of them the reckless Gauls – Hannibal knew it was a mighty victory. His brothers rejoiced. Hannibal was appalled at the enormity of slaughter. He stands gazing at the field of dead with a fascinated horror at what he has wrought. And what he plans to do.

A giant Gaul picks his way through the swathes of corpses. He approaches the three Barca brothers, clad only in a Roman helmet and his tribe's red plaid trousers. His wide bare chest is stitched with deep cuts and gashes, but he smiles happily as he lugs along a frayed woolen sack, dripping blood from its bottom.

Hannibal knows the man well and raises his hand in salutation. "Hail, Ducarius, chieftain of the Lingones." The enormous Gaul crosses his thick right arm across his breast and bows his head slightly. "Hail, King Hannibal, mightiest of generals."

Hannibal winces at the kingly honorific. "I am but a simple soldier, in service to my country."

Ducarius' head splits into a black, gap-toothed grin. "Simple soldier, eh? What a 'simple' surprise you sprung on the shit-eatin' Romans! My tribe had never beat 'em, but you wiped 'em out! They were like sheep out there, waiting for the club." He rubs his right arm, grinning. "My fuckin' arm's almost dead from all the choppin' I had to do … Arms and legs everywhere!"

Hannibal manages a tight smile, doing his best to be agreeable to Ducarius. The mighty chieftain is a man to be feared but not to be trusted, especially when there are other bidders for his tribe's services. "I see your men are gathering their share of plunder from the Romans," says Hannibal, glancing at the many Gauls pillaging the corpses.

Ducarius places his hands on his hips, watching the grisly harvest. "Aye, but the lot of 'em will barely fill an oxcart with treasure." The Gaul touches his helmet. "Some good armor, though. Shields too." He sweeps his hand towards a distant group of pillaging Gauls. "Too good for those Leuci over there, running around naked with their dicks hanging out. Barbarians, they are!" Ducarius laughs.

Hannibal spreads his hands optimistically. "There will be more treasure when we head south and take over their allies' towns.

Much, much, more!"

Ducarius' smile widens. "Ah! That is good news. Killin'
Romans is fine as far as it goes, but there are few gold coins to
be had, and no women at all!" He pulls forcefully at his crotch to
emphasize his joke, as Hasdrubal looks sideways at Mago and
rolls his eyes. "So what is your purpose here?" asks Hannibal.

Ducarius blinks, as if remembering what he came for, and
shoves his bloody sack out in front of him. "I brought you a
present – an ornament for your tent." Ducarius reaches inside the
bag and extracts a blood-spattered head with a split eye socket
where his sword had penetrated it. He holds it high, grinning
with delight. "General Hannibal, meet Consul Gaius Flaminius,
leader of the Roman army. He has come to pay homage to you!"

Hasdrubal crows and slaps his thigh. "Ah, shit! Good work,
Ducarius! That's one general won't be making up stories in
Rome about how he defeated us!" Mago turns to Hannibal.
"Let's send it to the Senate, see what those old farts say about
that!"

Ducarius drops the head back into the sack and gives it to
Hannibal. The general nods his thanks and holds the sack at
arm's length, gesturing for one of his Sacred Band to take it.
With a parting grin, the Gaul strolls back through the rows of the
slain, shouting jokes and ribaldries at his plundering tribesmen.
Mago watches him go and shakes his head. "I do wonder how
you hold all these lunatics together, brother."

Hasdrubal starts to mount his horse, but Hannibal raises his
hand. "Hasdrubal, my apologies. I do hate to tell you this now,
but you must return to Iberia."

Hasdrubal cocks his head at Hannibal. "What? Who says? You
don't think you need me anymore?"

Hannibal shakes his head. "Gnaeus Scipio has defeated our Iberian armies and gained control of the north. Carthage's mines are in jeopardy." Hannibal walks about with his head down, avoiding Hasdrubal's eyes. "The Council of Elders has decreed that you will sail back to Carthage to secure some recruits and thence sail to Iberia, to the port town of Carthago Nova. You will join General Gisgo there."

Hasdrubal's mouth is open. "Me? What about Mago?"

Hannibal shrugs. "He has no orders to leave."

Hasdrubal's eyes widen. He looks at Mago, then at Hannibal. "We can finally head for Rome's gates, and they drag me off to Iberia? What a load of oxen droppings!"

"It is not total madness," Hannibal says. "The Council is very worried about losing their profits from the mines, that is true. But Iberia is our army's supply line for money and food. If Iberia is cut off from us, we cannot feed or pay our mercenaries. They will desert us as they did to Publius Scipio, or rebel and crucify the lot of us. We need to retake northern Iberia from the Romans, before they cut us off."

Hasdrubal grimaces in disgust. "I feel like I am the one who is deserting, deserting you two in the midst of a war."

Hannibal watches the cloud shadows creeping across the charnel landscape, drifting black cloaks that cover the dead. "Our battles are over for a while. Rome has lost some fifty thousand men since we crossed the Alps. They will be loath to fight us again. Mago and I can set up camp and prepare for the spring campaign."

Hasdrubal glares at the ground. "I lose the chance to dance at Rome's burning just to save Hanno's ass. Fuck!" He mounts his horse and turns to leave. "I will worry about you two. You are the finest generals I have ever seen, but you are alone out here, outnumbered by Rome's allies." He grins. "Besides, how could you win without me to pull your ass out of the flames?"

Hannibal walks over to Hasdrubal and slaps him on the leg. "You have done well here, but you go to where you are most needed. Just keep the money coming to us, and we will take care of the rest. We will recruit more troops on our way to Rome."

Hasdrubal rides off, and Mago sadly watches him depart. "May the gods speed his mission, for we are undone without Iberia." He jumps on his horse. "I will see to the victory feast tonight. Let us have many bonfires to ward off this damned cold!" Mago heads off for camp.

Eschewing his horse, Hannibal hikes back to his command tent in the distance. As he does in every victorious battle, he walks through the battlefield, studying the concentrations of the dead, to determine what aspects of the battle rendered the greatest casualties. His aide follows him, leading Hannibal's horse and carrying his grisly sack.

As Hannibal nears his tent, cavalry leader Maharbal strides up to the general, leading a contingent of Hannibal's Sacred Band. Maharbal frowns at him. "So this is where you are hiding! Unprotected! Your guards told me that you sent them away!" He lowers his voice. "It is not wise, General. The Romans are gone, but I fear the Gauls more than them, truth be said."

Hannibal jerks his head toward the battlefield. "The Gauls are busy looting, they would not care if Baal himself had descended to meet them! But I am glad you came, I have another mission for you." He fetches his sack and pulls Flaminius' head out of the bag, holding it aloft by the hair. Maharbal wrinkles his nose and looks quizzically at Hannibal. "This is the head of General

Gaius Flaminius. I will sorely miss his gullibility. Have it cleaned as best you can, Maharbal," says Hannibal, "and send it to Rome. Perhaps this will incline them to bargain for peace."

Maharbal's eyes widen. "Peace? Why peace? We win every battle with them, we do not need peace. We need to feast on victory until we have consumed our enemy!"

Hannibal shakes his head. "I vowed I would never be a friend to Rome, and I will keep that vow. But I will not ruin Carthage to destroy Rome." Hannibal reads Maharbal's face. "Do not fret my words. If they do not wish for peace, we will throw down their gates and be done with this war." He smirks. "It will be on their heads, you could say."

Maharbal's mouth remains a tight line. "It will be as you wish."

Hannibal watches his breath fog in front of him, and scowls. "I am done with this northern cold. The Numidians and Libyans will not bear this misery much longer before they revolt or desert... and all our elephants are dead from it, except for Surus. We will move south along the eastern coast and camp where food and warmth are plentiful. The Romans have subjugated many of the tribes down there. We can recruit them as allies."

"Go south?" Maharbal laughs. "You will have no argument from me on that idea. Let us leave this shit pit as soon as we can!" He jerks his heels into his mount and gallops off.

Hannibal pauses before he enters his tent. He looks back at the acres of dead he has just walked through. He reaches into his belt pouch and gently retrieves a wad of soft, thick leather, and slowly unfolds it to gaze at the thumb-sized figurine of his dead father.

"I do your bidding. I labor to fulfill my promise to you. Must

Rome fall to do it? Would it be enough that Carthage stands?"
He gazes long at the figure, as if waiting for an answer. "Victory
is sweet no more, it only lacks the bitterness of defeat," Hannibal
says to the figurine. He carefully wraps it up and eases it back
into his pouch.

Hannibal pushes aside the tent flaps and walks inside, sitting at
a stool in front of his battle map. He looks at the figurines of
Roman and Carthaginian figurines. Abruptly, he sweeps them off
the map with his hand and looks upward. "War, war, where is
thy glory?" he says, as if in supplication. And he covers his face
with his hands.

*　　*　　*　　*　　*

Inside the walls of Rome, crowds of plebs churn about the
massive main gates, waiting for them to open. A wide spectrum
of the Roman working class paces about: blacksmiths, artists,
architects, nurses, farmers, clerks, and merchants. The plebs are
here to await the remnants of Flaminius' once-proud army,
hoping desperately that their loved ones are among them.

The rumors had trickled into Rome days ago: Flaminius'
invincible army has met some misfortune up north against the
Carthaginians. Then the rumors grew worse, rumors that many
thousands had been killed, and that Flaminius was nowhere to be
found. Soldiers' loved ones began to roam the streets, grabbing
passers-by and asking them if they had heard anything of a battle
being fought at Trasimene. Men and women slept at the gates,
beseeching any who entered the city for news. The furor grew
with each passing day, and the city's operations slowed to a
standstill. Fear became a pestilence that spread through Rome,
infecting everyone within reach. Its only antidote would be the
truth, however bitter its taste.

One moonless night, a phantom rider hurled a sack over the city gates. The guards reached into the sack to find the head of Gaius Flaminius carefully wrapped in virgin sheepskin, a figurine of Baal tied about the stub of Flaminius' neck. Word of the consul's fate flashed through the populace, and wailing rose throughout the neighborhoods. Thousands of plebs surrounded the Forum during the Senate's next session, screaming for them to come out and reveal what they knew about Trasimene.

The shouts rang through the Forum's stone halls, and the senators glanced nervously at one another. They had hoped to suppress the news of Flaminius' monumental defeat from the people until they could muster another army against Hannibal. But now they must face the plebs or risk a public strike. In Rome's history, the plebeians have twice refused to provide any goods or services until their demands were met. The city ground to a halt, riots broke out, and the Senate acceded each time. The senators know this time would be no different.

The present uprising has pleased some senators, however. The Latin Party leaders anticipated this furor and took steps to capitalize upon it. Led by Fabius and Flaccus, the Party developed a plan to seize power from the pro-Hellenic factions, which would enable them to pass their financial and moral austerity measures – all in the name of winning the war. The plan's execution began with Latin Party members cultivating the rumors that both the consuls were killed, that Hannibal would be at the gates within days, and that a dictator must take command of Rome to save it, as Cincinnatus and Dentatus once did. Now, as the frenzied citizens besiege the Senate chambers, the Party implements the final part of their scheme.

Thousands of plebs chant for the Senate to come forth, while hundreds more drift in from the surrounding apartment houses. The hills upon which Rome was founded are carpeted with its people, crying for news, shouting for action, and demanding audience with the Senate patricians. Finally, the senators stream out from the Curia. They line up along the upper steps of the Forum entrance, nervously eyeing the sea of angry faces before them.

Praetor Marcus Pomponius, a popular civil judge, pushes his way forward from the group of senators. He walks up to the Forum's rostra, a massive speaking platform built from the arched prows of enemy ships. The praetor faces the crowd and raises his hands for silence.

Pomponius' stentorian voice rings out, still powerful after four decades of public oratory, piercing the crowd's murmuring undercurrent. "We have lost a great battle."[v] With these words, a howling lamentation breaks loose from the crowd, their anger turning to anguish. After Rome's defeats at Ticinus and Trebia, this third disaster strips away their last vestiges of self-deception about Rome's superiority. Their army is no longer invincible, their city no longer a haven, and their lives no longer safe. Many sob and fall into each other's arms, seeking consolation. Others shake their fists at the senators, yelling for them to kill Hannibal. Marcus Pomponius signals the guards along the Forum steps, and they shout for silence as he continues.

"I will not hide the truth from you. The Carthaginians are northwest of Rome near Spoletum. Hannibal marches through our fertile fields, taking all he desires and burning the rest." Another wave of curses and lamentations breaks out, but the guards shout them down as Marcus raises his hands for attention. "Not all my news is dire, citizens. I do bring hope. Though Hannibal distresses our allies in Italia, they remain steadfast to Rome ... so far. But with each defeat this cheating trickster inflicts upon us, their loyalty weakens. The time is upon us to act, fellow Romans, the time for us to act decisively – and gain victory!" The praetor raises his fist heavenward to symbolize victory and garners a wave of cheers, many of them from Latin Party plants within the crowd. Most of the citizenry remain silent, awaiting details.

"The Senate has been meeting day into night, conferring with your tribunes and strategizing with our generals. We have devised a plan to win this war, to purge the Carthaginian stain from our sacred shores." The crowd roars it approval and Marcus allows it to build before he continues. "But the road to victory will be arduous, and you must know that – all of us will be faced with sacrifices. We cannot spend any more money on luxury, arts, and entertainment. That money is needed to equip our legions. New armies will be born from our efforts. Rome will rise as the Phoenix rises from the ashes of its burning. We will recapture the glory of our earlier days, when we repelled the Etruscans and Latins who were once at our gates. And victory will be ours!"

The plebs erupt with deafening cheers. Pomponius smiles and waves at them, but he casts an inquisitive eye toward Fabius and Flaccus. They nod their heads, and he knows it is time to make the final gambit. "Yes, we will raise a mighty army, the largest ever seen, to wipe out the Carthaginians. But we need a powerful leader to direct them."

Pomponius paces along the front of the crowd, hands spread apart. "Two hundred years ago, when the Sabines threatened to destroy Rome, Cincinnatus walked from his fields to become dictator of Rome and to save it from ruin. Now, as in the times of Cincinnatus, Rome must have a dictator – one with absolute power so that he may act quickly and decisively. To act without permission from you, or me – or even the Senate!"

The crowd cheers louder at this last statement; there is much enmity between themselves and the Senate patricians. When the acclaim dies down, the praetor continues. "As you know, only the acting consuls may appoint a dictator, relinquishing their duties to him. So we in the Senate propose that we send an envoy to Gnaeus Servilius in northern Italia, to petition our surviving consul. We will ask him to appoint a dictator immediately."

The crowd becomes quiet because they are uncertain about this proposal's implications for them. Pomponius stands patiently at the rostra, letting the idea sink in. "Of course, this will take some time, I fear. And time is of the essence. We have just received this message." Marcus unrolls a small linen scroll and reads it to the audience, his voice trembling. "The cavalry force of co-consul Gnaeus Servilius, acting under the command of officer Gaius Centenius, encountered a superior Carthaginian force near Umbria. All four thousand men were killed or captured. The fate of Gnaeus Servilius is as yet unknown."

Men and women cry out again, many breaking down in tears as Pomponius rolls up the scroll. "Another tragedy, yes. All the more reason we act immediately and get our consul to appoint a dictator, wherever he may be. What say you, citizens of Rome?"

Within the crowd, a dozen Latin Party hirelings take their cue. They begin to chant, "Fabius, Fabius, Fabius…" while pumping their fists in the air. The crowd picks up the chant. It spreads and rises to a deafening, urgent, pitch. The Senate members are taken aback at the crowd's reaction. Fabius looks innocently at his fellows, apparently bewildered by this turn of events. The senators huddle for discussion and then withdraw into the Curia chambers. Pomponius follows them, gesturing for the crowd to wait. The Forum platform is empty and the rostra unoccupied. But the crowd remains, waiting, in the hot afternoon sun.

Once inside the chambers, the senators engage in a furious debate about designating Fabius as dictator. Led by Flaccus, the

Latin Party members argue that it is the will of the people for Fabius to be elected. The Hellenic opposition party, led by an ailing Publius Scipio, argues that the Senate cannot legally elect a dictator, that only consul Servilius, who is a Hellenic sympathizer, can make that nomination. Many senators are not members of either party, and they are indecisive. They want to placate the plebs by giving them a dictator, but fear the ire of the Hellenics, especially the powerful Scipios. Eventually, a compromise is reached with a historic compromise of dictatorial powers. Fabius will be designated dictator, but he cannot pick his Master of Horse, his second in command of the army. Instead, the Senate gives the office to Marcus Minucius, a senator with Hellenic sympathies.

As the sun begins to set, Marcus Pomponius emerges and walks up to the rostra, a triumphant smile on his face. "By popular acclaim, for a period of half a year, the Senate appoints Quintus Fabius Maximus as dictator, supreme commander of the Roman army and chief executive of Rome!" The crowd cheers as Fabius slowly walks to the rostra, and he waves in acknowledgement. Flaccus stands behind him, grinning with satisfaction. A knot of Hellenic senators stands off to Fabius' left, their faces masks of repressed anger. Fabius raises his arms for quiet.

"Fellow citizens, I am deeply honored that you have picked me to be dictator, yes, honored! I will do my utmost to rid Italia of the Carthaginian menace, once and for all!" He pauses to let the cheers crescendo and then resumes. "As Marcus Pomponius says, we will raise a great army against this Hannibal, the largest ever seen, I say. And we will remedy this insult to our foully murdered consul, Flaminius. We will put Hannibal's head on a spear outside our very gates – yes, our gates – and see how he likes it!" Many laugh and roar their approval. "We will summon our best legions from home and abroad to become part of our mighty force. But that takes time, and I need men to engage the

Carthaginians as soon as possible, to keep them from our gates. So I ask you, every man among you, to join our legions, join the army now. And march with me to defeat Hannibal and drive the Carthaginians from our land. On to victory!"

Fabius raises his fist above his head in a stiff salute before he strides back into the Senate ranks, his aged eyes gleaming with triumph. He knows his party has won a crucial battle in its war against the modernist Hellenic forces in the war to control Rome.

A WEEK LATER, Fabius is addressing the senators inside the Senate chambers. He has wasted no time in exercising his new dictatorial powers. To increase Rome's war chest, he has taxed women's jewelry, banned cultural events, limited feasts, and, much to Cato's irritation, increased farm levies. With urging from Cato and Flaccus, he has mandated restrictions on finery, artistic performances, foreign tutors, and doctors. None of these proposals would have passed a vote by the Senate, but Fabius has a dictator's power to decree them, obviating that problem. The Latin Party rejoices in a return to austerity and morality for the citizens of Rome, even though the patricians maintain their own lavish lifestyle of parties and feasts.

Fabius' political agenda has been attained, so he turns his attention to mustering three new legions for the campaign against Hannibal. He knows the Carthaginian is slowly marching south through the fertile Tuscan valleys, rewarding allied towns that aid him and pillaging those that refuse. His trail of disaster has alarmed Rome's allies in the regions of Umbria and Apulia. Their leaders rush to the Senate pleading for help. Fabius knows that if he does not help these regions, they will defect to Hannibal. So Fabius goes to the Senate and pleads his case to leave Rome and attack Hannibal's minions.

Even though he is dictator, Fabius is obliged to present a plan for the senators to approve. He stands in front of them and explains his plan, using a giant map of Italia sprawled across three tables.

"We estimate Hannibal's force at thirty five thousand men, most of them Iberians and Gauls, with thousands of Libyans, too. That is a force of considerable size, yes considerable, and most of them are battle-hardened veterans of Trebia and Trasimene. It is a formidable army, I say." Fabius gestures to some nearby slaves, and they hold up the map so the Senate can better see it. Fabius runs his finger along it from Rome to the western coast of Italia.

"I will lead six of Rome's legions against Hannibal, along with several thousand cavalry. We will confront Hannibal here, in the fertile Apulia region. He will go there to forage grain and fruit for his army."

An older senator stands up in the front row, wearing the grass crown that testifies of his heroic military service. "Fabius, the fate of Rome is in your hands. Who is to say that your army will not suffer that of the last four against Hannibal?"

"Regulus, you know me as a general with many victories against Rome's enemies, a man who has been consul to Rome twice before – twice! And so it is with no small measure of experience, no small measure that I say that I will not confront Hannibal. I will not engage him in battle!"

A score of senators rise to their feet, shouting their disagreement with this strategy. Regulus looks inquiringly at Fabius for several long moments before he sits down to await the dictator's explanation.

Amidst the uproar, Publius Scipio walks over to stand next to the rostra and faces Fabius. "Honored Fabius, I do understand your logic. If Hannibal defeats you, there is no one to keep him from Rome." Fabius nods his assent as Scipio continues. "But you must know that Hannibal will burn his way to our gates. If we do not stop his progress his army will grow. Surely, you do not plan for our six legions to act as observers, perhaps to write epic poems of his victories over our allies! The Italia tribes will not read them, I am certain!"

Amidst some sarcastic laughter and comments, Fabius resumes. "My motto is *festina lente*. We must make haste slowly. I am not fool enough to fight the Carthaginian with the last of our troops, especially when most of them are novices! No, our worst mistake would be to rush into battle. There is no need for that, no need at all."

Fabius turns to the rows of senators, spreading his arms as if entreating them. "If we but harass him and if we keep nipping at his heels, we can defeat him. The Gauls will eventually desert him. They will grow bored or homesick as they always do. We will attack any of his men who wander from his force, reducing his numbers and consoling our allies. Then, when Hannibal is at his weakest, we will strike. We will be like a pack of hounds, worrying the bear. And like the hounds, we will eventually prevail."

Marcus Minucius rises to speak, and all fall silent. Fabius' new Master of Horse is a fiery young military officer, known for his bravery in battle – and for his rashness. He shouts at the Senate, his voice quavering with anger. "As second in command, I feel I must make my disagreement evident. Romans never hide from a battle. What would our ancestors say about such a plan? They led our armies right at our enemies, head first, and always they prevailed!"

A score of senators stand and cheer Minucius' words. Fabius, however, shakes his head. "Yes, perhaps that would work if we met Hannibal 'head first,' as you say. But Hannibal will not meet us that way, have you learned nothing from our defeats? He will contrive, and trick, and ambush. He will do anything to win, and so he does! I do not fear Hannibal, no, but I do not underestimate him as others have done before me. We must defeat him through a war of attrition, not a war of battles."

Voices of protest rise again, but Scipio raises his good arm for quiet. "I accept Fabius' plan. It has merit. We must give it a chance." Ignoring the outraged looks of his Hellenic Party fellows, Publius turns to Fabius. "General, your dictatorship expires in six months. This should be time enough to prove your strategy is effective." Publius raises his palm, and his voice booms through the chamber. "Let us brook no more discussion. The dictator has the right to act as he sees fit."

Fabius bows his head to Publius, knowing how difficult it was for him to say those words. "General Scipio, I would be honored if you would accompany me. I value your wisdom."

Publius shakes his head. "Apologies, dictator. When I am well, I will join my brother Gnaeus in Iberia, to cut off Hannibal's supply lines. I will send my son Cornelius with you. You will find him more than useful."

As the senators exit the Forum, Publius beckons Minucius to his side. "Do not detest me for supporting Fabius' strategy. He is bent on protecting Rome, not defeating Hannibal to gain glory." Red-faced Minucius starts to reply, but Scipio raises his hand. "I know you would do otherwise, but *alea iacta est*, the die has been cast. We now have a greater concern. Fabius' overall strategy is sound, but his tactics may not be inventive enough to cope with The Carthaginian's mind. He is a Roman traditionalist at heart, and this much I have learned from my son Cornelius:

we must think like Carthaginians, not Romans, if we are to avoid Hannibal's traps."

Scipio puts his arm around Minucius' shoulders. "I would ask you to let my sons Cornelius and Lucius be part of your cavalry. Cornelius is very imaginative. In truth, he has anticipated Hannibal better than any of my tribunes. He would be a useful advisor to you. And Lucius … well, he will be a good officer. He just needs more experience."

Minucius gives a curt nod. "Agreed. But I like not that Fabius wants our men to be hunting dogs, we have always been the bear."

Scipio reaches up to adjust his bandages and grimaces, then he forces a dry smile. "This Hannibal is more like a country fox, Minucius, the animal that outwits both the hound and the bear. I do fear that the Carthaginian will bring the battle to Fabius, whether he wants it or not. And when he lest expects it!"

* * * * *

Amelia strolls around the family peristylium, a large open-aired courtyard in the center of the Paullus domus, holding hands with Scipio. Her lover wears a dark blue tunic and the simple papyrus sandals favored by philosophers, while she is adorned in soft leather boots and a forest-green sleeveless dress, one that matches the foliage of her beloved gardens.

Amelia visits the peristylium every day. As a child she often sat here with her father, General Lucius Aemilius Paullus. Being there now makes her feel closer to her absent father. But for now, Scipio fills her mind as they admire the garden's bounty of roses, lilies, petunias, and lavender. Scipio and Amelia have been lifelong friends, and they are comfortable being silent as they walk together. But Amelia's distress eventually prompts her to speak.

"So, you will be leaving ... soon? Again?"

Scipio looks apologetic. "Father says I have to keep an eye on 'old Fabius,' to make sure he doesn't blunder into some ambush. As if he would listen to me!"

"Do not demean your gifts," chides Amelia. "You have a way about you. You speak of dreams and visions but people still listen to you, because your words have the ring of truth." She laughs. "But I can't imagine you being a senator!"

Scipio looks sideways at her, grinning. "Oh? Your father is a senator, and he is known as a temperate and reasonable man. And now I hear he will be the next consul, right after Fabius' dictatorship ends."

"Perhaps so. But he was never happier than when he was out of the Senate and in the battlefield where there was 'truth in action,' as he likes to say. I just can't see you enduring the chamber's lies and intrigue – it could corrupt you or break you."

He squeezes her hand. "I did not see myself as a soldier, either. But a Scipio is a Scipio – the military is my family's destiny. So, I will do the best the gods allow."

Scipio pauses with her by one of the garden's enormous rosebushes, one with scarlet blooms the size of saucers. He draws a step closer and mutes his voice. "Did I tell you I almost fled to Greece? After the battle of Ticinus, I thought of following that sailing dream I've told you about. I could see myself on that boat, sailing out across the Adriatic and on to Athens." Scipio looks away from her, looking at the flowers but not seeing them. "But I made a promise to defend Rome at all costs." He reaches out to touch one of the roses. "And when I touched that poor little rose you gave me, I realized I had two promises to keep."

Amelia kisses him on the cheek and leans her head on his shoulder. She sighs. "This war seems so different than the ones against the Gauls. It is so … out of control. I never worried that my father wouldn't come back from those conflicts. I knew the Roman army would prevail. Now I wonder if I shall ever see him again." Amelia plays with the silver-embroidered sleeve of Scipio's tunic. "And I wonder the same about you."

Young Scipio looks into her worried face and averts his eyes, embarrassed at what he will say. He reaches out and breaks a large rose off its bush. "Fortuna sent me a dream. In it, I saw the two of us as an old couple, together in some small town far from city or Senate. There is both sadness and joy in our moment, though why, I cannot say. But old as I am, you are there helping me prepare for some great battle, the most important one of all, against some great enemy of Rome." He cups her face with his hand. "I believe that we will survive this war. There is some greater purpose for us." He gives the rose to Amelia, holding it forth with both hands, as if in a ceremony. "The rose is the flower of Eros, God of Love. I swear by Eros, that I will always return to you, bearing a flower of our love. For I do love you, Amelia."

Amelia pulls Scipio's mouth to hers for a deep, lingering kiss. She looks about her to ascertain they are alone. She shrugs off a shoulder of her gown, baring a full, perfect breast, her nipple rosy with the first blush of maiden sexuality. She takes Scipio's hand and places it on top of her breast, closing his fingers about it. Scipio gently squeezes Amelia as he kisses her, feeling the nipple rise against his callused palm. Amelia leans her head into his shoulder, gasping with the pleasure. Her hand inadvertently wanders down to stroke her center before she forces it back to cup Scipio's face.

"Cornelius Scipio, rose of my heart, I do give you myself and my love. Now and forever."

Scipio pulls up the shoulder of her gown, places his hands on her shoulders, and leans forward to kiss her one last time. He walks from the courtyard as Amelia holds the rose in both her hands.

THE COCK CROWS at the rising sun. Amelia walks out of her doorway and heads toward the Scipio domus two streets away. As she turns onto the cobbled street, she can see Scipio standing there with his horse, preparing to ride out with Fabius' legions. Laelius is mounted next to him, brilliantly arrayed with his shining armor and glossy black stallion. Pomponia, Publius, and Asclepius are there bidding their goodbyes to the two young men, giving words of encouragement and final embraces. The mastiff Boltar wanders about in the dusty street, chasing geese, scavenging street scraps, and enjoying the commotion.

Scipio hugs his mother and gives her a final kiss. He and his father grasp wrists and shake their arms, nodding farewell. Scipio notices that his father no longer winces when his arm is moved. His wound is healing, and he will soon be leaving for Iberia to join his brother. Publius sees Amelia coming to meet his son, so he steps over to join his wife in bidding Laelius goodbye.

Amelia rushes toward Scipio, but Laelius dashes over to intercept her, whirling her off her feet. "Ah, my beautiful girl!" he exclaims as he kisses her forehead. "I wanted to say goodbye before that scruffy boy takes all your time!" Amelia kisses her childhood friend on the cheek and cups his chin with her hand, giving his head a playful shake. "I am so proud of you, Laelius, you have come so far! Take good care of yourself" She smiles impishly, "And take care of that scruffy boy, too."

Laelius hugs Amelia tightly and trots back to Publius and Pomponia. After a farewell embrace from them, he mounts his horse and turns about to leave. Laelius glances over his shoulder at Scipio. "Do not tarry long, general, they might win the war without us!" Scipio fakes a spit at his friend and turns to Amelia, enveloping her in his arms.

"Carissimus, you will be with me every step."

Amelia buries herself into his armored breast as if seeking to merge with him. Minutes pass, and she slowly detaches herself and pulls his head down for a final, lingering kiss.

"Go in peace, my love. I shall sacrifice to the gods for your safety, every day."

While all say their goodbyes, tutor Asclepius stands apart from them, waiting for Scipio to be alone. As Scipio turns around to mount his horse, Asclepius walks up and swats him on the back. Scipio turns and Asclepius leans into his face, intent on giving one final lesson.

"You listen to me, boy. Your father has told me that you are to be the mind of Hannibal, advising Minucius about The Carthaginian's plots. And advice to that ass Fabius, if he will listen. Remember always that this 'barbarian' is a brilliant student of military history. He has mimicked Alexander and Cyrus, using nature's elements against you, and he will do it again!"

"I do think he will, too," says Scipio. "I will try my best to anticipate him."

"Good. You are not to think about how you would defeat the Carthaginians, you are to think about how you would defeat your own army! Ask yourself what the great generals would do in this situation – because Hannibal will be asking himself that very question!"

Scipio nods respectfully. "I will, honored tutor. I promise." He slaps Asclepius on the shoulder and vaults onto his horse. As he turns to ride off, he points his finger at the leathery old man. "I will become the Carthaginian – I will see his mind!"

Laelius rolls his eyes in mock impatience. "Yes, yes, we all know you're brilliant, Scippy. Now let's get going. There's a war waiting for us."

Scipio and Laelius gallop off through the stony streets and disappear into the morning mist as Boltar chases after them. Two childhood friends, heading for war.

*　*　*　*　*

Fabius shepherds his army south along the coastal plains of Apulia in southeastern Italia, heading for Hannibal's camp. With the green-shouldered Apennines on his right and the turquoise Adriatic to his left, the scenery would be dazzlingly beautiful were it not for the ravaged wheat fields and olive groves beside him. The General's mind buzzes with plans to thwart Hannibal's pillaging march through this once-verdant countryside.

The dour centurion Marcus Silenus rides with Fabius, volunteering for this campaign while Publius Scipio recuperates in Rome. Minucius rides near Fabius and Marcus Silenus, with cavalryman Scipio trailing behind him, ready to advise the Master of Horse if he should ask for it. Scipio can hear the threesome discussing options for confronting Hannibal.

"We will be upon the Carthaginians by dusk, Fabius," says Minucius. "If we are within two miles of them we can easily attack the next morning."

"And they can easily attack us, too," retorts Fabius, "before we have established a secure camp. No, I think not, no. We will approach their camp two days hence, and build a fortress, one they dare not attack!"

Minucius frowns with disappointment and slows his horse, distancing himself from Fabius. He gestures for Scipio, who quickly rides up to him. Scipio notes Minucius' dour expression. "Do not fret, Minucius, there is some wisdom in Fabius' words. Hannibal always exploits vulnerability. He might very well attack if we showed up tired. "

"And milk in his spine," retorts Minucius. "He fears Hannibal, you can see it in his face."

"I do fear him, too. He is unpredictable. He never does the same thing twice."

"Young Scipio, you have a reputation for bravery. Would you have us follow Hannibal about like we were a bunch of camp prostitutes, waiting for him to plunge into us?"

Scipio is hurt by the jibe but he maintains his calm, knowing Minucius speaks from his temper. "I do not think we will have to follow him, Minucius. I think he will come to us. Look here." Scipio pulls out a much-fingered little scroll and shows its contents to Minucius. "I have kept a record of his battles through Italia. He only fights when he thinks he has a distinct advantage in manpower or terrain." Scipio tucks the scroll back into his saddle. "He must know we are an army of raw recruits, just as we were at Ticinus. It would be to his advantage to come after us before we acquire more veterans."

Minucius shrugs. "Perhaps, but it would surprise me if he did."

Scipio smiles to himself. "Just so, Commander. He is a man of surprises!"

Minucius rides up to rejoin Fabius, giving Scipio the chance to look for Laelius, who is riding behind him with an adjoining squadron. Scipio wanders back and waves over to his friend who returns a mock salute, holding his arm high in the air. Scipio grins and returns the salute, and resumes his place within his own squadron.

As midday turns into late afternoon, the Romans halt and set about building their base camp on a flat plain, five miles from the Carthaginian army. Fearful of Hannibal's penchant for ambushes and traps, Fabius settles on a spot where water is scarce but where anyone approaching is visible from a half-mile away. Hundreds of legionnaires set about digging a wide circular trench, while others fetch food and wood. Scores of disfavored soldiers are sent to shovel out the new latrines, denied food or rest until this vital task is complete. Soon the evening is filled with the firefly glow of cooking embers and the raucous games of men bored with inaction but terrified of impending battle.

*   *   *   *   *

Hannibal enters his command tent, pulling off a blonde wig and Gallic helmet. Mago and Maharbal stand inside waiting for him, and Mago cannot help but laugh as Hannibal divests himself of his disguise.

"Oh, so now you are dressing up as a Gaul? Is this perhaps to attract yourself a boyfriend that you may enjoy some barbarian dick without threat to your reputation?"

Hannibal glowers in mock anger. "Have a care, Mago. I have crucified men for less disrespect."

"Ah yes, those mutinous Iberian chieftains. They deserved it. I am but your loving brother, concerned with you improving your impoverished social life." Mago grins slyly. "But perhaps you have other reasons for your disguise. Have you dreamed of being a Gaul, running around naked with blue streaks all over your body?"

"You know why, buffoon. I can go about the men and take their temper without being recognized. And well I did. Now that they are healed from their wounds at Trasimene, the Iberians and Gauls grow restless for battle and plunder. We must occupy them with some fighting, or they may desert."

Maharbal opens his arms wide and looks heavenward. "Then the gods are indeed propitious, for they have brought our men some entertainment!" Maharbal unrolls a sheepskin map, freshly drawn with octopus ink. "Our western scouts have just returned with news. Rome's new army approaches, and it is led by Fabius." He stabs his finger into the middle of the map. "They are right here, at the northern end of the plain, and are moving closer. The scouts estimate forty thousand infantry and three thousand cavalry."

Hannibal shakes his head in wonderment. "These Romans, their armies are like the heads of the Hydra – you cut one down, and two more spring up to bite you."

"But these new heads are toothless," says Maharbal. "Most of these 'legionnaires' were walking the streets of Rome but a month ago, while our mercenaries have been fighting for three years. We should attack them now, while they are still battle virgins. Once we are rid of them, we can head to Rome and kill the Hydra's body."

Hannibal weighs his cavalry commander's words. Maharbal is a fearless fighter who is at the front of every battle, but perhaps too fearless as a strategist. Hannibal's eyes cloud with thought for a minute and then focus back on Maharbal. "True enough. We will strike these soldier-boys while they are still dribbling from the teat. If we wipe them out, there would be no army between us and Rome. They would have to sue for peace."

Maharbal looks at Mago, who nods his satisfaction. Maharbal rolls up his map and heads for the tent's exit. "I will send scouts to map the terrain between us."

Hannibal gestures for Maharbal to pause. Hannibal goes to a nearby table of food, breaks off a piece of bread and chews on it while he ruminates. After a minute, he turns to his two officers. "Put the infantry and cavalry on battle alert. Everyone sleeps with his sword. Fabius may venture from his little mouse-hole to come at us, and we must be ready to pounce." He grins. "The Romans will find that they are not the only ones that eat mice for breakfast!"

THE ROMANS BUSTLE ABOUT, building a permanent camp in sight of Hannibal's own emplacement. The new camp is a sturdy rectangular garrison, fortified with thick earthen walls that are fronted with a deep trench and backed with fearful palisades of sharpened stakes. By camping so near to Hannibal, Fabius is sending a clear message to him and his generals: from now on they will remain at the Carthaginian army's side. For five days the two camps coexist without incident, save for some skirmishes between foraging parties. On the sixth day, however, the Carthaginian army emerges at dawn, heading for the Roman emplacement. Within hours, Hannibal's force is arrayed across the plain in front of the Romans, inviting them to battle. Hours pass and the Romans' camp remains quiet, its closed gates acting as a mute refusal.

Hannibal bursts from his army's front ranks, charging his elephant Surus toward the camp gates as a score of his Sacred

Band gallop next to him. They halt abruptly within a spear's throw of the front wall. Glaring at the stolid legionnaires in the watchtowers, Hannibal hurls his sarissa into the log gates. The ten-foot spear thuds into the timbers and remains, quivering.

Hannibal rumbles Surus along the front of the wall. "Come out and fight," he bellows. "Is this the pride of the Roman army, hiding behind walls like old women?" He pulls out his sword and sweeps it behind him, taking in the Carthaginian lines. "Behold, we await you! You outnumber us, what do you fear?" Hannibal stares at the Romans lining the walls. They gaze back, impassive. Long moments pass in dead silence.

"Cowards!" Hannibal shouts, and he spits on the ground in front of them. He turns Surus about and lumbers back to the Libyan and Gallic infantry lined up in the center of his army line. He stands in front of his men, facing the Roman camp, inviting an attack.

More hours pass. The Roman camp is still quiet, the only sounds are those of horses neighing and blacksmiths pounding out weapons on their hastily rigged forges. As dusk approaches, Hannibal waves over to his officers who signal the trumpeters to sound a withdrawal. Two short blasts echo across the army lines, and the Carthaginians slowly head back to their own camp.

As the army marches into camp, a fuming Hannibal summons Maharbal, Mago, and all his Gallic and Celtiberian chieftains. "See to your men and meet me at the command tent at nightfall."

The puzzled chieftains shuffle off. They return several hours later to find food and wine waiting for them in Hannibal's tent, a rare departure from the asceticism of their past meetings. Hannibal greets the chieftains in a long, white woolen robe striped with Phoenician purple-red. It is the first time they have seen him without armor or cuirass. He motions for his officers to recline on the tent's robes and pillows as servants bring them wine and food. Once everyone has relaxed, he begins.

"Our spies in Rome were correct. They said the Senate had approved Fabius' delaying strategy, that he might avoid a battle with us until Rome regroups. Twice we have challenged them before their gates. Twice they have stayed inside." He stares into each of the commanders' faces. "The truth is, the Romans will not fight us."

A Gallic chief vaults up. "They do attack us, but only when we go out to find food, or wood … or women." He turns his head to the other chieftains, his voice rising angrily. "I am tired of these games. I say we put the ram to their gates. Then we will see who will fight!"

Several chieftains echo their approval of his words, but Maharbal shakes his head. "We cannot. The camp is too well fortified now. It has walls, trenches, and stakes. We would lose thousands just getting inside it! We need another way."

Hannibal walks to a nearby table and grabs a handful of grapes, chews them as he paces about. "I know what Fabius plans to do. He means to wear us down with attacks on our foragers, to block our path to Rome, to prevent us from getting the food and money we need." He slams his fist into his palm. "And to demoralize us by denying us a chance for victory! Do you not see that?"

"I can see that, Hannibal," exclaims a grizzled Iberian chieftain, "but I know not what to do about it." Other leaders mutter their assent, stirring about in frustration.

Hannibal paces about while the others watch silently. They know he will soon make a decision. It is clear that they trust the man who has led them to so many victories, who has brought Rome to its knees. After several more minutes of pacing, he stops in front of them. "Fabius is not our main enemy right now. Time and terrain oppose us, because winter will come before we know it. We must go for Rome."

A Celtiberian chief is the first to speak. "You want to conquer Rome?"

"Yes, before winter stops us from doing it. We will head over the mountains to Campania, where the Romans have built the Via Appia." Several tribesmen exchange puzzled looks, and Hannibal spreads his arms wide. "It is a hundred-mile road that goes straight to Rome, a paved roadway through the most bountiful farms and groves in Italia. We could gather supplies on our way, even with Fabius harassing us."

A Gallic chieftain raises his fist and pumps it excitedly. "That is well! We are tired of raiding farms where bumpkins have hidden all their food and women! We Gauls have burned Rome once, we would be happy to do it again!"

Several Iberian chiefs roar their support, then Hannibal raises his hands for quiet. "You know I live for Rome's fall, but our victories have taken their toll. We are grievously outnumbered. But, Campania has a dozen cities that resist the Roman yoke. They would make powerful allies, and give us many men. We need to challenge Fabius again, in Campania, and see if he backs down again. If he does, the Campanians will see that their hated Roman masters do fear to fight us. Then, when we promise them freedom and protection, they will come to our side."

Mago leaps up. "I speak not as Hannibal's brother, but as a warrior weary of this womanish life we lead. Let us away to Rome, to win this war and rid us of Romans! Now!"

Hannibal steps closer to the barbarian chiefs. He studies each man's expression, taking their measure and looking for those who blink or turn away. "If you would away to Campania and thence to Rome, raise your right arm." As one, everyone's arms thrust up. Hannibal nods. "Very well, we will break camp for Campania, the day after the half-moon rises."

A wizened Celtiberian chief grimaces as he chews on half a pomegranate. "The Roman camp is within pissing distance, Carthaginian. They will see us leaving and catch us on the march." He spits several seeds from his toothless mouth. "You should know that."

Hannibal nods, unperturbed. "That is true, Leukon. But they will not know we have left. I have a surprise for them."

AS NIGHT FALLS, Minucius stalks along the rude catwalk bordering the inside walls, inspecting the sentry towers and stake walls. Scipio follows him, hurrying to stay near the frenetic consul. Minucius finally pauses over the main gates, looking out to the Carthaginian camp strung across the plain in front of him. Hundreds of campfires burn there, a constellation of earthbound flickering stars.

Scipio's eyes roam across the lights. He ponders the animated beauty of the scene and thinks of the times spent as a boy in front of his household fires with Amelia and Laelius. There they would play the board game of Troy until dawn's cock crowed. What fun it was, rolling dice to move the Greeks and Trojans forward to battle on the board, cheering their victories and laughing at their defeats. How exciting conquest seemed then, eons removed from the stink and horror of this forever war.

Minucius flings a stray pebble at the Carthaginian camp. "Gods be cursed, I cannot bear this eternal lingering, just waiting for Hannibal to make a move. I swear before the gods, Cornelius. If Fabius does not come forth against the Carthaginian, I will lead our men out when that old dog returns to Rome to supervise the religious rites."

Scipio shrugs. "We have taken our toll on them, though it be not in battle. Thrice our scouting parties have caught Hannibal's' men foraging through the countryside, and thrice inflicted heavy losses. The only ones to escape us were those slippery damned Numidians." Scipio pitches a rock at the Carthaginian camp. "They ride away so fast you can't get near enough for a javelin cast!"

"Scouting parties, pah!" snarls Minucius. "We prick the lion while he devours our flock. How many towns has he plundered, how many grain stores raided? Our allies lose faith in us. Look at those barbarians, boy, sprawled out there in front of us like cats before a mouse hole!"

To humor Minucius, Scipio leans over the parapet, and peers into the dark. He scans the Carthaginian camp from end to end, trying to stare through the campfire lights to see what the men are doing there. He frowns in puzzlement and his right hand twitches. Then he leans back abruptly, bemused.

"By Jupiter's cock, they are not there."

Minucius turns toward Scipio. "Who is not there?"

"Who? The Carthaginians! And the Iberians, the Gauls, and the damned Numidians – they are all gone! Do you not see what they did?" Scipio sweeps his hand across the line of fires and tents. "I have been watching those campfires in the front, and I saw guards riding in front of them a while back. But lately, not once has any shape blocked the fires. Not once has any fire grown in size with someone throwing wood on it. Not once has a new fire sprung up. They built the fires and left!"

Minucius smiles patronizingly. "You think their army moved

out in the time it takes a fire to burn?" He smirks. "Is this one of your dreams?"

Scipio's reply is tart. "Xerses, Xerses of Persia. He used that trick two hundred years ago to escape the Greeks. I have read about it!" He grins ruefully. "That one-eyed demon tricked us again!"

Minucius' voice takes an edge of sarcasm. "So you believe this … this desert savage knows the history of some ancient Persian war? You do flatter the man, Cornelius! More like he is out there preparing to attack our fort and end this timid waiting game. I wager he detests it as much as I!"

With a scornful laugh, Minucius scrambles down a wooden ladder and heads for his tent. Scipio lolls on the parapet for hours, watching as the fires dim to ashes as the sun tints the horizon. His head droops with disappointment and weariness. Scipio goes to his group tent, stoops, and enters it. A sleepy Laelius raises his head and blinks curiously at Scipio. Scipio gestures him outside. They crawl out of the tent and walk apace from their dozing comrades.

"Where have you been all night?" asks Laelius, rubbing his eyes. "Were you out visiting village women again?" He grins. "You could have taken me to visit the husbands!"

Scipio smirks. "If only that were true! I think the Carthaginians are all gone. They left under the cloak of darkness. Old Hannibal, he left the campfires burning to fool us. I remember that trick from military history."

"Ah, yes, I'm sure it was in one of your hundreds of scrolls about ancient battles! You do live in the past, I swear. And what did Minucius say to all that?"

"He does not believe me."

Laelius yawns and smiles reproachfully. "Well, it does seem a bit … illogical, Scippy. We have scouts all over the place. What did you expect him to say?"

Scipio looks at Minucius' dimly lit command tent. "If you mean I do not follow Roman logic, I pray to the gods you are right!"

Laelius laughs and follows him back to their tent, where they immediately fall into sleep.

Within two hours, Scipio is shaken awake by a guard, who drags him out of the tent. Scipio opens his drowsy eyes to see Minucius and Fabius standing in front of him. Scipio looks from one to the other, bewildered. Minucius glowers at Scipio while he points to Fabius.

"Tell him!"

Scipio blinks. "Tell him what?"

"The story of the fires – what that Cursees or whoever did, curse you!"

Scipio rubs his eyes, blinks, and recites patiently, as if to a slow child. "Xerses had his army retreat, rear lines first, under cover of darkness. He left only the tents and equipment of the front line soldiers, and some of his men maintained the fires until dawn." Scipio yawns again. "Apologies, I am half asleep … and then those last soldiers rode away, and everyone escaped." He smirks into their grim faces. "He is gone, is he not?"

Fabius' lips tighten. He casts a disapproving glance at Minucius before he addresses Scipio. "Yes, Hannibal is gone. And our scouts are missing. Nothing remains of his camp but smoldering ashes and fetid garbage. He is away from us, only Jupiter knows where. How did you know?"

Scipio looks from one man to the other. "The fires were too …
uniform, the same size and distribution. Then I could see that all
the fires were burning down, but none were replenished." Scipio
glances at his two commanders, regretting what he will say next.
"Actually, he may have been gone for several days." He smiles
to himself. "A clever trick."

Fabius looks reprovingly at Scipio before he turns to face
Minucius. "Find them immediately. We must catch him as soon
as possible." He turns back to Scipio. "Cornelius Scipio, in the
future you will apprise us of any other 'tricks' you anticipate, is
that clear?"

With a glance at Minucius, Scipio nods. The two consuls leave,
arguing as they go. Scipio turns to see Laelius' head sticking out
of the tent flap, grinning with delight. "That's one for you,
Scippy!" chortles Laelius.

BY THE TIME the Romans have finally broken camp,
Hannibal's massive force is ascending the pass over the
Apennine Mountains, destined for the fertile paradise that is the
Campanian valley. The Carthaginians and their allies will leave a
trail of scorched fields and plundered towns on their eighty-mile
journey to the western coast of Campania, a path that will mock
Fabius' pursuing army.

Even though the pillaging enemy horde is out in the open, no
local armies venture out to halt their depredations. The peoples
of Italia are well aware of Hannibal's feats against the Romans.
None dare oppose him, while many consider joining him to
overthrow the Roman yoke. Only their fears of Roman
retribution keep them from switching allegiances – so far.

The enemy force's progress is implacable, but slow. Hannibal's army is an armed city, populated with craftsmen, healers, prostitutes, cooks, and merchants – and all the families of his Gallic and Iberian allies. Hundreds of shepherds lead large herds of oxen and horses behind the army-town, a moving livestock ranch. Hannibal and his officers must keep his army constantly on the move to replenish the vast amounts of food it requires. It is a task as tactically formidable as winning a battle, with routes planned for fertile foraging as much as military advantage. Every day, every living thing must be roused, fed, and watered before the army set outs. Food must be foraged from the countryside or taken from the neighboring boroughs. Every camp item must be disassembled and stored. Only then can Hannibal's town move on.

Once down into the fertile fields of Campania, the Carthaginian force weaves through it for months, feasting on the region's bounty and gathering plunder to pay their mercenaries. Fabius' legions eventually catch up to them and dog their steps, attacking the foraging parties and blocking any direct routes to Rome. Still, the legions can only slow and divert, they cannot halt this menace in their heartland. The dogs hound the bear, but the bear raids the countryside, gorging itself for a winter's hibernation.

It is not an easy time for Dictator Fabius. Messengers come from Rome, telling of a rising panic among its citizens – rich and poor alike. The city fears Hannibal will soon turn his destructive path down the Via Appia toward them. Everyone in Rome is aware of his fearful presence. Roman parents quiet naughty children by warning them, "Hannibal is at the gates!"[vi]

The people of Rome stridently voice their displeasure with Fabius' delaying tactics. Many plebs and patricians call for Fabius' deposal, so many that even the powerful Latin Party cannot silence them all. Fabius' honorific of Cunctuator, the Delayer, has become a term of derision. The local comedians boldly mock him in the public theatre, portraying him as the gullible and cowardly soldier that they often employ in their comedies. In the blink of an anxious eye, the city's hero has become a scapegoat, targeted by a people eager for a quick and easy resolution to their fears.

The dictator's Senate colleagues push him for a change in strategy. The senators appreciate that his plan has helped divert Hannibal from Rome, giving them time to recruit new legions. But that success matters little to a citizenry hungry for a Roman victory over the African demon who haunts their dreams. Fabius' plan is militarily brilliant but politically destructive, and politics are on the senators' minds.

The dictator realizes he must show some type of decisive victory before he returns to report to the Senate. He watches Hannibal's every step, hoping for a weakness, an opening, into which he can strike.

*   *   *   *   *

Hannibal and Mago walk past a dozen oxcarts piled with treasure as they follow a bent old man in a flowing gray robe. He is Cargon, the chief accountant for Hannibal's army, a man as powerful and important as any commander. Cargon carries a clay tablet that he frequently marks upon, updating his record of the army's resources. Today he is showing the Barca brothers the evidence of his latest tally. Cargon taps the tablet impatiently with his stylus, waiting for the two generals to finish their meandering conversation.

"Hasdrubal sends word from Iberia, Mago. He has driven Gnaeus Scipio from the gates of New Carthage. The fortress is still secure."

"Excellent," exclaims Mago. "While we still have control over the Campanian ports, we should ship him some of our treasure and exchange it for coinage, that would make it easier to transport."

Cargon sees his opportunity. "Speaking of treasure and coins," he says irritably, "perhaps I may finish my report now?"

Hannibal winks at Mago. Cargon's fussiness constantly amuses them. "Of course, Master of Numbers! Proceed with all due haste!"

Cargon clears his throat. "Very well. You can see, Masters Barca, we have substantial amounts of gold, silver, and gems. And a noteworthy collection of art, for what that is worth."

"Yes. And what of money?"

"After the sack of Laertenium, we have enough coinage for two years' pay. But the Gauls will prefer the treasures." He gives the brothers a despairing look. "And the Balearics will want women, of course. They must be collected as we go, a considerable impediment."

Mago nods, winks at Hannibal. "A people after my own sympathies! And what of the food stores?"

Cargon scowls. "With our present number of soldiers and captives, we require sixty five thousand pounds of grain, thirty thousand pounds of meat, and twenty thousand gallons of water per day. And the draft animals and horses require twenty tons of oats and barley per day, and almost three hundred thousand pounds of grazing pasturage." Cargon stares accusingly at Hannibal. "Your elephant Surus consumes two hundred pounds a day by himself."

"Our fearsome friend is worth every bit," retorts Hannibal. "If for nothing else than stepping on traitor's heads!" Mago giggles, and Cargon scowls at him. Hannibal continues. "How many days' food do we have for our men?"

Cargon looks at his tablet. "At the present time we have ten days' worth of grain and meat for us. And six days of oil and fruit."

Hannibal scratches his head and turns to Mago. "Baal help us, it is more difficult to feed an army than to defeat one! According to sage Cargon here, we have a higher chance of starving to death than being slain by the Romans!"

Mago nods. "We can double the men on foraging detail and extend our foraging range from camp." He turns to Cargon. "Do not inform the Gauls of our food scarcity. They talk enough already of returning home, though they think we do not know."

"The way they have been complaining for a fight," quips Hannibal, "I might help them pack their belongings!"

Mago rubs his chin, thinking. "Certainly, we must gather much more food for winter." He turns to Hannibal. "Perhaps Maharbal was right. We should attack Rome before it gains more military strength."

Hannibal slowly shakes his head. "It is not possible. We do not have the siege engines to overthrow Rome's walls." He walks over to a cart and picks out a gold snake bracelet with eyes of blood-red carnelian. Absorbed in its beauty, he tries to fit it around his sinewy scarred wrist, running his fingers along the bracelet's intricate scalework. "A wonderful piece, I can see the Greek influence in its design." He laughs. "Perhaps I should get a Greek to design me a new eye patch. I can put a big red eye on it!"

Mago presses him. "Back in Apulia, you spoke of taking the

Via Appia to Rome, what of that?"

Hannibal spreads his hands apart. "I have reassessed our situation, brother. We do not have the siege engines. We do not have the power to fight through Fabius' blockade of the Via Appia and then conquer Rome. We need more allies from Italia."

He flings the bracelet back into the cart. "I thought the Samnites would have joined us by now, or the Latins, once they saw that Fabius feared to stop us. What in Baal's name are they waiting for? Are they all cowards?"

"We cannot remain here, regardless," says Mago, "We have been up and down this valley, and taken everything within miles. There's nothing left for us, unless we encamp at the shores of the Mediterranean and take up fishing."

Hannibal gives him a sarcastic eye. "Yes, let's put the Gauls to work building boats. I'm sure that will keep them happy! We'd be murdered within a fortnight!"

"You know what I mean. We can't stay here."

"Not here, no, not here. We should return to Apulia. There is grain and feed in the southlands, more than enough for the winter. Plundering the towns that resist us would also placate the Iberians and Gauls. That is what we should do."

"Go back over that damned pass again? With Fabius' legions roaming around it?"

"Fabius will not fight us if we divert our path from Rome." Hannibal rolls his eyes. "Our greater battle will be convincing the Gauls and Iberians to do it again!" He crooks his head at Mago. "And what is this bleating about going over the pass? It was naught compared to our venture over the Alps, have you forgotten? Or have you just grown fat and lazy?"

Mago snorts. "Hah! Not so fat that I cannot throw you, Cyclops!"

Mago jumps on his brother and grabs his neck in a wrestling hold. Hannibal breaks it and trips Mago onto the ground, leaping on his back to pin him. For the briefest of time, the two careworn generals become boys again. Cargon stares over them, tapping his tablet as they roll about in the dust.

*   *   *   *   *

Scipio leads a scouting party on a reconnaissance mission along the base of the Apennine Mountains, out on his first military command. Laelius rides next to him. They exchange comments about women, wine, and war as their eyes roam the countryside for raiders. Laelius has proven to be a born cavalryman. He guides his stallion so effortlessly with his knees, he seems more centaur than soldier. His bronze armor is polished to a mirror finish, and his eyes gleam with the excitement of adventure. He knows this war is his best chance for notoriety, upward mobility, and financial security. He embraces this rare opportunity, whatever the risks.

A cloud of dust swirls along the main road far to the west of them, signaling that Hannibal's men are out there and on the move. Scipio puts his hand over his eyes, peering in to see more details. "It looks like they are heading this way, toward the mountains, back along their old route."

"That does not make sense," says Laelius. "There is nothing left there, the fields are ravaged. Are you sure?"

"We have but one way to find out. Let us get closer so we can study them."

"As you wish, Scippy. You're the one in charge, though only

the gods know why!"

Scipio shoves Laelius in the shoulder. "I can always count on
your support, can't I?" Scipio turns to face his twenty men and
waves his arm forward. The party moves along a ridge at the foot
of the mountains. Scipio keeps them within the trees to avoid
detection, something he learned from Hannibal at the Battle of
the Trebia. The art of disguise has become his favored stratagem.

The Romans draw within a half-mile of Hannibal's troops.
They can see the Libyan and Iberian infantry marching forward
in their Greek-style phalanxes, ready for any attack. The heavily
armored Iberian cavalry ride in formation behind the phalanxes.
The Numidians swirl randomly about the army's flanks, chasing
each other, scooping objects from the ground in full gallop, and
reveling in the sheer joy of riding. A gigantic mob of Gauls
walks at the back of the formations, trudging along with their
families and livestock, more a nomadic tribe than a company of
warriors.

Scipio stares into the Carthaginian army, memorizing their
formations. He gasps, and his eyes start from his head. In front
of them all is the unmistakable figure of Hannibal, his back
ramrod straight and his lacquered linen cuirass shining like a
polished egg. He rides a small Numidian pony while towing an
enormous elephant behind him on a rope, as if he were taking a
pet out for a walk. The two men beside him can only be the
formidable Mago and Maharbal. Scipio knows their appearance
well from all the scouting reports.

The Carthaginian army nears the crossroads and slowly edges
right to move southwest, trundling between fields stripped
during their original foray into the valley. Scipio observes their
progress from his sanctum within the trees, his men waiting for
his next order. He turns abruptly to Laelius, eyes wide with

amazement.

"They're leaving Campania. They're going back the way they came!"

"Why would they do that? Rome's the other way."

"Don't you see? Winter's coming on, and they need a place for supplies, a place with more grain and livestock. They're not going to Rome. They are going south, I'm sure of it!"

"Then we'd better get word back to Fabius and Minucius," says Laelius. "Hannibal's only a couple days from the pass!"

Scipio hustles his turma back along the ridge. They descend onto the plains and ride north beside the Apennines, heading for their main camp. After several miles of hard riding, the squadron sees a thick plume of smoke ahead of them. Scipio feels his heart pound. If that smoke comes from a burning field, there could be a raiding party ahead – and they will not be Romans. As the turma rounds a bend in the road, they see a wide patch of grain fields smoldering in the distance, surrounding a large village.

Scipio slows the squadron's pace as they approach the village so that he can decide what to do next. If there are Carthaginians, does he attack them? If the Carthaginians kill all of them, Fabius will not know about Hannibal's escape. Does he circumvent the conflict and leave the villagers to their fate? Then he remembers the Roman motto that Asclepius had drilled into him: *parva sub ingenti* – the weak are under the protection of the strong. His right hand twitches with his anxiety. He swallows, and yells back at his turma.

"Remus! Get up here!"

Small, spry Remus, the party's ablest rider, draws up to Scipio's side. "Stay near me," says Scipio. "I will need your speed, very soon."

Several heartbeats later, Scipio sees them. An Iberian raiding party is plundering the village. They lug out food and belongings from the evacuated village houses, throwing everything into their saddlebags and carts. The villagers are sprawled about the town square, a score of corpses with severed limbs and split skulls. He can hear cries of those still in distress, shrill screams of rape and murder. Scipio turns to Remus. "Run to camp as quickly as you can – but stay in the trees. Tell Fabius that Hannibal is going back over the pass. Now go! "

Remus salutes and races back toward the forest. Scipio takes a deep breath and chops his hand down. As one, his men charge the village.

The pillaging Iberians spy the Romans' approach. They drop their plunder and dash for their shields and spears. Once armed, the raiders scramble to the village entrance and straddle the road with two lines of a dozen men each. The chieftain orders the horses to be chased off. He wants his men to fight on foot, knowing the Romans always dismount and fight as infantry. He is also determined to prevent any retreat. It is kill or be killed.

As the turma closes in on the Iberians, Scipio screams at his men. "Do not dismount! Ride through them! Use your javelins!" He had his men practice this new attack tactic, but he never thought he would use it in a real fight. Nevertheless, he drops his reins and pulls his pilum back for a throw while he holds the second one in his left hand.

Scipio barks, "Now!"

The Romans arc their six-and-a-half foot spears into the shielded Iberians, concentrating their onslaught on the men in the center, so there are too many javelins for them to deflect. Four raiders are pierced through the chest and face and fall to the ground. Another has his eye lanced and runs screaming into his fellows, bouncing off them until he careens into the flaming fields, after which he is heard no more.

Then Scipio's squad is upon the Carthaginians, pushing through the barbarians that close about them, thrusting their remaining pila into the soldiers below. The Romans surprise the Iberians by staying on their horses, but these battle-hardened veterans quickly adjust. They stab the Roman's horses with their lances and bring several Romans tumbling to the ground. An Iberian scrambles over to a fallen Roman and crunches his falcata into the side of his skull before he can rise. Another swings his falcata low and chops a legionnaire's leg off at the knee, leaving him to bleed out and die.

One of the fallen is Laelius. Two Iberians immediately rush at him, prizing his gleaming armor. Wide-eyed with fright, Laelius nonetheless fights with his characteristic élan. Aping the superb gladiators he has watched at home, Laelius spins to avoid the first man's javelin thrust, turning in a complete circle to thrust his sword into the side of the surprised Iberian's chest. The man falls upon his knees and begins puking blood, embarking on his death journey.

The second Iberian, a bear of a man with arms as thick as legs, is quickly upon Laelius. He swings his cleaver-like falcata down upon Laelius' shield and splits it to the middle. His next blow hews a large chunk from the shield, and his third splinters it into worthless shards, knocking Laelius onto his back. Stunned and bleeding, Laelius frantically scrabbles backwards, rolling sideways to dodge the barbarian's murderous swings.

By this time, Scipio has charged through the Iberian lines and is turning for another assault. He sees Laelius' impending doom and digs his heels into his horse's side. He gallops straight at the massive Iberian. Scipio throws his pilum at the man, but it flies wide, serving only to distract him enough for Laelius to rise and plunge his sword at the man's chest. With one swipe of his thick sword, the Iberian knocks Laelius' weapon from his hand. He rams his thick oval shield into Laelius' body, knocking him flat and stunned.

Shaking with fright, Scipio vaults from his horse and rushes at the warrior, knowing he cannot reach him in time. He grabs the smallest throwing knife on his belt, a thin, leaf-shaped blade that is perfectly balanced and razor sharp. As he pulls it back to throw, Scipio remembers Marcus Silenus' instructions from months before, as the centurion placed his man-killing hands on Scipio's shoulders, guiding his practice throws.

"Aim for the neck, or someplace where there is no armor. The head does not move."

Scipio whistles the six-inch iron at the Iberian, just as the man raises his falcata for a killing blow. The knife thunks into the man's ear, its blade sticking halfway out of his skull. The Iberian's face bulges with shock and agony. The sword drops from his hand as he screams and contorts, grappling to pull the knife out. Quick as a striking serpent, Laelius stabs his blade up under the man's chin and into his brain. The massive Iberian crashes to the earth, kicks, and lies still.

Laelius pushes up and dusts off his armor, his hands shaking violently. He looks at Scipio and opens his mouth to speak but Scipio interrupts him. "To battle! Our work yet remains." Scipio jumps on his horse and returns to his men.

The Romans dismount and pair up against the surviving Iberians. The fighting is fierce nonetheless, as the tribesmen suffer mortal impalements for the sake of gashing an arm or throat before they die. After the last Iberian is cut down, four Romans lie dead among them. Scipio stands over his lifeless charges. His young eyes are glazed at the spectacle of men with whom he recently shared a joke lying dead at his feet. Minutes pass while he stares at them, his lips moving soundlessly. He hears the restless shuffling of his squad, and he wipes his face and turns about.

"Bu ... bury our men behind the village in a field where they will not be found and desecrated. Quickly now!" The men drag their compatriots off to the fields, their severed limbs resting on their torsos.

A somber Laelius watches his fellows go about their macabre task while he ties a scrap of tunic onto his arm gash. He studies Scipio's face, and he can only see misery on it. He quiets his nerves and summons enough enthusiasm to stride jauntily over to Scipio.

"You did wonderfully, Scippy ... Cornelius. You caught them totally by surprise when we stayed on our horses, and we got them all! Now we can make it back to camp."

Scipio turns to face him and Laelius winces at the sorrow in his friend's distant eyes. "Yet four men dead will remain," mutters Scipio. "Catullus there was but a boy, even younger than I." Scipio grimaces with reproach, his right hand twitching. "I should have set an ambush for them. That is what Hannibal would have done. Maybe we'd all be here then."

Laelius places his hand on Scipio's neck, squeezes it once, and withdraws it. "You saved many of us from death," he says softly. "And a village from being set to flame. There was no better way to do it. None." His voice becomes brisk. "What next? Put out the flames?"

"We have no time to stop the fires, the villagers will have to come back from the woods and do it. We return to camp. Hannibal has a new plan, and I fear I know what it is."

As the men jump onto their horses, Scipio wanders over to the corpses of two dead Iberians, one of them the bear-man he killed. He bends over and pries the falcatas from their rigored grip, cleaning the weapons on their linen tunics. Scipio hefts the bear-man's sword, admiring the balance of its thick, curved blade. He puts his hand inside the hooked handle and swings it about, listening to it swoosh through the air like an ax. He wraps the weapons in cloth and stuffs them into his saddle pouch. With a wave, he leads his men forward. They ride from the ravaged village, hastening back to camp.

*　　*　　*　　*　　*

As the sun arcs toward the horizon, Hannibal leads his army west, approaching the base of the mountain pass to Apulia. Riding his tireless Numidian stallion, he talks with Mago and Maharbal as they start up the long switchback trail. The three are arguing about the best camp location for the night when they hear a sentry's trumpet, the signal that someone is approaching. The brothers look over to the east and watch a small dust cloud approaching them. Soon, four figures materialize within it, Numidian scouts rushing back from their morning mission. They ride up to their commander, Maharbal. A rangy Numidian dismounts in one bound and strides toward him. Maharbal raises his hand in greeting.

"Hail, Juvo. What say you?"

"Hail, Maharbal. I bring distressing news. The top of the pass is occupied by the Romans."

Hannibal frowns. "That is not a complete surprise. How many

there?"

Juvo turns back to his men and there is a muttered discussion.
"A legion."

Maharbal stares intently at him. "A legion? Four thousand men
are there? You must be mistaken."

Juvo's face does not change expression. "We did move about
them to make our count. There are thousands of men on each
side of the pass. I also saw the legion banner of the spread eagle
flying there." He turns to Hannibal, points to a long ridge far to
the left of the pass. "More Romans are coming, filling that ridge
yonder. Cavalry are there now. Infantry will be there soon.
Fabius leads them."

Hannibal turns to Mago. "So Fabius' army is here. That old
man can move quickly when he wants to." Hannibal studies the
landscape about him and points to an open expanse behind their
army, near a wide stream. "Set camp immediately, over there, by
the water supply. Triple the sentries. Keep all men on alert,
weapons at the ready. Do not unpack anything but fighting gear.
Everything must be ready to move. Check back with me at dusk,
and bring the allies." Without another word, Hannibal returns to
the center of his army, his Sacred Band guards following.

Hours later, the mercenary allies file into the command tent.
There are Iberian chieftains, Gallic clan leaders, Numidian
captains, the priest-chief of the Balearic slingers, and the Libyan
commander. They arrive to find Hannibal pacing about, acting
uncharacteristically anxious, with Mago and Maharbal standing
by the map table. Hannibal gestures for the leaders to remain
standing. He has goblets of wine brought to them. After all have
quaffed deeply, he commences without preamble.

"The Romans have taken the pass to Apulia. They have enough

men there to inflict heavy damages if we dare to cross it. And there are at least three legions mustered on the ridge above us. I think general Fabius is finally willing to fight us." A ripple of enthusiasm breaks from the battle-hungry Gauls and Iberians, but Hannibal raises his hand to continue. "I know we lust for their destruction, but it would not be to our advantage to fight them now. Fabius has the high ground and superior numbers, with more men arriving. Winter is coming, however, and we must get over that pass."

Several chiefs push forward to speak, but Hannibal thrusts his palm out – an imperious command for silence. The tribesmen bristle at the gesture, but they see the determination in Hannibal's face and they know he has a plan.

Hannibal goes to an urn in the tent corner, and withdraws several fruited olive branches from it. He bends the branches to affirm they are not too dry, picks up a candle from the map table, and waves its flame under the leaves. The limbs flare into a torch that burns slowly and steadily. Hannibal watches the flickering flames for a moment, nods approvingly, and holds the flaming brand in front of his rapt audience.

"Do you see how the branches burn bright and long when they have some oil in them? They make fine torches, do they not? Hear me now: we can take the pass tomorrow night, when there is no moon. We can do it by preparing an 'inducement' for the Romans to attack us."

"You say the Romans are too numerous to fight, then you talk of inducing them to battle. You talk in riddles, Carthaginian," blurts an irritated Gaul.

"All things will become clear," says Hannibal, with a wry smile. He gestures to one of his guards. "Bring in the ox…"

A NIGHT LATER, near midnight, two Roman guards stand atop a massive boulder at the entry point of the pass, looking down into Campania's Falernan Fields, a place once abundant with grain and fruit but now a sea of ravaged stalks. The guards can see the Carthaginian camp sprawled across the plain at their feet, dotted with the twinkling specks of campfires. A long thread of lights suddenly springs to life on their right. The thread weaves up the trail between the pass and Fabius' camp on the high ridge. Hundreds of flickering lights snake in and out of the thick tree stands on the mountainside as they approach Fabius' main encampment. As one, the two sentries turn and race to report to the centurion of the guard, who walks over to check the sight, and then dashes to the legion commander's tent.

Within an hour, the superbly disciplined legion is marching rapidly down the pass, led by the legate Montanus. Believing this is Hannibal's army on a night attack, Montanus plans to intercept this army of lights moving several miles away below him. Two messengers fly past the marchers, rushing to warn Fabius about the threat, even though the ascending river of flame would be visible from Olympus itself.

After scrambling down the rocky trail, the legion draws within bowshot of the ascending enemy. Montanus hurries his men onward, savoring the thought of dropping down upon Hannibal's army while it is on the march and strung across the trail, perhaps leaving Hannibal himself exposed to capture or death. He orders his maniples to attack when the signal horn blares, and to give no quarter to those below.

The legate starts to give the order to his trumpeter, but then he pauses. Something is amiss. The torches seem to be held too close to the ground, and they weave back and forth, as if their bearers were drunk and scrambling about bent over. The flames crash about as if heedless of being discovered, not a tactic the wily Hannibal would employ. The commander's brow creases with puzzlement for a minute, but he shrugs it off, confident that his Roman legion can overcome any ruse Hannibal may try, especially when his legion has the upper ground. He shouts to the trumpeter, the cornu sounds, and the Romans descend upon the flowing flames.

The legion bursts through the trailside brush, ready to massacre the unwary Carthaginians. Instead, they find they are attacking a herd of two thousand oxen. The beasts rumble along with flaming brands tied between their horns, driven on by hundreds of Iberian light infantry. At once embarrassed and outraged, the legion storms down upon the trotting barbarians, determined to wipe them out.

Fighting among the mountainside rocks means the Romans must break formation and fight as individuals. The mountain-wise and lightly armored Iberians are much more mobile than the Romans, giving them a tactical advantage. They dart agilely between the oxen and scramble about the boulders, using darkness as their ally. Even so, the Romans are unrelenting in their pursuit, and the two infantries duel evenly for hours.

Through sheer determination, the Romans take a heavy toll on their elusive foe, scrambling after them wherever they go. The Romans begin to surround the remaining Iberians for the final conquest. As they begin their encirclement, the legion finds itself attacked from behind, back along the trail from whence they came. A division of Libyan heavy infantry has come down from the pass the Romans vacated. That can mean only one thing. Hannibal has taken the pass.

After the Roman legion evacuated the high pass, a thousand of

Hannibal's light infantry sprang from trees around its pitch-black main trail. They quickly overcame the skeleton force of Romans left behind and stationed themselves along the top the pass to guard it. Then the rest of Hannibal's army – livestock, camp followers, and thirty thousand men – emerged from the trees about the main trail to file over the pass and down into the bountiful lands of Apulia.

From their camp along the high ridge, Fabius and Minucius have been watching the mysterious river of torches moving up the trail near them. The scouts they have sent out have not yet returned, and they are squabbling about what course of action they should take. Minucius' tone is urging. "This may be our final chance to catch him at a disadvantage! We have him between our army and the legion at the pass! The messenger said that Montanus was going to intercept him!"

Fabius shakes his head. "Why would Hannibal show himself so blatantly, else he had a trick in mind? I smell a trap, I say, smell it!"

Minucius looks at Fabius with thinly veiled contempt. "You are becoming as bad as young Scipio, always smelling a trap or a trick! Hannibal needs torches to light his way, because the trail has steep drops on it. That is all." Minucius looks sideways at Fabius. "And he knew you would not attack him, even if you knew where he was, *Cunctuator*…"

Fabius ignores the insult. "Summon that boy Scipio. He warned us about that last trap. We will see what he has to say, yes, see what he says."

Minucius fumes with disappointment, but he gives the order to a guard. Within minutes, Scipio approaches the tent. He sees Fabius and Minucius out front of it, studying the torchlight parade. Fabius gestures out toward the torches.

"What do you think of that, boy? Is Hannibal attacking?"

Scipio looks carefully at Minucius and Fabius' faces, trying to determine their attitudes. He looks out at the flames and shakes his head. "That is not Hannibal."

Minucius can barely contain his frustration. "Who else would it be? The townspeople on a night parade to the gods?"

Scipio shrugs. "I know not who, or what, it is. But this looks like one of Hannibal's diversions, using that mountainside for some kind of trick. Hannibal will be up near the pass. That is where he must go."

Fabius nods. "Thank you, boy." He waves his hand for Scipio to leave. As Scipio turns to go, Fabius turns to Minucius. "We shall stay here until the dawn to see this anomaly in the light of day. Montanus will send word of what he encounters there."

Scipio halts and his mouth drops open. "Montanus' men are out there?" Scipio blurts. "Who is guarding the pass?" A puzzled Fabius simply looks at him. Scipio's eyes widen. "Oh, gods! I would wager my life Hannibal is at the pass now! Those torches are bait!"

Minucius rolls his eyes. "I doubt Hannibal is moving an entire army about in the dark! He is not a magician!"

Scipio merely looks at him. "Yes he is, sir. Yes he is."

Fabius face shows his irritation at Scipio's impertinence. "You may go."

Scipio does not reply to Fabius, but he glances at Minucius and gives the barest of head shakes. Then he walks outside to watch the lights streaming up the mountain trail.

AS DAWN BREAKS, Montanus reaches Fabius' camp with dire news. He has lost over a thousand soldiers in the trail battle, and Hannibal's men command the pass. The Carthaginians are moving down into Apulia, and Roman pursuit is blocked. Fabius staggers to a stool beside the map table, collapses onto it, and covers his face with his hands.

* * * * *

Within days, all Rome hears the word. Hannibal has tricked Fabius and escaped to the southlands. Another uproar by the plebs engenders a quick decision by the Senate. Fabius' term as dictator will not be extended at the end of his six months' term. He is to return to Rome immediately to supervise the upcoming religious rites and to oversee the election of consuls to replace him and Minucius. Ever the good soldier, Fabius silently packs his belongings and departs within the week. Before he goes, however, he warns Minucius not to fight Hannibal in a pitched battle, fearing that Minucius' blind ambition has made him deaf to Fabius' words.

As soon as Fabius departs, Minucius starts making changes. One of his first acts is to make Scipio his advisor on military strategy. Minucius immediately weeds out all the Fabian sympathizers from his advisory group, replacing them with officers who are more aggressive strategists, ambitious men of his own temper. He then meets with his inner circle to develop a plan. Four days later, Minucius leads the Romans over the now-unguarded pass, resuming the pursuit of Hannibal.

HANNIBAL HAS GUIDED HIS MINIONS southwest to the ancient town of Luceria in the midst of the most abundant grain fields in Italia. It is autumn, and the Carthaginian needs ample winter food stocks for his men, women, and animals. The army soon builds a winter camp with walls of thick tree trunks and a deep trench surrounding them. Organizing into armed raiding bands, most of the camp sets forth to plunder the cornucopia around them, ferrying in oxcarts of wheat, barley, hay, grapes, and olives. For a short respite, life is peaceful and full

But the peace is soon shattered by the murder and terror brought on by Hannibal himself, much to his detriment. Seeking to win allies, Hannibal travels to the nearby fortress town of Gereonium, offering to buy its vast stores of grain and to provide them protection from war's ravages. When the town officials refuse his offer, an angry Hannibal decides a lesson is in order for the region's inhabitants. He breaches Gereonium and slaughters everyone in it. He then commandeers it as an outpost and storehouse, establishing his control of Apulia. From then on, his troops roam at will throughout the countryside. His men gather strength for a spring assault on Rome. In spite of the Carthaginians' imposing presence, however, the locals refuse to ally themselves with them. Instead, they huddle fearfully behind their town walls, fearing reprisals from the Romans if they join with Carthage, and fearing the Carthaginians if they do not.

After negotiating their way over the vacated pass, the Romans move quickly across the plains towards the Carthaginian army and set camp nearby. The legionnaires immediately attack the enemy foraging parties, and skirmishes erupt throughout the area. The Romans win most of these small battles, and Minucius' confidence soars. He brags to his officers about storming into Hannibal's main camp, of running the Carthaginians into the sea.

Scipio likes Minucius' daring and confidence, and he is grateful for Minucius' trust in his ideas. However, when Minucius speaks about destroying the Carthaginian army, Scipio hears the voice of Flaminius at Trasimene, and Sempronius at Trebia. He worries over the fate of Rome, and the thought of yet another battlefield disaster often keeps him awake at night.

One evening the nightmares return. Scipio is on a wide plain at sunset. He stands in a field of slain Roman soldiers, the bodies so thick he could walk a mile upon them. Scipio is picking his way through the carnage, calling for Laelius, when he freezes in alarm. Beneath his feet lies Paullus, Amelia's father, his dead eyes closed to the horror about him.

Scipio stares at Paullus' peaceful face, and his eyes cloud with tears. Paullus' eyes fly open, and the dead man stares pleadingly at Scipio – begging him to do something, although Scipio does not know what.

Scipio is terrified. He runs wildly away, stumbling and slipping among the dead's intestines and feces, rushing to the top of an unsullied hillock. As he nears the top, he sees mighty Hannibal in front of him, genuflected before the murdered legions, studying the destruction he has wrought. The Carthaginian's face is a mix of triumph and sorrow. Hannibal looks at Scipio with deep regret, as if he must perform an unwelcome task. He draws his shining sword and steps down toward Scipio.

Scipio vaults up from his blanket gasping for breath, his body bathed in sweat. He looks at his sleeping comrades and waits for his hammering heartbeat to subside. For once, the sign of the dream is clear to him. It is a portent of what will be, if nothing changes. But how does he change the future?

At dawn's light, Scipio writes a letter to his father. He sends it with a messenger bribed for the utmost speed and confidentiality. Scipio walks off from camp to a clear stream nearby, takes out a cloth tunic scrap, and scours the sour night sweat from his body.

*   *   *   *   *

Minucius and Scipio are at each other with swords. They thrust, dart, and parry, each seeking a killing thrust. Their trainer, a respected doctore, circles them slowly. He shouts encouragement and makes corrections to their swordplay He stops Scipio in mid-thrust and takes his wooden sword, demonstrating a defensive move to Minucius' overhand cut. Scipio and Minucius repeat the maneuver until the training master approves.

In the midst of their dance, two Roman officers arrive, flanked by a score of guards. Minucius and Scipio immediately drop their swords and face them. Minucius frowns in dismay when he recognizes who they are, because he realizes their purpose for coming to camp. The leading officer dismounts and raises his arm in a greeting salute as he walks toward Minucius.

"Salus, Minucius."

"Salve, Gnaeus Servilius Geminus. How be you?"

"I am well, consul. You know my partner, Marcus Atilius Regulus. We are here as the arm of the new consuls, Gaius Terentius Varro and Lucius Aemilius Paullus."

Minucius grudgingly raises his hand. "Salve, Atilius."

Out of respect, Servilius speaks so softly no one can hear him except Minucius. And Scipio. "Minucius, we are here to assume your command. We are to replace you until the new consuls arrive."

Minucius stares at them and his face stiff with resentment. "I did know replacement would happen, but I did not expect it so soon."

Atilius dismounts and walks over toward Minucius. "Varro and Paullus are eager to put their stratagems to effect. We have come ahead as their arm of decision until they finish their obligations in Rome.

Servilius interjects. "You have the option of joining our staff or retiring to Rome, Commander. But we would welcome your counsel here."

"Join your staff?" Minucius repeats the words out loud, amazed at the turn of affairs. "Act as a 'counsel'? I think not."

"Then the matter is settled," says Servilius.

Minucius turns and starts to walk away, crestfallen. He turns back. "I did but want a chance to battle Hannibal – to defeat that monster once and for all. That is all I desired, though death takes me in the trying."

Servilius casts a wary glance at Atilius, who nods at Minucius. "Yes, that is what we would expect you would do, Master of Horse."

Scipio watches his Minucius leave. His wooden sword still dangles from his hand. Atilius turns to study Scipio, staring hard at him. Then a smile of recognition creases his face. "Ah, my gods, I almost did not recognize you." He turns to Servilius. "It is Cornelius, son of Publius Scipio!"

Servilius grins. "Look at you. By Hades, the boy has become a man! You have become quite the figure among the people of Rome. They know of your gift for sniffing out Hannibal's tricks." He calls Atilius to his side, and there is a whispered discussion, ending with Atilius nodding in agreement. Servilius steps up to Scipio. "We want you to stay on with us, as a leader of your own cavalry unit. And to provide counsel. What say you?"

Scipio thinks fondly of returning home to his family, to a year's respite of study and teaching. Then he remembers the dream, of Paullus face, his promise to protect Amelia's father from harm.

Scipio nods. "Th-...that would be an honor. But I would like to return to Rome for a bit, if I may."

Servilius slaps him on the back. "Excellent. We have much need of you. Of course you can return to Rome. You can leave with Minucius and return with Varro and Paullus. But return soon. There is a storm approaching, a Roman storm. And it will bring lightning upon Hannibal, night and day..."

*   *   *   *   *

The rising sun shimmers the ocean as a fleet of Carthaginian warships glides quietly to the shores of Barulum, a port town a half-day's ride from Hannibal's camp. Maharbal waits by the docks, sitting on one of his Numidian horses. He prepares to welcome the new arrivals, and they are welcome indeed.

The quadriremes stroke into the docks and immediately throw down their gangplanks. Thousands of Libyan infantry emerge, stern veterans marching proudly in formation down the wide wooden planks. Maharbal grins to see them, but for him the best is coming from the ships still out in the bay.

The infantry ships empty their passengers and moor out in the bay. The remaining quadriremes drift in and dock in their place. The ships' holds open, and hundreds of lithe Numidians lead their wiry little horses to the dock. This is Maharbal's new cavalry, the fierce and elusive desert riders that are the curse of the Romans. Soon, a small army fills the docks and streets of the town, milling about as they await orders. Maharbal locates the Libyan and Numidian leaders, and they quickly convene before Maharbal rides over to his cavalry. Orders are given, and the entourage departs for the Carthaginian camp.

By nightfall the convoy arrives at camp. The Libyan and Numidian leaders are directed to go to Hannibal's command tent.

They find Hannibal out front with his men, casting dice with them while he cooks his porridge on a small campfire. When the new chieftains approach, he springs up and gives each of them a bearlike hug, overjoyed at their arrival. The tribal leaders are taken aback with the embrace of this one-eyed man wearing the rough wool tunic of the common infantry, until Maharbal assures them it is Hannibal. The general leads them inside his tent, and introduces them to his brother Mago.

"I am delighted you are here," says Mago. "I trust your trip went well?"

"The sea trip was uneventful," replies a Libyan. "We evaded the Roman blockade and the seas were calm." He laughs. "We had no trouble at all until we were on our way to your camp!"

Hannibal looks at Maharbal for an answer. "Cannae. Again," says Maharbal testily. "When we passed through its hills, some cavalry ambushed our rear forces. They vanquished ten of our men before we ran them off."

Hannibal stares into space, thinking. "The Romans came from Cannae?"

"More than likely," Maharbal says. "That storehouse is where the Romans keep all their provisions, so of course it is heavily manned. They have been harassing our foragers from for months."

"Yes, yes," Hannibal says. "We should have put an end to that place a long time ago. But we shall talk of that later." He turns back to the Libyans and Numidians, pouring them a glass of wine that he personally serves to them. He points to a food-laden table. "We are delighted to have you. Please refresh yourself. When you have had your fill, my men will show you to your quarters. We shall meet on the morrow, but I must now attend to other affairs."

The leaders bow to Hannibal as he exits the tent, Maharbal and Mago following him with several Sacred Band guards. They walk through the center of camp.

"I am relieved they finally arrived," Hannibal says. "With these new recruits, we exceed our original force that set out for the Alps. We now have about thirty five thousand infantry and ten thousand cavalry."

Maharbal interjects. "More important, most of those cavalry are Numidians! They will be the bane of the clod-footed Romans."

Watching some slaves herding oxen past him, Hannibal nods. "Ah, if only the Council of Elders saw fit to send us some elephants! They would thrive in this warmer clime."

"Elephants are expensive," Mago says. "We had no chance to get them. We only received half our manpower request as it was. May Baal take me if I lie, the Elders are more worried about filling their purses than winning a war!"

Maharbal smirks. "They are motivated to protect the silver and gold mines in Iberia, the source of their wealth. And source of the pay for our mercenaries, to be fair."

"That may be," says Mago. "But with twice that purse we'd be dining in Rome. I guess we will get nothing more until we take the city."

"True, and they will get their wish," Hannibal says. "Spring comes, and we are as strong as we will ever be. This time, nothing will delay us from our trip to their gates."

Mago smiles darkly. "Well, those two new consuls, Varro and Paullus, they may have something to say about how fast we get there!"

"I expect we shall finally have our decisive battle, and soon," Hannibal says. "The people of Rome want a fight. Varro was elected because he pledged to rid Italia of the 'Carthaginian menace,' as he calls us. But he is just another smooth-armed politician. That Paullus, now he is the dangerous one. A military veteran." Hannibal smirks. "Difficult bastard to trick!"

Maharbal barks out a hoarse laugh. "That old fart Fabius was smarter than the rest of 'em. He knew we'd cut their balls off if they fought us!"

"They will have the advantage in numbers, again," says Mago. "They have four new legions joining the ones already here, and four more of their Italia allies. I wager they will bring them all after us."

"Then we'd best get to them while they are still raw!" Maharbal gives Hannibal a challenging look. "You once mentioned forcing them to make peace. It does not appear they want to discuss peace, would you say?"

Hannibal sighs and shakes his head. "I underestimated them. They will fight until we kill them all, or we are all killed." He sighs. "A peace treaty is not an option – gods save us all."

Hannibal reaches into his purse and extracts the figurine of his father, Hamilcar. He holds it in his palm, tumbling it in his fingers, studying it. The laughs and crude jests of the men echo around them. Hannibal lifts his head up and turns to Mago.

"Now we will use one of old Fabius' tactics. We starve the beast and provoke it to attack us." He looks at the figurine as he pockets it. "To kill them before they kill us all."

Maharbal knits his brows. "How can we 'starve the beast,' as you say?"

Hannibal looks up with feigned surprise. "Did you not reveal it earlier when you told me about your trip yesterday? We go to Cannae, of course."

V. CANNAE

Gaius Marcellus, governor of Apulia and legate of Cannae, is just finishing his breakfast, sitting upon a couch in the large stone cottage that functions as his office. His slave cuts the last portion of roast pork for him, and Gaius pops the slice into his mouth. Then he picks up some bread and spreads honey on it with his fingers. The slave brings him a moist towel, and the governor is wiping his hands when the legion's First Centurion barges into the room, his face drawn and anxious. Gaius calmly throws the towel to his slave and waves in his trusted lieutenant.

"What is it, Martinus?"

"There is something you should see, Commander. At the wall."

"I will be there in a twitch," replies Gaius. The centurion hurries out the front door. Gaius waves for his armor, ties it on, and hurries to the main gates of Cannae. The legate scrambles up a heavy wooden ladder onto the wide plank walk that borders Cannae's sixteen-foot walls. Martinus is already at the top. He motions for Gaius to look over the wall. The legate cranes his neck over the parapet and beholds a very unwelcome sight.

A column of horsemen rapidly approaches. They fly a dark blue flag with a golden crescent, indicating they are part of the Carthaginian army. Gaius can see the sun glinting off armor and chain mail, a sign that these men are heavy cavalry, most formidable combatants. The legate shouts for the town gates to be closed, and for his legionnaires to be on full battle alert. *This will be a good day spoiled*, he thinks.

As the cavalry approaches Cannae, it spreads out into a double line and encircles the town. Gaius can see their bossed circular shields and pointed helmets. They are Iberians. He scratches his head, puzzled. Why would heavy cavalry come here? They cannot hope to break Cannae's walls, and they are certainly not equipped to mount them. Several hours later he has his answer. The plain is filled with the machine-like sound of infantry marching in step. Thousands of Libyan and Gallic infantry appear on the horizon. They stamp toward the Iberian cavalry encirclement. The Iberian riders have dismounted and crouch next to their horses, watching the town. Gaius realizes the cavalry was not there to get into Cannae. They had been sent to prevent anyone from leaving for the main Roman camp. He feels his stomach knot – these men did not come to parley.

Cannae's legionnaires look out over the walls, watching a daunting spectacle unfold. By dusk, ten thousand infantry have arrived to join the two thousand Iberian cavalrymen. A thick ring of warriors surrounds the town's sturdy walls. The Carthaginian army sets about pitching tents and building cook fires. Mules and oxen rumble into the makeshift camp, bringing food, armament, cooks, and blacksmiths. This army is preparing for a lengthy stay.

Gaius immediately orders his men to reinforce the gates with timbers, and to place fire-fighting supplies along every part of the walls. The legate is very worried. The walls were hastily rebuilt after last year's fire reduced them to rubble. The stone blocks are thick, but not high enough to repel a siege.

That night, Gaius sends five messengers out at different times, hoping one will get through to the main camp. Then he sits at his desk to write a farewell message to his wife and children in Rome, sending it with his most elusive messenger. He makes a second copy, seals it, and addresses it to Hannibal for delivery to his family. He knows Hannibal will deliver it in the event of his death. The legate is a veteran of many battles. He does not fear dying, but he fears losing Cannae's rich resources to the dread Carthaginians, seriously weakening the Roman army. To prevent this, he is prepared to fight until the light departs from his eyes.

The sun rises, and Hannibal trots out from camp with a score of his Sacred Band. He pauses at the main gates of the Cannae depot, just out of javelin range. Within an hour, the gates open and Gaius Marcellus rides forth, accompanied by Martinus and several senior tribunes. Hannibal raises empty hands to show that he comes in peace. He rides forth alone, and Gaius does the same, each raising their hand in salutation as they meet. They stop at arm's reach from one another. Hannibal's face is stern when he addresses Gaius.

"Legate, I offer your men safe departure from Cannae if you go now. Otherwise, I will throw these walls down around you."

Gaius nods slightly, acknowledging he has heard. His eyes drill into Hannibal's. "You think we would depart meekly and turn all our stores over to you? We are Roman legionnaires. There will be no surrender." He hands Hannibal the letter he has addressed to him. "If Fortuna does not smile upon me, could you see this to my family?" With the briefest of nods, Hannibal takes the papyrus.

Seconds pass as Hannibal silently stares at Gaius and then he sighs. "Ah, Commander, I expected you would say as much. Admiration for your courage." His pitying eyes take on a feral, determined glare. He bows his head slightly as he gives Gaius a grim look. "Fare you well in the next life."

Without another word, the two commanders return to their men. Gaius summons his officers, and they prepare the defense. He fills the catwalk with soldiers and loads them with javelins and stones. From a guard tower, Martinus monitors the enemy's activities. He watches the Carthaginians moving about into battle formation, with scores of them entering two enormous tents that have been set up behind the front lines at Cannae's gates. Within the tents, there is a clamor of hammering and banging. Martinus' eyes narrow with rueful expectation. He has been through sieges before.

After several hours, Hannibal emerges from the serried ranks of his waiting infantry, riding his war elephant Surus. He pauses in front of his men, facing the depot's main gates. He raises his right hand high and chops it down.

A trumpet blares three notes, and other trumpeters echo it along the circle. A group of Carthaginian shepherds lead out a herd of armored oxen and distribute them in pairs about the troop circle. When all the oxen are in place, the trumpets sound again. The Iberian riders spring into action. They rush to the base of the town walls and dismount to throw multi-pronged siege hooks onto the top, concentrating on overlapping them onto a single section. The riders tug on the thick ropes to snag them into the wall, and loop the other end to the oxen's neck yoke. They drive the oxen out from the wall, yanking down the top wall stones. The Romans rain a torrent of javelins upon the Iberians but they persist, holding their shields over themselves as the armor-clad oxen tug down the next layer of stones, and the wall gaps spread.

Hannibal's infantry tramps forward. A large phalanx of Libyans leads the charge; men grouped in a hundred squares of thirty-six men. The Libyans use the curved rectangular shields the Carthaginians scavenged from the Roman dead at Trebia and Trasimene, along with the Romans' helmets and breastplates. It is an eerie sight to the Romans. It looks as if their own men are attacking them. As the Libyans close in on the front walls, the Romans hurl missiles down upon them, prompting the Libyans to cluster into a tortoise-shell of shields, just as the Romans do with their scuta – Hannibal is never too proud to learn from his enemies.

Looking down from a front gate tower, Gaius sees the Carthaginian lines part by the main gates. A roofed platform rolls forward, pushed by scores of muscular Gallic infantrymen. The legate's eyes start from his head. The platform is an exact replica of the famed Greek aries. The massive iron turtlehead of the battering ram pokes out from the front of the A-shaped roof. Its bulk is suspended on ropes inside the shelter. A shiver of dread runs down Gaius' spine. The ram's pole is a thick as a ship's mast. He knows that the town gates cannot long endure this timbered monster.

The ram trundles toward the gates as Gaius shouts for his men to attack it. The Romans on the wall hurl javelins and stones but they only succeed in killing the few Gauls who venture outside the roof. As the ram comes to the portal, the soldiers above the gate put torches to pots of Greek Fire, the infamous green liquid whose burn cannot be quenched. They hurl the flaming pots on top of the ram's roof, and upon any luckless soldiers caught outside of it. No scream from sword cut or spear thrust can match the terrorizing shriek of a man doused by this fire. But the shrieks only intensify the stern Gauls' determination to break in and escape the hell raining upon them. Onward they push.

The ram's head is pulled back and disappears inside the roof. Then it torpedoes forward, booming into the gates, again and again. The battering ram roof is an inferno but still the ram pounds into the gate, and a splintering sound becomes a counterpoint to the fearful thuds. Legionnaires and townspeople rush to brace the gates with timbers, but the gates split nonetheless. A few final blows and the gates splinter inwards. Mobs of Gauls scramble over the wreckage, screaming their battle-lust, eager for revenge and glory. They leap into the gates' defenders, and a free-form fight erupts on both sides of the Cannae entrance.

As the Gauls storm the main gates, the Iberian cavalry ride up the earthen ramparts outside the wall and vault through the holes they made, beating back the foot soldiers at the openings. Groups of Hannibal's infantry dash forward, some toting hooks to tug down more wall stones, and others rushing to clear the blockage at the gates. The remaining cavalry stampedes through the openings, and hundreds of pitched battles erupt in the streets of Cannae.

Gaius Marcellus fights in the main street with a contingent of his guards, desperately shouting orders for his cohorts to organize and maintain ranks. The veteran officer cuts down several Gauls with his sword before a falcata-wielding Iberian chops into the back of his neck. The legate falls, his head dangling from his body by a thin scrap of skin.

Riding his seven-ton elephant, Hannibal bursts through the wreckage of the main gates, clearing a wide swath for his elite Sacred Band cavalry. He plows into the maniples defending the entrance, breaking their ranks. Seeing their pila bounce off the elephant's thick skin and body shields, several courageous Romans rush forward and spear the beast's ears. The pain maddens Surus. He bellows in pain and rampages among the terrified legionnaires, bowling them over and trampling them beneath his trunk-like feet.

Hannibal hastily scrambles down from Surus to fight on foot. His Sacred Band dismount with him and shield his blind side. Even with only one eye, the general is still a superb fighter, parrying sword thrusts with his shield and skewering attackers with undercuts of his sword. The Carthaginians and Iberians grind through their unyielding but outmanned foe, moving toward the headquarters in the center of town. Maharbal rides over to Hannibal.

"We have taken the side streets and are going house to house. It's bloody work, but it will not be long."

Hannibal nods, wiping the sweat from his face. "Guard all the granaries and feed stores, if anyone with a torch approaches, kill them outright. Tell Mago he is to repeat this order to all his men. Slay all the Romans, but do not harm the townspeople."

By late afternoon, the fight has dwindled to the tall stone block praetorium near the center of Cannae, where the surviving Romans hurl missiles from the windows and doorways. The Carthaginian army surrounds the edifice and settles down to watch, for the battle has turned into a deadly spectator game. Iberian and Gallic tribes sally forth one at a time, seeking the glory of breaching the praetorium entryway. Each venture is beaten back, but the army cheers them on.

Hannibal understands the morale value of letting his mercenaries have their fun, and of the various nationalities cheering together. He allows the grim game to continue, until he notices that several of the tribesmen are limping back with knife throw wounds, some with blades still embedded in their backs.

Hannibal remembers hearing about a fearsome centurion who

defended Publius Scipio at the Battle of Ticinus, killing all he faced with sword and knife, just as he remembers the stripling who fearlessly rode in and saved Publius. Could this be the same centurion? Could the stripling be in there, too? Just as a group of Gauls prepares for a run at the praetorium, Hannibal calls them back. He gathers a cordon of his Sacred Band and walks toward the headquarters with hands raised and empty. He shouts out to the men inside.

"Romans, I would talk with your leader! Will you allow me to enter in peace?"

There is a hushed mumbling within before the reply comes. Bloodied but unbowed, a short muscular man walks out from the main door, helmetless. Hannibal looks into the man's piercing yellow-green eyes and sees no fear, only aggression. The Roman's hands are empty of weapons, but Hannibal can see a single knife blade still attached to his belt, a final throw being saved – for whom?

"I am Marcus Silenus, First Centurion of the tenth legion."

Hannibal nods his acknowledgement, starts to speak. "I am–."

Marcus interrupts. "I know who you are, Bane of Roma. Were it not for a soldier's honor, I would gladly kill you where you stand."

Hannibal grins at the centurion, and fingers the pommel of his sword. "Or at least die trying, eh?" He points to the knife on Marcus' belt. "You were at Ticinus?"

"I served under Consul Publius Scipio."

"So I have heard, Silenus. You saved your consul's life that day – you and that boy. Is he inside, too?"

"The boy was his son, Cornelius Scipio. He is with Fabius."

Hannibal blinks in surprise. "That was a Scipio? A patrician? Hmm, I shall watch for him in the future... but to the matter at hand. How many men remain to you?" Hannibal sees Marcus' wary look. "I have five thousand men surrounding you. It is not a strategic question."

"Twenty or so, depending on who has died from his wounds since I have been out here wasting time with you."

Hannibal cannot help but grin at the audacity. "Well, I had best get to the matter! Centurion, I will let you and your men go. You may keep your weapons and return to your main camp. I ask but one favor."

Marcus Silenus sneers. "I want not your mercy, Carthaginian. I will fight you for their freedom, with whatever weapons you desire."

Hannibal laughs. "Yes, I am sure you would. I would be delighted to accommodate you in other circumstances, centurion. But I have need of you, alive. As I said, I will spare your men for a favor."

Marcus stares at him, his face a stone.

"You will deliver this message yourself in the presence of the new consuls. Tell Aemilius Paullus that I look forward to meeting such a respected general on the field of battle. That is all I ask of you. Will you do that?"

Marcus looks away, searching for the trick in the favor. He shrugs, and looks back at Hannibal. "It will be done. And what words for Varro?"

Hannibal answers with disdain in his voice. "I have nothing to say to Varro. Nothing."

The centurion looks at the stone house where his men are quartered. "So be it." He heads back into the headquarters. Soon he leads eighteen soldiers out from the praetorium, a half dozen of them supported by their fellows. Hannibal and his guard stand to the side as the men file past. He waves over Maharbal.

"Give these warriors horses and safe passage to their camp."

Hannibal watches the Romans limp toward the main gates as Mago walks up to join him.

"Why are you letting those pricks escape? You said 'kill all the Romans,' and they're the only ones alive!"

"Life and death should serve our purpose. We leave the locals alone that they may look kindly upon us and become our allies. The legionnaires will carry the word of Rome's defeat with no lies from the Senate to taint their message. Marcus Silenus is a most respected warrior. There could be no better messenger."

Mago glares at his brother. "That 'messenger' asshole killed at least six of my men. We should have crucified him in the town square!"

"Our fate may hinge on the message he gives Paullus from me," Hannibal says. "And what he tells Varro that I did not say."

Mago stares quizzically at his brother and shrugs. "I know you like your little mysteries, but I don't understand 'what he did not say.' And I don't have time for this crap. We have spoils to divide!"

"Very well, I shall be clear. Now that Cannae has fallen to us, Varro and Paullus will have to destroy us, or risk losing their Apulian allies. Varro is the weak link. His vanity and ambition will be our allies, and we must use them before we battle the Romans again. And for that, the centurion will play his part."

Maharbal rides up and dismounts. "The scum have departed. They were the last of the Romans."

The Carthaginian reaches into his pouch and fingers the clay figurine of his father. "Then we must act quickly. We only have three days. Mago, organize the burial details for our men. Burn the Romans outside the gates. Maharbal, gather all treasure and weapons in the town square that we may allocate shares to the tribes. Fetch Cargon. We need an accounting of what we have captured. We return to camp on the morrow. Another battle will be soon upon us. All too soon."

Hannibal turns to leave, then he catches himself. He reaches into the pouch at his belt and extracts Gaius Marcellus' final letter. "See that this is send by peace messenger to Fabius," he says to the captain of his Sacred Band. The veteran officer immediately sets out on his task. Hannibal watches him go, and sighs.

*   *   *   *   *

Gaius Terentius Varro wads up the papyrus scroll and throws it into a corner of the elegant Senate waiting room, as Lucius Aemilius Paullus and Marcus Silenus calmly watch. Red-faced Varro stomps about the marbled anteroom in his purple-bordered Senate toga, spitting out his words.

"That fucking Hannibal has taken the Cannae depot! All our money and food, all our weapons and armor! Hades take that bastard!" He looks about the chamber. "And why are these walls decorated with marble? Greek frippery, it should be good Roman stone! We have grown weak from these womanish indulgences – that is why we lost!"

Paullus and Marcus wait quietly for Varro to finish his tirade. Paullus wears the same honorific toga as Varro, but Marcus wears only a sleeveless gray soldier's tunic, his veined shoulders bulging out from its openings. Varro ceases his rant, and Marcus speaks. "Hannibal did give me a message for consul Paullus. He said that he looks forward to competing with such a distinguished general on the field of battle."

Varro waits for Marcus to say more. When he says nothing else, Varro blurts out. "Well, did he say anything else?" Marcus merely shakes his head, prompting Varro to continue. "Did he address anything to me?"

Marcus stares into the distance, impassive. "He had nothing to say to you."

"He said nothing at all?"

The centurion shakes his head. "More exactly, he said he has nothing to say to you."

Varro becomes apoplectic. "What? That vulgar barbarian does throw his disdain in my face!" He stomps about the room again, sputtering curses.

"Now is not the time for pride," says Paullus. "We have to figure out how to suppress the news of this disaster." He eyes Marcus Silenus. "The plebs must not find out about this. They would riot if they heard of another defeat. We must have a plan of action to give them before they learn about Rome's loss."

"Action?" Varro says, "I'll give them action. I'll destroy that sheep-fucking savage!"

"Well, we should certainly mount another campaign before a panic sets in," Paullus says. He ticks off the numbers on his fingers. "Let's see... we have over four legions that can leave

Rome, with one to guard the city. So we have more than twenty thousand men. According to the latest barracks count, we have at least that many Italia allies. We could get almost forty thousand men together."

Varro nods, his temper cooling. "Our proconsuls Atilius and Servilius have almost that many in Fabius' old army, near Cannae. If we combine forces, I would have an army twice the size of Hannibal's."

Paullus points a finger at Varro. "We, not you, would have an army twice that size, consul. From day to day, we will alternate leading the army, as is customary. Is that not right?"

Varro waves his hand impatiently. "Yes, yes, we take turns. Let us explain our campaign plan to the Senate today, so we can move immediately." As the two consuls leave for the Senate chambers, Marcus Silenus takes Paullus aside.

"General, apologies for my intrusion, but I did not think you would be so ... motivated to act quickly. A battle now may just be what Hannibal wants – a fight while he still has food and money for his mercenaries."

Paullus waits for Varro to exit through the senaculum doors, and then he speaks. "I do not share Varro's eagerness for an immediate battle. But Fabius' delaying strategy has become very unpopular, however wise. If Varro hawks for a fight, and I do not, the people of Rome will think the Hellenic Party is weak."

Marcus looks sideways at Paullus. "Is that your concern, party politics?"

"For the sake of Rome's future, it is," says Paullus. "I would rather face the spears of the enemy than the votes of the angry citizens." [vii]

Paullus walks out of the senaculum as Marcus Silenus watches him go, his hands on his hips.

THE SHRINE OF VULCAN is a small, round temple adjoining the Forum where an eternal flame burns in homage to the god of fire. Worship services do not start for hours, so the temple area is empty and is the perfect place to converse unheard. Flaccus, Cato, and Fabius gather here, basking in the early spring sun. They sit on the wide stone steps encircling the columned shrine and talk in low tones. As often happens, the Scipios are a major topic of discussion.

Fabius nibbles at a loaf of ciabatta bread, dribbling crumbs down his toga. "Publius has almost recovered from his wounds. At the last Senate meeting, he submitted a request to join his brother in Iberia."

Flaccus shrugs. "I regret I was not there to oppose him, purely on party grounds. Nevertheless, we should let him go. If he goes over there he would not be blocking our austerity proposals or bothering us about land reform." Flaccus shakes his head. "The man is always fussing about more land for the farmers and soldiers. And giving them some of our land to do it, if you can imagine such nonsense!"

Fabius snorts. "The Hellenics cannot leave well enough alone. We should let Publius go, but on one condition: that he take that pestilent wife of his, Pomponia. She and that cunt Amelia have been painting campaign slogans all over the city walls. She almost prevented Varro from being elected the new consul, writing that he was a 'vainglorious legion-killer.' The bitch!" He leers and waggles his finger. "Now, if she had herself a good clit-licking dwarf, she wouldn't have frustrations to vent, no, and not be venting them upon us!"

Cato is still burning over Flaccus' remarks. "Cincinnatus was a humble farmer, as was Dentatus. Both saved Rome from certain destruction. They deserved to have a say in their government. And more land than they were given."

Flaccus flaps his hands in protest. "Oh no, I do not question the valiance of our rustic citizens! Many of our plebs have proven themselves in battle, dying for the cause and such. But Publius speaks of giving them more voting power, and they are just too ignorant to make sound decisions." Flaccus sniffs. "Besides, Cincinnatus was born a patrician, that was what made him the man he was!"

Cato gapes at this patronizing patrician, again wondering what kind of bedfellows he has made with the Latin Party. "He was an aristocrat deposed by his own kind," growls Cato, "and thence became a farmer. As such he became a man of earned worth instead of worthless privilege. That is what the Latin Party is about, conserving our values of simplicity and austerity. Is that not so?"

Flaccus waves his hand dismissively. "Oh, yes, that is the party saying." He breaks into a sarcastic singsong chant. "To restore the austerity and discipline of the past, as long as it does not detract from the status quo of the present. Is that what you wanted to hear?"

Fabius looks at Cato's face and sees it is best to change the subject. "We will not oppose Publius' assignment to Iberia, but we will limit the amount of legions we send with him. We have five legions now, we could raise another four by the time Publius Scipio is ready for Iberia next year. But we should give most of our men to Paullus and our man Varro. They will be the ones fighting Hannibal – fighting him here in Italia, yes!"

Flaccus nods, but makes a face. "The Scipios are popular with the citizenry, Fabius. And the boy's a war hero. The Senate may not be willing to deny Publius his troop request and risk the plebs' disfavor."

"Cornelius Scipio a hero?" sneers Cato. "I saw him after the battle at the Trebia River, and his armor was as clean as if it had just come from the armory! Hero, indeed!"

After hearing Cato's comment, Flaccus' eyes light up. "That's it. We'll start a rumor that Scipio did not save his father, that someone else did, a ... a loyal attendant to Publius who gave the credit to his son Cornelius. The people will love that story because it has a commoner as the hero. We can discredit the boy and Publius, too."

Cato studies Flaccus, who avoids his eyes. "I did not hear anything such as that, Flaccus. I only saw him unsullied after the second battle. It would be a lie to say otherwise."

Flaccus shakes his head pityingly. "You have much to learn about the ways of politics, young man. The beauty of a rumor is that it does not have to be proven. Because no one knows who started the rumor, it will be difficult to challenge its veracity – or us. We have but to raise the issue, to say, 'I heard that young Scipio did not rescue his father, an attendant did it,' and the rumor will move faster than Mercury." Flaccus spreads his hands. "We are not lying. We do not say that it happened, only that we heard that it might have happened, understand? Then we will..."

Cato interrupts. "I think the first virtue is to restrain the tongue. *'He approaches nearest to gods who knows how to be silent, even though he is in the right.'* *"viii* He points his finger sharply into Flaccus' face. "You would have us spread empty words and put us in the wrong."

Flaccus shrugs. "If we restrain our tongues, we may find

Publius as our next dictator, and the Hellenic party will be taxing us to pay for their social programs, and bringing in their Greek doctors and tutors. Would it satisfy you then that you were in the right?"

Cato turns to Fabius. "Do you condone such tactics, General? Do you think these actions are worthy of us? Of you?"

Fabius turns away from Cato's stare, his brow furrowed in thought. He turns back and waggles his finger at Cato. "It is not as if we know that young Scipio saved his father – that is only a rumor itself, a rumor. We merely raise an alternative explanation so the people do not get so, so carried away about this rescue nonsense. Yes, carried away!"

Flaccus nods approvingly. "Excellent. I will be meeting with some senators before the next session, and I will tell them what I heard about young Scipio's 'heroism' at Ticinus. We have some plebs in our pocket. For a few sestertii, they will spread the rumor among the citizenry."

Fabius bobs his head. "I will be talking to some senators about troop allocations for the attack on Hannibal. I can urge them to allot extra legions to Varro and Paullus." Fabius cackles. "The Senate will be most receptive to that request. Hannibal has them scared pissless!"

Cato frowns. "I cannot countenance such rumor-mongering. My place is elsewhere than in this party."

Fabius puts his arm around Cato's shoulder. "Be not so hasty, boy. You have a noble character, although you are a bit too serious about it. You embody the Latin Party values -- you have a future in the party yes, a bright future! I will recommend that you join Varro's army as a centurion. I am sure Varro will approve it. Does that change your mind?"

Cato looks from one man to the other. He is both delighted and dismayed. "I – I would be happy to serve."

Fabius and Flaccus depart, out on their political missions, but Cato stays behind. He looks out past the Forum to the edge of the city. There he can see the farmers toiling, plowing clean straight lines in the furrowed fields.

AT ROME, SCIPIO RECLINES on the atrium couch at home, bouncing a leather ball off the marble walls. His mother and brother are on an adjoining couch, playing a lazy game of Knucklebones. Lucius drops his four bones and reads them. His placid face splits with a broad grin.

"I scored a Venus. Mother, look! Every number is different." Pomponia smiles encouragingly at him and drops two coins in the pot.

"So you did!"

Scipio flings the ball faster, catching and returning it in one motion and beating a noisy tattoo on the wall. Lucius hisses at him to be quiet, but Scipio just makes a face at him, "Gods be damned," Scipio blurts, "I miss Laelius. When will his squadron return?"

Pomponia reaches over pats his arm. "Your father said it will be just a couple days, they had to check the road to Cannae before the legions start out on it. Now stop bouncing that ball, you'll hit one of the frescoes."

Scipio begins flipping the ball into the air and grabbing it overhand. "Everyone seems so scared. It seems like everyone has someone who was killed at Ticinus, Trasimene, or Trebia. When I went to the gymnasium, the boys talked about nothing but the war, how they wanted to join the army and fight the

Carthaginians."

"People are very scared," Pomponia says. "Our legions once defeated all who opposed them, including Carthage. And now they fall, time after time."

Scipio looks anxiously at her. "Do you think Rome will fall?"

Pomponia walks to the front of the atrium. She looks out the vestibule's open front door at the passing citizenry. "Someday, in the future, as all nations do. But no, we will not fall to the Carthaginian. Fabius has kept Hannibal from Rome while we mustered new legions. We will wear him down, eventually." She looks at her son's surprised face and smiles. "I know, the people call Fabius the Cunctuator because he would not attack Hannibal. That was a smart decision, and we should give him his due. But I fear that Fabius the politician will exploit the people's fear for his party's purposes. The Latin Party's mischief is already afoot. They would send your father to Iberia with one hand tied behind his back."

"Father said he requested five legions for his Iberia campaign with Uncle Gnaeus, but the Senate might only give him three. With half the money!"

Pomponia hugs him. "I know, son. It is frustrating to us all. Flaccus and Fabius say Rome needs the legions to repel Hannibal. What they really mean is their man Varro needs the legions to win glory." Pomponia reaches down to stroke Boltar's head. She watches the dog pant happily, her face pensive. "Your father may have no recourse but to take what the Senate gives him and use mercenaries, at least until the money runs out."

"Who would he recruit? The Gauls? They deserted him before our battle at Ticinus and almost got him killed. The Iberians? They are out fighting with Hannibal! I would not trust any of them to fight for us. Gods know how Hannibal does it. We fight for our homeland while his hirelings fight for money. We have such disciplined and organized fighters, but each of his groups fight their own way. Yet he defeats us at every turn." Scipio shakes his head. "I must learn his genius."

Pomponia walks over to a fresco of some pears and pomegranates and uses the hem of her dress to wipe a stain off its border, rubbing assiduously until it is gone. "I suspect that Hannibal knows far more about us than we know about him. We caught one of his spies at a Senate meeting, in the citizens' section. They cut his hands off and sent him back to Hannibal, but I'm sure there are many more here. Perhaps you should return the favor and spy on them."

Young Scipio cocks his head at his mother. "Me? Shouldn't Father find that out? He can command men to do anything, go anywhere."

Pomponia shakes her head. "Your father is too proud to 'sneak about,' as he would call it. Even if he did, he would use his toughest soldiers, not some wily commoners. For this we need a snake, not a lion. Someone who can slither through their camp without notice." She smiles ruefully. "Deception, now that is something we could learn from the Latin Party! They are spreading rumors even as we speak."

"What rumors?"

Pomponia shrugs, and looks away from Scipio. "Oh, nothing of import. Do not let it trouble you." She sees Scipio is about to speak and raises her hand. "No, Cornelius, I know what you are thinking. It is not upon me to do this spying. I will not be the next general in the family, will I? This intrigue is yours to do, the skill will prove quite useful to you."

Scipio wrinkles his nose. "I believe what you say about using this ... this intelligence from insiders. But I wouldn't know where to start."

"Talk to Asclepius. He knows the ways of the Persians and the Egyptians, they were expert spies. He told me the Greeks regard spying as an art, what they call 'espionage.' They think it as important as warfare." A predatory smile creases her face. "He has certainly taught me a few things. I have invited some of the unaffiliated senators here for the purification festival of Februarius. As the wine flows, I will take their measure, to see if they support the Latin Party's 'purity' of ignorance and isolationism. It will be a good time to learn more about them."

Pomponia reaches into a pottery bowl near the couch, pulls out some grapes, and chews on them, thinking. "When they are properly stuffed and drunken, we will extract some promises to oppose Fabius and Flaccus. As the proverb says, *Ancipiti plus ferit ense gula.*"

"*Gluttony kills more that the sword; wine has drowned more than the sea,*" Her son echoes. He looks wonderingly at his mother. For the first time he grasps that she is more than a wife and mother to the Scipios, she is a political force in her own right, plotting the defense of her homeland against the enemy within. "Very well, Mother," he says, "I shall talk with Asclepius about this intelligence gathering."

Pomponia stands to leave, motioning for Lucius to follow her. As he passes, she bends and kisses Scipio on his forehead. "You are a Scipio, love. You will do more than talk…"

AS THE SUN SETS behind him, Publius enters the family domus, returning from the Senate meeting. He walks upright and steady, his wounds almost healed. As he walks he slaps a small scroll against his palm.

Publius walks into his bedroom and motions for a slave to help him shed his purple-striped toga, which he exchanges for a simple white tunic. He walks into the atrium, where he sees Cornelius and Lucius playing at dice, happily jibing each other's losses. They take one look at his face and rise to face him, knowing something serious is at hand. Publius walks over and embraces each of them before he speaks.

"It is done. I leave for Iberia at the dawn of the new year. The Senate has promised me three legions and money to recruit the native Iberians." He puts his hand Lucius' shoulder. "You are to go with me, as a member of the cavalry. It will be a valuable experience for you."

Lucius grins genially. "Whatever you say, Father. On to a new adventure!" Young Scipio looks at his father, waiting for his reply. "And what of me? I am to go to Iberia?"

Publius frowns, turns to Lucius. "Lucius, go find your mother and bring her here." As Lucius exits, Publius says. "You will go with Paullus and Varro, as a tribune in their army."

Scipio's' mouth is agape. "Why? I thought we would all go together! I would fight under you!"

"Would that you could come with me," Publius says ruefully. "But you can be of greater service if you join the fight against Hannibal. You know his mind better than anyone." He frowns. "And you must pursue your own path now, apart from me."

"Am I such an encumbrance to you?"

"There are lies spreading about Rome that someone else saved my life instead of you, that the Scipios are making false claims to glory. Few believe them, but we cannot give the Latin Party any more fodder. No one doubts the word of Varro or Paullus.

Your deeds with them will be unquestioned."

"I don't care about some rumors! Besides, Lucius is going with you."

"Yes, well, you know your brother," Publius says. "He requires some ... attention, if he is to make his way as a Scipio." Publius smiles. "He was not a war hero at seventeen."

Young Scipio shrugs. "The die is cast, then."

"There is good news." Publius continues. "Your victory over the Iberian raiders has been lauded by the people and the Senate. Even old Fabius applauded it! Henceforth you will be a tribune, commanding your own alae of five hundred men. And Laelius will accompany you as a decurion in charge of a turma of thirty-two." He kisses his son on the cheek. "I am proud beyond words at what you have done, as one so young."

Pomponia enters the room with Lucius. Publius gives her his news about himself and her sons and watches her face alternate between worry and joy. As they talk, Scipio departs for the house of Paullus Aemilius, eager to share his news with Amelia.

*   *   *   *   *

It is late morning in the Carthaginian camp near Cannae. Hannibal lies back on the wide cushions of his command tent, his face a rictus of pleasure-pain. He pounds his fists into the thick pillows around him. He can feel the pressure surging up from his loins to the shaft of his phallus.

"Ah, ah gods! Do not stop!" he exclaims.

He looks down to see luminescent blue eyes staring coyly back at him, shining from a tangle of jet-black hair. They are the eyes of beautiful Diomedia, the famed fellatrix of Altamura. She can feel Hannibal's shaft throb in her stroking hand, and she knows his end is near. Diomedia moves her mouth expertly over his large phallus and she swirls his shaft with her almond-oiled hands.

Hannibal bucks and comes explosively. He collapses into the pillows as Diomedia rises from between his legs, smiling triumphantly. The fellatrix starts to pull on her robe but Hannibal pulls her down on top of him, stretching her nude willowy body against his, cupping her buttocks with his broad calloused hands.

"You were worth all the battles it took to get here, madam. You are justly famous."

Diomedia smiles and reaches down to lightly brush his spent shaft, eliciting a final shudder. "I am honored that I, of all the people in Italia, was able to lay low the mighty Hannibal."

Hannibal slaps her bottom and grins. "And a mighty lay it was!"

Just as his mouth moves down to her breasts an anxious voice insinuates itself through the thick linen walls. "Hannibal … are you in there?"

Hannibal rolls his eyes toward the tent entrance. "Can this not wait, Mago?"

"Put your dick back in your tunic, brother. There is news about the Romans."

With a heavy sigh, Hannibal heaves himself up and searches for his cloth. He pauses to watch Diomedia bend over to pick up her clothes, admiring the sway of her pear-like breasts as she rises up. *If I had just another hour*, he thinks. With a sigh of regret he grabs a bag of coins from the table and tosses it to her. "Would we had time for more, enchantress. But duty does call. My men will see you home."

Diomedia bows and glides out of the tent, passing Mago as he enters. He enters, pauses to admire her as she passes, and pulls his stare away to face his brother. "Zaracas and Salicar have returned from Rome. They say the Romans are on the march with over forty thousand men. They are heading directly at us."

Hannibal strokes his chin stubble. "The Romans have moved quicker than I expected. I will need to know how many cavalry and infantry they have, both Roman and Italian."

Mago nods. "It will be done." He heads toward the exit.

"Mago!" Hannibal shouts. "What about the insignias?"

"Oh yes. Zaracas said there were two men with a spread eagle on their armor, both riding at the front of the cavalry."

Hannibal's eyes shine with excitement. "Varro and Paullus! They are both coming. Do you know what that means?"

"We have two consuls to kill?"

"We have two generals who will take turns leading the army. And one is naught but a politician!"

"Two taking turns?"

"Remember their rule of command," says Hannibal. "When two consuls are within a single army they take turns leading it, on alternating days. Do you not recall your Roman history?"

Mago wrinkles his nose. "I had no time for womanly studies, I was learning to fight! So these Roman generals, they take turns running the same army?" He shakes his head in amazement. "By Baal's balls, how did they win that first war against us?"

"They won because they are superbly disciplined and organized. Remember how those two legions fought to the last man at Trasimene? At the Cannae depot? They are the best infantry I have ever seen. And this time they will come at us with an even larger force."

"You make it sound like we might as well bare our buttocks and let them have their way with us, because they are so big and strong," Mago says. "Their infantry may be tough, but their cavalry fight like those Celtiberian dung-eaters, jumping off their horse first chance they get. That is their weak spot."

"Defend against your enemies' strengths," Hannibal says, "and attack his weaknesses. Paullus is an accomplished soldier. He is one of their strengths. From what our spies have told us, this Varro is as ambitious and headstrong as Flaminius was at Trasimene. Varro is their greatest weakness, not the cavalry. We must use him to our advantage."

"So this Varro will be eager to defeat us and make a name for himself," Mago says. "But we cannot try the same tricks we used at Trebia and Trasimene. Even those arrogant bastards will be wary of an ambush by now."

"Yes, he will be eager to defeat us," Hannibal muses. "A victory could make him dictator of Rome. A legend."

"So what can we do?"

Hannibal gives Mago one of his rare impish grins. "Fetch Maharbal. We must prepare for victory – by the Romans!"

VI. AND CANNAE

Scipio and Laelius ride along the right wing of the massive
Roman army, moving toward the Carthaginian encampment at
Cannae depot. Varro and Paullus have commandeered the forces
of Atilius and Servilius, the proconsuls they sent here last year to
slow Hannibal's progress. They now lead an army of Eighty
thousand Romans and Italians. It is the largest Roman force ever
assembled. Many senators have joined the campaign, over a third
of them are there as tribunes and other officers. Rome has
invested every available man to stop Hannibal – once and for all.

The two friends serve under cavalry commander Servilius, but
Scipio is often at the right hand of Paullus himself, speculating
about Hannibal's plans and tactics. Scipio knows that the heavily
outnumbered Carthaginians will depend on Hannibal's tactical
genius to give them an advantage. But what tactics he will use,
Scipio cannot yet imagine, and that sorely vexes him.

"I wonder what he has for us, Laelius," says Scipio. "Cannae
doesn't have any forests near it, no lakes or mountains. He can't
use any of his old ambushes."

"Who knows, Scippy? Maybe he'll just come out and do battle, man to man. Or maybe he will call down the moon and sun to help him this time, or the wind. Or run burning oxen at us because he doesn't have any elephants! I do know we have forty thousand legionnaires behind us, so why should we care?"

Scipio makes a disgusted face. "Now that is the thinking that got us into trouble in the first place, as the poet Simonides would say. These Carthaginians will be desperate. Their backs are to the sea and they have nowhere to run. I fear for us more than I did at Trebia or Trasimene."

Laelius rubs the back of his neck, grimacing. "I do not worry about him. I worry that I will not give a good account of myself to my men. Most are older than me!"

"Your men know you have been in several battles, they will listen to you. Just don't dress too ... elaborately around them. They are soldiers, after all."

Their conversation is interrupted as one of Paullus' guards rides over to them. "Cornelius Scipio! Consul Aemilius Paullus would meet you after we set camp, at the twelfth hour."

Scipio rolls his eyes. "Ah, delightful! Another quarrel session with Varro and Paullus – the butcher's son versus the aristocratic general."

"Do not be so patrician," chides Laelius. "I came from common stock, and look how brilliant I have become!"

"Aye, and pretty, too. You are so superior you will never find a worthy lover, Laelius. I think you should just go fuck yourself!" Scipio laughs as Laelius waggles his tongue at him. "But I do hear you. It is not that Varro came from the citizenry, it's that he has no fighting experience. He is a pot slave driving a chariot of thoroughbreds!"

Laelius grins. "A pot-slave with some powerful Latin Party connections. Do what you think is best, Scippy, you seem to know what Hannibal is about – most of the time."

"Yes," agrees Scipio, "but those other times that give me nightmares."

"Ah, friend, you are a man of nightmares – and visions and dreams!" says Laelius, shaking his head.

As the sun eases toward the horizon, the Romans turn from building camp to building campfires, fetching armfuls of twigs and branches from the mound foraged for them by camp slaves. Scipio weaves through the scattered fires, watching the soldiers cook supper in their small iron pans, most chewing on their daily allotment of cheese and bread while they watch their porridge cooking. He stops to share a drink of vinegar-wine with a few familiars and finally heads to the consuls' command tent. As he enters, he finds the two commanders in the midst of a familiar dispute.

"We must attack Hannibal within the next several days, Paullus. As soon as our fortifications are complete."

"Not from here," says Paullus. "The land is treeless and flat, the perfect setting for his cavalry."

"What do we care about his cavalry? We outnumber him two to one. He has no place to ambush us. What do you fear?"

Paullus looks at Scipio. "Cornelius, you have been in three battles with Hannibal. What say you?"

Scipio fidgets. "Hannibal would only be here if he sees some natural advantage to it. He would not fight us otherwise."

Varro arches an eyebrow. "And what is that advantage, boy?"

Scipio shrugs. "I do not know. We have not yet scouted the terrain enough for me to guess. There are four miles between our camp and Hannibal's, and we know little about that area. On the other hand, Hannibal knows every twig and puddle in the Apulia region. If there is an advantage there, he will find it"

"The man's words have wisdom," says Paullus, nodding towards Scipio.

Varro sniffs. "He is a boy of, what, nineteen years? Pfuff!" He turns to Paullus, his voice menacing. "Tomorrow is my day of command, then your day, and then mine again. Tomorrow we shall complete our preparations for war. And I swear before Mars, on that third day I end this Carthaginian menace, if you do not do it sooner!"

Varro stomps out of the tent as Scipio and Paullus stare at one another. Paullus finally breaks the silence. "By the twelfth hour tomorrow, our scouts will have more details of this area. We shall talk about this again, with or without Varro."

Scipio starts to leave when Paullus calls to him. Scipio turns to see a changed man, his stern visage softened with concern. "On your oath, if anything happens to me you will see to Amelia, that she will be well?"

Scipio clasps Paullus' forearm and nods solemnly. "She will be my life, whether yours end or not." And he leaves.

Two days later, Paullus addresses the legions with a brief speech. He knows that Varro will send them to battle the next day, and he seeks to motivate them by appealing to their moral duty. They surround him in a semicircle, silent as camp mice. Paullus assumes his best oratorical stance and shouts out to them, arms spread wide.

"Those who, like you, are about to fight not for others, but for yourselves, your country, and your wives and children, and for whom the results that will ensue, are of vastly more importance than the present peril, require not to be exhorted to do their duty but only to be reminded of it. For what man is there who would not wish before all things to conquer in the struggle, or if this be not possible, to die fighting rather than witness the outrage and destruction of all that is dearest to him? Therefore, my men, even without these words of mine, fix your eyes on the difference between defeat and victory and on all that must follow upon either, and enter on this battle as if not your country's legions but her existence were at stake. For if the issue of the day be adverse, she has no further resources to overcome her foes; but she has centered all her power and spirit in you, and in you lies her sole hope of safety. Do not cheat her, then, of this hope, but now pay the debt of gratitude you owe to her and make it clear to all men that our former defeats were not due to the Romans being less brave than the Carthaginians, but to the inexperience of those who fought for us then and to the force of circumstances."[ix]

After Paullus' speech the men cheer heartily, shouting, "Roma! Roma! Roma!" until the camp horses circle nervously at the din. The men depart but Paullus signals for Scipio to stand next to Servilius Geminus and Marcus Silenus. Scipio scurries over, anxious about being among high-ranking officers. Servilius, the tall and haughty cavalry commander, is speaking to Paullus.

"The men seem emboldened by your speech, especially our new recruits. May your words bear bitter fruit for the Carthaginian."

Paullus frowns. "I hoped to give them courage, but the proof will be in their first battle. And I fear that will be tomorrow. Varro is rabid to assault Hannibal's camp. Look here..." Paullus unrolls a map scrawled with outlines of rivers and hills. "The scouts drew this up from their first reconnaissance. It is crude but it suffices." He puts his finger on a tent drawing, and runs it along the map toward another tent. "When we set out tomorrow we will march across an open plain, past these hills, and cross this river onto the plain in front of Hannibal's camp. Varro means to have the army there by midday to engage the Carthaginians with a direct infantry assault."

The three officers study the map, with Servilius the first to speak. "How is the river?"

"According to the scouts," Paullus says. "It is a spear-cast in width but shallow enough to march through."

Marcus nods. "Good. It cannot be used as a trap, such as the Trebia was."

Scipio looks at the rudely drawn map. "If Hannibal were to attack, he might try to catch us on the march, as he did at Trasimene. He could come at us from these low hills about the plains."

Paullus nods. "Yes, I have considered that. I will have an advance scouting party sent out today. They will survey the hills before Varro leads us out." He looks at Marcus Silenus and Servilius. "You two are known for your battle wisdom, and it will be sorely needed tomorrow. Do not disobey any direct orders from Varro, but use your judgment in all circumstances." He rolls up the map. "We meet with the allied officers this afternoon in Varro's tent. Do not mention this conversation. You may go."

Scipio heads back to his cavalry unit, where he finds Laelius grooming his black stallion. He gives Scipio a prideful grin. "What do you think, is she not beautiful? A bit lean and rangy, but she carries me well in spite of all the armor I wear. Oh, to ride like the Numidians: half naked and quick as the wind. And they have beautiful bodies, do they not?"

"You would notice their bodies," Scipio grumps. "And if you had your way you'd ride completely naked, like some undersized Gaul."

"But I would be much cleaner, and have a gold-trimmed saddle on my horse to make her beautiful, too! I would be the most glorious decurion in the army!"

Scipio smiles. "Yes, I'm sure you would. But it is good you are preparing yourself. I suspect we will have some concerted action tomorrow. Varro musters us out after breakfast."

"Good. I know he is a foolhardy, Scippy, but camp life bores me. I grow as restless as a virgin at an orgy!"

Scipio waggles his finger at Laelius. "Remember Aesop's moral about the herdsman and the bull, be careful what you wish for! Hannibal will doubtless have a surprise for us, though I cannot fathom what it might be. The land is almost featureless, and the weather is calm. What can he exploit?"

"Perhaps it is best to just expect the unexpected, and be ready to adjust to the circumstances. Just as you should do in life!"

"Perhaps so," says Scipio, "but we are not leading the army, Varro is. I fear him as much as the Carthaginian…"

BY LATE MORNING the Roman army has organized its battle formations, infantry in the middle and cavalry on the wings. Laelius' turma of thirty two men is on the right side, a part of Scipio's alae of five hundred, both within Servilius' division of two thousand. The army rumbles out towards the Carthaginian camp, Varro leading the way on his magnificent white gelding.

Cato trudges along in the infantry center, directing his century of sixty men. Although he is a novice centurion he has already won his men's respect by being a strict but fair leader. He is a man without nuance, but a man without bias. Cato affirms that his men are in order, then looks to the front of the army, watching Scipio as he rides along.

By midday Scipio can see the outline of the tree-lined hills in front of them, islands in a sea of ripening grain fields. Scipio's heart pounds as they near the hills. His right hand twitches, betraying his anxiety about what awaits them. He knows the scouts reported the area free of enemy, but he can imagine thousands of cavalry hiding in that forest. He should warn someone, he thinks, but what can he warn them about?

The Romans file along the wide road between the hills, moving into the spacious plains that lead to the Carthaginian camp. The silver strip of the Aufidus River gleams a half mile in front of them – their last crossing before they approach Hannibal's camp. Scipio admires the lush waves of grain fields about him. He muses wistfully about living there, having a life of farming and study, far from war and politics.

A distant trumpet blast startles Scipio to alertness. Hundreds of Numidians rise from the fields in front of him, along with hundreds of Iberian light infantry, as if the fertile farmlands were sprouting warriors. The nimble Iberians organize into narrow columns and trot down the road toward the Romans, carrying only a small round shield, a sword, and a spear. The Numidians jump onto their horses and dash toward the Roman flanks, hurling javelins as they close.

The Romans scramble into battle formation. A wide-eyed Varro yells for his tribunes to counterattack, and plunges toward the enemy. As the tribunes rush to battle, Paullus stops several senior officers and speaks briefly to them. They nod their heads and shout orders to their men. Immediately, the heavy infantry forms a shield about the edges of the front columns, blocking the Numidians from penetrating. The velites rush forward to engage the Iberian light infantry, a battle that turns into hundreds of individual duels of men hurling javelins and clashing swords.

Servilius leads his cavalry wing out toward the Numidians, with Scipio and Laelius guiding their men into the fray. The heavily armored cavalry rumble toward the Numidians to crash them down. Before Servilius' riders can reach them, the Africans gallop away, easily outdistancing their foe. The Romans spread out in pursuit, and the Numidians spin about and dash into their pursuers, only to turn and flee again.

Scipio and Laelius call for their men to stay on their horses to maintain their mobility. Even so, the Numidians are difficult to kill. More than once a Roman raises his sword for a killing stroke, to find his opponent has spun out of reach. The Numidians, on the other hand, have their deft spear thrusts deflected by the Romans' tough armor. Only the most precise stab can penetrate their defenses. The cavalry fight winds through the waving grain fields, scores of men dying in its lush sea of life.

Scipio looks over to see Laelius fencing with a tall Numidian who wields the leopard skin shield of a chieftain. Laelius swings his sword at the Numidian's head but the barbarian blocks it with his short sword, knocking Laelius' blade from his grasp. The Numidian instantly wheels about and closes for the kill. Scipio frantically gropes for one of his throwing knives, but before he can find one Laelius dives from his horse and tackles the man, knocking him from his mount. Laelius crashes on top of the African and slips his razor-sharp dagger into the side of the stunned man's throat, pulling it across his neck until the bright arterial blood spouts. Scipio looks on in amazement as Laelius calmly wipes his blade and remounts his horse, making a face at the bloodstains on his armor. He sees Scipio staring at him and grins. "That jump worked, just like when we were boys!"

Scipio glares at him. "Are you mad? He could have killed you in midair!"

"He didn't expect surprises from a Roman," Laelius crows. "Besides, these bastards are too tough to catch on horseback." Laelius glances at the dead warrior. "Handsome devil, though."

Scipio can only shake his head.

The battle rages evenly, both sides advancing and being beaten back. Varro sends three maniples of a hundred twenty heavy infantry each to join the light infantry at the front of the conflict, hoping to turn the tide. Cato leads his century at the Iberians, walking in front of them so he will be the first to fight.

The heavy Roman infantry slowly hews through their lighter counterparts, leaving a wake of bodies as they advance. Many of the outnumbered Numidians are eventually encircled and killed, and the survivors begin to defend more than attack. As dusk approaches, the Carthaginian forces make an orderly retreat toward their camp, and Varro calls his men back. Over a thousand Iberians and Numidians lie dead, with a barely a tenth of than number on the Roman side. It is an overwhelming victory for Varro.

The Romans cheer and pound each other on the back. They have bested the mighty Hannibal's army. Varro, in particular, is delirious with joy at his army's success. He directs his men to head toward the Carthaginian camp. As the sun goes down, Varro is still leading the army toward Hannibal's emplacement when a bloodied and weary Paullus catches up to him.

"We had best stop now, Varro. It is too far to return to our base."

"What? Now is the time to burn his camp! Wipe them out once and for all!"

"Varro, look at the sky. It is a moonless night. Soon we will not be able to see our hand in front of our face. We can build camp by the river, use it to protect our men."

Varro sucks his lip for a minute. "Very well," he says. "I suppose we would end up killing each other if we went on." He clenches his fist. "But we cannot let that bastard escape again!"

Paullus looks at him soberly. "You are right about that. In spite of our victory over him, Varro, I have a sense he is not going anywhere."

The elated Romans march to a spot near the Aufidus River and set about constructing their camp. As night comes, Scipio looks toward the Carthaginian camp, now near enough that their largest bonfires are visible. He walks through the Roman tents, amidst the shadowy clanks and scrapes of men making food and sharpening weapons. As he rewraps a wrist cut from today's skirmish, he recalls his daydream of living among peaceful fields, but these fields were hiding their treacherous enemy. *There is no escape from war*, he thinks, *only a delay in when it will find you. Rome will not make peace with Carthage; one of us must destroy the other before the killing stops.*

THREE DAYS LATER, Paullus and Varro lean over a large leather strategy map spread out the ground in their command tent. The map is populated with clay figurines of Roman and Carthaginian forces: cavalry, infantry, slingers, and velites. Scipio stands in the rear of the tent, acting as the consuls' attendant. He holds several small papyrus maps while he watches the consuls argue over their conflicting battle plans.

Paullus moves several Roman figures to a spot just in front of Hannibal's forces. "If Hannibal stations his men near his camp we will have to attack uphill. That will be to his advantage."

Varro shrugs. "It is but a slight rise, nothing taxing. We have many more infantry than he has. We would overwhelm his lines with a frontal attack."

Paullus stares at the map again. "Yes, but he has many more cavalry, and that is what worries me."

Varro sighs with exasperation. "Who cares about how many cavalry? They are naught but infantry on horses! Let us attack now, I will not be a Cunctuator, like old Fabius! Hannibal may get more reinforcements if we wait any longer. We attack now, while we have the advantage!"

"Tomorrow is your day to lead the army, so it is your decision. But I think it is foolish." Paullus says, as he paces about the tent, bouncing a horse figurine in his palm. "You say we have the advantage, but why has Hannibal not retreated in face of our superior numbers?"

As the two generals glare at each other, Scipio hesitantly steps forward. "Forgiveness, generals, I think Hannibal plans a trap of some kind, using his camp's elevated position. It is the only anomalous terrain nearby. There has to be some advantage to it that he will exploit."

"Here we go again! Why should we worry about trickery, boy?" Varro sneers. "Our infantry can cut through any tricks or traps. Did you not see what we did to his last ambush? Were you not there when we ran them off?"

"His ambushes have given him the advantage in battles where

he was outnumbered, General." Scipio says. "And we fall into them because we are predictable. He knows we will attack with our infantry in the center and our cavalry on the flanks," Scipio shrugs. "That is what Romans always do, and that is just what he wants."

"Perhaps the boy has a point, Varro. Hannibal won at Trebia and Trasimene, though we had superior numbers."

Varro looks angrily at Scipio. "I know of your heroics at Trasimene: how you rode through the enemy and rescued your father. I respect your bravery but I must tell you, those men lacked the will to win. If I had been leading them instead of your father, we would not have lost."

Scipio stiffens as if slapped, throws his maps on the floor, and stalks from the tent without a backwards glance.

Varro turns to face Paullus. His face is set. "I have heard nothing today that would dissuade me from completing our mission. Tomorrow, I will rid us of this Carthaginian canker!"

Paullus stares at Varro for several long moments. He shrugs with resignation. "Very well, let us prepare for tomorrow's assault. I will return momentarily." Paullus strides from the tent to find Scipio. He locates him several paces away, seething at Varro's remarks. Paullus puts his hand on the young man's shoulder.

"Pay him no heed, son. Sometimes Varro's temper controls his mind. Your father fought bravely and wisely. Gallic treachery undid him, not Hannibal."

Scipio nods. "I think we take Hannibal too lightly. He will somehow surprise us, and we are not prepared to react to it. I fear the worst."

Paullus nods thoughtfully. "Your father has told me of your gift of foresight, Cornelius. Tell me, have you had a dream about this battle? Have the gods sent you any premonition about our fate?"

Scipio fidgets, thinks of his dream with Hannibal victorious at the battlefield, and avoids Paullus' eyes. "I have seen Hannibal with a look of dismay on his face, but why I do not know."

Paullus searches Scipio's face. "There is more to your dream than you reveal, I suspect. Just remember your promise. If Fortuna does not smile on us – on me – tomorrow, promise you will return to Amelia and care for her."

"I do promise. And if I should perish, tell her she was always the flower of my life."

Paullus turns from Scipio. "I must go back and help him. If Varro cannot be dissuaded from attack, I must do my best to help him win." He looks toward the command tent as he speaks. "The gods have touched you, son, you have the promise of greatness. But remember, great generals have great enemies, and most are not on the battlefield."

That night, as the summer winds susurrate across the darkened plains of Cannae, the old dream returns. Scipio stands in the front of the Grecian sailboat, gliding out into the rising sun. Asclepius smiles as he guides the boat, lazily pulling the tiller from side to side. This time the boat is filled with a cadre of legionnaires in bloodied armor, their faces haunted.

Scipio looks back to the docks and sees Amelia forlornly watching him, a petal-less rose in her hand. Publius is next to her with a crowd of Roman citizens behind him. All somberly watch him depart. Scipio rushes to seize the tiller from Asclepius, but he cannot wrest it from the sturdy old man. As he struggles, the boat sails on, and Amelia fades from sight. Scipio sits up from his blanket, gasping and disoriented. He sees Laelius lying next to him, watching him with knowing eyes.

*   *   *   *   *

A man in Roman armor rushes through the dawn-lit camp toward Hannibal's command tent. The Sacred Band guards let him pass without a second glance. They know it is Shafat, Hannibal's finest spy and one of his most trusted friends.

Shafat walks into an empty tent and steps back out to the guards. "I have news for Hannibal. Where is he?"

A voice comes from behind him. "Over here, Shafat."

Shafat sees Hannibal rising up from the rows of sleeping soldiers, clad in the tunic of a common infantryman. Shafat looks at Hannibal, puzzled. Hannibal grins at him.

"I sleep with my men. My command tent is a decoy to avoid assassination attempts. Not that the Romans have the wit to attempt anything so 'ignoble', but some of our allies ..." Hannibal goes inside the tent, as Shafat follows. "What have you to reveal?"

"Something is afoot in the Roman camp," Shafat says. "I have heard nothing, but the soldiers are tense. They spend much time tending to their weapons and armor, practicing swordfights. I think they prepare for an attack upon us."

"How many troops have they?"

"I gather about eighty thousand infantry, and four thousand cavalry. We are outnumbered by tens of thousands."

"Ah, but we have the cavalry advantage," Hannibal says, as he stalks about, thinking. "Twice their cavalry, at least!" He turns to

Mago. "Who leads tomorrow, Varro or Paullus?"

"Varro. I overheard some tribunes say he is rabid to attack us."

"As we had hoped," Hannibal smiles. "He is inflamed with his victory in that skirmish we staged for him." Hannibal's smile fades when he looks about the camp, sees his soldiers laughing and talking. "If it gives the Romans an arrogant confidence, the sacrifice of those men in that little drama will not have been in vain."

Hannibal walks over to the guards at his command tent. "Summon Mago and Maharbal, fetch the tribal chiefs!" He turns to Shafat. "We will give Varro another 'victory' tomorrow. For a while."

SUNRISE LIGHTS THE CAMP as an Iberian scout hurtles through the open gates, scattering the guards like geese. "The Romans come! They come!" He barges through the troops drilling along the main camp road and leaps from his horse in front of Hannibal's tent. Mago and Maharbal emerge, followed by Hannibal. All are armored and ready, anticipating what the scout will say.

"The Romans approach, in battle formation," exclaims the scout. "Their infantry in the center and cavalry on the flanks!" Hannibal raises his arm in acknowledgement, and the scout departs for his place in the cavalry. Chewing on his breakfast steak, Mago picks a bone from his teeth and grins.

"Infantry in the center and cavalry on the wings, same old shit! By Baal's balls, those Balearic slingers have more imagination!"

Hannibal shrugs. "Perhaps. And perhaps they have a surprise for us." He turns to Maharbal. "Double the trumpeters, our commands must be quickly passed today. Get the cavalry into attack formation!"

The Roman army soon arrives, halting a quarter mile away from the bustling Carthaginian camp. The Carthaginian troops are arrayed at the top of a wide shallow hill, looking down at the Romans on the plains. The Romans and their Italian allies march a short distance and stop, and then repeat the routine. They are blatantly challenging the enemy to attack.

Riding behind the front lines, Varro and Paullus can see that the Carthaginians have thousands of Numidian cavalry on one side of the infantry center, with an equal amount of Iberians and Gauls on the other. They watch Hannibal riding along the top of the incline, his white linen cuirass glinting in the sun. He waves his sarissa above his head, exhorting his men. Paullus turns to Varro and points up the hill.

"Look there, at the Gauls. That is where the attack will come."

Varro sees that there are thousands of Gauls clustered into the center's front lines. They pace about, cursing and shouting to each other, impatient to storm the Roman lines. Behind the milling Gauls are phalanxes of the stolid Iberian heavy infantry, immobile and silent.

Following Hannibal's directive, the Gauls and Iberians are spread out in wide, thin lines that make it appear most of his army is there in the center. But Hannibal's elite Libyans, ten thousand strong, stand on each side of the center, packed into narrow and deep columns that roll over the hill and disguise their numbers. Over a hundred thirty thousand men face each other on the plains of Cannae, eager to see the battle start, and eager to see it end.

The sun rises. Hannibal returns to the Carthaginian center and again surveys his lines of men. He nods at Mago, who shouts an order. Trumpets sound throughout the acres of infantry and cavalry, echoed by the Roman signal horns. The Iberians and Gauls beat their tribal drums and take the first step forward, screaming insults and bragging to their stone-faced enemy. The armies march toward each other as their cavalry surges ahead of them along the flanks. The Gallic and Iberian infantry are in the advancing center. They forge ahead of the Libyans at their sides, forming a crescent that is bowed out toward the grim Romans who are advancing up the rise.

The howling Gauls trot forward, clans of enormous painted men eager for the glory of battle. Most are naked on this hot, humid day and others wear only a chain mail tunic, at once obscene and frightening. The steady Iberians are squared up behind the tempestuous Gauls, arrayed in dazzling white tunics with a thick purple border. The Iberians proceed steadily, maintaining their phalanxes, as the Gauls storm toward the Roman lines. Clad in their plundered Roman armor, the Libyans continue to move slowly along the sides, allowing the center to advance well ahead of them.

Varro rides as the head of his men, leading eighty thousand infantry into the conflict. The Romans march on in their characteristic checkerboard of maniples. The legionnaires are in the middle, with the socii, their Italian allies, in maniples on each side of them. As the infantry nears Hannibal's oncoming force, the men in the first rows raise their shields high, preparing for the shock of the onrushing Gauls.

Varro gives a quick wave to his Master of Horse and rides back behind his lines. The Roman cavalry race toward the Iberian heavy cavalry, while their Italian allies head for the light and swift Numidians. Thousands of velites dart from between the maniples to hurl their pila and darts into the Gauls, felling hundreds. In response, Hannibal's Balearics emerge from the scattered clusters of Gauls. Six thousand slingers hurl stones and lead balls into the velites, blotting the sun with their deadly hail. Many of these poorly armored young Romans fall, their bones shattered and skulls crushed, but the velites remain in front until they have hurled the last of their projectiles, and then retreat behind their maniples. The Balearics reload and rain more stones upon the infantry, but they form a testudo or 'tortoise' of shields to ward them off. The two armies forge ahead, thundering towards a collision.

Paullus is on the flank leading the Roman cavalry attack. As they near the front, he is stoned on the shoulder and falls from his horse. His guards dismount and help him back onto his steed, and he pushes on. Varro rides through the space between the maniples, heedless of the stones and spears flying about him, intent on lashing his men to victory. He screams at the tribunes to push their men forward. The tribunes shout to the centurions, who shout for the legionnaires to maintain formation.

Now the Gauls are upon the Romans. They swarm onto the well-disciplined hastati in the maniples' first row. The barbarians swing their broadswords like axes, aiming to cleave a shield or helmet. The Romans parry with their shields and jab their swords at the Gauls' unprotected chests and limbs. Amid the deafening metallic din, men fall screaming yet unheard.

After a short and furious fight, there is a lull. The Gauls step back to catch their breath, and the centurions shout for the principes to step forward and the hastati to retreat behind them. For a quarter hour the two sides stand apart, the Romans shouting orders, the Gauls shouting insults. The Gauls plunge forward again, hammering at the principes, determined to break their lines.

The Romans hold through several cycles of attacks, and the day waxes hot. The tribunes direct a second set of maniples forward to replace the ones at the front, and Cato strides up with his century of men. Now a battle-hardened veteran, Cato calmly reminds his men how to duel with the enemy, telling them to strike first, then step back and move to the right so they do not trip over any fallen bodies.

The new maniples fight with great energy. The large barbarians grow exhausted in the heat and begin hold their shields low, giving the Romans the opportunity to make more telling thrusts. A number of unenthused Gauls simply leave the battle and walk toward the rear lines, content with a severed head or plundered souvenir as their day's work. The Roman lines advance, pushing their enemy backwards.

Mago sees that the Gauls are losing their shock value, so he summons the Iberians. The tribesmen march forward in tight rectangles. They clash with the advancing maniples: hacking and thrusting with their deadly falcatas, jabbing with their armor-piercing iron javelins. The fierce Iberians repel the tiring hastati and principes, but fresh maniples step forward to relieve them, and the Roman lines stiffen. The Iberians step back, regroup, and rest. Then they attack the waiting Romans again. And again. But the Romans hold, and then slowly advance.

Fighting with machine-like efficiency, the infantry pushes the Carthaginian army's center inward, reaping heavy casualties. Hannibal's lines gradually turn into a reverse crescent, bowing inward as his infantry gives ground. Directing his men behind the center ranks, Varro's eyes gleam with triumph as his men cut through the middle of Carthaginian army. He can see Hannibal and Mago in the center, drawing ever nearer to him. Through the noise of a hundred thousand weapons clashing, Varro shouts wildly for his commanders to press the advantage.

"Onward, you have them! Drive them into the river!"

Proconsul Atilius is riding over from the allied cavalry when sees an opening in the Carthaginian lines, a space between the Gauls and Iberians. Atilius can see Hannibal through the opening, and he quickly changes course and races toward the Carthaginian. Hannibal is pulling his sarissa from a fallen socii and does not see Atilius approaching from his blind side until he hears the thud of approaching hoofs. He spins about to see Atilius' javelin flying toward his chest. Quick as a flash, he deflects the javelin with his shield. Undaunted, Atilius rams into the side of Hannibal's horse and knocks him to the ground. Hannibal lies stunned. He gropes for his sword as Atilius dismounts and straddles him, raising his blade for the killing blow.

Atilius pauses with his arm in midair, eyes wide. He stares wonderingly at the spear point sticking out of his chest. Even as blood burbles from his mouth, the proconsul hacks at Hannibal, who easily deflects his weakened blows. Atilius crumples to the earth as a Sacred Band soldier steps from behind him and bends to help Hannibal.

"Are you injured, General?"

Hannibal raises himself and wipes Atilius' blood from his face. He slaps the short and rotund youth on the back. "My gratitude, Hiram. You saved me."

Hiram's dark eyes flash with pride. He bows his head slightly. "My honor to serve you."

Hannibal grins. "Then serve me one more time. Help me get back on this damned horse!"

Hannibal remounts and moves into the center of the retreating

Iberians, and Hiram follows along with the rest of the Sacred Band. As he directs an orderly withdrawal of his center lines, Hannibal seems strangely unperturbed by his men's retreat. He instead casts worried eyes to his cavalry on the flanks. He can see that Rome's Italian allies are battling the Numidians to a standstill, swirling about them in a melee. Looking to his left, however, he sees a different scene, one that pleases him mightily.

The outnumbered Roman cavalry are fighting for their lives against the heavy cavalry of the Iberians and Gauls. Scipio has commanded his alae of five hundred men to stay on their horses and use their lances, killing enough riders that the enemy avoids them for the easier prey of dismounted Romans. The Roman cavalry down many foes, but they are too outnumbered to win.

Laelius has dismounted to fight hand-to-hand with a Gallic cavalry officer he has speared from his horse. The wounded, red-bearded giant swings his long sword at Laelius' head, but he deftly deflects it by angling his shield downward, guiding the heavy blade toward the earth. As Laelius arcs his sword at the Gaul's head, Scipio's mouth opens in amazement. Laelius brandishes a falcata, one of the Iberian swords that Scipio retrieved from the vanquished scouting party. Instead of stabbing at the Gaul's body, Laelius chops at the man's sword hand, cutting his cabled forearm to the bone. The broadsword drops from his enemy's nerveless hand, and Laelius coolly administers a disemboweling twist to kill him. As the Gaul hits the ground, Laelius jumps back into his saddle.

Scipio rides over to him, eyes wide with curiosity. "What in Jupiter's name are you doing with that falcata?"

Laelius smiles. "I lost my other sword, so I borrowed one of yours. And I love it! It's tougher than ours and it's perfectly balanced." He winks. "This is your present to me, for being such a great soldier!"

Scipio starts to say more when he hears a trumpet from the surrounding enemy cavalry. He looks over and sees that Gisgo is leading his Iberian cavalry away from the present engagement. He is heading for the Roman army's back lines.

In a flash, Scipio sees Hannibal's plan. He screams at Laelius, pointing at the departing Iberians. "They're going to surround us! Where is Paullus?"

"I saw him near the river."

"Oh my gods! Help me find him. We have to get out of here!"

Hannibal's trap is now being sprung. The Roman infantry pushed the Carthaginian troops into a deep V-shape, back up the hill from whence they came. As the Romans crested the incline, their ranks narrowed and packed closer together, limiting their mobility. The sun has risen up behind him, glinting in the Roman's eyes and making them squint and turn their heads. This is the moment Hannibal has been waiting for.

Hannibal rides down behind the infantry's front lines and urges his Iberians and Gauls to keep fighting. As the maniples advance toward him, Hannibal calls his trumpeter to his side and tells him to remain. In spite of the glare in their eyes the resolute Romans gain more ground, exulting in their progress, and they eagerly push forward to break through the Carthaginian center. Defeat is imminent, but still Hannibal watches and waits, as thousands of Romans draw ever nearer to him.

Hannibal hears a rushing sound behind him, feels his hair stir, and a hopeful grin starts on his face. He looks behind him across the open plains, and his smile broadens. Swirling dust clouds are blowing toward him, borne by winds off the Adriatic Sea. The coastal wind comes, coming at the same time it has come every day, coming in answer to his prayers to Baal that it come one more time.

The strong winds bring a dusty cloud with them, composed of the upturned plains soil that Hannibal had his men till up over the last several days. The dust blows into the legionnaires' faces, further impeding their vision. Some swing wildly at nonexistent foes, others react too slowly to enemy strikes, sealing their doom.

Hannibal rides over to Mago. "Now, Mago. Now!"

Mago waves his arms back and forth. The trumpeter blasts four rhythmic notes that the others resound. Immediately, the dormant Libyans pound in from each side of the center lines, spreading out to envelop the Roman infantry's flanks. Several Libyan phalanxes reinforce the Iberians in the center, halting the Roman advance. Jabbing with their iron spears and short Roman swords, the Libyans delve into their compacted, blinded, foe. The legionnaires are now assailed on three sides. The maniples disintegrate into disorganized groups, and men fall with greater frequency as they lose room to maneuver and fight. Hannibal's infantry implacably closes in, ignoring the many comrades who fall beneath the desperate blades of the unyielding Romans and Italians.

As he looks for Paullus, Scipio watches in horror at the trap being sprung on the main Roman force. He spies Paullus' silver spread-eagle standard shining out from a mass of Gallic cavalry. Scipio tugs at Laelius' bridle and waves for his men to follow him toward the standard. They rush forward and hit the Gauls from behind, downing a score of them before they even know they are attacked. Scipio can see Paullus in the center of his men.

exhorting them to resist and striking down any Gauls that dare attack him. Scipio dodges through the enemy riders and draws within earshot of Paullus. As he nears, Scipio screams at him. "General Paullus! To the rear, ride to the rear lines!"

Paullus pauses to look over at Scipio. He starts to speak, but a Gallic cavalryman charges through Paullus' protectors and shoves his long spear at the general's head. Paullus deftly parries the thrust, but as he does an enemy foot soldier pads up behind him and shoves his long sword into the back of his skull. Paullus' eyes start from his head, blood streams from his eyes and nose, and he slumps in his saddle, scrabbling at his face as he topples from his horse.

"Oh Gods, not the dream!" Scipio screams. Reckless with alarm, he rams through the remaining Gauls until he reaches his fallen friend. Scipio spears the dismounted Gaul in the back and hurtles into the chieftain, whirling blows on him like a madman and bellowing his rage. They duel until Laelius rides up from behind the chieftain and plunges his falcata into the man's liver. The Gaul stumbles away, screaming his death agony.

Scipio stares at Paullus' limp form sprawled in the dirt. He starts to dismount but Laelius grabs his reins. "Scippy, he's gone. We have to get out of here!" Scipio shrugs off his friend's hand. He jumps down and kneels to close Paullus' bloody blue eyes, and wipes the gore from his face before he kisses him goodbye. Scipio remounts and heads back to join the main cavalry force, tears so blurring his eyes that Laelius must warn him where he is going.

Inflamed at the loss of their leader, the remaining cavalry swarm into the Gauls and drive them from the field. A leathered old tribune named Tullius directs the men in Paullus' stead, as calm in the carnage as if he were in a training exercise. Tullius calls Scipio and the other officers together, and Scipio frantically explains Hannibal's plan. Tullius defers to Scipio, and soon the Roman cavalry are pursuing Gisgo's men, looping toward the Roman's rear lines.

In the distance, Scipio sees the allied cavalry being chased from the field by the combined force of the Numidians and Gisgo's Iberians. Gisgo's men leave the Numidians to finish chasing down the Italian allies. The Iberian riders speed toward the rear of the beleaguered Roman infantry. As Scipio and his men watch helplessly, thousands of armored Iberians storm into the legions' back end, sealing the circle and closing the trap.

With the encirclement complete, the Balearic slingers and light infantry trot out to the front lines and unleash another projectile storm upon the compacted Romans. The stones and javelins come from every direction, so many the infantry cannot block them with their shields. Thousands fall, wounded and dead, and the circle shrinks so dramatically the slingers cannot throw again for fear they will hit their own men on the other side.

Cato and his fellow soldiers fight in every direction, so close together they are more mob than maniple. Knowing their fate, the veteran triarii of the third line put down their spears and draw their swords. They join the principes on the front line, intent on killing as many enemies as possible before they fall. Hundreds of Romans eventually cleave through the Carthaginian circle and run away, but they are ignored for the larger game in the center. The Carthaginian army relentlessly tightens their murderous noose, walking over so many Roman dead their feet do not touch the ground.

Within hours, the epic battle is finished. Thousands of Romans and allies scatter from the battlefield, running for their camps, running for town, running for their lives. They flee through enemies so exhausted with killing they cannot raise a hand to stop them, so blood-sated they do not even venture a curse.

Cato pulls a handful of his surviving century from the slaughter. They kill as they go, some breaking lines to join any lone soldiers who are still in a fight. As they cut through the last infantry resistance, Cato can only think that his death would mean the loss of his family name and of his chance to rectify the slight to his ancestors who died in these battles. And that must not happen. Fighting demonically, he tows his cadre through the border of the slain and out into the open plains, where they head for the main Roman camp. A knot of Numidians gallop towards them, intent on disposing of survivors. Cato's eyes flash angrily.

"Halt," he shouts. "Gods take you cowards, form ranks!"

Several terrified men try to run. Cato grabs one and strikes him down with the flat of his sword. "I will kill the next man who runs," he shouts as the man grovels on the ground. "Form ranks! Draw your swords"

The men organize into an open square and face the onrushing savages. Seeing a determined opponent with swords at the ready, the weary Numidian chieftain raises his arm and directs his men to follow him, away from Cato's men. He has no wish to die fighting some desperate stragglers after a great victory has been won. There is more vulnerable prey to pursue. And greater plunder to collect.

Off to one side, Scipio's Roman cavalry fight a company of Iberians that intercepted them before they could ride to the back of the Roman infantry. The two groups battle back and forth for over an hour. Tullius falls, bled to death from multiple wounds, and Scipio assumes command. The outnumbered Romans face annihilation until the Carthaginian trumpets blow. Their weary opponents rush back over the hillside, racing to reinforce the

Carthaginian army. Scipio calls his men together to regroup and staunch their wounds. They soon ride over to join the main battle, which is only visible as distant dust clouds, faint shapes moving in the dirty haze.

When Scipio's men crest the hill they stop, frozen at the spectacle before them. Several soldiers break into sobs. The men see no fighting legions to join, only a sea of dead Romans and Italians. Below, the victorious Carthaginian infantry staggers over the corpses and farther up the hill, heading back to their camp. Scipio's mouth moves but no words come forth, he can only gape. He looks all over the plains, looking for some Roman resistance to support, but he sees only the retreating scraps of the mightiest force in Rome's history. Laelius draws next to him, sobbing unabashedly, tears washing streams down his blood-grimed face.

Scipio's eyes cloud, but he summons himself. "Return to camp! There is nothing we can do here." The cavalry trots slowly toward camp, picking up survivors as they go.

IT IS SUNSET at Cannae. Hannibal is back upon the rise where he led his troops this morning, looking down upon the plain of battle. His brother Mago stands next to him, for once subdued. The brothers gaze out on a scene from hell: below them sprawl more than sixty thousand Romans and allies, strewn like rows of new-mown wheat and layered with thousands of Hannibal's own dead troops. The field rings with cries for help from the wounded, screams of death from those being dispatched by the Carthaginians, and the cawing of the carrion crows rejoicing in their grisly feast. The copper smell of blood is all about, punctuated with the viscous stench of feces and urine.

As if in a trance, Hannibal steps down into the stink and horror. He pauses to study a lifeless Roman, head buried in a hole he dug with his hands, suffocating himself to escape the terror and shame.[x] He watches a Numidian pull a wounded comrade from under another dead foe. The Numidian has pieces gnawed from his nose and ears, evidence that the dying soldier tried to chew off the face of his opponent when his arms failed him, using his teeth as his last weapon.[xi] Hannibal gazes in horrified wonder: *I swear by the flames of Baal*, Hannibal thinks, *if I had a division of men like that Roman I could conquer the world.*

Hannibal hears a soft, quavering voice to his right. "General Hannibal. Please, please..."

He steps over a mound of bodies to come upon Hiram, his savior, his Sacred Band guard. The young Carthaginian lies there with his intestines in his small, thick fingers. His life's dark blood pools beneath him, anguish glazing his pleading eyes. Hiram's final words come out as a sickly whisper.

"My G- General...please..."

The youth fixes his dark eyes on Hannibal and slowly raises his chin, exposing his bare neck. Hiram's eyes beg Hannibal for his surcease, but his commander can do nothing but bend over and look at him, eyes wet with sorrow for the young man who rescued him but hours ago.

Mago comes to Hannibal's side and gently pushes him away. "Go. This is for me." Hannibal pushes Mago aside and kneels next to Hiram. He reaches into his purse and retrieves the clay figurine of his father. He presses it into Hiram's palm and closes his fingers about it.

"This has the spirit of my father, The Thunderbolt. He will guide your trip to the Land of Mot. Paradise will be yours, my son."

Hiram clasps the figurine to his heaving breast and manages a slight nod of gratitude. With a deep and trembling sigh, the Carthaginian bends to kiss the boy, and slowly rises as Mago takes his place. Hannibal trudges back up to the hilltop. He pauses when a weak scream sounds behind him, slumps, and stumbles on. At the top of the rise a handful of his Sacred Band await him, but he gruffly waves them off. He sits down and covers his face with his hands. After a few minutes, Mago comes and stands over him. Mago fidgets silently, not knowing what to say. Then he bends to Hannibal's ear, speaking softly.

"I return to camp. We have captured eight thousand Romans. Ransoms must be arranged for them as soon as possible, so we don't have to feed them. Are you coming?"

Hannibal does not respond. Minutes pass. Mago places his hand on his brother's arm.

"We lost few men and killed many Romans. Tonight there will be a big victory celebration. You must be ready for such a joyous occasion. To rejoice in front of the men."

Receiving no answer, Mago squeezes Hannibal's shoulder and rises. He vaults onto his horse and canters off, giving his brother a final, worried, glance. Hannibal sits silent among the carnage until the sun creeps down the horizon, its angular rays glinting off the fallen warriors' bloodied bronze. Maharbal gallops up to Hannibal, who looks at him blankly.

"A brilliant victory, General! Now the way lies clear to Rome. We can hold our next victory celebration in the Forum!" He slaps his knee gleefully, and points northwest, toward Rome. "I shall go ahead with the cavalry – so the Romans will know of our arrival before they are aware of our coming!" [xii]

Hannibal blinks at him, and looks back upon the plains of

Cannae. "How fare the men, Maharbal?"

"Most of our cavalries are intact, except for the Gauls."
Maharbal says. His expression darkens. "Gisgo is dead. He fell
to some knife-throwing centurion." His eyes flash again. "But
we killed Paullus and his two proconsuls, Atilius Regulus and
Servilius Geminus. Only Varro escaped us, but he is worthless."

Hannibal slowly rises up to face Maharbal. His voice is weary
but decisive. "I ... we are not ready for Rome. We will plunder
their camp and ransom the prisoners. And salvage all the
weapons from the field. And then we will rest. Rest from the
killing. No one dare attack us now."

"Of course they won't attack. We have killed them all! We have
the advantage, General. You always said we must exploit our
advantages. What should we do with this one?"

Hannibal rubs his face, blinks his eyes open. "I will send a
peace delegation to the Roman Senate. Perhaps now we can end
this war."

"Peace? We do not need peace, we have them! They have not
the legions to oppose us!" Maharbal splutters with frustration.
"You know how to win a battle, Hannibal, you do not know how
to use the victory!" [xiii]

As Maharbal storms off, Hannibal walks over to his horse. He
slowly strokes its neck as the sun finally sets on the battlefield at
Cannae.

*   *   *   *   *

Led by Scipio, three hundred Roman cavalry ride through the
wide portal of Canusium, an allied stronghold nine miles from
Cannae. The gates are left open for the knots of infantry and
cavalry that stagger in from the disaster. Many collapse in

exhaustion when they enter the security of the town walls. The town overflows with thousands of soldiers: they wrap their wounds, search for missing comrades, hone their weapons, or lie in the makeshift hospitals among townspeople's homes. Some just sit on street corners, sobbing uncontrollably.

Scipio halts his men when they enter the town square. Laelius queries one the local militia, who points him to a side street. The riders quickly trot down the street to the town stables, where they dismount and disperse, seeking shelter and food. Scipio stays to haggle with the stable master, eventually giving him a handful of quadrigati. As the stable master carefully counts out the silver coins, Scipio heads back toward the main gates. He enters the town hall, shoving open its creaking timbered doors.

A large group of Roman and allied officers are inside, standing around a roughshod feasting table – there are tribunes, decurions centurions, and chieftains. Several Romans jump to greet Scipio, overjoyed to find a friend who is still alive. The conversation runs loosely about the horrors and exploits at Cannae. There are many angry declamations and mournful stories. After an hour of commiserating, a pale young nobleman stands up at the head of the table.

"I am Lucius Caecilius Metellus, a tribune of the equestrian guard. You know my father, Proteus Caecilius, a senior member of the Roman Senate." Metellus looks carefully at everyone there before he speaks his next words. "I have met with my fellows," he says, nodding at a half-dozen young noblemen behind him. "We have all come to the same conclusion, though it so pains us to admit it. Hannibal will soon assault Rome, and he cannot be stopped. Rome will fall."

A protesting outburst drowns his next words until Metellus' colleagues shout for quiet. Then he resumes.

"Rome has but a few untried legions. Think you they can stop the Carthaginian army? The people of Capua will likely join them. They have resented our control for years. Our army in Gaul has been decimated, and it is too far away to get here in time, anyway. There is no succor."

Scipio looks at the men's faces, seeing that even the dauntless centurions nod their heads in acquiescence. A few men shake their heads but say nothing. All is quiet for a moment, then a leathery, middle-aged centurion raises his angry voice.

"And what of it, Metellus? What option do we have but to fight and die in service to Rome?" A handful of men voice agreement with the centurion, but Metellus shakes his head.

"We do not have to bow to the inevitable, we can avoid it. The coast lies near us, and Greece awaits. We can sail to Greece and escape certain death."

Scipio cannot believe his ears. He hears Metellus proposing his heart's desire, to leave the war madness for a life of repose and scholarship. To save men, not kill them.

"I am holding three ships at the coast of Apulia." Declares Metellus. "We can leave tomorrow, and escape before the Carthaginians arrive."

Scipio imagines himself sailing on the sunny Adriatic, free from care. The image brings a smile to his haggard face. Then he recalls his dream; sailing away with bloodied men as Amelia and his father watch him go. And he thinks of Paullus, Amelia's father, and of Scipio's final words to him at Varro's tent. And Laelius, would Laelius go with him? What would Scipio do if he didn't? What of his vow?

Scipio's right hand twitches and his arm begins to shake. He jumps up and strides to the head of the table. He pauses next to Metellus, glaring at him until he looks away. Scipio leans his hands onto the table and looks out into the crowd.

"Men of Rome, of Italia, hear me now! The eve before battle the gods sent me a vision. I saw the destruction of Hannibal at the gates of Carthage! Our legions had thrown down its gates, its rulers were begging for peace! And Carthage, Carthage was burning, drowning in flames!"

The crowd mutters uncomfortably, trying to make sense of Scipio's words. One of the Italia chieftains speaks out. "You say, Roman, you saw this in a dream? These are sacrilegious words. Our gods only send dreams to our priests."

"Those of you who know me, know that the gods often visit me when I sleep. Is that not so, Romans?" Several officers murmur their agreement before Scipio continues. "I saw Carthage clear as day and I tell you, this war is not over. If we but persevere, we will triumph in the end!"

Metellus interrupts, his voice sharp. "Any who cares may stay with you to 'save' Rome. But if you would sail with us, I ask you to step over here with me and my men."

Metellus rises and starts to push Scipio aside. Scipio yanks out his sword and presses it against the tribune's throat. Metellus stretches his neck backwards to avoid Scipio's blade, his eyes glassy with fright.

Scipio grabs the front of Metellus' tunic. "On my sacred oath, I swear that I myself shall not abandon the republic of the Roman people, nor will I allow any other Roman citizen to do so. If I knowingly break my oath, may Jupiter Optimus Maximus visit the most terrible destruction on my home, my family, and my possessions! Lucius Metellus, I demand that you, and the rest of you here present, take an oath using these words of mine. Anyone not swearing – let him know that this blade is drawn against him!" [xiv]

Scipio's eyes bore into each man in the room. "Will you let Hannibal sack Rome and sell your families into slavery? Will you die as cowards? All who can walk, follow me to Rome!"

The room is quiet for several heartbeats. The aged centurion pushes himself up from the table and limps over to stand next to Scipio, his seamed face firm with resolution. "My blade is drawn against any who would forsake our mother Roma."

Within minutes, the remaining centurions have joined their comrade. Standing in front of the group with drawn swords, they take the oath. The decurions step forward and finally the tribunes. The senior tribune, a large portly man, raises his voice.

"This matter is settled. No one leaves for Greece, upon pain of death. Is this agreed?" Hearing no dissent, he continues. "We have a new matter to decide. There are thousands of us in this town but no order of succession for command. We must elect someone to lead us. What say you?"

The tribune sees many nodding their assent. "Very well, we will take a vote" He waves his hand at the officers and chieftains. "Who will you nominate…?"

THREE DAYS AFTER the fateful town hall meeting, the Roman army survivors gather outside the gates of Canusium. The scouting parties have indicated the Carthaginians are moving south, away from them. It is a good time to journey the two hundred and fifty miles to Rome. The new commander rides to the front, next to his designated second in command.

"Everything is in order, oh exalted leader!" says Laelius with a broad grin.

Scipio raises his fist heavenward and arcs it down. The trumpeters sound the call. Four thousand soldiers follow him out into the rising sun, heading for Rome, heading for home.

VII. GATHERING STRENGTH

Amelia sweeps the front doorstep of her family home. She pauses to wipes her tears with the edge of her black mantle and resumes her chore. She has slaves for sweeping but she feels better being busy, doing even the most menial tasks. The work distracts her from the sorrow of her father's death – and her anxiety about Scipio's fate.

The family greyhound wanders past her out to the street, wagging its tail at two black-robed undertakers who are passing by. They will certainly get rich this year, she thinks. Amelia snaps her fingers and the dog trots back inside, past the *cave canem* (beware of the dog) sign her father placed there as a private joke about their overly friendly pet. She smiles at the memory of her father's jest, and then she weeps again.

As Amelia sweeps her way down the front sidewalk, she sees Pomponia approaching, her wan face evidencing her concern for her son. Amelia carefully studies Pomponia's face, looking for any sign she has some news of Scipio. As Pomponia draws nigh she looks at Amelia and shakes her head – nothing to report. Even so, Amelia cannot restrain herself.

"Have you heard anything new?" she says. "Anything?"

Pomponia grimaces. "Rumors, damned rumors, all: he was seen at Capua, he was taken prisoner for ransom, he was killed by Numidians. The torture of hearsay is all I hear!"

Amelia bows her head and sighs deeply. Pomponia places her hand next to Amelia's on the broom handle. "Do you sweep to keep busy?" she says, with a kind smile. "To keep from thinking too much?"

The girl wipes the corner of her eye and nods. "It is the ninth day since my father's death. Tradition says it is time to sweep out the ghosts and move on with life. I would do that task myself, to renew my spirit and resolve. By all our gods, Pomponia, first Mother gone last year, and now Father! It is almost too much to bear."

"Ah, chasing out the ghosts is the Roman way, is it not?" Pomponia says. "To face forward and move on? But how can we forget about Cornelius' uncertain fate? What has Fortuna decreed, is he dead or alive?" Seeing Amelia's head droop, Pomponia hastens to add, "I do feel that he is still out there, and he is safe."

"I pray it is so. I sacrifice at the temple every day for Cornelius, and for ... for my father, that he has made favorable passage to our ancestors." Amelia looks intently into Pomponia's face. "If Cornelius were gone, too, I could not live. I would not."

Pomponia embraces her. They linger together until a boy slave trots up to Pomponia. "Mistress, a scout has returned. He says many men are coming to Rome, they will get here tomorrow. And they are legionnaires."

"Did he speak about Cornelius?" Pomponia demands. "Did he

say he was there? Speak!"

The boy cowers, taken aback by her uncharacteristic anger. "No, nothing about the young master. But Cassius is there waiting, he will let us know."

Pomponia bows slightly, shamefaced. "Forgive me, Patroclus. My grief does bear me down. Go back and join Cassius. Come to me if you hear anything, even a scrap."

As the slave runs off, Pomponia turns back to Amelia. "More rumors to pull at our hearts. All we can do is pray that the gods will bring him back to us."

"Do you think the gods take part in the affairs of men, as the scrolls tell us?"

"On that, I am not sure," Pomponia says, "but I am sure I must continue to appeal to a higher power for help, so I feel I am doing everything possible to bring him back to us. I have to pray, to make sacrifices – to do anything, instead of waiting helplessly for fate's hand to show itself." She smiles gently at Amelia. "It hides the pain, like your sweeping does for you."

"Then let us go to the public mourning this afternoon and join our prayers to theirs," says Amelia. "I would find much solace in giving solace to others."

Later that day, Pomponia and Amelia return from the temple, joining thousands of the citizens who file back to their homes from the latest sacrificial rituals. Many have a haunted look because they return from witnessing the rarest and most ghastly of all Roman rituals, a human sacrifice.

After news of Cannae, the temple priests consulted the ancient scrolls called the Books of Fate. They determined that the gods were angry at Rome, and that the deities must be appeased with human life, life in the full flower of living.

All of Rome convened at the Forum Boarium, Rome's oldest public gathering place. Two Greeks and two Gauls were brought into the forum grounds. There, at the Temple of Hercules, the four captives were placed in front of a deep pit dug at the bottom step. After a series of prayers for forgiveness and succor, the priests pitched the bound youths into the pit. Chanting over their delirious screams and pleadings, the priests threw shovelfuls of dirt on top of the captives, until the screams were muffled – and then heard no more. By the ritual's end, many attending were crying, and others had fainted. All felt a guilty hope that these deaths might somehow stay the dread hand of Hannibal.

Pomponia is stupefied with the horror of what she has just witnessed. Even as she stumbles away, sobbing, she can hear the strident voices of Latin Party candidates excoriating the citizens for displeasing the gods with their decadent lifestyle. The Party has exploited Rome's citywide fear as an opportunity to advance their agenda of austerity. They claim the gods are angry at Rome's decadent Greek pursuits, and they pillory its people for everything from excessive education to lavish dinners.

Pomponia listens to their diatribes against Rome, against their own people. She realizes that the real war for Rome is with the Latin Party, not the Carthaginians, that the Party will use any means to advance its agenda of austerity and ignorance. And she knows that she has found a war in which she can fight.

As Amelia and Pomponia head toward the Scipio domus, they see Cassius pushing his way through the crowd, shouting for Pomponia. They hail the slim youth and run to meet him, breathless with excitement.

"Mistress!" exclaims Cassius. "Legionnaires are coming! Many come!"

Without a word, the two women hurry toward the main gate, joining an excited mob that was morosely walking home just minutes ago. The city's capacious entryway is jammed with frantic and hopeful people, all waiting for the portal to open. They push about and gossip excitedly to one another, doing anything that relieves the tension of knowing they might finally learn of their loved ones' fate.

An eternity later, a sentry sounds three long notes on his trumpet, signaling that a large force approaches. Scores of guards rush out to channel the swarming citizenry into two lines along the main promenade, as other guards open the towering gates. Pomponia and Amelia push to the front line of the crowd. They crane their necks to see through the dust, looking into the approaching cavalry.

Consul Terentius Varro is the first to enter the gates, leading a force of eight thousand Cannae survivors, ever after referred to as the Legiones Cannenses. At his right hand rides twenty-year-old Publius Cornelius Scipio, who led his men from Canusium to join with Varro's army on their way to Rome. The consul nods and smiles at the populace, acting as if he were returning from a glorious victory. Scipio is solemn and dignified, but his eyes betray his joy at returning home.

Amelia is the first to see Scipio. She shrieks with joy, and grabs Pomponia to point him out. Scipio's mother can do naught but stare open-mouthed, not trusting her eyes. She claps her hands to her face and falls to her knees, babbling her teary thanks to the gods. Scipio's face splits into a broad grin, all solemnity gone as he waves furiously at them. The two women's happy cries join the chorus of others who have recognized a loved one. Pomponia and Amelia shove through the retaining guards to trot next to Scipio's horse. He leans from his saddle and grasps their hands.

"I love you! I love you," cries Scipio. "I will see you soon!"

As the guards push them back into the crowd, Pomponia and Amelia watch him parade toward the Forum, amazed and overjoyed at this turn of Fate. The boy who left at the back of a squadron returns as a man in the front of an army.

SCIPIO IS SOON at the family home, joyfully reunited with his loved ones. They lounge on the couches in the dining room as he relates his adventures, revealing everything but the battlefield horrors of Cannae. When it comes time to talk of Cannae, Pomponia peppers him with questions, wanting to know the reasons behind Varro's fatal battle strategy. Her son may have information she can use in her own newly declared war against the Latin Party, especially against Varro, the Party hero.

Amelia says little as she sits beside Scipio, content to feel his body next to hers and to hear his voice as proof he lives. Her sorrow at her father's death has vanished for now. Scipio fills her heart.

The evening wears on, and all retire but the two young lovers. Scipio walks Amelia out the door and down the cobbled street to her quiet house. They enter and go to the atrium, to sit on a couch by the fishpond. The household slaves bring out wine and bread but she waves them away. They are only hungry for each other. Amelia strokes his shoulder and looks wonderingly into his face.

"I heard you had escaped," she says, "but I so feared it was untrue. I could not endure losing you, after ...."

Scipio puts his fingers to her mouth before she can finish. "My heart weeps at your sorrow, my love. Your father was a great and noble man. He died bravely. He did always think of you. His only fears were for your welfare."

Amelia nods gratefully, and grasps Scipio's hand. As she does she stares at his wrist in alarm. "Are you well, Cornelius? Truly? You are so thin!"

"Ah, there were some hardships on our way back to Rome. But I knew every step brought me closer to you, so it was nothing."

She hugs him close. "And you are back! You have so lightened my spirit, carissimus!"

Scipio takes her hand and gently kisses her. "You endure your father's death with such strength and dignity. I cannot imagine what I would do if mine were gone."

"I pray you never find out. And that you will ever be here with me."

Scipio smiles ruefully. "I promised to defend Rome, and to protect you. For now I will stay here and help rebuild our armies. But someday I will have to join my father in Iberia." Amelia's frowns at his words, but Scipio raises her chin with his finger and smiles into her eyes. "We have now and tomorrow, many tomorrows. We can make that our forever time."

He holds her close for a moment, then draws back to face her. "This is not the most propitious time, but I have been carrying this for months. I had it fashioned before I left Rome."

Scipio reaches into the pouch on his belt and pulls out a gold ring. The ring is fashioned as two arms with hands clasping one another, the Roman symbol for betrothal. He holds it next to her left hand. "May I, Amelia?"

Overcome, she can only nod. He slips the ring onto the third finger of her left hand, the finger with the nerve that connects to the human heart. "With this ring I declare my intention to marry you, to be my wife 'til time's end."

Scipio presses his mouth upon Amelia's. She puts her hand onto the back of his head and gently presses his mouth deeper into her. Soon, Scipio's hand parts the folds of her robe, to cup her breasts and to feel them swell. Amelia moans. Abruptly, she pulls back to look at Scipio. Her face is at once loving and wanton. She takes his hand, leads him into her bedchamber, and stands before him. As he watches, she disrobes until she is completely nude, a young Venus standing before him. Scipio draws in his breath, entranced with the rounded hips and wide, full breasts he sees for the first time. The roughhouse girl he grew up with is gone, replaced by this sensuous woman before him.

Amelia helps him slip off his tunic and subligaculum, and she leads him to her sleeping platform. They lie together, caressing each other until Scipio can bear no more of his tumescent pain. He straddles Amelia as she lies on her back and pushes his hips forward, preparing to enter her. She puts a hand to his chest, stopping him before he can descend, and touches his face.

"I would not anger the gods by taking your seed into me before marriage. My brother still fights in Sardinia. But there is this, for now…"

Amelia reaches to her bedside for one of her vials of olive oil. She pours a little into her palm and caresses it about his blood-darkened phallus. He gasps and strokes her hair, twitching as she scrapes his testicles with her fingernails. When he is about to erupt, she pulls back and gets upon her hands and knees, presenting herself to him. "For now, the lioness position is ours, and its rear portal is yours. Whenever you desire."

Scipio moves behind her, places his hands on her shoulders, and strokes her back. Very soon, Amelia's hands clench the linen covers.

*   *   *   *   *

Carthalo, emissary from Hannibal, rides down the broad Appian Way to Rome, accompanied by a score of Sacred Band guards. The guards are not there to protect Carthalo, but to guard his precious political cargo. Carthalo is transporting ten prominent tribunes captured at Cannae.

The Carthaginian emissary is intent on striking a peace treaty with the Senate. He carries a list of Hannibal's terms, which focus upon returning Sicily and Sardinia to Carthage. For a man who has destroyed the Roman army, Carthalo thinks, Hannibal's terms are very lenient. Was this the man who had sworn to destroy Rome?

The negotiating group draws within three miles of Rome when they encounter a squadron of Roman soldiers straddling the road. Standing in front of the group is a lictor, the leader of the Roman magistrate's personal bodyguard. The stocky ex-centurion is wearing the scarlet robe of his office, and cradles a pilum in one arm. As Carthalo's group nears him, he raises his pilum to command them to halt.

"I am Martinus, lictor of Rome. Are you Carthalo, messenger of Hannibal Barca? If you are, state your business here."

"I am Carthalo. I come in peace, to negotiate peace terms with the Senate at the behest of Hannibal Barca. You have received a messenger to that effect, is that not true?"

The lictor takes several steps forward until he is within arm's reach of Carthalo. His face is a mask of stone. "The Senate did receive the message. At their behest I do tell you, turn around and depart now. On pain of your life, be gone from the city limits before nightfall."

Carthalo is flabbergasted. "I come with a peace proposal, a proposal with no loss to Rome, though you be at your weakest. Surely the Senate will want to hear these terms!"

The lictor remains impassive. "There will be no peace between Rome and Carthage, while both still stand." He points at the Roman captives. "They may proceed to Rome. We promise they will be sent back to you. But you are to leave now, emissary."

Angered at the insult to Carthalo, several Sacred Band guards start toward Martinus and grasp their jeweled sword hilts. Carthalo raises his arm, halting them. "In the interests of cooperation, the captives are released to you. I will return your words to Hannibal the Great, though you will rue the day you said them."

The lictor gestures the captives forward. Without another word, he turns his back on the Carthaginian emissary and rides off with his cortege. Carthalo is left to watch them go, still seething.

The next day, the ten captives stand at the rostra in front of the Senate. The chambers are filled to overflowing with Roman citizens. They know the captives are here to ask that their eight thousand fellows be ransomed back to Rome. Many onlookers hold out hope that their spouse, father, or friend is one of the prisoners. It is their last hope.

The captives' leader pleads for them to be released, while the citizens cry out from the galleries, beseeching the Senate to free their loved ones. At the end of the leader's speech, the Senate clears the chamber and the debate begins. Many senators are inclined to ransom their countrymen. Others protest that a ransom for eight thousand men would greatly increase Hannibal's war chest.

Titus Torquatus, a leader of the Latin Party, steps up to the rostra. His argument is succinct and forceful. If the Senate ransoms these men, who surrendered rather than fight to the death in battle, future soldiers will also be prone to surrender in difficult circumstances, knowing they may be ransomed and freed rather than sold into slavery. The Senate hears his words and votes against ransom. They send the ten captives back to the Carthaginian camp, under guard to guarantee they return.

As the ten captives shuffle out, a senator runs up to the rostra, glaring at his fellows. "By condemning them to slavery, you have eliminated two legions of our best fighters. All for preserving some romantic notion of 'heroic traditions!' How do you propose to replace them?"

An aged senator stands. "We can use the Cannenses instead, the men Scipio and Varro led back from Cannae. Two legions of veteran infantry. They would be a powerful asset for us."

"No, not those cowards!" yells a young senator. "They are being exiled to Sicily, by the command of Dictator Junius Pera. And I support him. True Romans would have fought to the death!"

"And in doing so, achieved nothing in their dying!" shouts Young Scipio, who has vaulted from his seat. Scipio knows he is but an onlooker and should be quiet, but he cannot restrain himself. "Rome is no longer a kingdom of farmers, fighting against the hill tribes of Etruscans and Latins. We are becoming a world power, with looming conflicts against other nations. We have to utilize every available man if we are to survive Carthage, or Macedonia, or Persia. We become much more powerful if we use the Cannenses."

"And we become much more cowardly if we do," hisses Torquatus.

The aged senator interjects. "My colleagues! We cannot recall our legions in Italia and Gaul, they guard our borders. We should find another source for our legions. And quickly build another army, before Hannibal is at the gates. If we cannot use the Cannenses, who can we recruit?"

"STAY IN FORMATION! I swear to the gods, I will have you buried alive if you don't keep in your rows!"

Cato walks through a roughshod maniple of a hundred slaves sporting battered Roman armor and wooden swords – the rudiments of Rome's next legion. In concert with Cato's barked orders, the slaves move to their right and shove their shields into an imaginary enemy, thrusting their swords horizontally to maximize the imaginary wound they inflict, and then step back. They do this while maintaining the required three-foot space between their line mates, so everyone has room to maneuver. It is a well-coordinated dance of death, a combat routine that has made the Roman infantry the world's most efficient killing machine.

Cato monitors the spaces between the lines, checking that the rows and columns are evenly arranged, that no one steps out of turn. An uneven line means someone is not keeping his distance from his fellows, and that merits a smack from Cato's vitis, the yard-long cudgel that symbolizes the centurion's authority. Cato brooks no excuses, and eventually the men all fall into line.

Rome is so desperate for new legions it is training slaves and youths to become Hannibal's next opponents. From the lowest pot boy to the most elevated patrician, the Romans are determined to fight to the end before they capitulate to the Carthaginian, the man who has slain so many of their loved ones.

Although the Senate hawks for any available man to join the war, they continue to exclude the Cannenses, the men led back from Cannae by Scipio and Varro. Those legionnaires are reviled as cowards and are summarily exiled to Sicily for the remainder of their service. However, not all who returned from the disaster are shunned. Scipio's heroism is well known: the plebs worship him. To maintain the Latin Party image, Varro's associates have hosted celebrations and laudatory speeches for him, and his impetuous blunders are lost among the wine and food.

Scipio speaks out for the Cannenses at several Senate gatherings, praising the men who battled their way from the slaughterhouse fields. But the result stays the same: the officers are honored, and the soldiers are reviled.

To help fulfill Rome's need for soldiers, Scipio turns his attention to training four turmae of new cavalry. Most of them are sixteen- and seventeen- year-old youths from families wealthy enough to afford their sons' horse and armament. After the recruits have learned the basics of horsemanship and weaponry, Scipio trains them to fight on horseback, contrary to the Roman penchant to dismount and fight on foot. He shows them how to use the Numidians' swirling tactics, to engage, disengage, and turn about to engage again. Laelius shows them how to use the falcata, and many grow to prefer the hefty Iberian weapon over the traditional Roman sword. A new type of Roman soldier takes shape under Scipio's tutelage, one designed to combat the varied fighting styles of Hannibal's mercenaries.

Scipio's unconventional methods do not go unnoticed. Several days after Scipio implements his new tactics, Cato notices the aberrations. Cato is working his infantry on a training field next to Scipio's area. He spies Scipio's trainees practicing with the falcata. With a muttered curse, Cato stalks across the training fields toward Scipio, who is directing his men atop his warhorse.

"Cornelius Scipio! What are you doing to these men?"

Scipio stares down at the blocky youth glowering at him. He suppresses his irritation with Cato's churlish manner, knowing he is now a respected Latin Party member.

"Ah, friend Cato. It has been a while since last we talked. The Senate chambers some years ago, was it not?"

"No matter that. Your men have an alien weapon." Cato's voice takes a mocking turn. "Is that of Greek origin? Something acquired by the Hellenic Party?"

Scipio cocks an eye at him. "You know what it is. You have seen it kill enough of our comrades. It is the Iberian falcata. A superior weapon!"

"Pah! You Hellenics think anything from a foreign country is better than what we have here. But the foreigners all fall beneath our good Roman iron."

Scipio shakes his head. "Our 'good Roman iron' is not as good as this material. Those Iberians do something special to iron. Our blacksmith told me they temper it into what he calls 'steel.' It makes their swords stronger than ours." Scipio swooshes the sword in an arc. "The design is better, too. It's thicker in the back – good for chopping as well as thrusting."

Cato sneers. "It is a poor craftsman who blames his tools, patrician. Is that not the old saying? I bet I could defeat you with one of our 'inferior' Roman swords."

Scipio vaults from his horse with his eyes shining with anger. "Well, friend farmer, let us give you that chance." He beckons to a nearby trainee. "Fetch us some pads and armor, a sword, and a falcata. But not the wooden ones." The youth goes over to some large wicker bins and brings back two caged helmets and two heavily padded leather coats. He runs back and fetches two shields and two blunted metal practice swords. Cato and Scipio's trainees gather round, confused but excited.

Cato grabs the Roman sword, and Scipio takes the falcata. The two silently don their coats and helmets. They turn to face each other, raise their weapons in a combat salute, and step forward to engage.

It is a brief but furious fight. Cato moves agilely in classic infantry maneuvers, crashing his shield into Scipio's to gain an opening, stabbing with his gladius to score a kill spot. Scipio plays a waiting game by staying behind his shield, deflecting Cato's jabs by parrying them off his blade. He swings his falcata toward Cato's midsection, which Cato blocks with his sword. They parry and feint for several minutes, each scoring stinging blows on the forearms and shoulders. Scipio finally sees the move he wants when Cato essays a strong looping swing at his helmet. Scipio arcs the falcata upward to clash against Cato's swing, throwing his body weight into it. There is a loud clang, and Cato's sword shatters into pieces. Cato is left holding a stub of his blade, staring at the shards around his feet.

"That is enough for today." Scipio removes his helmet and coat and turns to walk off, casting a final comment as he goes. "As I said, superior metal for a superior weapon. That is why we practice with this sword."

Marcus Silenus watches Cato and Scipio duel. The old centurion's face betrays no emotion throughout the conflict, but his mouth registers the slightest of grins when Scipio shatters Cato's blade. As the overseer of all recruit training, Marcus has command of all who teach and practice on the field, regardless of rank. He uses that privilege now.

Marcus walks over to Cato and Scipio, who both turn to face the famous soldier – a man who could kill them both with his bare hands. He stares into their eyes until they look down, abashed. "That is quite a demonstration you put on for your men. What was your message, to settle their differences with a swordfight? Our forces are lean enough without these pups trying to kill each other!"

Scipio bows his head slightly. "I was demonstrating the falcata's superiority. No more was intended than that."

Marcus turns his head and looks sternly at Cato, giving a curt nod toward Cato's men. Cato walks off without another word. The centurion turns back to Scipio. "I have seen enough of my men chopped up by that sword not to respect it. But it does not suit fighting in maniples, as a coordinated group. I do not wish to see it on the training field again."

"As you will," says Scipio. "But perhaps with some modifications to the maniple formation it could be…"

Marcus cuts him off. "Perhaps, with some modifications. But we are in the midst of a war, and we have no time to change legionary fighting tactics. I am clear, am I not?"

Scipio nods in acquiescence, but he thinks how ably the young men adapted to his new stratagems. *When I am a general,* he muses, *we will revisit this…*

FOR THE NEXT two years, Scipio and Cato join with the other veterans to prepare six new Roman legions from every part of the Roman region. Scipio's batches of recruits are ever younger and poorer, many showing up with decrepit armament and horses. Cato turns from training slaves to training convicts, men who will be freed from their sentence if they survive their first campaign. Picking from the pieces of a shattered city, Rome gradually aggregates and army of twenty six thousand new legionnaires to fight in Italia.

Amelia turns her genius at message design to restoring the spirit of her beloved city. She develops a banner emblazoned with the purple-red Phoenix, the mythical Egyptian bird that rose from its own ashes. Amelia enlists Pomponia's political skills to help her promote her new symbol. Soon facsimiles crop up across the city: banners flying from the third and fourth storeys of the apartment buildings for the poor, signs stuck in front of the baths – even posters nailed to the front doors of wealthy patricians from both parties. Rome rises from the ashes of its mourning and fear, a city burning with the fires of defiance.

The legions of roughshod recruits merge with those of the remaining veterans, and the new army is finally ready. The force heads out for the Carthaginians, its generals commissioned to follow the once-reviled Fabian strategy of harassing Hannibal instead of confronting him. With his spies relaying the Romans' every move, Hannibal incubates a new strategy to defeat Rome's latest attempt to vanquish him.

HANNIBAL AND MAHARBAL lounge on a hillside near the ancient Mediterranean town of Naples, watching a gladiatorial contest with their men. Inside a thirty-foot ring, two Roman senators duel in mortal combat, with the survivor being set free for Rome. These middle-aged combatants were drawn from the captives whom Rome refused to ransom, leaving Hannibal with eight thousand prisoners to sell into slavery. The pair was given a choice: fight to the death with the winner going free, or both would be killed on the spot. The two readily agree, even with the macabre stipulation that the winner returns to the Senate with the loser's head.

Maharbal jokes that it is so the Senate will know who to replace. But Hannibal created this grim contract in a desperate attempt to provoke a ransom or treaty from Rome, before he embarks on another devastating campaign against them. The portly senators fight desperately if not skillfully, and the soldiers enthusiastically cheer them on. Maharbal jeers at the opponents' swordsmanship, thoroughly enjoying the brutish spectacle.

The younger senator plunges his sword into the face of his exhausted opponent, a thoughtful man who had once helped him develop an aqueduct proposal for Senate approval. The patrician falls on his back and gurgles out his life as the crowd cheers another Roman death. Hannibal watches the action without expression, seeming to endure more than enjoy it. Maharbal finally notices Hannibal's silence and leans toward him.

"Do you not enjoy seeing one Roman kill another?" Maharbal grins. "Or would you rather do it yourself? I see not a man that is match for you, though you have but one eye!"

Hannibal merely stares into space. "I did this for peace, not for sport. Those soft-handed senators in Rome may change their ways when their colleagues' heads are delivered to them. I know not what else to do." Hannibal rises to leave. "Use three more pairs of senators, then save the rest for another day."

A new ferocity burns from Hannibal's cold determination. When Carthalo brought back news that Rome would accept no peace terms, his face flushed with frustrated anger, and then turned grim. "Those stubborn fools seem to hate compromise," he said to Maharbal. "We have no choice but to drive them into the ground, as my father always said. The survivors will sign a treaty with us – if there are any left to do it."

"I told you," chides Maharbal, "we should have headed to Rome right after Cannae."

"And how would we get there?" Hannibal retorted. "Eat our own men on the way? We had no food left and no prospect for attaining any on the march. How do you feed fifty thousand men when every town is walled up against you, every grain field burned along the Appian Way? I had to reconsider." Hannibal shakes his head. "And suppose we made it there? The Romans would have stayed behind their walls until they starved us to death. No, we need a larger force, that we may storm their walls and avoid a siege. That is why I sent Mago to Carthage."

Maharbal shakes his head. "It is a puzzlement. You sent one of our best generals to beg for troops and food."

"The Elders are more concerned with protecting their Iberian mines than winning the war in Italia," Hannibal says. "It had to be one of us Barcas, to muster our friends against those ... businessmen."

Maharbal stretches out his hand, and a slave places a chalice of dark red wine into it. He drinks deeply before he replies. "We don't need more men from the homeland. Look at all of Rome's allies who have come to us: the Bruttii, the Lucanians, and the Samnites. Every one of them adds to our force and subtracts from theirs!"

"We need even more," says Hannibal. "Most of Rome's allies still fear reprisals -- they far outnumber the ones who have come to us. Mago's journey will determine how soon we can attack Rome, and what peoples we must recruit or conquer before we go. Pray he does well, or we are undone."

*   *   *   *   *

Mago leads his army toward the glittering hilltop citadel of Byrsa, perched within the mighty empire-city of Carthage, commercial hub of the world's nations. Many of the region's two million inhabitants have filled its wide avenues to cheer the hero of Cannae, and he passes by throngs of elegantly dressed residents standing among Carthage's many exquisite stone temples, amphitheaters, and apartment buildings. Mago's guards and officers are resplendent in fresh linen cuirasses and shining armor. Mago, however, wears his bloodstained armament to show the citizens the price paid for Carthage's safety. On the back of his saddle, the tall and wiry general carries two large heavy sacks that jingle loudly as he clops along the wide cobbled street.

Mago finally arrives at Byrsa's massive city square, to attend a homecoming celebration in his honor. After many prayers, speeches, and performances, the festival winds down and the citizens head for home. Mago rides wearily to the sprawling Barca complex, there to reunite with his royal family and to plot a convincing strategy for the morrow's presentation.

The next day, Mago stands before the Council of Elders, the hundred men who comprise Carthage's Senate. He is there to report on the progress of the war against Rome and to request men, money, and grain. He knows this mission is as important as any battle he has fought.

Mago bows to the august body, and commences with his summary of the war in Italia, detailing all the battles won by Carthage. When he comes to the topic of Cannae, he stops and waves for two of his guards. They drag forward the two large sacks that were on the back of Mago's horse. At his command, the men upend the sacks. Thousands of glittering gold rings chime across the Senate floors, bejeweling the thick marble slabs with their splendor.

Mago sweeps his hand over the scattered pools of gold. "These rings are from the hands of the knights slain at Cannae. They were taken off Rome's finest cavalry and soldiers, most of them senators and tribunes. Twenty times this number died at Cannae and just as many at Trebia and Trasimene." Mago steps closer to the semicircle of Elders. He raises his fist high, as if it were a hammer prepared to strike. "Rome's losses are mortal, they have few men left. Now is the time to give them the death stroke and end this war. You have that in your power, if you but grant us the men and money for the death blow."

A tall, saturnine man stands up, attired in rich silks and gems. He gives Mago a sour look before he turns sideways to speak to his fellow Elders. It is Hanno the Great, one of Carthage's richest men, a veteran commander of the first war with Rome.

"Let me ask you, Mago," Hanno says. "Have the Romans sent Hannibal any ambassadors to sue for peace? Have you received a report of peace being talked about in Rome?" xv

"No, I have not," says Mago.

Hanno nods his head as if he has heard a great truth. He paces about, bent over as if he is thinking deeply. He turns back to Mago. "Have any of the thirty-five tribes of Italia deserted to Hannibal?"

Mago stares at him defiantly. "No, not yet. But I have been gone. It could have happened."

Hanno ignores his comment and turns back to the Elders. "There are many of us still alive who remember how victory shifted back and forth in the first Roman war. I do not think it serves any purpose to send assistance to a force that is already victorious with the men they have now, much less one that is hoodwinking us with false and groundless hopes!"

Scores of Elders jump to their feet with cries of "Nay!" and "Lies!" Others shout against the naysayers, and a loud debate erupts. Mago stands and watches, gritting his teeth in frustration.

*   *   *   *   *

Hannibal and Maharbal stand at the docks of Bruttium, waiting for Mago's returning quadrireme to tie up at the main pier. The ship docks and an elegantly dressed older man steps down the gangplank, and shuffles over to him. Hannibal smiles at the sight of an old friend. He and Maharbal walk over to greet him.

"Hail, Shafat," says Hannibal. "I trust your family is well."

"Hail, Hannibal, mightiest of all generals! Mine eyes rejoice at your visage!"

"You are truly welcome here, comrade." Hannibal looks up at the ship's deck. "Where is my brother Mago?"

Instead of answering, Shafat hands a sealed scroll to Hannibal. "From the Council of Elders. An official decree."

Hannibal unrolls the scroll and reads it. He gapes at Shafat. "Mago has been sent to Iberia? His army with him?"

Shafat nods, his mouth a line of reluctance. "To join your brother Hasdrubal. To combat Publius and Gnaeus Scipio." He sees Hannibal staring confusedly at him, and his voice softens. "You have not heard, perhaps. The Scipios scored a great victory at Dertosa. Many of our men were lost and many of our Iberian allies deserted us. Our control of Iberia is in serious jeopardy." The messenger frowns. "More importantly to the Elders, our control of the mines is in jeopardy."

Maharbal barges into Shafat's face. "What say you? We are on the verge of conquering Rome, and those squat-to-piss shop keepers take our men away?"

"There was a long debate in the Council about who most required reinforcements, you or them. But in the end, it was decided that twenty six thousand troops will be sent to Iberia, to be distributed to the three generals there: Mago, Hasdrubal, and

Gisgo the Elder."

"And I receive nothing?" Hannibal exclaims. "I, who command the regions of Campania and Bruttium?"

Shafat shrugs. "Not exactly nothing. As it says there, you will have four thousand Numidians and forty elephants coming. Your orders are to commence a holding action, to occupy the armies in Italia until Iberia is under control again. And then more can be sent to you."

"A holding action? Am I to become another Cunctuator, and skirmish about Italia like a coward? Gods above, I am ready to throw down their walls! There would be no war in Iberia, Rome would be ours! Now they have taken Mago and his men from me! Who perpetrated this madness?"

"Hanno the Great," says Shafat.

Hannibal grimaces. "I should have known. That gutless incompetent has hated the Barcas since our father rescued him from disgrace in the last war. Baal take him. I shall go to Carthage myself!"

"It will do you little good," Shafat says quietly. "Hanno leads the Aristocratic Party, and they have the majority."

Hannibal stands quietly for several moments and places his hand on Shafat's shoulder. "I know you would have this news be otherwise, honored friend. The Elders who sent you know the love I bear for you. No doubt they hoped to sweeten a bitter message, that I might swallow it whole. Go now. We shall share wine tonight, and many stories."

Shafat heads back to the ship, and Hannibal watches until he boards. Maharbal stands silently, knowing his commander is already devising a new approach. Finally, Hannibal sighs, scratches the back of his neck, and turns to Maharbal.

"There is only one way. We will build our army from Rome's allies. As you said, every addition to our force is a subtraction from theirs." He glowers. "It will take years, but we will thresh through the peoples of Italia until we finally have enough men to conquer Rome." He throws Shafat's scroll into the water. "Our politicians would have us fighting in chains, but we fight nonetheless. And win."

Maharbal looks at him, bewildered. "Where do we start?"

"At Capua," Hannibal says. "The richest and most powerful of Rome's allies. The one that hates Rome the most."

*   *   *   *   *

Scipio is stretched out on a couch in the family atrium with a dozen scrolls piled around his feet. He unfurls one, scans it, and rolls it up to fetch another. After perusing a half-dozen of them, he lingers on one tattered yellow roll of papyrus. As he runs his finger over its scrawled characters and diagrams, his mother Pomponia enters the room. He looks up at her eagerly.

"Look here! I finally found it! That encirclement Hannibal used on us at Cannae? The Athenian general Miltiades used it at the Battle of Marathon, two hundred years ago! It's called a pincer movement. Hannibal used it against us at Cannae. He knew Varro wouldn't have studied Greek history." Scipio rises to show her the scroll but he pauses, seeing a concerned look on her face. "Is Father all right?"

Pomponia spreads her hands and smiles. "He is excellent, son, be not alarmed. His message says he has allied himself with the tribes of some chieftains called Indibilis and Mandonius. So he has recruited Iberian allies to add to the few legions the Senate gave him, may the Latin Party be damned."

Scipio makes a face. "I do not trust paid allies. Remember how the Gauls deserted him?"

Pomponia raises her eyebrows. "Yes, but they were Gauls. Your father is recruiting men to defend their homeland, not to fight alongside their sworn Roman enemies."

Scipio shrugs. "Perhaps so. I hope he has appealed to these chieftains' concern for their own tribe, rather than calling it a threat to Iberia. They are loyal to their tribe, not their country. That is how I would do it, anyway."

Pomponia strokes his head. "You have changed so much. Four years ago, you were talking about how you would become a teacher. Now you talk about how you will wage war."

"It is not a change I would have made," says Scipio, "had I the choice. But I will fulfill my vow to Father, as best I may."

"I know you will, but you do not have to fight Carthage to do it. There is another war to be waged. A political war against the Latin Party."

"Ah, a political war," Scipio sighs. "Your specialty."

"It has been three years since you returned from Cannae. You have become an exemplary military trainer and a respected tribune. Perhaps it is time for you to resume the Course of Offices, so that you may become a Senator for the Hellenic Party." She takes a deep breath. "I think you should run for aedile through the Hellenic Party, while the people remember your heroism at Cannae."

Scipio makes a wry face. "Where you are concerned, it is more me becoming a politician against the Latin Party than becoming a politician for the Hellenic one!"

"You know I have a distaste for the way they treat women and the poor," Pomponia says. "The choice to run is yours, but you have an opportunity to do much good for Rome."

"It is moot, Mother. I cannot run for magistrate. You have to be twenty-five years old."

Pomponia shrugs. "Rome has broken their election rules before in times of desperation. Besides, your cousin Marcus is also running. He doesn't stand a chance on his own, but if you ran alongside him, you might carry the day for both of you."

Scipio laughs, and shakes his head. "And here I thought Father was the strategist in the family!"

"Your father is a brilliant man, strong, moral, and noble." She fiddles with the hem of her gown, avoiding Scipio's eyes. "But perhaps a bit too noble. His Senate enemies employ tricks and ambushes even Hannibal would envy! If we are to prevail, we have to repay them using their coin."

"You mean with their same dirty money," says Scipio edgily.

Pomponia takes Scipio's ancient scroll from his hand, reads it, and holds it out to her son. "As you have said about Hannibal, you can't just blunder into his traps and expect to win. You have to use your own tricks. Or lose."

Scipio takes the scroll and rolls it up. "I promised to defend Rome against its enemies," he says, "whoever they were. But being a plotting politician is even farther from my heart than being a soldier. Even farther from my dream."

Pomponia's voice takes a sterner edge. "I love you with all my heart. And I hope you will become the scholar you have dreamed of being – someday, in peacetime. But Rome is at war on two fronts, within and without. If you would fulfill your vow to defend it, you must defend its people from those who prey upon them under the guise of patriotism and tradition. Hannibal will fall, but I am not so sure about Fabius and Flaccus."

Scipio just shakes his head. "I wouldn't know where to start."

"Amelia and I will help you with the campaign. She is very good with slogans. Remember the one on Epidius' villa last year? 'Epidius with his household want and support Helvius Sabinus as aedile.' xvi That was her creation."

Pomponia grins at Scipio's expression. "Do not look so incredulous. Did you expect her to sit home and pine for you while you were off fighting? She is her father's daughter, a warrior for Rome. We fight in different ways than you, that is all."

Scipio takes a deep breath. "I must say, it has been boring for the last couple of years, while Hannibal lies quiet. I try this new war, and run for office. If I cannot fight with Father, I can fight with you and Amelia!"

Pomponia kisses his forehead. "And we will win, my son. We will win."

*   *   *   *   *

CAPUA, CAMPANIAN REGION, 214 BCE. Hannibal sits bolt upright in a sea of pillows. He plays with his wine cup as bodies swirl in front of him on the stage. The nobility of Capua recline about him, enjoying the performance given in his honor. The nobles watch raptly, laughing and joking while they swill large chalices of mulsum, a honeyed wine. Only Hannibal seems unmoved by what transpires in front of him.

On stage, three men and two women are coupling with each other in a sex circle. The woman rides atop one man while she is being penetrated from the rear by another, and as she gives fellatio to the third, who is performing cunnilingus on a petite girl who has her legs wrapped around his neck. Like trained acrobats, they vary the pace and style of their ministrations until they climax together, their screams chorusing through the small stone room adjoining the main banquet hall.

Calavius leans toward Hannibal, unctuously close. "It is a very worthy show, is it not, General? Such orgasmic coordination! It took them years of practice!"

Hannibal's face is an unreadable mask. "I have not seen the like before. I shall never see it again, I am sure. You must excuse me now. General Maharbal awaits me."

Hannibal rises, nods to his bleary-eyed associates, and strides out into the expansive main banquet hall, hurrying through the opium smoke to the exit. He passes scores of his officers and chieftains. Many roll about with naked women or boys, others stumble about drunkenly, and some are passed out in their own vomit.

Hannibal pauses in mid step to take in the entire room, looking it as if it were the aftermath of a battle. He quickens his pace until he breaks out into the cool night air. He stops to take in several deep breaths and looks up at the stars as the hall's raucous noise fades from his notice. Hannibal stands quietly until a low chuckle interrupts him. A familiar figure steps out from the building's shadows.

"You could not stand it anymore, could you? I would wager a goat on it!"

Hannibal gives Maharbal a rueful smile. "All that free food and fucking, and all I could think of was how it was ruining our men."

"I swear, those hedonistic Capuans are more dangerous than the Romans," laughs Maharbal. "Two years ago we came here as battle hardened veterans, capable of defeating Rome's best, even when they outnumbered us. Now our Gauls and Iberians are fat and happy. Their skills are dull, and their enjoyable lives have become too precious for them to fight like they used to. Even some of our Sacred Band are doughy and lazy! I would not trust us to beat a bunch of downy recruits, much less a legion of Roman veterans!"

Hannibal nods. "We have to get out of here. These wealthy Capuans are a powerful ally, but they will be our downfall."

Maharbal grins expectantly. "So on to Nocera?"

"Nocera has rejected our overtures for an alliance," Hannibal says, as he stares back up at the stars. "Now they will become a lesson for those who resist us. Their crops are still in the field, so their food stores will be low. We can starve them out."

"Then we could harvest their grain and winter there," Maharbal urges. "We could have a more austere lifestyle than here at Capua, one befitting a soldier."

"It is more important that we let the Gauls and Iberians ransack the city," muses Hannibal. "When they regain their taste for plunder, they will slaver for more fighting."

"And what can we do with a horde of slavering Gauls?"

"We move north through the cities of Campania, making allies or removing enemies. The Campanians will scream to Rome, and Rome will have to confront us. Then we can break them, once and for all."

Maharbal laughs. "These Romans are as thick-headed as mules. How many times must we destroy them before they quit?"

"If it were any other nation, they would have come to terms after they lost their first major battle. That has been the way of the Greeks, the Persians, and us." Hannibal shakes his head. "They are like a bunch of stubborn farmers, seeding crops while a dust storm approaches. But this storm will be Carthage, and it will storm their gates. Because they gave us no choice. "

*   *   *   *   *

ROME, 213 BCE. The chariots race around the turnpost, heading into the seventh and final lap. The Pompeii team is a short distance ahead of the Romans and Foggians, but they are both closing fast. The Foggia team spills sideways, hurling its drivers into the dust of the Circus Maximus. Tens of thousands of plebeians cheer wildly, filling the Circus with the cacophony of their mad enthusiasm. The circus games are sponsored by the new curule aedile (public works magistrate) of Rome: Cornelius Scipio.

The new magistrate has wasted no time in fulfilling his duties as manager of festivities and holidays, declaring a citywide festival. Working behind the scenes, Pomponia has organized the event as a commemoration of Publius and Gnaeus' Scipios' victory at Dertosa last year. Cornelius Scipio then declared the commemoration as a citywide holiday, one of a hundred thirty that the festival-loving populace would have that year. Pomponia is overjoyed. She knows the Dertosa celebration will promote the image of the Scipio family as well as the Hellenic Party, and help move Cornelius further into the political limelight.

The Scipios have added a twist to these games, one to combat the Latin Party's cultural jingoism against the plebs. Groups of professional orators and actors are stationed about the circus entrances, lecturing on Greek art and philosophy and performing Grecian tragedies and comedies. Many of those patricians attending the games mutter among themselves, uncomfortable with Scipio's public dispensation of knowledge and art. But they know it wise not to confront him, a man who is clearly the people's new favorite.

Scipio, Amelia, and Pomponia are seated in the first-row boxes reserved for patricians and senate members. Flaccus, Cato, and Fabius sit on their far right, dourly observing the enthusiastic crowds. As the chariots race about, Pomponia looks proudly at her son and leans next to his ear, to be heard over the din. "I still cannot believe it. You are the youngest man to ever enter the Senate. You have done well."

"If I have done well, it is because of you and Amelia. All those parties and meetings you hosted–we had half of Rome at our house!" He playfully squeezes Amelia's shoulder. "I cannot believe you wrote that slogan 'Vote Isidore for aedile. He's the best at licking cunt.' [xvii]My gods, people were laughing all about town!"

"He had it coming," says Amelia. "All those lies he was spreading about you and Laelius being lovers. About some slave saving your father at Ticinus instead of you. He is a scoundrel!" She giggles. "But we should be glad that women can't vote – that slogan would have got him elected!"

Scipio laughs, and cocks an eye at his mother. "I am learning this war of politics has its own attack and defense tactics. Not all are moral or cerebral."

Pomponia nods. "You should think of politics as a military campaign. In fact, that is what we should call it, a 'political campaign!'" She smiles grimly. "In a campaign you do many things you are not proud of to keep the enemy from the gates."

"Therein lies the problem, Mother. In breaking rules, do you become the person you decry? The rules say I could not have run for office until I was twenty-five, but here I am at twenty-two!"

She pats his cheek. "It is as you told those who objected to your running 'If all the Roman people want to make me aedile, I am old enough.' [xviii] You had to run now to exploit your reputation for valor and devotion."

"I do not enjoy the idea of exploiting anything." Scipio throws his hands into the air. "I fear I am not a true politician, Mother."

Pomponia draws herself up to her full height, and speaks to Scipio with a tinge of outrage in her voice. "Every man who wields power is a politician. There is always someone to placate or coerce. To save Rome from Carthage – and from itself – you must learn to do that."

Scipio can feel his right hand twitch. "I know this office is a means to a higher end, so I will do my best. But it is not the noble undertaking I thought it would be, however necessary. That philosopher Plato was right. The virtuous man would never seek to be king.'" Scipio sighs, and looks out upon the hurling chariots rounding the bend. "I would rather be with Father and Lucius in Iberia. There you know who your enemies are, and who is winning."

Pomponia laughs. "I suppose so, but the real war may be here. Your father has oft commented that he was more worried about the enemy within than the enemy without! But whatever his worries, he is conquering Iberia." She adds, wistfully, "Perhaps he will soon end this war, and come home."

*　　*　　*　　*　　*

BAETIS RIVER, IBERIA, 211 BCE. Publius Scipio can feel

his time running out, even as the sun rises in the sky. His army must defeat these rebellious Ilergetes before Mago's and Gisgo's armies arrive. Publius has marched his men all night to intercept this powerful Iberian tribe before they join the Carthaginians. Now he has caught them here by the Baetis River and has backed them up against its rocky shores.

The Ilergetes are the fiercest fighters in all Iberia, but the implacable Roman infantry are thinning their ranks. Indibilis and Mandonius, the chieftain brothers, will not surrender. They race back and forth behind their infantry's front line, screaming for their men to resist the Roman advance. The chiefs hope to buy enough time for the Carthaginians to rescue them, but Rome's maniples press them ever backwards. Each time the Romans step forward they step over dead Iberians. It is only a matter of time.

As Publius watches his men press in, he notices a dust cloud off to his right, swirling toward his cavalry on the flanks. He raises his hand to feel for wind, but feels none, and he feels dread creep into his heart. That cloud moves too fast to be infantry, he thinks. It can mean only one thing. He mutters a curse and quickly sends an order to his Master of Horse to prepare the cavalry for a counterattack.

A spearhead of riders takes shape within the dusky cloud; half-naked men riding like the wind was beneath them. Masinissa, Prince of the Numidians, is leading thousands of his fleet riders into Publius' cavalry flank. They rush into the outnumbered Romans and quickly surround them, joining the Ilergete cavalry to form a thick wall around the Roman horsemen. Publius has no choice but to send a legion over to aid them. The Iberian infantry sees the legion leave their fight, and their resistance stiffens. The battle becomes a stalemate, which is a victory in time for the desperate Iberians.

Soon, all too soon, they come. Mago and Gisgo appear on the horizon, leading their armies toward Publius' unprotected rear lines. Within an hour, Publius' men are engulfed by a force twice their number. The Romans struggle to maintain lines as they are pushed together, fighting as individuals rather than maniples. Cannae repeats itself.

Publius is in the center of the encirclement, within a defensive circle of his elite guard. He assesses the enemy surrounding his army, and his dread becomes regret. He quickly calls his son Lucius to his side. "Lucius, you are to leave with these members of my guard. Take a message to Tiberius Fonteus back at our camp. Tell him to retreat to the Ebro and join Nero's men." He sees the confusion on Lucius' guileless face and knows this is no time for the truth. "Go now, through that gap in the northeast, away from the Numidians, and circle around to the north!"

A bewildered Lucius nods and hugs his father. Publius clings fiercely to him for a moment and then pushes Lucius away. "Go!" he shouts sternly, his eyes clouding.

One of Lucius' accompanying guards catches Publius' eye and nods his understanding. "It was an honor serving you, General. I swear I shall get him to camp."

Publius watches Lucius until he has ridden out of the melee. After his son is out of sight, Publius slowly dismounts from his horse, and draws his sword. He will end his fighting on foot, among his men. It is not long before Publius is the center of a small island of Romans, with waves of Iberians crashing into them. As he thrusts his dagger into an onrushing Ilergete's throat, he thinks of Pomponia and his two sons, all safe back at Rome. The relentless Ilergetes cut through the last of the men about him, and he can think no more.

VIII. SCIPIO RISING

Here in Northeastern Iberia, the Ebro River is strong, eighty feet wide and flowing as forcefully as the mountain streams that feed it. The river charges through valleys and canyons in a thick swirl of grey-brown water, challenging any who are foolish enough to impede its rush toward the Mediterranean. Yet cross it they do, Roman survivors wading, swimming, and floating in their desperation to reach the citadel of Tarraco on the other side. Most of them cross, others drown, but none tarry on the side of defeat.

First come the remainders of Publius Scipio's devastated army. Hundreds trudge in from the forests and hills, while others gallop to the shores in lathered horses. Amazingly, a small legion soon appears on the desolate plains, marching defiantly toward the riverbank. They are led by the hulking legion commander Tiberius Fonteius, a deceptively jovial man who has whipped the disheartened remnants of Publius Scipio's army into a vengeful force. The legionnaires march with determination, ready to destroy any who stand in their way, preferring to die in battle than live with the shame of allowing their commander to perish. Their only aim is to attain Tarraco and redeem themselves by renewing their fight against the Carthaginians. Tiberius has reminded them of the Cannenses' disgrace and exile. After decimating a Numidian pursuit party with the hubris to attack them, they proceed unchallenged across the Ebro.

Weeks later, two maniples of Gnaeus Scipio's force limp to the banks of the Ebro, led by a courageous and clever equite, the commoner Lucius Marcius. The men are the only maniples from that once-proud army, for Gnaeus has suffered the same fate as his brother Publius.

Once they overran Publius Scipio's army, Mago and Gisgo hurried to join Hasdrubal's divisions near the town of Ilorca, to assault Gnaeus' army with the superior numbers of their combined forces. There at Ilorca, on a hill overlooking the town's picturesque groves of olive and orange trees, Gnaeus and his army met their end at the hand of the Three Generals.

In the space of a month, the Three Generals have killed the Scipios, massacred their armies, and wrested control of Iberia from Roman hands. Tarraco is the last bastion of Roman strength in Iberia, the sole haven for the remains of the Scipios' mighty legions.

When they cross the Ebro, the Romans regroup into a makeshift army. Tiberius Fonteius collects what officers he can find and holds a vote about their next course of action. Rather than rush to the safety of Tarraco, they elect to remain by the Ebro and search for stragglers, to leave no man behind. The legionnaires quickly construct a fortified camp and throw down a rude bridge for the scores of men that trickle in every day.

The camp soon grows into a defensible garrison of almost eight thousand men, all that remains from the thirty two thousand that marched out to conquer Iberia just six days ago. Now they wait to see if help from Rome will arrive in time to save them, or if the armies of Hasdrubal, Mago, and Gisgo will find them first.

* * * * *

Scipio strolls from the Senate chambers, conversing with two fellow senators about Rome's public grain supply. Now twenty-four, Scipio is a young politician with the scarred and muscled body of a veteran warrior underneath his finery. He wears the purple-bordered toga of his magisterial office, the curule aedile, carrying himself like a man older than his true years.

Scipio is explaining that he returned the wheat the Sicilians sold to Rome because they were providing the city with an inferior product, selling chaff-filled bags of grain. When the senators give their approval of his decision, Scipio moves to capitalize on their support. He presents his proposal to change the allocation rules for grazing on public land to provide more acres to small farmers and less to the patricians. The wealthy senators receive his proposal with some enthusiasm after Scipio provides figures to justify its economic benefits to Rome – and to themselves.

As curule aedile, it is Scipio's duty to oversee food supplies for the public and the military. For the time being, Scipio the auditor has replaced Scipio the warrior and Scipio the scholar. He has become a man obsessed with the details of food and finance because he has learned how vital these details are to Rome's continued welfare. They are weapons as potent as any legions.

"I will make the land allocation proposal immediately," Scipio says to the two senators. "My time in office will be up soon. I want it done before I depart."

"You have done well for one so young," says Senator Fluvius Gracchus. "You should consider running for praetor."

Scipio bows slightly, acknowledging the compliment. "I have enjoyed my time away from the war, but I must join my father in Iberia and assist him in finalizing his campaign against the Three Generals." He smiles. "Unless he has already driven the Carthaginians into the sea!"

The other senator laughs. "You will certainly be allowed that, you are still a hero to the people. They remember how you led our legions back to Rome when the city was so defenseless."

The second senator makes a disgusted face. "Nevertheless, those Cannenses disgraced themselves. Thank the gods we sent them to Sicily where they will do no harm."

"I saw them at Cannae," says Scipio, with a measure of irritation. "They fought bravely. They did not leave the field until the battle became a slaughter."

Embroiled in his conversation with the senators, Scipio does not notice the approach of his Greek tutor Asclepius, an incongruous presence in the staid Roman chambers. The regal old man walks purposefully toward Scipio, his face sorrowful. The two senators see Asclepius coming. They see his expression and immediately fall silent. Scipio looks over his shoulder and sees his teacher. His face breaks into a welcoming smile. He sees his tutor's expression, and the smile vanishes.

Asclepius lays his hand on Scipio's shoulder. "My son..."

"What? Is Mother all right?"

Asclepius nods, but his expression remains doleful. Scipio's hand twitches at his side. "Is it Father? It's Father...?"

"Your father's army was betrayed by his allies. Your uncle was lost. Your father..." Asclepius spreads his hands as if something has escaped them.

Scipio falls to the floor, writhing in anguish. "Father! Oh my gods! Father! Aaaah!"

Asclepius and the senators bend to comfort Scipio. They mutter soft and soothing words, but he is inconsolable. Asclepius helps him up and leads him from the Forum. Knots of senators look on and exchange glances, their partisan attitudes faded in light of their all-to-familiar sorrow for another fellow Roman who has lost a loved one to war.

The Scipio domus is hushed that afternoon. Slaves tiptoe about, doing their chores as quietly as possible, ignoring the cries and sobs that waft from Pomponia's room. Hours later she emerges, as queenly as always, wearing a dark blue mourning robe, her hair undone and disheveled. Her deeply shadowed eyes betray the agony of her loss, but she moves with purpose. She makes her way to the atrium to alleviate her son's grief. When she enters the atrium she finds Scipio sobbing face down into the atrium couch, his toga rent and hair askew. Amelia sits next to him, stroking his hair. Pomponia stands next to her son and rests her hand on his back. "Cornelius, dear, you should go to you room. You must rest now, so you can go on. Rome needs you."

Scipio's head lurches up, his face a rictus of tearful anger. "For what? To die in a war for silver and gold, every ounce purchased with a gallon of blood?"

Pomponia's voice is so soft it can barely be heard. "If Iberia falls, Rome will be conquered. We will all meet tragedy. Your father swore he would prevent Rome from falling, but he cannot stop it now. It is time for you to assume his duties."

"Whom will I save? The senators who gave him only a handful of soldiers so he had to bribe those treacherous fucking savages? Save those sheltered cowards in the Senate who refused peace when Hannibal offered it, so that others may die? Is that who I vowed to protect?"

Amelia strokes his damp brow. "Your mother speaks true, my heart. Think no more of war and politics for now. It is time for you to rest, before the fevers come upon you again."

Amelia and Pomponia gently ease him up, but Scipio shrugs free and stalks around the room, shouting. "Why bother? Why? Carthage is unstoppable! They defeat us at every turn! Ah, I should have heeded the betrayers at Canusium and taken us all to Greece! What folly this fight! What madness this war!"

Pomponia stands in front of her son and slaps his face, a short stinging blow. Scipio rubs his cheek in amazement. Her eyes blaze with staring anger.

"Speak no more of others' treachery when you so cherish your own! You are a Scipio, born to lead our legions! If you have not the will to fight, spend your efforts in the Senate you so despise. But you will not dishonor your father by talking of treason. You will not shame my husband!"

Scipio composes himself, angry and embarrassed. "It is a sham war," he growls, "posed as the defense of Rome, used to make the rich that much richer. How do you have the strength to wage it?"

Pomponia stares defiantly at him. "Because I must. My heart is broken forevermore; my life's love is gone. But duty remains. People will suffer if I do not do what I am supposed to do, it is that simple." She touches the cheek where she struck him. "Heed no more tonight. Let events provide your healing. Saturn is not only the god of time, he is the god of renewal. Both are so conjoined in human nature."

"I shall sacrifice to Febris tonight," says Amelia. "That she will not visit you in your despair. Let us go now, love – the time for words is past." Amelia takes Scipio's hand, and leads him down the hallway to his room. She gently pushes him in, pausing at the entrance. "I know your true heart's desire is study and teaching," Amelia says, "as you are my heart's desire. And if you must leave to pursue yours, be that to Greece or Persia, I shall be at your side. Where you go, I will follow."

Amelia kisses him once, lingeringly. "Now rest," she says, and departs.

Late that night, Febris comes to Scipio in full force. He shivers, sweats, and thrashes, muttering to his father, shouting warnings as if in the midst of battle. Soon he hears two faint voices arguing. The voices become louder, and two bickering spirits appear over his bed. One is Voluptas, goddess of pleasure. She is a buxom young woman with flowing golden hair ringed with a flower wreath, clad in diaphanous saffron. The other is Pietas, the goddess of duty to parents and country. Pietas is a severely attractive woman, clad is a long, thick stola of glowing white, with a veil over her tightly-bound brunette locks. The spirits hover about the foot of Scipio's platform bed, speaking to him with entreating, desperate voices.

Voluptas: Scipio, your time is short to leave this madness. Soon you will become a general. Then it will be too late to change your course. Your life's path will be set!

Pietas: Heed her not, Scipio! Your father is gone. Paullus is dead. Rome's generals are old and timid. They cannot defeat the crafty Carthaginians. Only you. Rome needs you more than ever.

Voluptas: Have you learned nothing from Rome's defeats? It is folly to oppose Hannibal and his brothers! Look to your heart's desire while breath yet remains. You are a scholar, not an ox for a businessman's yoke. Go to Greece and study war no more.

Pietas: Remember noble Cincinnatus? He was but a humble farmer until the barbarians came. He put down his plow and led Rome to victory, and then returned to the fields he loved. You are fated to save Rome twice, once as a general and once as a scholar. Your destiny lies in Iberia, not Greece.

Voluptas: Many brilliant officers have fallen to Hannibal and the Three Generals. Do you think you can beat them all, that you are wiser than all who came before? Than your father? Be not a fool for duty!"

Pietas: You swore to preserve the Republic. Will you do it by abandoning your countrymen? Will your father have died for nothing? Do not spend your days in dishonor, haunted by the violation of your trust. Only you know how to defeat our enemy, only you have the genius of invention. Do your duty or be damned, son of Publius.

Scipio moans, sweats, tosses – and finally sleeps.

At dawn, a rooster crows and Scipio rises. He stares about for a minute until he gains full consciousness. He hears the rooster crow again, challenging daybreak as he does every day. Scipio's eyes light with sweet determination. He knows what he must do.

*　*　*　*　*

"You stupid fuckers! We have to stick it in their ass! Now!"

Hasdrubal is storming about the main meeting hall of Cissa, a town near the Romans' base at Tarraco. He flings battle figurines against the walls, swipes maps off the table, and rages against the three austere Carthaginian senators sitting around the hall's banquet table. Gisgo and Mago finally grab him and halt his ranting movements, but he continues to scream at the aged officials.

"Pardon my brother, Senators," says Mago. "He is angry – but he is also correct. We are at the doorway to Italia. All we have to do is bring down Tarraco, and the route is open to Hannibal – and Rome! We can end this war!"

"Do you buggering old farts not see that?" spits Hasdrubal, before Gisgo glares him to silence.

The senators betray no emotion or gesture. The chief official, an aged merchant dressed in gold-embroidered silk robes, waits until the Three Generals are still before he speaks. "We have discussed this for two days, and nothing has changed. Your mission is to protect the gold and silver mines in Iberia. If you attack Tarraco, you act contrary to the Council's wishes. We are sending a peace envoy to Rome. Further conflicts with them would be … unprofitable."

Hasdrubal is further incensed. "Peace? Baal take you, can't you get it into your fucking heads? Rome will not rest until Carthage is destroyed! Hannibal has tried peace already! They will make no treaty, brook no settlement, and spare no life! All you do is buy time for them to regroup while they are at their weakest. Carthage must burn Rome before Rome burns Carthage! Rome must be destroyed! Assholes!"

Short and sturdy Gisgo steps in front of Hasdrubal to grin placatingly at the senators, his thick hands spread entreatingly. "Senators, we want to protect the mines as much as you, because we need the money for our mercenaries. But Hasdrubal speaks the truth. Rome is at its most vulnerable now. We must strike before they rise from the ashes like the Phoenix, and peck out our eyes! We greatly outnumber the force at Tarraco, we can take it within days. Then Mago and I can take our armies south to protect the ports and the mines, while Hasdrubal joins Hannibal in southern Italia. Everyone will have what they want, is that not true?"

One official shakes his head. "I admit we would like to end this war and reopen Carthage's trade routes. But you make this big 'victory' sound all too easy."

Gisgo angrily thrusts out his fist out toward the politician. "Remember, Senator, we occupied Tarraco before the Scipios took it back. We know its vulnerabilities. Yes, it can be held with only a few legions, but not with the few thousand stragglers they have there now."

"It is an act of further aggression," exclaims another senator. "If you fail, we lose all chance for peace, as well as any chance for a victory!"

Mago places his hands on his hips and smolders at the three officials. "This becomes tiresome. We are the commanders of Iberia, is that not so? Attacking Tarraco is a military decision, so it is ours to make, is that not so?"

The youngest senator flushes and snaps back. "True enough, General. But you must come to us for more reinforcements or provisions – or money. I beg you to remember that before you take any action on your own. The Peace Party controls affairs in Carthage, and they do not hold the Barcas in high esteem. You will find no support without first securing ours."

Gisgo starts to reply when the senior senator rises. "We have made Carthage's position clear. Whatever you decide, you know the consequences of your actions. We remain seven more days to record what transpires. Now we take our leave."

The three senators file out. When they are gone, Mago turns to Hasdrubal and Gisgo. "Well, what do you think?"

Hasdrubal looks at Gisgo, and Gisgo breaks into a wide smile.

"We go for Tarraco," Gisgo says, "before the Romans put in reinforcements!"

Hasdrubal frowns at the door from which the senators exited. "Those money-grubbing pisspots think everyone can be bought. To hell with future reinforcements and provisions, let us kill the Romans before they kill us!"

Mago nods. "Tarraco, four days hence."

LUCIUS MARCIUS STALKS around the low walls that border the beachside town of Tarraco, planning his conquest of it. *If I were Mago,* he thinks, *where would I attack first?* He looks to the right and nods to himself. *These low seaside walls, of course. If he comes at them with several phalanxes, it will take all of Tarraco to defend them.* He strolls along the shore to the front of the town. *Mago will assault the front gates, too, so we have to divide our defenders. And then he will take the city.* Marcius kicks the sand and sighs, shaking his head. *We have to stall the attack. Reinforcements must be coming. They must.*

At sunrise, a trireme beaches nears Tarraco, and a kingly old man marches down the gangplank to the beach, resplendent in his purple-bordered toga. The man is a nuntius, an official Roman messenger who speaks the voice of the Senate. The nuntius hustles along the beach with a retinue of guards, heading for Tarraco's main gates. As soon as he enters, he demands the whereabouts of Lucius Marcius from a surprised sentry. The sentry points, and the messenger stalks over to the town meeting hall. Without ceremony he walks into Lucius Marcius' planning session with the town officials.

"I bear news from Rome," intones the nuntius.

Marcius nods toward the attendees. "All may hear. Speak."

The nuntius scrutinizes each member of the town gathering before he continues. "Gaius Nero will land north of Tarraco in two days. He brings reinforcements."

Marcius sighs with relief. "Good news indeed, honored nuntius. How many legions does he bring?"

The nuntius shifts uncomfortably. "Six thousand Roman infantry and three hundred cavalry. And a like amount of allies."

Marcius' eyes widen. "That is all?"

The nuntius raises his eyebrows. "All? It is all Rome can bear. Hannibal stalks Italia, and the Macedonians have risen against us." The nuntius turns to go. "I must return to Nero's fleet while the coastal lanes are open. May the gods be with you."

After the nuntius leaves, the people at the meeting erupt in a mix of relief, excitement, and disappointment. Marcius waits for them to vent their feelings, and then he stands at the head of the table to address them.

"It is good news indeed that Nero is coming with his seasoned veterans. But it is disappointing that there are not more of them. We have upwards of eighty thousand Carthaginians to the south of us, and the Three Generals will not be dissuaded by an army a tenth of their size. We have to think of something to keep them from attacking Tarraco."

A veteran centurion rises to speak. "I was with Fabius when he hounded Hannibal throughout Italia. Hannibal tricked us time and again, making us think he was present when he had left, and that he had more men than he did. We should use that trick on his own brothers, I say!"

The table is quiet, as the soldiers and officials consider his words, then Marcius breaks the silence. "We have been too proud to resort to Hannibal's deceptions, and we have paid dearly for it. Perhaps it is time for us to be the fox. And your words do remind me of one of his stratagems, centurion." Marcius gestures to a nearby soldier. "Tell the nuncio to tarry. We will have a message for Nero forthwith, about a visit from us to him…"

When Nero docks two nights later, he encounters a group of soldiers as large as his own. This Roman "army" is a blend of Roman legionnaires and the citizens of Tarraco. The locals have been given castoff armor and weaponry, and were quickly trained to march and ride in formation. They act enough like soldiers to deceive unwary eyes.

Emulating Hannibal, crafty Marcius has marched out this military hodge-podge under the cover of darkness to meet Nero's reinforcements at the dock. Nero grasps Marcius' plan as soon as he sees the men he has brought with him. He surrounds Marcius' mock legions with his own, so that thousands of Tarraco's citizens are concealed within Marcius' veterans and hundreds of local horsemen ride with his cavalry. Nero then sets out for Tarraco, with an "army" that is twice the size of the one with which he arrived. With Marcius at his side Nero parades toward the city, making a point to arrive at the height of day when it is easy to perceive the size of his force.

That afternoon, the Carthaginian scouts deliver their report to The Three Generals: Nero has come to Tarraco with twenty five thousand men. The three leaders talk for several hours, but it is obvious that now Tarraco cannot be taken without a costly siege. They decide to move their three armies back into Iberia and cement their control of it, where allies and resources are readily available. The Three Generals set out for different parts of Iberia. Tarraco remains a Roman stronghold and Carthage's northern portal to Italia closes, never to reopen.

*　　*　　*　　*　　*

With the defeat and death of the Scipio brothers, Rome has swung from festive optimism to anguished apprehension. Everyone knows that the Three Generals control Iberia, and that Hannibal threatens Rome. The people fill the Forum grounds and rail nonstop against the Senate, blaming them for everything from selecting the wrong commanders to angering the gods. Conciliatory speeches from the Senate are met with angry cries for action. The plebs' approval of their politicians has never been lower.

The senators know they must quickly find a new commander for Iberia, but one who is chosen by the people, in order to avoid blame on themselves. They hastily call a public election for the new Iberian proconsul, or governor, who will lead the offensive against the Three Generals. The call goes out to every major elected official in Rome to declare his candidacy.

Four days later the city empties into the Campus Martius, a five hundred acre field at the city's edge. There, on the top steps of the altar of Mars, is a line of all the executive magistrates of Rome: praetors, censors, quaestors, tribunes, and aediles.

Marcus Buteo, the Senate leader, stands in front of the officials. He is a statuesque, white-haired, ex-consul with thirty years of Senate service, a man respected for his fairness and morality. The senator calls for interested candidates to step forward and speak on their behalf, to declare their credentials. Long minutes pass and none step forth. The lack of response is not surprising. Most candidates regard the assignation as certain failure, while others see it as certain death. Several veteran generals know they are too old for an arduous campaign against overwhelming odds – they, too, remain in the pack. Many of Rome's most valiant leaders are absent, fallen beneath the Carthaginian blade.

The Senate leader calls again for candidates to step forward and declare their qualifications. The crowd murmurs anxiously, confusedly. Several commoners make jokes about the size of the candidates' phalli and testiculis, provoking many laughs. Others shout the names of their favorites, urging them to step forward. None do.

Minutes later, Publius Cornelius Scipio walks to the forefront of the altar. He is arrayed in glistening battle armor, cradling a tall lance in his left arm. The bright sun flames his mirrored bronze. To the crowd below it appears as if Mars himself has descended from Olympus. He stands at the edge of the altar platform, there gazing upon the thousands in front of him. He abruptly shouts out at them in his best oratorical voice.

"I am Publius Cornelius Scipio. I declare my candidacy for the consulship. I do swear to you now, I will defeat the Three Generals and restore Iberia to Rome!"

His remarks prompt scattered cheers from the crowd and a number of jeers that bring satisfied smiles to Flaccus and Fabius – the sesterces they paid to their plants in the crowd was money well spent. Scipio walks along the wide altar, staring into the eyes of the citizenry, his youthful face a beacon of unquestioned resolve.

"Heed me, fellow citizens! Rome has the greatest warriors in the world, by the gods we know it is true! Yet we have lost many battles because we fight two enemies at once: Carthage and ourselves! We always fight the same way, regardless of terrain, climate, or weaponry. Hannibal and his brothers know that, and they exploit our stupidity with their ever-changing ambushes and stratagems. We refuse to adapt, to innovate – even though we fall victim to them in every battle. But no more!"

"I have new ways of fighting the Carthaginians, new weapons

and tactics. I cannot tell all here, since spies are everywhere, but know you this. I plan to defeat the Three Generals and regain control of Iberia's mines. That is how we will defeat Hannibal! If Hannibal does not have money, his mercenaries will desert him and his allies depart. His army will weaken. He will become ripe for defeat!"

Fabius looks uneasily at Flaccus. He can see every face in the crowd staring up at Scipio, as if watching a great actor upon the stage.

Scipio can sense the crowd's support for him. He knows it is time to seal their favor. "The gods sent me a dream last night! I was on a great, wide plain in Africa. Yes, Africa! And there was Hannibal, and there was I – leading our legions against him. Scores of monstrous elephants stampeded toward us, and hordes of Numidians flew toward our men. Yet we turned Hannibal's elephants against him, and the Numidians flew over to join us in battle. And the Carthaginians were destroyed!"

The crowd roars their enthusiasm, overwhelming the scattered jeers. When they have quieted, Cato steps forward from the crowd of magistrates, wearing his simple white toga. He stands near Scipio and speaks in the ringing, powerful voice for which he will become famous.

"Heed not Scipio, his is the voice of weakness and defeat! Verily, he has told me he would make peace with Hannibal. He would negotiate with this rabid bear! Scipio speaks of using lies and deceptions to win a battle, but I ask you, is that the Roman way? Are we to copy the ways of cowards and liars, to abandon the forceful courage of Cincinnatus and Dentatus? No! If you send another Scipio to Iberia, we will have another massacre and thousands will die again!"

The crowd is quiet, the citizens are murmuring among

themselves. Scipio stands in the center of the altar and spreads his arms. He speaks without oratory, as if to a friend. "You know my conduct in battle, do you not? Did you not honor me for saving my father when Hannibal's warriors surrounded him? Did you not praise me for leading thousands of soldiers back from the slaughter at Cannae? Did you find me to be soft, then?"

There are scattered replies of "No!" until Cato interrupts. "Yes, Cornelius Scipio has shown his bravery as a soldier, his willingness to risk his life. But Rome does not need a brave young soldier to lead them. It requires a wise old general, someone such as our revered Fabius!" Here Cato pauses as cheers for Fabius ring out from parts of the crowd, then he resumes. "We need a general well versed in leading an army against our enemies, something which Cornelius Scipio has never done. And yet this green general, this Scipio, would not even fight like a true Roman. He rejects our time-honored strategies, though he has never led an army!"

Before the crowd can react, Scipio steps in front of Cato, teetering on the very edge of the steps above the crowd. "Young Cato repeats himself," Scipio says, with a smirk, "but he is somewhat on the mark. Our 'time-honored strategies,' as he calls them, worked well against the barbarian tribes of centuries past. Carthage, however, is not a tribe, it is an empire, one with vast resources, new weapons, and unexpected stratagems. Hannibal has necessitated new tactics to defeat him, which we refuse to employ. The Three Generals have thousands of seasoned veterans in their army. We cannot just charge forward and conquer all. Not anymore." He turns to Cato with a mocking smile. "Besides, charging forward is an old *Greek* tactic, Cato, and its time has passed!"

Many laugh. They know the long-standing dispute between Scipio and Cato, between the Hellenics and Latins.

Marcus Buteo steps forward, and the two combatants fall silent. "Enough has been said, your positions are clear. It is time to vote, unless there are other candidates." When there is no further response, he continues. "I might remind you, young Cato here is not eligible for election, but Fabius is. Citizens, proceed to your centuria and vote."

The citizens move to one of the many roped-off areas within the Campus. Each group of a hundred has one vote, which they cast after discussing the candidates. By late afternoon, the election is complete.

AS AMELIA WALKS among the flowers in her garden, Scipio appears behind her in the doorway. Sensing him, she plucks a violet bloom and turns to hand it to him.

"Congratulations on your commission to Iberia," she says, giving him a forced smile. "I heard the people's vote was unanimous! I am so proud of you."

"You know already? That was but an hour ago."

"Gossip travels faster than Mercury, Commander Scipio."

He bows. "I am but the man who loves you, no more."

Amelia shakes her head. "Ah, but there is much more, isn't there? You will be leaving. And leaving me."

"Would I could stay here with you forever. But we cannot escape the Carthaginians by hiding from them, I know that now. Wait for me, my heart, that we may wed upon my return."

Amelia walks over to examine some buttery daffodils, cradling them between her fingers. "You ask much of me. I still grieve for my father, must I also spend years wondering if I will add your ashes to my brow? That I could not bear."

He stands close behind her, places his arms around her waist and softly embraces her. "I cannot promise that I will return. But I can pledge you my heart and my life, if you would have me."

Amelia fingers the thorns on a rose stem while she talks, looking away from Scipio. "Do you think it would lessen my pain to know that the man fighting the stone-eyed Africans is pledged to be my husband? It would but deepen the sorrow that now wounds my heart, were you to die."

"There is no other recourse, beloved. The Fates have made this course for me. And duty bids me to follow it."

"No recourse? You can stay here without dishonor. You are a hero, my love. "

Scipio sits down on a garden bench, and looks up at her, his eyes challenging. "A hero who sends others to do his duty, to risk their own loss of life and love? I swore to Father that I would preserve Rome, and I promised your father I would care for you. I cannot do either if I stay."

Near the two lovers there is a spindly rose bush that has stretched its branches to reach the sunlit part of the garden, pushing its small red blooms into the light. Scipio cups one of its flowers and looks at Amelia, his face pensive. "To live is to strive. Even this dainty flower fights for its place in the sun. I would strive against those elements that would darken the flowering of our love and our future family. I cannot do that if I stay here. Or flee to Greece. I have finally, finally learned that. My die is cast with Pietas."

Without plucking the flower, he proffers it to her. Amelia draws herself up, heaving a deep sigh. "I know your purpose. And know this, son of Publius – Cornelius Scipio. I will be one with you, in this world and the next, in this world unto the next. Go, and return to me."

As Amelia and Scipio envelop each other, sunset falls across the garden. The spindly rose glows in the final spot of sun, ever brighter for the shadows that surround it.

*   *   *   *   *

Only two hundred senators are in the Chambers, fully a third of them are missing. All those killed at Cannae have since been replaced, but the slaughters at Ilorca and Castulo have again decimated their ranks. They lie as piles of ashes on foreign soil, but each empty seat is a gravestone for he who occupied it. Every living senator attends, however. No one would dare miss the new consul's plan for Iberia. The Senate meeting is closed to the public at Scipio's request. He knows that Hannibal's spies are about, even in the Chambers. What he says must be kept secret.

Scipio stands at the Senate rostra, discussing his departure schedule. Senator Vilarius, a senior senator, bends over to murmur to young Senator Pastorus next to him. "The stripling had better have a good plan if he wants to get all those legions I've heard he wants!"

Pastorus shrugs, and nonchalantly pushes back a lock of his thick curly hair "Do we want to win back Iberia or not? That is the correct question for determining troop allotments."

"It is a question of winning Iberia versus losing more legions in another defeat," retorts Vilarius. "That boy has some strange ideas about warfare."

Pastorus bores into Vilarius' eyes. "Of certitude, it is time for some 'strange ideas.' The familiar ones have not sufficed!"

Their conversation halts when Scipio resumes outlining his

strategic plan. He returns to the topic of recruiting new allies, a central point of his budget request.

Flaccus rises to confront Scipio, his voice dripping with sarcasm. "Did you say that we need to add Africans to our army? What kind? Would you recruit some African elephants to join us?" The senators laugh, but Scipio's face does not change expression. He is the essence of gravitas.

"We need horsemen. Our cavalries are slow and stiff; they fight like infantry on horseback. I will recruit Numidians, the best riders in the world."

"The Numidians!" blurts a red-face Vilarius. "Those devils are Carthage's allies! They destroyed our men at Cannae, hunting them down as if they were wild hares!"

"I know, Vilarius. I fought against them three times. They whirl about you like a breeze, and are just as elusive. However, I do not speak of the Numidians allied with Hannibal. I seek a rebel tribe that has long fought Carthage to gain their freedom. They could soon come to our side. My spies have met with them in secret, and they tell me these Numidians are amenable to joining us."

"This is how you mean to defeat mighty Carthage?" Flaccus declaims. "Sneaking about and spying on people?" He looks at his fellows, his face full of false incredulity. "Is this the 'general' you send at the Three Generals?"

Scipio looks defiantly at Flaccus. "Yes, exactly. I intend to defeat them by spying and sneaking about. I call it gathering 'intelligence' about your foes and to help us make intelligent decisions about defeating them. The Carthaginians have been spying on us for years, and it has profited them, would you not say?"

Amid several rueful chuckles from the Senate, Vilarius speaks. "So, Cornelius Scipio, you say you can defeat Hannibal by taking Iberia from the Three Generals. Which army would you first challenge: Mago, Hasdrubal, or Gisgo?"

Scipio shrugs. "Whichever one is farthest from the other two, most likely. But defeating the generals is not my only objective. As I have said before, we can best defeat the Carthaginian beast by starving it. We must take away its source of nourishment."

Scipio beckons two slaves bearing a large map. "You know that the Carthaginians command the citadel of Saguntum, south of Tarraco. That is where many of their troops are stationed." Scipio moves his finger below Saguntum. "But I have found the true source of the Carthaginians' strength. Here..." Scipio points to the map.

The senators crane in to see the dot. One draws back in surprise. "Is that New Carthage? It is but a dot on the map, a small port town in southern Iberia. There are no armies there."

"Correct," says Scipio excitedly. "But that town has a garrison of Carthage's best troops. Do you know why? New Carthage is where their resources flow from, their money, food, weapons, and animals. It is the lifeblood of the Three Generals' armies." Scipio pauses. "And of Hannibal's! Capturing that 'dot' will be one of our objectives."

Fabius peers in. "Your idea has merit, yes, merit. But the Carthaginian armies are not far from New Carthage. When they find out you are there, they will rush to save it."

"Agreed. I plan to engage the armies of the Three Generals one at a time, before the other two can join the battle. We will go faster than any army has gone before and catch them by surprise. And ambush them!"

"Ambush? Surprise?" Flaccus sneers. "There you go again. You propose to sneak about in battles, too?"

"Hannibal has bested us in three major battles, and each time we blundered into his traps. Now, we will spring our own on his brothers. They will never suspect trickery from Romans." Scipio smirks at Flaccus. "We do not have the imagination for it."

Before Flaccus can say anything, Scipio brandishes a rolled parchment at the senators. "Send me to Iberia. I will finish my father's mission and return victorious." He steps forward until he is at the front chamber row, looking eye to eye with the Senate. "Or I will not return. This I pledge on my family's honor."

The Senate is briefly quiet as the senators mull Scipio's words. Fabius raises his voice. "Scipio speaks of defeating the Three Generals. I tell you, that is the route to our defeat! They have beaten all who oppose them and outnumber us. Consider, fellow senators, we can initiate a delaying action with them, as we are doing with Hannibal."

Scipio bows his head slightly toward the aged consul. "Fabius, you are called 'The Delayer' for good reason: your skirmishing strategy slowed Hannibal's advance to Rome. It was a wise strategy – for him, for that time." Scipio unrolls another part of the map and points to a cluster of three Xs on it. "The Three Generals are garrisoned near each other on terrain that allows for quick passage from one to the other. If we should continuously nip at one army without defeating it, it will only be a matter of time before the other two would catch up to us because we would lose the element of surprise. We must defeat each decisively, at the first encounter."

Fabius stares stolidly at Scipio. He turns to his Senate fellows while still addressing Scipio. "And how many men will your 'conquest' require?"

Without blinking, Scipio replies. "Four legions, an equal number of allies, and two thousand horses."

The Senate waits for him to say more, but he leaves his statement lingering in the air. Flaccus finally breaks the silence. "Four, you say, four legions? Did I hear you aright? And how will you deploy this army in a head-to-head battle?"

"I will not know until I get there. I have to study the opposing force, the weather, and the terrain. For every battle, we will invent a new stratagem, suited to its conditions. We will be ... unpredictable. That much I can predict!"

Tiberius Longius, a young Hellenic Party senator, vaults up from his seat, red-faced with frustration. "Give him the legions! Give us the chance to settle this forever war!" Tall, dark, and muscular, the veteran soldier faces the Senate like one of the Furies personified. "Do you not see that his genius is invention? He will find a way to conquer them!"

Marcus Buteo, the Senate leader, steps next to Scipio. All is quiet when he speaks. "Senators, we thank our newest consul for outlining his plans. General Scipio, it is time for us to consider your words. Three days hence we will meet and finalize troop allotments. We will call you before us for our decision."

The leader bows to Scipio, who gathers his maps and exits the Curia Hostilia. When he is outside The Forum, he exhales deeply and leans against one of its thick columns, waiting for his trembling to subside.

FABIUS, CATO, AND FLACCUS dine on a stone table outside one of Rome's ubiquitous open-air restaurants. They break off chunks of a large cheese and onion pizza and grab pieces of the restaurant's specialty, roast pork covered in fish sauce. There is festive chatter in the diner, but their mood is somber as they discuss Scipio's new appointment.

"It defies logic," exclaims Flaccus. "The youngest commander in history, and we send him to fight three veteran generals – with three veteran armies! He'll be wiped out! We should have let Gaius Nero take over. He is there at Tarraco."

"I do not favor the young pup's appointment, either," chuckles Fabius. "But Nero? He would have been even worse! You know he despises the Iberians, and they despise him." Fabius drains his goblet of wine. "The boy was willing to go, at least. And he has some good ideas, such as making our maniples more flexible. I may have been too hard on him, I say, too hard!"

"You should have gone instead of him, Fabius," says a petulant Cato. "Your delaying strategy is popular again, now that our armies are back to nipping at Hannibal's heels, as you like to say."

"Yes, yes, time has proven me right," preens Fabius. "But I'm too old to take on three generals at once. I am not so sure my 'hounding' strategy would work, anyway. Scipio has a point. While you are hounding one bear, the other two could sneak up on you! No, this is a fight for a younger man, much younger…"

"But is it a campaign we want to give to a Hellenic Party member?" says Flaccus. "If Scipio should somehow win a skirmish or two, or a battle, his glory redounds to the Hellenics. Their power will grow, and we are back to fending off their proposals for equal land distribution and public education. We barely passed our tax on women's jewelry as it was!"

Cato grins. "Ah, the Oppian Law. I am proud to have fought for it. The law has limited some of this Grecian frippery in our women, though they like it not."

Fabius cocks his head. "We have to be careful with doling out legions. That pup Philip of Macedon has declared war against Rome, doubtless encouraged by Hannibal's victories. And Sicily needs more men. So there is just cause to limit young Scipio's forces, yes, just cause!"

Cato looks earnestly at Flaccus and Fabius. "The answer is simple. We will allot Scipio enough men for a holding action but not enough for a victory. He asks for four legions, give him two – the same as his father received. That will be enough for him to guard Tarraco until Hannibal falls. Or one of our veteran generals becomes available."

Fabius heaves himself up and plops a final slice of pork into his mouth. He starts to walk off, casting a final comment. "The plan has merit, young Cato. As long as Tarraco stands, Hannibal cannot receive reinforcements. Sooner or later, he will have to return to Carthage. And the Latin Party will receive the glory."

"I do admit that I have concerns of conscience with such a plan," says Cato. "Would shackling our Iberian army spell Rome's downfall?"

Flaccus leans back, grinning deprecatingly at his young charge. "The Hellenics are Rome's worst enemy. If this boy should win a battle with his little army, then it is well and good. If he should lose, at least we have not wasted more legions, and we can elect a new consul. And his loss will be the end of the Scipio family's influence. That is a true victory!"

SCIPIO STANDS BEFORE his fellow senators, awaiting his orders. As the new proconsul and governor of Iberia, Scipio is wearing an elaborately designed toga palmata, resplendent with gold-embroidered palm leaves throughout. Laelius is watching from the citizen's gallery, and he smiles at his friend's uncommon grandeur. *There is hope for him yet*, Laelius muses.

Five seats over from Laelius, Cato frowns in disgust at Scipio's regalia. *I bet that pretty boy takes it in the ass.*

Marcus Buteo steps to the rostra and hands a scroll to Scipio who reads it as the Senate leader speaks. "General Publius Cornelius Scipio, this is your approved budget and troop assignation. You are allotted two infantry legions and one thousand cavalry, totaling Eleven thousand men. You will sail to Tarraco and assume command of the remaining armies under Marcius and Nero. From there you are to proceed as best you see fit. You have thirty quinqueremes for transport and battle with their accompanying crews. The money and grain allotments are as specified in the budget you have in your hand."

Scipio scans the figures and looks accusingly at the Senate members, his eyes lingering on Flaccus and Fabius. "Two legions," he says loudly. "I have only two legions?"

"Two legions, as I just said," replies Marcus Buteo, testily. "With the addition of Marcius and Nero's men in Iberia, that is approximately twenty two thousand men."

Scipio laughs bitterly. "In other words, I have less than half the force of the Three Generals. Is that not right?"

There is no response in the chamber. All are mutely watching Scipio.

Scipio unrolls the scroll and stares into it again, while the senators shift about impatiently. He looks up, his voice ringing with accusation and anger. "I will accede to this preposterous assignment on two conditions. First, that I have leave to recruit the Numidians as allies, and second, that I may choose my own senior officers."

Marcus Buteo quickly scans the senators' faces, reading their reactions and turns to Scipio. "Agreed. And fare you well." He turns back to face the Senate. "Now, to the next order of business…"

Scipio silently exits the chambers. As he goes, he steals a look at Flaccus, noting his smug satisfaction. He looks at Cato in the citizen's gallery and is taken aback at the anger in his face as he glowers at Scipio. By Mars' spear, Scipio thinks, that stern little farm boy hates me.

An excited Laelius intercepts Scipio as he descends the forum steps. "Scippy, you are the commander of an army!"

Scipio manages a wry grin. "Such an army – half of what I requested! They provided a token army for a token general, Laelius, someone to occupy the Three Generals until they find a senior commander. I suspect Flaccus had a hand in this."

Laelius throws up his arms. "Then to Hades with them! It is your right to refuse, is it not?"

Scipio laughs and slaps Laelius on the back. "What? And deny you the opportunity to be a legate? I think not!"

"The leader of a legion? In truth?"

"In truth, I knew I would not receive the men I asked for – the men I needed. But I used their denial as a bargaining chip for the most important choices, choosing my allies and officers. I need you to accompany me, as one of my lieutenants!"

"Hahaha! Look out, Hannibal, you have nothing on Scippy the fox!" An ecstatic Laelius pounds Scipio on the back until the new governor's eyes bug out, and he begs him to desist.

They walk across the Forum grounds, and Scipio unexpectedly turns west, heading away from the Scipio domus.

"Where are you going?" Laelius asks.

"To secure the final piece of the puzzle. I go to the legionary training grounds, for Marcus Silenus. It is time for Rome's greatest warrior to return to battle."

* * * * *

"More wine, slave, and be quick about it. I find myself growing sober!" Gisgo waves in mock desperation from his spot among the cushions on the wide, low couch. Brothers Mago and Hasdrubal grin at his dramatics. The Three Generals have just commandeered the large festival hall at the coastal citadel of Saguntum, halfway between Tarraco and New Carthage. The commanders are celebrating the Scipios brothers' demise, which is a major step in their quest to drive the Romans from Iberia. In a few days, they will be out on recruiting visits to the Carpetani and Celtiberi, but tonight they relax in worn tunics and sandals, savoring a last chance to laugh together. Several musicians play a soothing mix of progressions on their harps and flutes.

The generals' guest is the regal Masinissa, prince of eastern Numidia and staunch ally to Carthage. He is a rangy young man with a close-cropped black beard and studious brown eyes in a finely defined face. He is the man who doomed Publius Scipio with his surprise cavalry attack.

Gisgo sips his refilled goblet and spits it out. "Ptah! This wine is horse piss. I need something fit for a salutation to our friend Masinissa. Sophonisba! Are you out there? Bring a pitcher of the Rioja. It is time for a toast!"

Hasdrubal glowers in mock anger, playing with the Roman dagger in his belt. "So, bastard, you save the good stuff for last? Are you hoping we will be too drunk to consume much? I will disappoint you on that matter, I assure you!"

"I am here, Father." Sophonisba enters the hall carrying a large bronze pitcher. Masinissa glances over as she approaches and is struck dumb. He had heard stories of Sophonisba's captivating beauty, but he believed himself to be above such mortal concerns – a man more preoccupied with defeating his rival Syphax for control of all Numidia. But all thoughts of conquest are driven from his mind. He can only stare at the lithe, raven-haired vision before him: a sloe-eyed goddess whose every step is a swaying grace of curved hip and fulsome breast. Sophonisba walks over to stand next to her father. Gisgo dumps the wine from his cup and proffers it to her.

"Pour for us, daughter."

"As you wish," she says, with a voice sensuous beyond her fifteen virginal years.

Sophonisba fills Gisgo's cup, then those of the Barca brothers. She comes last to Masinissa, standing before him with her eyes modestly averted. It takes all of Masinissa's willpower not to stare into the swell of her dusky bosom as she bends to her task. He awkwardly draws the cup toward his lips.

"Gruh, uh, gratitude, Sophonisba."

The girl looks up and meets his gaze. Masinissa sees a flash of desire in her light blue eyes before she looks away from him. She retreats to her father's side, and Gisgo kisses her before he gestures for her to leave.

"There she is, my jewel! She is here visiting from Carthage. She came over with those damned meddling Elders. I was so glad to see her. I cannot bear having her long from me!"

Masinissa mutely nods his assent. As he watches her go, he knows he will do anything to have this child-woman by his side, even if it means abandoning his kingdom or his life. He stares dazedly into his cup, as if it may hold answers on how to win her. Mago and Hasdrubal exchange wry glances. The brothers have seen Sophonisba's effect on men before, including themselves.

Gisgo smiles broadly and raises his cup toward Masinissa. Mago and Hasdrubal follow suit. "Honors to our ally Masinissa. Without your charge into the Roman flanks, we might all have our heads on spears by the gates of Rome! To the future king of Numidia!"

The generals raise their cups to Masinissa, but he barely notices. His eyes are fixed on the door through which his Sophonisba left, as if he can still see her there.

*   *   *   *   *

OSTIA, 210 BCE. Thirty ships sail out from the Rome's seaport, their sails filled with the morning wind. Scipio and Laelius stand at the lead ship's helm, trying to act like officers but childishly excited about their great adventure.

A dour Marcus Silenus stands behind them, looking back upon the troop ships following them, assuring that all is in order. When all seems right, he withdraws one of his throwing knives and arrows it into the main mast, practicing his throws. Scipio joins him, challenging him to a throwing contest. Scipio jokes at every score or miss, enjoying his last carefree days before he lands and begins the quest to reclaim Iberia. To reclaim it as Proconsul Publius Cornelius Scipio, governor of Iberia, commander of the Iberian armies, and Rome's final hope.

ABOUT THE AUTHOR

Martin Tessmer is a retired instructional design professor who taught at the University of Colorado and the University of South Alabama. He lives in Denver, Colorado. This is his ninth of ten books.

Volume Two of the trilogy, <u>The Three Generals</u>, was published in 2015. The third volum, *Scipio's Dream*, will be out in January 2016.

[i] Cato, Marcus Portius. *De Agri Cultura*. 160 BCE. Books 1-2, page 5.

[ii] Livius, Titus (Livy). *Hannibal's War: Books 21-30*. Translated by J.C.Yardley. Oxford: The University Press. Book 21, Chapter 42, Page 42.

[iii] Livius, Titus (Livy). *Hannibal's War: Books 21-30*. Translated by J.C.Yardley. Oxford: The University Press. Book 21, Chapter 46, Page 46.

[iv] Gabriel, Richard. *Scipio Africanus: Rome's Greatest General*. Washington, D.C: Potomac Books, 2008.

[v] Polybius. *The Histories*. Translated by Robin Waterfield. Oxford: The University Press. 3, 86, 196.

[vi] List of Latin Phrases (H). The Wikipedia. http://en.wikipedia.org/wiki/List_of_Latin_phrases_(H)

[vii] Livius, Titus (Livy). *Hannibal's War: Books 21-30*. Translated by J.C.Yardley. Oxford: The University Press. 22, 40, 110.

[viii] http://en.wikiquote.org/wiki/Cato_the_Elder.

[ix] Polybius. *The Histories*. Translated by Robin Waterfield. Oxford: The University Press. 3, 109, 214-215.

[x] Livius, Titus (Livy). *Hannibal's War: Books 21-30*. Translated by J.C.Yardley. Oxford: The University Press. 22, 51, 147.

[xi] Livius, Titus (Livy). *Hannibal's War: Books 21-30*. Translated by J.C.Yardley. Oxford: The University Press. 22, 51, 121.

[xii] Livius, Titus (Livy). *Hannibal's War: Books 21-30*. Translated by J.C.Yardley. Oxford: The University Press. 22, 51, 120.

[xiii] Livius, Titus (Livy). *Hannibal's War: Books 21-30.* Translated by J.C.Yardley. Oxford: The University Press. 22, 51, 120.

[xiv] Livius, Titus (Livy). *Hannibal's War: Books 21-30.* Translated by J.C. Yardley. 22, 51, 122.

[xv] Livius, Titus (Livy). *Hannibal's War: Books 21-30.* Translated by J.C.Yardley. Oxford: The University Press. 23, 12, 147

[xvi] *Ancient Encyclopedia of History.*
http://www.ancient.eu.com/article/467/

[xvii] Varone, Antonio. *Erotica Pompeiana: Love Inscriptions on the Walls of Pompeii.* "L'Erma" di Bretschneider, 2002. p. 81.

[xviii]
http://www.thelatinlibrary.com/imperialism/notes/scipio.html

CPSIA information can be obtained at www.ICGtesting.com
Printed in the USA
LVOW10s1103080516

487241LV00031B/854/P